Blood Beneath Daybridge

Blood Beneath Daybridge: The Making of a Monster - *The Butcher's Tale*

Author's Note

Blood Beneath Daybridge: The Making of a Monster is the official prequel to *Shadows of Daybridge*, the first book in the Ethan Reeves werewolf detective series. While *Shadows* introduced readers to Detective Reeves and his investigation of supernatural crimes in present-day Daybridge, this prequel reveals the dark origins of the city's most infamous legend—the Ogre of Daybridge Bridge.

The events chronicled here span more than a century, from Guthrie Knox's childhood in the 1870s through his transformation into the monstrous entity that would haunt Daybridge for generations, culminating in the final confrontation with Detective Reeves that connects directly to the opening scenes of *Shadows of Daybridge*.

Prologue: The Butcher's Apprentice

Guthrie Knox was seven years old when he first understood that he was different from other children.

It wasn't the circumstances of his birth or his residence at Blackwell Orphanage that set him apart—many children in Daybridge's industrial quarters were orphaned by accident or disease, abandoned by parents who couldn't feed another mouth, or simply lost in the administrative chaos of a city expanding faster than its institutions could manage. The gray stone building that housed sixty-three unwanted children was a common enough feature of the cityscape, neither particularly brutal nor especially kind in its administration of young lives.

No, what made Guthrie different was something more fundamental, something that caused the caretakers to watch him with wary eyes when they thought he wasn't looking, something that made the other children maintain a careful distance despite the overcrowded dormitories.

It was the way he watched.

On that particular autumn morning in 1878, he stood in the orphanage courtyard, a slight figure with serious gray eyes, observing with clinical detachment as the butcher's delivery boy unloaded a half carcass of pork from his cart. Most children would have been repelled by the sight of the splayed ribs, the exposed muscle tissue, the lingering bloodstains on the burlap wrapping. A few might have been morbidly fascinated, giggling nervously or daring each other to touch the cooling flesh.

Guthrie simply watched, his gaze steady, his expression betraying neither disgust nor excitement—only intense, focused curiosity.

"What are you staring at, boy?" The delivery assistant, a red-faced teenager named Thomas, had noticed Guthrie's unwavering attention. "Never seen meat before?"

"Not like that," Guthrie replied, his voice oddly mature for a child so young. "Only after Mrs. Smithson has cooked it."

Thomas snorted, heaving the pork carcass higher on his shoulder. "Well, it doesn't start out as chops and roasts, does it? Something's got to die for you lot to eat."

"I know that," Guthrie said with a slight frown, as if offended by the suggestion he might not understand such a basic principle. "I've seen dead things before. Cats and pigeons and once a dog by the canal. But they were whole. This is... opened."

Something in the boy's tone—the complete absence of the squeamishness Thomas expected—made the delivery assistant pause. He studied the small, solemn-faced child more carefully.

"You're not squeamish, are you?" he observed. "Most kids your age would be green around the gills, looking at fresh slaughter."

Guthrie shook his head. "It's interesting. How it all fits together inside. Like machinery but made of meat."

Thomas barked a laugh, genuinely amused by the unusual response. "That's one way of looking at it, I suppose. You should see a whole pig come apart. Now that's something—watching a skilled butcher turn a carcass into all the different cuts. Like a puzzle in reverse."

The boy's eyes widened slightly, the first real expression of emotion he had shown. "Do they let children watch that?"

"Not generally, no." Thomas adjusted his burden, preparing to carry it into the orphanage kitchen. "Health regulations and all that. Plus, most kids would either faint or be sick all over the shop floor."

Guthrie took a step closer, his gray eyes fixed on Thomas with unsettling intensity. "I wouldn't be sick. I'd be quiet and stay out of the way. I just want to see how it works."

Something about the boy's seriousness, his complete lack of childish squirming or pleading, made Thomas consider the request more seriously than he might have otherwise. He studied Guthrie for a long moment, noting the careful stillness, the focused attention, the absence of the manic energy that typically characterized children his age.

"Tell you what," Thomas said finally. "I'll speak to Old Silas—he's the master butcher I work for. If he says it's alright, maybe you can come by the shop sometime. No promises, mind you. Silas is particular about his workspace."

Guthrie nodded solemnly, as if they were businessmen concluding a serious negotiation. "Thank you. I would appreciate that."

As Thomas disappeared into the kitchen with his burden, Matron Smithson emerged from the building's side entrance, her sharp eyes immediately finding Guthrie standing alone in the yard.

"Guthrie Knox! What are you doing out here? You should be in the dining hall with the others, setting tables for lunch."

"Yes, Matron. I was just watching the delivery." Guthrie turned toward the building, his expression once again neutral, revealing nothing of the conversation that had just transpired or the anticipation he felt at the possibility of visiting the butcher's shop.

"Always watching, that one," Matron Smithson muttered to herself as she followed him inside. "Never playing, never laughing like a proper child. Just watching everything with those old eyes. It isn't natural."

Three days later, Thomas returned to Blackwell Orphanage with the regular delivery and a message: Old Silas had agreed to allow one visit from the curious orphan, provided he stayed out of the way and followed instructions precisely. Matron Smithson was reluctant—allowing a child to leave the orphanage's supervision was irregular, particularly for such an unusual purpose—but Silas Holloway was a respected businessman and significant donor to Blackwell's perpetually strained resources. Permission was grudgingly granted for Guthrie to accompany Thomas back to the shop the following Saturday morning.

The anticipation that filled Guthrie during the intervening days was unlike anything he had previously experienced. He had always been a studious child, preferring books to the rough games that occupied most orphanage residents, but this was different—a focused excitement that manifested not in the fidgeting or chattering that might have betrayed another child's eagerness, but in an even more intense stillness, a heightened attention to detail in his chores and lessons, as if proving his worthiness for the opportunity ahead.

Saturday dawned clear and cold, a perfect late autumn day in Daybridge. Guthrie was awake before the bell, dressed in his cleanest clothes, his hair carefully combed with water from the dormitory basin. When Thomas arrived, the boy was waiting in the entrance hall, standing straight-backed beside a suspicious Matron Smithson.

"Now you mind your manners, Guthrie," she instructed sternly. "Mr. Holloway is doing you a great kindness in allowing this visit. I expect you to be on your best behavior and return by noon precisely."

"Yes, Matron," Guthrie replied, his serious gray eyes meeting hers directly. "I'll be good."

The walk to Holloway's Meat Emporium took them through Daybridge's commercial district, a section of the city Guthrie had rarely visited. He absorbed the sights with his characteristic quiet attention—the shop fronts with their polished windows, the street vendors hawking hot chestnuts and meat pies, the carts and carriages navigating the cobblestone streets with varying degrees of success. He asked no questions, made no childish observations, simply processed everything with the same detached curiosity that had first caught Thomas's attention.

Holloway's occupied a prime corner location, its large windows displaying an array of cuts arranged with artistic precision on beds of fresh straw. The shop front, painted a deep burgundy that disguised the inevitable small bloodstains, bore the establishment's name in gold lettering along with the founding date: 1842. A small brass bell tinkled as Thomas ushered Guthrie through the front door.

The shop's interior was impeccably clean, the tile floor scrubbed to a dull shine, the marble counters wiped free of any residue from the previous day's business. Glass cases displayed premium cuts—crown roasts, tenderloins, specialty sausages—while hooks along the back wall held larger pieces awaiting further processing. The air carried the distinctive metallic scent of fresh meat mingled with the sharper notes of spices used in Holloway's signature preparations.

Behind the main counter stood a man who could only be Old Silas himself—though the nickname, Guthrie would later learn, referred more to his position as the oldest established butcher in this district than to his actual age, which was perhaps fifty. Tall and barrel-chested, with forearms corded with muscle beneath rolled-up sleeves, Silas Holloway possessed the physical presence of a man who had spent decades working with carcasses weighing as much as he did. His face, framed by muttonchop whiskers just beginning to show threads of gray, conveyed both the sternness of a master craftsman and a hint of genuine curiosity as he regarded his unusual visitor.

"So, this is the boy who wants to see how a carcass comes apart," Silas said, his voice a deep rumble that suited his imposing frame. "Thomas says you've got an unusual interest for one so young."

"Yes, sir," Guthrie replied, meeting the butcher's gaze with his customary directness. "I want to understand how things work. Inside."

Silas studied the child for a long moment, noting the serious expression, the controlled stillness, the complete absence of the nervousness or exuberance he would have expected from a boy this age. Then he nodded once, decisively.

"Understanding is a worthy pursuit," he said. "Too many people go through life never questioning what's beneath the surface. Come through to the back, then. We've got a hog to break down this morning, delivered fresh from the Hargreaves farm yesterday. You'll see the process from start to finish."

He lifted a section of the counter, creating a passage to the workshop behind the retail space. Guthrie followed without hesitation, Thomas bringing up the rear with an expression that mingled amusement and lingering curiosity about this unusual orphan.

The workshop was larger than the front shop, designed for the practical business of transforming animal carcasses into retail products. A massive butcher block dominated the center of the room, its wooden surface-stained dark from years of use despite regular scraping and sanding. Various tools hung from hooks on the walls—cleavers, saws, knives of different shapes and sizes, each meticulously maintained and arranged in order of use. At the far end, a large sink and drainage area provided facilities for the necessary cleaning, while a heavy door presumably led to cold storage where carcasses were kept before processing.

"First rule in my workshop," Silas said, turning to face Guthrie with sudden sternness, "is absolute attention to instruction. One wrong move around these tools can cost a finger or worse. You'll stand exactly where I tell you, move only when I say you can, and touch nothing without explicit permission. Understood?"

"Yes, sir," Guthrie replied without hesitation.

"Second rule is cleanliness. Butchery is not a dirty business, despite what some might think. It requires precision, care, and proper hygiene. Thomas will get you an apron. It'll be too big, but it'll keep your clothes clean."

Thomas fetched a canvas apron from a hook by the door, helping Guthrie tie it behind his back. The garment indeed engulfed his small frame, the bottom edge nearly touching the floor, but the boy made no complaint.

"Now," Silas continued, "I'll explain each step as we go. Questions are permitted, but only between steps, not during cutting. Sharp tools require complete concentration."

With these preliminaries established, Silas nodded to Thomas, who disappeared through the heavy door at the rear of the workshop. He returned moments later, struggling slightly under the weight of half a pig carcass, already split lengthwise down the spine but otherwise intact from snout to tail. With practiced efficiency, he hoisted it onto the butcher block, positioning it precisely according to some system Guthrie didn't yet understand.

Silas studied the carcass with a professional eye, running his hand along certain sections as if confirming what his vision told him about the quality and condition of the meat. Then he turned to a sink, washing his hands thoroughly before selecting a specific knife from the array on the wall.

"We begin with the separation of the primal cuts," he explained, positioning himself at the butcher block. "Observe the natural seams in the muscle structure. A good butcher works with the animal's anatomy, not against it. The knife follows the paths already present in the carcass."

What followed was a revelation to young Guthrie Knox. With movements that combined raw strength and balletic precision, Silas began transforming the uniform mass of the carcass into distinct sections—shoulder, loin, belly, ham—each separated along natural divisions in the muscle tissue with minimal sawing through bone. His commentary was sparse but precise, identifying each cut, explaining its characteristics, noting its best culinary applications.

Guthrie watched with unprecedented fascination. His already remarkable focus intensified, his gray eyes tracking every movement of Silas's hands, every incision of the blade, every separation of muscle from bone. He absorbed the terminology without effort—Boston butt, picnic shoulder, baby back ribs, pork belly—connecting each name to the specific part of the animal's anatomy as it emerged under Silas's skilled hands.

Most striking to both Silas and Thomas was the boy's complete comfort with the process. Where most children might have flinched at the occasional snap of cartilage or the subtle resistance of the knife against gristle, Guthrie showed only deepening interest. There was no disgust, no squeamishness, not even the morbid fascination that sometimes drew boys to bloody spectacles. Instead, there was only pure, clinical curiosity—the satisfaction of seeing a complex system revealed and understood.

As Silas moved from primary separation to the more detailed work of trimming and final preparation, he began to direct occasional questions to the unusually attentive child.

"Why do you think I'm cutting along this line here, boy?" he asked, his knife poised above a section of loin.

Guthrie studied the exposed muscle structure, his brow furrowed in concentration. "Because the fibers change direction there," he replied after a moment. "They run lengthwise on this side, but crosswise over there."

Silas's eyebrows rose slightly. "That's exactly right. Different muscle groups have different fiber orientations. Cutting against the grain gives you tender meat for quick cooking. Cutting with the grain gives you pieces that hold together during long, slow cooking." He nodded approvingly. "You've got a good eye."

The work continued, Silas occasionally testing Guthrie's understanding with similar questions, the boy responding with increasingly accurate observations as he began to grasp the underlying principles of the butcher's craft. Thomas, initially amused by the unusual situation, found himself impressed by the child's aptitude and seriousness.

When the final cuts had been wrapped and set aside for transfer to the shop displays, Silas turned to the cleaning process, demonstrating the same meticulous care in maintaining his workspace and tools that he had shown in the butchery itself. Guthrie assisted where permitted, his small hands surprisingly capable as he helped wipe down surfaces and organize tools for proper storage.

As they completed these final tasks, Silas studied the orphan with renewed interest. "You've got an uncommon mind, young Knox," he said finally. "Most boys your age couldn't sit still for ten minutes of this work, let alone a full morning. And still fewer would understand what they were seeing."

Guthrie looked up from the cleaver he had been carefully drying. "It makes sense to me," he said simply. "Everything has a structure. Once you see it, you can understand how it works."

"Indeed, it does," Silas agreed, taking the cleaver and hanging it in its designated place. "And that understanding is the difference between a butcher and a mere meat-cutter. Anyone can hack a carcass to pieces with enough strength and sharp tools. But to do it properly—to respect the animal's design, to maximize the value of each part, to create cuts that will cook well and taste good—that requires knowledge and precision."

He paused, studying the serious-faced child before him. Something in the boy's focused attention, his natural affinity for the systematic approach that characterized good butchery, resonated with Silas in a way he hadn't anticipated when agreeing to this unusual visit.

"How would you like to come back next Saturday?" he asked abruptly. "There's a lamb scheduled for processing. Different animal, different muscle structure. Might be educational to see the comparison."

Guthrie's eyes widened slightly; the first real expression of emotion he had shown all morning. "I would like that very much, sir," he replied, his voice carefully controlled despite the obvious eagerness beneath the words.

"I'll speak to your matron, then," Silas said with a decisive nod. "If she's agreeable, perhaps we can make this a regular arrangement. Saturday mornings before the shop opens to customers. You'd help with cleanup afterward, of course—earning your education, as it were."

"Yes, sir," Guthrie agreed immediately. "I'd work hard. I wouldn't be any trouble."

"I believe you," Silas said, and realized with some surprise that he meant it. There was something in this unusual child that inspired confidence—a seriousness of purpose, a natural discipline, that belied his seven years. "Thomas will walk you back to the orphanage now. We'll see about next week."

As Thomas escorted Guthrie back through the shop toward the front entrance, Silas Holloway watched the small figure in the oversized apron with thoughtful eyes. In his forty years as a butcher, he had trained several apprentices, but never one so young—and certainly never one who had shown such natural aptitude from the very first observation.

There was something different about Guthrie Knox, something in the way those serious gray eyes watched and analyzed and understood. Silas couldn't quite name it, this quality that set the boy apart, but he recognized its value. In his profession, such clinical detachment, such precise attention to structural detail, was not merely useful but essential.

The butcher nodded to himself; decision made. He would speak to Matron Smithson about a formal arrangement—Saturday mornings to start, perhaps expanding as the boy grew older and more capable. Blackwell Orphanage was always in need of financial support, and Silas had no children of his own to inherit his business. It was an unconventional arrangement, certainly, but one that might benefit all concerned.

As the shop door closed behind young Guthrie Knox, Silas returned to his workshop, unaware that his impulsive decision would shape not only the boy's future but, decades later, the very fabric of Daybridge itself. He could not have known that the skills he would teach—the precise dissection, the intimate understanding of how living things were constructed, the methodical transformation of once-living flesh—would one day be applied in ways he could never have imagined.

He saw only a serious child with unusual aptitude and focus—not the seeds of something that would one day become a monster.

In the years that followed, Guthrie's Saturday mornings at Holloway's Meat Emporium expanded into a formal apprenticeship. By age twelve, he was spending every day after school at the shop, learning every aspect of the butcher's trade under Silas's exacting tutelage. By fifteen, he had left school entirely to work full-time, developing skills that impressed even veteran butchers who visited from other districts.

Guthrie's quiet intensity, his meticulous precision, his absolute focus on mastering each technique—these qualities made him an exceptional apprentice. Where other boys might have been distracted by social pursuits or youthful rebellions, Guthrie remained singular in his dedication to understanding the structural intricacies of his chosen profession.

What neither Silas nor anyone else at the orphanage fully recognized was that this same clinical detachment, this ability to separate form from feeling, structure from sentiment, was developing in all aspects of Guthrie's interaction with the world. The emotional distance that made him an excellent butcher—able to transform living creatures into marketable products without distress or hesitation—was simultaneously creating a young man who moved through human society with the same analytical remove, observing social connections and emotional exchanges as systems to be studied rather than experiences to be felt.

By the time Guthrie Knox reached adulthood, he had become exactly what Silas Holloway had hoped for—a master butcher whose skills equaled or surpassed his own. But he had also become something neither of them had anticipated: a man whose understanding of physical structures far exceeded his comprehension of human emotion, whose precision with a knife was matched only by his disconnect from normal human bonding, whose perfect knowledge of how bodies were assembled existed alongside a profound ignorance of how hearts and minds connected.

It was this unique combination—technical mastery paired with emotional detachment—that would one day attract the attention of Eliza Blackwood, a woman whose own interest in the transformation of flesh extended far beyond conventional butchery. When she first observed Guthrie's work at Holloway's, she recognized something special in his methodical precision, his complete comfort with the intimate details of mortality, his natural talent for understanding how living things could be taken apart and, perhaps, put back together in new configurations.

In Guthrie Knox, master butcher and emotional outsider, Eliza saw the perfect candidate for a very particular kind of transformation—one that would require both his skills and his psychological distance from normal human concerns. She saw not just a craftsman, but a canvas for her most ambitious work yet.

She saw the man who would become the Ogre of Daybridge Bridge.

Copyright:

First Edition

Published by Live For Excellence Productions

ISBN:

Ebook: 978-1-998591-75-6

Paperback: 978-1-998591-76-3

Audiobook: 978-1-998591-77-0

Chapter 1: The Boy on Stygian Street

The air hung heavy with coal smoke as dawn broke over Daybridge in the spring of 1870. The city was transforming—brick factories rising like monoliths along the Shadowlair River, their chimneys belching black plumes that dimmed the morning sun. Horse-drawn carriages clattered over cobblestones while workers shuffled toward the textile mills and ironworks that had sprung up seemingly overnight, turning what had once been a sleepy river town into an industrial powerhouse.

On Stygian Street, in the shadow of the hulking Blackwell Orphanage, a woman's scream pierced the predawn quiet. Inside a small, filthy room at Madame Lowell's boarding house, seventeen-year-old Josephine Knox clutched at bloodied sheets, her labor having started hours earlier. The midwife—a withered crone who smelled of gin and carbolic soap—shook her head gravely.

"Push, girl," she commanded, her voice like rusted hinges. "The baby's comin', but you're losin' too much blood."

Josephine, a thin wisp of a woman with copper hair and emerald eyes now dulled with pain, summoned her remaining strength. With one final agonizing effort, she brought her son into the world. The newborn's first cry was powerful, almost unnaturally so for a baby born to such a frail mother.

"A boy," the midwife announced, wrapping the unusually large infant in a threadbare blanket. "Strong one, too."

But Josephine would never hold her child. Even as the midwife worked to stem the bleeding, the young woman's life ebbed away, her final whisper naming her son: "Guthrie... after my father."

By noon, the orphanage cart arrived, and Guthrie Knox—not yet twelve hours old—began his life as ward number 342 of

Blackwell Orphanage, a grim, Gothic structure that loomed like a sentinel of misery over the Eastern Quarter of Daybridge.

Seven years passed in a blur of gray walls, watery gruel, and the constant drone of children's coughs. Blackwell Orphanage operated less as a sanctuary for Daybridge's abandoned children and more as a warehouse for unwanted humanity. Headmaster Silas Blackwell—a cadaverous man with fingers like talons and breath that reeked of cheap whiskey—ruled the institution with casual cruelty.

Young Guthrie stood out from his earliest days. By age seven, he was already larger than boys several years his senior. His broad shoulders and thick limbs seemed at odds with the malnourishment that plagued the other children. While they grew pale and thin, Guthrie thrived like a stubborn weed, drawing strength from the same meager rations that left others weakened.

It was this physical vitality, combined with the unsettling intensity of his gray-eyed gaze, that first caught the attention of Thomas, the butcher's delivery boy. The encounter in the orphanage courtyard—Guthrie's unwavering focus as he watched Thomas unload the day's delivery, his odd maturity as he questioned the process of breaking down a carcass—marked the beginning of the boy's journey from mere orphan to apprentice butcher, from unwanted child to something far more ominous.

At seven, Guthrie Knox already understood that he was different. The way he watched, the things that held his interest, the detached curiosity with which he observed the world—all set him apart from the other children at Blackwell. When Thomas offered him the chance to visit Holloway's Meat Emporium, to see firsthand how death was transformed into sustenance, the boy seized the opportunity with a focus that belied his years.

That first visit to the butcher shop opened a door in Guthrie's mind, one that could never be fully closed again. The sight of carcasses being methodically disassembled, flesh parted from bone with ritualistic precision, blood flowing in controlled rivulets—it resonated with something deep inside him, some wordless hunger that craved understanding of how things worked beneath the skin.

Silas Holloway, master butcher and owner of the shop, recognized the boy's unusual aptitude immediately. The uncanny stillness, the unblinking absorption of each phase of the process, the penetrating questions that cut to the hidden logic of the craft—in Guthrie, the old butcher saw a kindred spirit, someone who instinctively grasped the sacramental nature of his work.

And so, the orphan became an apprentice, trading the gray misery of Blackwell for the cathedral of blood and bone that was Holloway's. Every spare moment—stolen from chores and lessons, earned through impeccable behavior—Guthrie spent at the shop, learning at the master's side. His hands, so clumsy with childish games, proved preternaturally deft with a blade. His mind, so often chided for inattention in the classroom, focused like a burning glass when presented with the intricacies of anatomy.

In the blood-spattered sanctuary of the butcher shop, Guthrie Knox found more than a trade. He found a calling, a purpose that resonated in his very marrow. The first time he made the killing cut himself—the long, precise slice that transformed a living creature into mere meat—something shifted inside him. A hunger long denied took its first full breath.

And deep in the shadowed corners of Daybridge, ancient eyes marked the boy's progress with avid interest. Wheels that had been turning since before the city rose from the riverbank mud clicked into a new configuration. A plan centuries in the making saw a new piece slide into place on the board.

Guthrie Knox, so young, so full of promise. The boy who watched, and learned, and hungered. He would learn to cut so much more than mere meat in time.

All the time in the world.

Chapter 2: The Apprentice's Blade

The summer of 1883 brought a blistering heat wave that turned Daybridge into a kiln. The sun beat down mercilessly on the cobblestone streets, baking the stench of horse manure and human sweat into a noxious miasma that clung to clothes and skin. In the slums and rookeries, the very air seemed to shimmer with fever, heavy with the groans of the sick and the dying.

Guthrie Knox, now thirteen, barely noticed the oppressive weather. His world had narrowed to the blood-slicked sanctuary of Holloway's Meat Emporium, where he spent every waking moment honing his craft under the watchful eye of Silas Holloway. Five years as the master butcher's apprentice had transformed the once-spindly orphan into a youth of impressive size and strength, his body forged by countless hours wielding cleavers and hauling carcasses.

But it was his skill with a blade that truly set Guthrie apart. His cuts were swift, precise, almost elegant in their economy of motion. He could disassemble a side of beef with a speed and surety that made even the seasoned journeymen shake their heads in wonder. For Guthrie, it wasn't just a matter of rote technique or practiced efficiency. It was an art, a calling, a form of communion with the fundamental workings of flesh and bone.

"The lad's got a gift," Silas Holloway often said to customers who marveled at the young apprentice's prowess. "A true feel for the work. He'll be a master in his own right one day, mark my words."

Guthrie accepted such praise with characteristic reserve, his expression seldom shifting from its habitual mask of composed detachment. But inside, each compliment kindled a fierce glow of pride, stoking the hunger that had first awakened when he watched Thomas unload that pig carcass so many years ago. It was a hunger not just for skill or recognition, but for a deeper understanding of the mysteries that lay beneath the skin.

That hunger found an outlet in the strays that haunted the alleyways behind the shop. Guthrie, who rarely showed warmth or empathy toward his fellow humans, developed a curious affinity for these wretched creatures. He would save scraps from the day's butchery and, when work was done, distribute this bounty among the assembled dogs and cats, his manner almost tender as he ensured each animal received its share.

One dog in particular—a scarred, one-eyed terrier he simply called Dog—became his special favorite. With infinite patience, Guthrie coaxed the half-wild creature to accept his touch, eventually training it to perform simple tricks in exchange for choice morsels. It was the closest thing to a friendship the solitary apprentice had ever known.

This idyll of blood and companionship might have continued indefinitely, had fate not intervened in the form of a trio of young swells out "slumming" one August night. Sons of wealthy industrialists, flush with gin and the arrogance of privilege, they amused themselves by tormenting the stray dogs with kicks and thrown stones.

Guthrie, making his nightly rounds with Dog trotting faithfully at his heels, turned a corner to find the three young men whooping with drunken laughter as they cornered one of the smaller strays. They had tied a string around the terrified animal's neck and were taking turns yanking it back each time it tried to flee.

Something ignited behind Guthrie's eyes then, a cold conflagration of rage that swept through him like a killing frost. He did not shout or posture. He simply strode forward, a tall figure in a blood-stiffened apron, and seized the nearest swell by the throat.

What followed was not a fight but an education. Using nothing more than his bare hands, Guthrie imparted a lesson in the frailty of human anatomy to the three young men. Bones cracked. Blood flowed. Screams rent the fetid night air. Through it all, the apprentice butcher's expression never wavered from its mask of icy composure, as if he were demonstrating a particularly tricky cut of meat rather than systematically dismantling three human beings.

When it was over, when the swells lay groaning and weeping in the filth of the alley, Guthrie calmly untied the string from the whimpering stray's neck and scooped the animal into his arms. He carried it back to the shop, where he cleaned its wounds and fed it a generous portion of liver before sending it on its way.

News of the incident spread quickly through the neighborhood. The wealthy victims, eager to avoid embarrassment, concocted a story of being set upon by a gang of "river scum" to explain their injuries. But the denizens of Daybridge's meaner streets knew the truth. They had seen the tall, silent figure in the bloodied apron, had heard the screams and the sickening crunch of breaking bone. And from that night forward, they accorded Guthrie Knox a wary respect bordering on fear.

For his part, Guthrie seemed unmoved by his newfound notoriety. If anything, he withdrew even further into the world of the slaughterhouse, speaking only when necessary and shunning all companionship save that of his beloved strays. Even Silas Holloway, who had come to view his apprentice with an almost paternal regard, found the boy increasingly difficult to read, his silences more loaded, his gaze opaquer.

And yet, the old butcher could not help but marvel at Guthrie's ever-growing mastery of their shared craft. The precision, the surety, the almost mystical communion between blade and flesh—it was as if the boy had been born to this bloody work, his hands shaped for the cleaver before they ever grasped a rattle.

What Silas Holloway did not know, could never have guessed, was that the incident in the alley had awakened more than just

Guthrie's rage. It had provided the first true taste of a hunger that had long lurked beneath the surface of the apprentice's tightly controlled facade. A hunger for dominion, for the hot, salt-copper tang of absolute power over living flesh.

In the blood-drenched world of the slaughterhouse, Guthrie Knox had found his calling. And in the savage lessons of the street, he had discovered a deeper truth—that he wielded the power of life and death not just over dumb beasts, but over men as well.

It was a truth that would shape the course of his life in ways even he could not yet imagine. A truth that would lead him inexorably into the shadow of the bridge, and the dark embrace of the being that waited there, patient as centuries, hungry as the Void.

Guthrie Knox, apprentice butcher, master of the killing cut. He had learned to slice flesh and shatter bone, to reduce the twitching intricacies of life to mere meat for the block. In time, he would learn to practice his art on a far grander scale, in service to appetites older and colder than any human hunger.

The blade was eager in his hand; its edge honed to a scalpel's keenness. All Daybridge lay spread before the blade, quivering and oblivious. Waiting for the cuts to come.

Chapter 3: Red Hands Rising

The spring of 1895 dawned on a Daybridge much changed from the city of Guthrie Knox's youth. The industrial revolution had tightened its grip, transforming the once-modest river town into a sprawling metropolis of brick and iron. Factory smokestacks dominated the skyline, belching black clouds that stained the clouds and settled like a shroud over the city's poorer quarters. The Shadowlair River, once clear enough to see fish darting beneath its surface, now ran thick with industrial waste, its waters taking on a different color each day depending on what the textile mills were dyeing.

Within this transformed landscape, Holloway's Slaughterhouse remained one of the few bastions of traditional craftsmanship. While newer, mechanized facilities had sprung up along the city's outskirts—vast, impersonal places where animals were processed with assembly-line efficiency—Holloway's maintained its reputation for quality over quantity. This was due in no small part to the skills of its head butcher, Guthrie Knox.

At twenty-five, Guthrie had grown into his considerable build. Standing six feet four inches tall, with shoulders broad enough to fill a doorway and hands that could crack walnuts without effort, he cut a commanding presence. Nine years of working with heavy carcasses had hardened his muscles into bands of steel beneath pale skin marked by a latticework of small scars—the inevitable badges of his profession. His face remained a study in harsh angles, now accentuated by a short beard that he kept meticulously trimmed. Only his eyes had changed significantly, their gray depths seeming to have receded further, as if the man behind them was retreating from the world even as his physical presence expanded to fill it.

Old Silas had passed away two winters before, leaving Guthrie as the undisputed master of Holloway's killing floor. The older man's final illness had been brief but painful, a wasting disease that had reduced his once-wiry frame to a skeletal husk in a matter of months. Throughout it all, Guthrie had visited his mentor daily, bringing small comforts—a bottle of decent whiskey, fresh bread, news from the slaughterhouse. On the final night, as Silas's breathing grew labored and his grip on life tenuous, he had pulled Guthrie close.

"Remember what I taught you," the old man had whispered, his voice barely audible. "About respect. For the blade. For the beasts. For death itself. It matters, lad. More than you know."

They were the last words Old Silas would speak. By morning, he was gone, leaving Guthrie with a hollow ache in his chest that he couldn't name. The funeral had been modest—a few fellow slaughtermen, Franklin Holloway himself looking uncomfortable in a black suit, and Guthrie, standing apart from the others, his face as impassive as always despite the unaccustomed moisture that blurred his vision as the plain pine coffin was lowered into the earth.

Now, two years later, Guthrie had assumed not just Silas's position but something of his mantle as well. The younger slaughtermen and apprentices approached him with the same mixture of respect and wariness that they had once shown his mentor. They sought his approval, flinched at his rare rebukes, and exchanged whispered stories about his uncanny abilities with a blade.

"Saw him take down a bull with one cut yesterday," a new apprentice would murmur. "Clean through the spine. Never seen anything like it."

"That's nothing," another would reply. "Last month he processed an entire wagon of pigs by himself when half the men were out with fever. Didn't even break a sweat."

These tales, passed from man to man like folk legends, only enhanced the aura of otherness that had always surrounded Guthrie. He was respected certainly—feared perhaps—but never truly accepted. He remained as solitary as he had been in his youth, speaking little except to issue instructions or correct a technique.

His routine had changed little over the years. He still lived in the small apartment above the slaughterhouse, though he had gradually improved it with simple furnishings built by his own hands—a sturdy table, a bookshelf filled with volumes on anatomy and butchery, a comfortable chair where he would sit in the evenings, reading by lamplight. His collection of knives had grown impressive, each one maintained with obsessive care. And he still fed the strays that gathered in the alley behind Holloway's, though the individual animals had changed over the years as the harsh realities of street life claimed them one by one.

What had changed was Holloway's itself. The financial pressures bearing down on the old slaughterhouse were impossible to ignore. Orders had decreased steadily as cheaper, mass-produced meat flooded the market. Even their loyal customers—the better restaurants and hotels that had always valued quality—were being forced to cut costs as Daybridge's economy stagnated.

Franklin Holloway, now in his sixties and battling gout that made his every step an agony, had become increasingly bitter about the changes. "No craftsmanship anymore," he would complain to anyone who would listen. "Just cheap goods for cheap people. Quality means nothing in this godforsaken city."

Guthrie said nothing during these tirades, but he understood the implications. The slaughterhouse was struggling, and with it, his own future. While his skills would certainly secure him a position elsewhere, the thought of leaving Holloway's—the only real home he had ever known—left him with an unfamiliar sense of dread.

It was against this backdrop of uncertainty that Jeremiah Crowe entered Guthrie's life, bringing with him an opportunity that would forever alter the butcher's path.

The day began like any other—before dawn, with Guthrie supervising the delivery of livestock that would meet their end under his knife. A late spring rain fell in sheets, turning the cobblestones slick and the holding pens into mud. The cattle lowed nervously, sensing what lay ahead in a way that never failed to impress Guthrie with its primal awareness.

"Knox!" Holloway's voice echoed from the office doorway. "Visitor for you. Important gentleman. Don't keep him waiting."

Guthrie looked up from the steer he was examining, his brow furrowing slightly. Visitors were unusual, especially ones that Holloway described as "important." He wiped his hands on his apron, trying without much success to remove the blood and grime that were the constant companions of his trade.

The office was small and cluttered, dominated by a battered desk piled high with ledgers and invoices. Seated in the room's only comfortable chair was a man who seemed as out of place in the slaughterhouse as a peacock in a chicken coop.

Jeremiah Crowe was in his late forties, though he carried himself with the vigor of a much younger man. His tailored suit of charcoal gray wool was clearly expensive, as was the gold watch chain that stretched across his vest. His face combined the ruddy complexion of a man who enjoyed fine living with the sharp, calculating eyes of one who knew exactly how to acquire the means for it. His hair, once dark but now salted with gray, was cut in the latest fashion, and his mustache was waxed to precise points.

"Ah, Mr. Knox," Crowe said, rising smoothly and extending a hand. "A pleasure to make your acquaintance at last. Jeremiah Crowe, at your service."

Guthrie hesitated before taking the offered hand, acutely aware of the stark contrast between his own blood-crusted appearance and Crowe's immaculate presentation. The businessman didn't seem to mind, his grip firm and confident.

"I'll leave you gentlemen to your business," Holloway muttered, shuffling out of the office with a grimace of pain as his gout-swollen foot touched the floor.

Alone with Crowe, Guthrie stood awkwardly, unused to social interactions that didn't involve the direct exchange of orders or the haggling of prices for meat.

"Please sit," Crowe gestured to Holloway's vacated chair. "I've been hoping to meet you for some time now. Your reputation precedes you, Mr. Knox."

"My reputation?" Guthrie's voice was rough from disuse; his social skills had atrophied over years of minimal conversation.

Crowe smiled, a gesture that didn't quite reach his calculating eyes. "Indeed. Throughout Daybridge, among those who appreciate true craftsmanship, your name is spoken with respect. 'The finest butcher in the city,' they say. 'Perhaps in all of New England.' High praise indeed."

Guthrie shifted uncomfortably. Compliments were as foreign to him as silk cravats and fine cologne. "I just do my job," he replied.

"With exceptional skill, by all accounts," Crowe countered smoothly. "I've spent my life recognizing talent, Mr. Knox. It's how I've built my various enterprises. And you, sir, have a rare talent indeed."

There was a quality to Crowe's voice—a silken persuasiveness that reminded Guthrie of the rare occasions when traveling salesmen would visit the orphanage, convincing Headmaster Blackwell to purchase tonics and remedies that inevitably proved worthless. It put him instantly on guard.

"What do you want?" he asked bluntly.

Rather than taking offense at the directness, Crowe seemed amused. "Straight to the point. I appreciate that in a man." He leaned forward, his expression becoming more serious. "I want to offer you an opportunity, Mr. Knox. One that would make use of your particular skills in a way that would be... exceedingly profitable for both of us."

"I'm a butcher," Guthrie stated flatly. "That's all."

"Is it?" Crowe's head tilted slightly, those calculating eyes seeming to see through Guthrie's impassive exterior. "I wonder. I've watched you, you know. Not personally, of course, but through the eyes of those who frequent establishments like this. The way you work, with such precision and detachment. It speaks of a mind that understands anatomy on an instinctive level. A mind that sees the underlying structures of things, the connections that others miss."

Guthrie remained silent, unsettled by how accurately this stranger had assessed his approach to his craft.

"Let me be direct, Mr. Knox," Crowe continued, lowering his voice though they were alone. "Daybridge is changing. The old ways—craftsmanship, quality, tradition—are being swept aside in favor of efficiency and profit. Men like you with genuine skill are being replaced by machines and unskilled laborers."

He gestured toward the window, where the outline of a massive new meatpacking plant was visible in the distance, its chimneys belching smoke into the already murky sky.

"Holloway's is dying," Crowe said, his tone matter of fact rather than cruel. "You must sense it already. Within a year, two at most, this place will close its doors forever. And then what becomes of Guthrie Knox and his extraordinary talents?"

The words struck Guthrie like physical blows, all the more painful for their undeniable truth. He had known Holloway's was struggling, had seen the ledgers awash in red ink, had noticed how the workforce had been reduced by half over the past three years.

But to hear it stated so baldly, to have the precariousness of his position laid bare by this elegant stranger, filled him with a cold dread.

"What exactly are you proposing?" he asked, his voice even lower than usual.

Crowe smiled again, this time with genuine satisfaction. "I have interests throughout Daybridge—properties, businesses, investments of various kinds. Occasionally, these interests generate... problems. Problems that require discreet handling by someone with specialized skills."

He reached into his coat and withdrew a small leather case, from which he extracted a card. It was simple but expensive, the heavy cream paper embossed with Crowe's name and an address in Graystone Heights, Daybridge's wealthiest district.

"I'm hosting a small gathering this Saturday evening. Nothing elaborate, just a few associates and their wives. I'd like you to attend. We can discuss potential arrangements in more detail then."

"I'm not a socialite," Guthrie protested, eyeing the card as if it might bite him. "I wouldn't fit in with your kind of people."

Crowe waved a dismissive hand. "Don't concern yourself with that. Come at eight o'clock through the servants' entrance at the back of the house. My butler will be expecting you and will show you to my study. No one else needs even to know you're there."

Reluctantly, Guthrie took the card, its smooth surface alien against his callused fingers.

"One more thing," Crowe added, reaching once more into his coat. This time he withdrew a small envelope, which he placed on the desk. "A token of my seriousness. Consider it an advance on our future association."

Without waiting for a response, Crowe stood and adjusted his immaculate cuffs. "Saturday at eight, Mr. Knox. I believe this will be the beginning of a most productive relationship for us both."

With that, he departed, leaving behind only the card, the envelope, and the lingering scent of expensive cologne that seemed jarringly out-of-place amid the abattoir's pervasive odor of blood and offal.

For a long moment, Guthrie stared at the envelope, wariness warring with curiosity. Finally, he picked it up and broke the seal. Inside was a stack of banknotes—more money than he earned in three months at Holloway's.

The implications were clear. Whatever "problems" Crowe wanted handled, they weren't legal. They likely weren't even moral. And yet, as Guthrie tucked the envelope into his pocket, he couldn't deny the surge of something like relief. Here, perhaps, was an answer to the uncertainty that had been looming over him like a storm cloud—a way to secure his future, even if that security came at a price he couldn't yet fully comprehend.

Saturday arrived gray and drizzling, the damp chill of late spring settling into Guthrie's bones as he made his way through Daybridge's winding streets toward Graystone Heights. He had spent his half-day at the slaughterhouse as usual, then returned to his apartment to wash away the blood and grime with painstaking thoroughness. He had even purchased a new shirt and coat for the occasion, the first such indulgence he had allowed himself in years.

Still, as he approached the imposing iron gates of Crowe's mansion, Guthrie felt acutely out of place. Graystone Heights was a world apart from the industrial quarters he knew—a realm of manicured gardens, gaslit streets, and houses that seemed to have been built for giants. Even in his new clothes, Guthrie knew he must look like what he was: a laborer, a man who worked with his hands, a denizen of Daybridge's grimier precincts.

Following Crowe's instructions, he circled to the rear of the property, where a smaller gate led to a service yard. A thin, austere man in a butler's uniform was waiting, his expression carefully neutral as he assessed the massive figure before him.

"Mr. Knox, I presume," the butler said, his voice as precisely modulated as his appearance. "Please follow me. Mr. Crowe is expecting you."

Guthrie was led through a maze of servants' corridors, the muffled sounds of music and conversation suggesting that Crowe's "small gathering" was well underway in the main part of the house. The contrast between the opulent glimpses he caught through partially open doors and the utilitarian passages they traversed was stark—a physical manifestation of the divided nature of Daybridge itself.

Finally, they arrived at a heavy oak door. The butler knocked once, then opened it without waiting for a response. "Mr. Knox has arrived, sir," he announced, then stepped aside to allow Guthrie to enter.

Crowe's study was a temple to masculine luxury—dark wood paneling, leather-bound books lining the walls, a massive desk of polished mahogany, and comfortable chairs arranged before a fire that cast dancing shadows across the room. The air was fragrant with tobacco smoke and the subtle scent of beeswax polish.

"Ah, Mr. Knox. Right on time." Crowe rose from behind his desk, a glass of amber liquid in one hand. "Thank you, Harrison. That will be all."

The butler bowed slightly and withdrew, closing the door with a soft click that somehow emphasized the room's isolation from the rest of the house.

"Brandy?" Crowe offered, gesturing to a crystal decanter on a nearby table.

Guthrie shook his head. "I don't drink."

"A man of discipline. I admire that." Crowe took a seat in one of the leather armchairs, indicating that Guthrie should do the same.

"I'm glad you decided to come. I believe we can help each other tremendously."

The chair creaked under Guthrie's weight as he sat, his discomfort obvious in the stiffness of his posture. "You mentioned problems that need handling," he said, getting straight to the point. "What kind of problems?"

Crowe smiled, swirling the brandy in his glass. "Direct as always. Very well." He leaned forward, his voice dropping to a confidential murmur despite the room's privacy. "I am a businessman, Mr. Knox. A successful one, with interests that span from textiles to shipping, real estate to mining. Such success inevitably creates rivals, some of whom are less than... ethical in their competition."

He took a sip of his brandy, his eyes never leaving Guthrie's face. "One such rival has recently caused me considerable difficulty. A man named Hargreaves, who has been systematically undercutting my textile operations, bribing my workers for information, and generally behaving in a most ungentlemanly fashion."

"And what do you want me to do about it?" Guthrie asked, though he suspected he already knew the answer.

"Hargreaves had an unfortunate accident this morning," Crowe replied, his tone as casual as if discussing the weather. "A fall down a particularly steep flight of stairs. Fatal, I'm afraid. The body is currently in a warehouse I own near the docks. It needs to disappear. Completely."

The implications hung in the air between them, as tangible as the smoke from Crowe's expensive cigar. Guthrie's mind raced, processing the request with the same methodical precision he brought to his work at the slaughterhouse. Disposing of a body would not be technically difficult for someone with his expertise. The moral implications, however...

"You want me to butcher a man," he said flatly, needing to hear it stated plainly.

Crowe winced slightly at the bluntness. "I prefer to think of it as solving a problem using your particular skill set. But yes, essentially, that is what I'm asking."

"Why me? There must be others who could do this for you."

"None with your abilities," Crowe countered. "This needs to be done efficiently, cleanly, and with absolute discretion. Your reputation suggests you are capable of all three."

Guthrie fell silent, weighing the proposal. He had never killed a man, though there had been moments—particularly during his youth at Blackwell Orphanage—when he had come close. He had certainly thought about it, had even mentally mapped out how he would do it if the necessity arose. But to actually take a human life, to apply his butcher's skills to a person rather than an animal...

And yet, did it matter? Hargreaves was already dead, according to Crowe. It wasn't as if Guthrie would be murdering him. And the money—that envelope of banknotes had been merely an "advance." How much more might there be for the actual work?

As if reading his thoughts, Crowe spoke again. "I'm prepared to pay five hundred pounds for this service. Half now, half upon completion. Additionally, should our arrangement prove satisfactory, there would be further opportunities in the future. Lucrative ones."

Five hundred pounds. It was an astronomical sum for a butcher who earned perhaps a hundred pounds in a year. It was security, independence, a buffer against the inevitable collapse of Holloway's Slaughterhouse. It was a future.

"If I agree," Guthrie said slowly, "I would need certain things. Tools. A secure location. Somewhere to dispose of the... remains."

Crowe nodded, clearly pleased by this shift from questioning to practical considerations. "All arranged. The warehouse has a section that's been prepared with everything you might require. As for disposal, the river is conveniently close, and the currents at that point are particularly strong. Anything entering the water there is quickly carried out to sea."

It was all so neat, so carefully planned. Guthrie wondered how many times Crowe had arranged similar "solutions" to his problems. But that wasn't his concern. His concern was the job itself, and whether he could do it.

"When?" he asked simply.

"Tonight," Crowe replied. "Now, in fact. My carriage is waiting in the mews. It will take you to the warehouse and wait to bring you back once you've finished."

The suddenness startled Guthrie, though he kept his expression neutral. He had expected some time to prepare, to mentally adjust to what he was agreeing to do. But perhaps it was better this way—no time to reconsider, to let doubt creep in.

"Five hundred pounds," he repeated. "Half now."

Crowe smiled and reached into his desk drawer, withdrawing a small leather pouch that clinked with the unmistakable sound of gold coins. "Two hundred and fifty pounds, as agreed. The rest upon completion."

Guthrie took the pouch, its weight substantial in his palm. He tucked it into his coat pocket without counting—a show of trust that wasn't lost on Crowe, whose smile widened appreciatively.

"Shall we proceed, then?" the businessman asked, rising from his chair.

Guthrie nodded; his decision made. Whatever moral line he was about to cross, he would do so with the same methodical precision he brought to every task. "I'll need an apron," he said. "And proper tools."

"All waiting for you," Crowe assured him. "Along with a change of clothes for afterward. Harrison will show you to the carriage."

As Guthrie followed the butler through the servants' passages once more, he was acutely aware of the weight of the gold in his pocket—and the heavier weight of the decision he had just made. By the time he returned to his apartment above Holloway's Slaughterhouse, he would be different. Not just financially, but fundamentally. The line between butcher and something far darker would have been irrevocably crossed.

The warehouse was near the eastern docks, a looming structure of corrugated iron and timber that had seen better days. The carriage pulled up to a side entrance, where a burly man with a face like a battered anvil stood guard. He nodded to the driver, then unlocked the door without a word, gesturing for Guthrie to enter.

Inside, the warehouse was cavernous and mostly empty, with a few scattered crates and barrels suggesting it was still occasionally used for legitimate purposes. The guard led Guthrie through the echoing space to a smaller room at the back, secured with a heavy padlock. Once inside, he handed Guthrie a key.

"Lock it behind me," he grunted. "When you're done, find me out front. Don't rush. Do it right." With that cryptic advice, he departed, leaving Guthrie alone in what could only be described as a makeshift butchery.

The room was perhaps twenty feet square, with a concrete floor sloping gently toward a central drain. Heavy plastic sheeting covered the walls and floor, secured with tape—a practical measure to prevent blood spatter from leaving evidence. Bright electric lights hung from the ceiling, illuminating the space with harsh clarity. A large metal table dominated the center of the room, beside which stood a smaller table laden with tools—knives of various sizes, saws, cleavers, all professional quality.

And on the table lay a body.

Hargreaves had been a man of middle years, with the soft physique of someone who enjoyed the finer things in life. His neck was bent at an unnatural angle, confirming Crowe's story about a fall. His eyes were open, glazed in death, staring at the ceiling with an expression of permanent surprise.

Guthrie approached slowly, studying the corpse with the detached interest of a craftsman assessing his materials. He had seen death countless times, had caused it with his own hands in the slaughterhouse. But this was different. This was a man, not a steer or a pig. A human being who had woken up that morning not knowing it would be his last day on earth.

For a moment, Guthrie hesitated, the full weight of what he was about to do pressing down on him. Then he remembered Old Silas's words: "Respect. For the blade. For the beasts. For death itself. It matters."

Perhaps it was a perversion of his mentor's teaching, but Guthrie decided that if he was to do this, he would do it with the same respect and precision he brought to his work at Holloway's. Not rushed, not careless, but methodical and clean.

He removed his coat and rolled up his sleeves, then donned the butcher's apron that had been provided. It was new, the canvas still stiff, but it would serve its purpose. Next, he examined the tools, testing the edge of each blade with his thumb. They were excellent quality, better even than his own collection. Whoever had procured them knew their business.

Finally, he turned his attention back to Hargreaves. The man had been dead for several hours, judging by the pallor of his skin and the beginning stages of rigor mortis. That would make the work slightly more difficult but not impossible.

"I'm sorry," Guthrie murmured, the words surprising him as they left his lips. He wasn't sure if he was apologizing to Hargreaves, to Old Silas's memory, or to some part of himself that he was about to leave behind forever.

Then, with a deep breath, he began.

The work was both familiar and alien. The basic principles were the same as with any large mammal—major blood vessels to be severed first, allowing what blood remained in the body to drain; joints to be separated; meat to be removed from bone. But the human form, while similar to the animals he butchered daily, had its differences. The proportions were wrong, the muscle groups arranged in subtly different patterns.

And yet, as he worked, Guthrie found himself slipping into the same focused trance that characterized his best days at the slaughterhouse. His hands moved with practiced efficiency, his mind mapping the anatomy before him with intuitive precision. There was no revulsion, no hesitation—only the pure, cold concentration of a master craftsman at work.

Hours passed, marked only by the soft sounds of his labor and the steady drip of fluids into the drain. Hargreaves, once a man with ambitions and appetites, was systematically reduced to his component parts, no different in Guthrie's hands than any other carcass.

When it was done, when what had been Hargreaves was packed neatly into weighted sacks ready for their journey to the river's depths, Guthrie stepped back and surveyed his work. The rubber sheeting had contained most of the mess, and what blood had escaped had been washed down the drain with the bucket of water provided for that purpose. The tools lay clean and gleaming on their table, wiped as meticulously as Guthrie cleaned his knives at Holloway's.

He removed the apron, now stained beyond salvation, and added it to one of the sacks. Then he washed his hands in the remaining water, dried them on a towel that would also go into the river, and changed into the fresh clothes that had been provided—simple workman's garb that would not attract attention.

Only then did the full impact of what he had done begin to register. He, Guthrie Knox, had dismembered a human being with the same dispassionate skill he brought to his legitimate work. And he had done it well. There had been no disgust, no moral queasiness, no sense that he was crossing a line that should not be crossed. Only the same satisfaction he always felt after completing a difficult job with precision and care.

What did that make him? The question echoed in his mind as he gathered the sacks and began the laborious process of carrying them one by one to the small dock attached to the warehouse, where he methodically dropped them into the swiftly flowing river. The current caught each one immediately, dragging it down and away toward the distant sea. Within minutes, all physical evidence of Julian Hargreaves had disappeared beneath the Shadowlair's murky waters.

Guthrie watched the ripples fade, his face as impassive as always. But inside, something had shifted, an internal barrier broken. He had discovered something about himself tonight—a capacity for a kind of work that few could stomach, fewer still could execute with such clinical detachment, and perhaps none could perform with his level of skill.

It should have horrified him. Instead, as he returned to the warehouse's entrance and found the guard waiting as promised, Guthrie felt something almost like peace. The rage that had been his constant companion since childhood, that had simmered beneath the surface of his being like magma beneath a volcano's peak, had temporarily subsided. The focused work, the absolute concentration required, had quieted it in a way even his regular butchery never fully achieved.

"All done?" the guard asked, his expression suggesting he neither knew nor cared about the specifics of what had occurred inside.

Guthrie nodded. "It's finished."

"Carriage is waiting. Boss says to tell you he's pleased. The rest of your payment will be delivered tomorrow."

And so, it was done. His first "special job" for Jeremiah Crowe, but not, he suspected, his last. As the carriage carried him back through Daybridge's darkened streets toward Holloway's Slaughterhouse, Guthrie contemplated the path that had led him to this point—and the one that now stretched before him.

He had crossed a line tonight, one that could never be uncrossed. Yet he felt no remorse, no self-loathing, no fear of divine judgment. Only a cold, clear certainty that he had found a new application for his skills, one that would ensure his survival in a city that cared nothing for traditional craftsmanship or the men who practiced it.

Old Silas had taught him to respect death, to make it clean and quick. In his own way, Guthrie believed he had honored that teaching tonight. Hargreaves was already dead when Guthrie received him. What followed was merely... processing. No different, really, then his daily work at Holloway's.

Or so he told himself as dawn broke over Daybridge, casting long shadows from the factory chimneys and turning the polluted river into a ribbon of fire. So, he would continue to tell himself in the days, months, and years to come, as Jeremiah Crowe's "problems" became a regular part of his life, and the name Guthrie Knox began to inspire a different kind of fear in Daybridge's shadowy underworld.

His hands had always been red from his work. Now they were simply red with a different kind of blood. And in time, he would find that the distinction mattered less and less.

Chapter 4: The Crimson Ledger

The summer of 1896 descended upon Daybridge like a fever dream, bringing with it oppressive heat that transformed the industrial quarter into a steaming cauldron of coal smoke and river stench. The polluted waters of the Shadowlair receded under the relentless sun, exposing muddy banks littered with the detritus of a city in flux—rusted machinery parts, broken bottles, and occasionally, the bloated corpses of dogs and rats. Sometimes, if rumors were to be believed, things far worse washed up when the tides were especially low.

For Guthrie Knox, the changing seasons meant little. His life had settled into a new pattern, as regimented and disciplined as ever, but now divided between two worlds that rarely intersected. By day, he remained the head butcher at Holloway's Slaughterhouse, his reputation for precision and efficiency unchallenged. By night, however, he had become something else entirely—a shadow figure known to only a select few among Daybridge's elite.

In the ten months since that first "special job" for Jeremiah Crowe, Guthrie had handled a dozen similar tasks. Each one arrived the same way—a sealed envelope delivered to Holloway's, containing an address, a time, and half his payment in banknotes or gold sovereigns. Never any details, never a direct connection to Crowe. Just the implicit understanding that a problem needed solving.

Most were like Hargreaves—already dead when Guthrie arrived, requiring only his skills at dismemberment and disposal. A few had been more complicated, involving transport of live subjects who became dead ones under circumstances Guthrie neither questioned nor particularly cared about. He performed each task with the same meticulous care he brought to his legitimate work, earning not just substantial payment but also a reputation among Crowe's circle as reliable, discreet, and thorough.

What surprised Guthrie was not the work itself but how easily he had adapted to it. The moral line he had feared crossing that first night with Hargreaves had proven to be far more permeable than he'd imagined. The emotional detachment that had been his survival mechanism in childhood now served him well, allowing him to compartmentalize these nocturnal activities as simply another form of butchery. The fact that his subjects were human rather than animal seemed a technicality rather than a fundamental distinction.

This ability to separate himself from the moral implications of his actions made him invaluable to men like Crowe. Unlike the typical thugs and cutthroats who populated Daybridge's criminal underworld, Guthrie brought a professional's precision and a craftsman's pride to his work. There was no sadism, no unnecessary cruelty, no messiness born of emotional involvement. Just clean, efficient disposal of problems that threatened the business interests of wealthy men.

As his reputation grew, so did his clientele. Crowe began to act as an intermediary, connecting Guthrie with others among Daybridge's upper echelon who required his particular services. Industrialists whose rivals suffered convenient accidents. Bankers whose debtors disappeared without a trace. Politicians who needed certain scandals permanently buried.

The money flowed steadily, far more than Guthrie could earn in a lifetime at Holloway's. He kept most of it hidden in a series of lockboxes beneath the floorboards of his apartment, using only enough to improve his living conditions modestly. A better bed. Some quality clothes for his rare ventures into the city's respectable districts. Books on anatomy, physiology, and medical procedures that expanded his understanding of the human body and its vulnerabilities.

To anyone observing him, Guthrie's life appeared unchanged. He still lived above the slaughterhouse, still worked the same grueling hours, still kept to himself. The stray dogs in the alley behind Holloway's continued to receive their nightly offerings, though now the scraps were supplemented with proper meat purchased from a butcher across town—a small luxury Guthrie allowed himself as his finances improved.

But beneath this facade of continuity, significant changes were taking place. The most substantial was the workshop Guthrie had created in a forgotten corner of Holloway's basement.

The slaughterhouse had been built in the 1840s, during Daybridge's first industrial expansion. Like many buildings of that era, it contained spaces that had been rendered obsolete by changing methods or forgotten entirely during renovations. One such space was a large storage room accessible only through a heavy iron door hidden behind stacks of rarely used equipment in the basement. The room had likely been used for aging meat in the days before mechanical refrigeration, but modern methods had made it superfluous.

Guthrie discovered it during his early years at Holloway's, when he was still exploring every corner of the building that would become his home. At the time, it had been nothing more than a curiosity—a damp, chilly chamber with stone walls and a floor that sloped toward a central drain, much like the killing floor above but on a smaller scale. He had noted its existence and then largely forgotten about it.

Now, however, it presented an ideal solution to a growing problem. The warehouses and abandoned buildings where he had been conducting his "special work" were becoming increasingly risky. Daybridge was changing, with development pushing into formerly derelict areas. Each new location required scouting, preparation, and afterward, thorough cleaning—all of which increased the chances of discovery.

Over several weeks in the early spring of 1896, Guthrie quietly transformed the forgotten room into a purpose-built workshop for his clandestine activities. He replaced the rusted old drain, ensuring proper flow to the sewer system. He installed a series of gas lamps for reliable lighting. He brought in a sturdy metal table, similar to those on the killing floor but smaller, and bolted it to the floor. Along one wall, he mounted a rack for his growing collection of specialized tools—some from Holloway's stores, others purchased with his newfound wealth, a few custom-made by a blacksmith in the industrial quarter who asked no questions about their intended use.

The finishing touch was a heavy lock for the iron door, the key to which never left Guthrie's person. The room was now secure, accessible only to him, and practically soundproof due to the thick stone walls and its location deep within the slaughterhouse's foundations.

The workshop solved several problems at once. It eliminated the need for external locations, reducing risk. It was already equipped with proper drainage for bodily fluids. And most importantly, it was located within Holloway's, where the constant sounds and smells of regular butchery provided perfect cover for Guthrie's darker activities. Who would notice an extra carcass being processed in a building where death was the daily business?

Franklin Holloway, increasingly consumed by his failing health and the slaughterhouse's declining fortunes, never ventured into the basement anymore. The few workers who might have occasion to go there were easily avoided by conducting the special work late at night, after everyone else had gone home. And if anyone did happen to notice Guthrie working unusual hours, they would think nothing of it—his legendary dedication to his craft was well-established.

The workshop became Guthrie's sanctuary, a space where he could practice his craft without constraint or observation. It was here, in the cold silence of that stone chamber, that he began to refine his methods, developing techniques specifically adapted to human subjects rather than simply applying his butchery skills.

And it was here that he began the journal.

The idea came to him after a particularly complex job involving a labor organizer who had been causing problems for one of Crowe's associates in the textile industry. The man had been brought to Guthrie still alive—gagged and bound, his eyes wide with terror. Crowe's associate had specific requirements about the disposal, wanting certain body parts preserved as warnings to other potential troublemakers.

The technical challenges had been considerable, requiring Guthrie to improvise solutions that combined his butchery knowledge with information gleaned from his medical texts. Afterward, he found himself mentally reviewing the procedure, identifying aspects that could be improved. On impulse, he purchased a leather-bound ledger the next day and began to record his observations.

The first entry was clinical, detached—a technical description of the methods used, the tools employed, the challenges encountered, and potential improvements for future reference. There was no mention of the subject as a person, no acknowledgment of the moral dimension of what had occurred. Just a craftsman's notes on a complex project.

That initial record evolved into a habit. After each special job, Guthrie would add to the ledger, documenting his techniques with the same meticulous attention to detail that characterized his work. Over time, the journal expanded to include sketches of the human anatomy, precise measurements of blood loss rates from various wounds, observations on the effectiveness of different disposal methods, and other technical details that might prove useful.

The ledger itself was kept in a false-bottomed drawer in Guthrie's apartment, secured by a lock whose key he wore on a chain around his neck. Not that anyone ever visited his sparse quarters or would have reason to examine his few possessions. The precaution was born not of practical necessity but of the same exacting thoroughness that defined all aspects of Guthrie's life.

To an outside observer, the journal would have appeared monstrous—the meticulous record-keeping of a man who had lost all connection to humanity. But to Guthrie, it was simply a professional tool, no different from the diagrams of cattle and pigs that guided apprentice butchers in their training. If his subjects were human rather than animal, that was a distinction that had ceased to matter in any meaningful way.

This emotional severance—this ability to regard human beings as simply another form of meat to be processed—had not come suddenly. It had developed gradually, nurtured by the isolation and abuse of his childhood, reinforced by years of slaughterhouse work, and finally perfected through his nocturnal activities. By the summer of 1896, Guthrie's capacity for empathy had atrophied to the point where it functioned only in the narrowest of contexts—primarily toward the stray animals he continued to feed and protect.

Toward humans, he felt... nothing. Not hatred, not anger, not even the cold satisfaction of power that motivates many who kill. Just a vast, echoing emptiness where such emotions might have resided in another man.

This emotional numbness was perhaps Guthrie's most valuable asset in his new line of work. It allowed him to approach each task with clinical detachment, untroubled by conscience or remorse. It was what made him so effective—and so frightening to those few who understood what he had become.

The change in Guthrie's status within Daybridge's criminal hierarchy was subtle but significant. Where once he had been merely a tool to be used by men like Crowe—a skilled craftsman hired for specific tasks—he was increasingly becoming a power in his own right, someone whose favor was sought and whose displeasure was feared.

This shift became apparent during a gathering at Crowe's mansion in late August 1896. Unlike the first time Guthrie had been summoned there, on this occasion he was invited to enter through the front door, not the servants' entrance. He was escorted not to a private study but to a well-appointed drawing room where a dozen of Daybridge's most influential citizens were engaged in what appeared to be a social evening but was, in reality, a council of sorts.

Industrialists, bankers, shipping magnates, and politicians—men whose names appeared regularly in the city's newspapers and whose decisions shaped Daybridge's future—greeted Guthrie with the cautious respect normally reserved for dangerous but necessary allies. They offered him brandy (which he declined), cigars (also declined), and then, more significantly, a seat at their table.

"Gentlemen," Crowe announced once they were all settled, "I believe most of you know Mr. Knox, at least by reputation. For those who don't, suffice it to say that he has been instrumental in resolving various... challenges that have confronted our business interests over the past year."

Murmurs of acknowledgment rippled around the table. Several men nodded to Guthrie, their expressions a mixture of respect and wariness.

"I've asked him to join us tonight because we face a situation that requires his particular expertise," Crowe continued. "The dock workers' union is becoming increasingly problematic. Their latest demands would increase shipping costs by nearly thirty percent—an unacceptable figure that would render Daybridge's port uncompetitive with New York and Baltimore/"

One of the men—a heavy-set individual with the florid complexion of someone who enjoyed the finer things in life—pounded his fist on the table. "Damned socialists! They'll ruin this city with their demands. We should bring in strikebreakers from Chicago, teach them a lesson they won't forget."

Crowe raised a hand. "Violence on that scale would attract unwanted attention. The newspapers, even those sympathetic to our interests, would be forced to report it. No, we need a more... surgical approach."

All eyes turned to Guthrie, who sat impassive and silent, his massive frame seeming out of place among these well-fed, well-dressed men of business.

"The union has five leaders," Crowe explained, sliding a folder across the table toward Guthrie. "They're the driving force behind the more radical elements. With them removed from the equation, we believe the rank and file would be more amenable to reasonable negotiations."

Guthrie opened the folder, examining the photographs and handwritten dossiers it contained. Five men, ranging in age from their late twenties to early fifties. Names, addresses, habits, routines—all meticulously documented.

"All five?" he asked, his voice quiet but carrying clearly in the hushed room.

Crowe exchanged glances with the others before responding. "Yes. Spaced out over several weeks, of course. Made to look like accidents or common crimes. Nothing that would suggest a pattern."

Guthrie considered the request. Until now, his work had primarily involved disposal or, at most, execution of individuals already detained by others. What Crowe was proposing was different—active hunting of targets who were not already in custody. It represented a significant escalation of his role.

"My usual fee would need to be adjusted," he said after a moment. "Given the increased complexity."

Relief visibly washed over several faces around the table. They had been uncertain whether he would accept the assignment—not for moral reasons, which they correctly assumed would not trouble him, but because it went beyond his established parameters.

"Of course," Crowe agreed smoothly. "Shall we say double the standard arrangement? Half in advance, as usual."

Guthrie nodded once, closing the folder and tucking it inside his coat. "I'll need two weeks for the first one. Preparation is essential."

"Understood. We leave the details entirely in your capable hands."

The meeting continued, moving on to other business matters, but Guthrie's role was done. He sat quietly, observing the interactions among these powerful men, noting the alliances and rivalries that surfaced in their discussions. It was educational, in its way—a glimpse into the machinery that truly drove Daybridge, far from the public facades these same men presented in newspaper photographs and civic ceremonies.

When the gathering dispersed shortly before midnight, Crowe took Guthrie aside, pressing an envelope into his massive hand. "The first installment," he murmured. "And my personal thanks. This situation has been... concerning."

Guthrie pocketed the envelope without checking its contents. Trust had been established between them over the past year—not friendship, certainly, but a professional understanding. "Two weeks," he repeated. "The first one will appear to be a robbery gone wrong."

Crowe nodded, satisfied. "Excellent. Oh, and Guthrie," he added, using the butcher's first name for the first time in their association, "I want you to know that your position in our circle is appreciated. You've become quite indispensable to Daybridge's prosperity."

It was a compliment, but also a recognition of the changing power dynamic. Guthrie was no longer merely a tool but a partner of sorts. A man who knew too many secrets to be treated as a simple hireling.

As he made his way back to Holloway's through the warm summer night, Guthrie considered this new development. He had never sought power or influence. His needs were simple—security, solitude, the freedom to practice his craft without interference. But power had found him, nonetheless, born from his unique skills and his willingness to use them without moral constraint.

The folder in his coat pocket represented a new chapter in his evolution. No longer just a butcher of the dead, but a hunter of the living. A harbinger of death rather than merely its processor. The distinction might have troubled another man. For Guthrie, it was simply a technical challenge to be approached with his usual methodical precision.

He would need to plan carefully. Study his targets. Learn their habits, their weaknesses. Develop methods that would appear as random street crime or unfortunate accidents. It was complex work, but not fundamentally different from breaking down a carcass. Just another form of butchery, with additional steps beforehand.

By the time he reached his apartment above the slaughterhouse, Guthrie's mind was already mapping out approaches, evaluating tools, calculating risks. He would record it all in his journal, of course. The Crimson Ledger, as he had come to think of it—a meticulous accounting of debts paid in blood.

The first target was Daniel Hewitt, treasurer of the dock workers' union and, according to the dossier, the most financially vulnerable of the five leaders. A man with a weakness for gambling that had left him deeply in debt to some unsavory characters in Daybridge's Eastern Quarter.

Guthrie spent a week observing Hewitt's routines, noting his regular visits to a particular tavern near the docks where illegal card games were held in the back room. The man would typically leave well after midnight, often intoxicated and either flush with winnings or, more commonly, depressed by losses. He would then walk the four blocks to his modest home, taking a shortcut through an unlit alley that ran behind a row of warehouses.

It was an almost laughably easy scenario—a drunk man, alone at night, in one of Daybridge's more dangerous districts. The perfect setup for what would appear to be a routine robbery gone violently wrong.

On the chosen night, Guthrie positioned himself in the darkest section of the alley, wearing nondescript workman's clothes and a cap pulled low over his face. He carried a lead-weighted cosh—a common weapon among Daybridge's criminal element—and had roughened his hands with coal dust to eliminate the possibility of leaving identifiable prints.

Hewitt appeared right on schedule, stumbling slightly as he made his way down the alley. From the slump of his shoulders and the muttered curses Guthrie could hear, it had been a losing night at the tables. Good—a robbery would seem even more plausible.

The actual deed took less than thirty seconds. A swift, silent approach from behind. The cosh brought down with precise force at the base of the skull—enough to stun but not kill. Hewitt dropped like a stone, unconscious before he hit the ground. Guthrie dragged him deeper into the shadows, then applied the techniques he had developed during his year of "special work."

A particular pressure point at the junction of the neck and shoulder, held for exactly two minutes and seventeen seconds—a method he had perfected through careful experimentation and documented in his journal. It left no marks, caused no trauma that would be visible during a cursory autopsy, and mimicked the effects of a heart attack or stroke. Hewitt's known drinking habits and the stress of his union activities would provide plausible explanations for such a medical event.

Once he was certain Hewitt was dead, Guthrie rifled through the man's pockets, taking his wallet, watch, and a small silver flask—items whose absence would support the robbery narrative. These he would dispose of in the river later that night. Then he arranged the body in a position consistent with someone who had collapsed suddenly, adjusting the limbs to account for the effects of rigor mortis that would set in over the next few hours.

The entire process, from initial attack to final arrangements, took less than five minutes. Guthrie left the alley the way he had come, encountered no one, and was back in his apartment above Holloway's within the hour. There, he meticulously recorded the details in his journal—the effectiveness of the cosh, the precise time required for the pressure point technique to take effect, observations about Hewitt's physical responses during his final moments.

The entry, like all those in the Crimson Ledger, was clinical and detached. There was no mention of the man's expression as death took him, no reflection on the family he left behind, no consideration of the moral dimensions of the act. Just technical details, useful for refining his methods for future assignments.

The next morning, Guthrie went about his regular duties at the slaughterhouse as if nothing had changed. When news of Hewitt's death reached Holloway's—brought by a dock worker who delivered a shipment of ice—Guthrie expressed the same mild interest as his colleagues, then returned to his work without further comment.

That evening, a messenger delivered an envelope containing the second half of his payment for the Hewitt job, along with a newspaper clipping about the "tragic death" of the union treasurer, apparently the victim of a heart attack after being robbed in an alley near the docks. The police were investigating but had no leads on the robbery. The medical examiner had determined the cause of death to be natural causes, likely brought on by the shock of the attack combined with Hewitt's known heart condition.

Guthrie read the article twice, noting with professional satisfaction that his techniques had achieved exactly the result intended. He added the clipping to his journal as a form of documentation, then began planning for the second target on his list.

Over the next two months, the remaining four union leaders met similar fates. A drowning in the Shadowlair River after a night of heavy drinking. A fall down a steep staircase in a tenement building. A tragic accident with a gas lamp that resulted in fatal burns. And finally, a mugging that turned deadly when the victim allegedly fought back against his attackers.

None of the deaths, viewed individually, aroused particular suspicion. Daybridge was a dangerous city, especially in its poorer quarters where the union men lived and worked. Such tragedies were commonplace enough to merit only brief mention in the newspapers, quickly forgotten as new misfortunes took their place in the public consciousness.

Only when viewed collectively did a pattern emerge—but by the time anyone might have connected these dots, the damage to the union had been done. Leaderless and demoralized, the rank and file voted to accept a much-reduced version of their original demands, effectively ending the threat to the shipping interests represented by Crowe and his associates.

For Guthrie, the successful completion of this complex assignment represented a significant evolution in his capabilities. He was no longer just a disposer of bodies or an executioner of captives. He was now a hunter, capable of identifying, stalking, and eliminating targets in ways that aroused no suspicion. His value to Daybridge's criminal elite increased accordingly, as did his fees.

By the autumn of 1896, Guthrie Knox had become something far more dangerous than a simple butcher with a side business in disposal. He had become a precision instrument of death—efficient, reliable, and utterly without moral constraint.

It was during this period of professional advancement that Guthrie committed his first truly independent kill—an act not commissioned by Crowe or any other patron but undertaken solely on his own initiative. The incident revealed aspects of his character that even he had not fully recognized, foreshadowing the more monstrous evolution that lay in his future.

The victim was Walter Simms, a dockworker known for his meanness when in his cups, which was most evenings. Simms lived in a run-down tenement near Holloway's and often passed through the alley where Guthrie fed his strays on his way home from whichever tavern had been willing to extend him credit that night.

On several occasions, Guthrie had observed Simms kicking at the dogs, throwing bottles at them, or otherwise tormenting the animals who gathered for their nightly feeding. Each time, Guthrie had stayed out of sight, not wanting to create a connection between himself and the strays in the mind of someone like Simms, who might drunkenly mention it to others at Holloway's.

But on a frigid November evening, with sleet stinging the skin and turning the cobblestones treacherously slick, Simms went further than mere harassment. As Guthrie watched from the shadows of a recessed doorway, the dockworker cornered one of the older dogs—a grizzled terrier mix that had been coming to the alley for years—and began beating it with a length of pipe he'd picked up from a pile of construction debris.

The dog's yelps of pain echoed off the brick walls of the alley, but it was the look in the animal's eyes that triggered something in Guthrie—a deep, visceral rage that bypassed his usual emotional detachment. The terrier's gaze, filled with confusion and terror, connected with some buried part of his psyche, perhaps reminding him of his own helplessness during the abuses of his childhood.

Without conscious thought, Guthrie stepped out of the shadows and moved toward Simms with the same silent, deliberate stride he had used when approaching Hewitt in that other alley months before. But this was different. This wasn't a calculated, professional act. This was personal, driven by an emotion that Guthrie had thought long extinguished.

"Stop," he said, his voice carrying the cold authority that had become his trademark at Holloway's.

Simms turned, the pipe still raised for another blow, his face flushed with drink and exertion. Recognition flickered in his bloodshot eyes—he knew Guthrie by sight, as did most who lived or worked in the area around the slaughterhouse.

"Mind yer own business, butcher," Simms slurred, lowering the pipe slightly but not relinquishing it. "This mangy cur bit me last week. Deserves what's comin' to it."

Guthrie said nothing, simply continued his advance, his massive frame blocking the feeble light from the single gas lamp at the alley's entrance. The sleet plastered his hair to his skull and ran in rivulets down his impassive face, giving him the appearance of a statue come malevolently to life.

Something in that implacable approach, or perhaps in Guthrie's expression, finally penetrated Simms's alcohol-fogged brain. He took a step back, then another, the pipe now held defensively rather than offensively.

"Now, look here," he began, his voice taking on a wheedling tone. "I didn't mean no real harm. Just teachin' the beast a lesson, is all."

Still, Guthrie said nothing. He closed the distance between them with two more long strides, then reached out with a speed that belied his size and wrenched the pipe from Simms's grasp. The dockworker stumbled backward, losing his footing on the icy cobblestones and landing hard on his backside.

"Jesus Christ," Simms gasped, real fear now evident in his face. "It's just a bloody dog, for God's sake!"

That was when Guthrie did something unprecedented in his adult life—he allowed his expression to change, to reveal the cold fury that had seized him. His lips drew back from his teeth in a snarl that had nothing human about it, a rictus of pure, predatory rage.

"It's under my protection," he said, each word enunciated with unnatural precision. "As are all the creatures in this alley."

Simms scrambled backward like a crab, trying to put distance between himself and the towering figure looming over him. "I didn't know," he babbled. "Swear to God, I didn't know they was yours. Won't happen again, Mr. Knox. You have my word."

In that moment, looking down at the pathetic, cowering form of Walter Simms, Guthrie made a decision. Not a calculated, professional assessment like those he made in his work for Crowe, but a raw, emotional choice driven by something primal that had awakened within him.

This man had hurt one of his creatures. Had taken pleasure in causing pain to a defenseless being under Guthrie's protection. Such an offense could not go unpunished.

"Get up," Guthrie ordered, his voice unnaturally calm now, the momentary display of emotion locked away once more behind his usual mask of impassivity.

Simms struggled to his feet, still babbling apologies and promises never to bother the dogs again. Guthrie listened without comment, then gestured toward the far end of the alley.

"Walk," he commanded.

"Where? I live the other way—"

"Walk." There was no anger in the word, no threat, just an implacable certainty that he would be obeyed.

Simms walked, casting nervous glances over his shoulder at the silent figure following a few paces behind. The sleet had intensified, reducing visibility and muffling sounds. Perfect conditions for what Guthrie had in mind.

They emerged from the alley onto a narrow street lined with warehouses, most of them dark and shuttered for the night. Guthrie directed Simms toward one particular building—a disused cold storage facility that had been abandoned when its owner went bankrupt the previous year. The heavy padlock on the main door had been broken months ago by scavengers looking for anything of value and never replaced.

"In there," Guthrie said, pointing to the gap where the door stood slightly ajar.

"What? Why?" Simms's voice had risen an octave, panic beginning to override even his alcohol-dulled senses. "Look, Mr.

Knox, I said I was sorry about the dog. Won't happen again. Just let me go home, yeah? Wife'll be wonderin' where I got to."

"In," Guthrie repeated, taking a step toward the increasingly frantic man. "Or I'll put you in there myself."

The threat, delivered in that same eerily calm tone, broke whatever resistance Simms might have been considering. He stumbled forward and pushed through the gap into the darkness beyond.

Guthrie followed, pulling the door closed behind them. The interior of the warehouse was pitch black and bitterly cold; the air heavy with the lingering smell of meat that had spoiled when the refrigeration failed. He heard Simms breathing raggedly somewhere ahead of him, could sense the man's mounting terror.

With the practiced ease of someone accustomed to working in darkness, Guthrie extracted a small tin from his pocket and struck a match, illuminating the cavernous space with a sudden flare of yellow light. Simms stood a few yards away, his face ghastly in the wavering illumination, eyes wide with fear.

"Mr. Knox," he began, his voice shaking. "Please—"

"Quiet."

Guthrie lit a stub of candle from the match, then placed it carefully on a nearby ledge. Its feeble light created a small island of visibility in the vast darkness of the warehouse. Within that circle of illumination, he could see hooks hanging from overhead rails—the remnants of the cold storage system that had once held sides of beef ready for distribution to butcher shops throughout Daybridge.

It was, Guthrie thought with cold appreciation, almost too perfect a setting for what he had in mind.

"Take off your coat," he instructed, his voice still devoid of emotion.

"What? It's freezing in here—"

"Take it off."

Simms, trembling now from both cold and fear, struggled out of his threadbare wool coat. Guthrie took it from him and hung it carefully on one of the hooks, then turned back to the increasingly desperate man.

What followed was a methodical application of the skills Guthrie had developed over his years of "special work." Not rushed, not driven by passion despite the anger that had initially propelled him into this situation. Just the careful, precise execution of techniques he had refined to an art form.

He worked silently, ignoring Simms's initial pleas and eventual screams. The warehouse's thick walls muffled the sounds, and the surrounding buildings were empty at this hour, anyway. No one would hear. No one would come.

When it was done, when Walter Simms had been transformed from a living man into what Guthrie clinically regarded as "material," he stepped back to assess his work. It was, he had to admit, some of his finest. A demonstration piece, really—the sort of thing Old Silas might have created to show apprentices the proper techniques for breaking down a complex carcass.

The candle had burned low, its light flickering as it neared the end of its brief life. Guthrie took a moment to record mental notes for later transcription into his journal. The effectiveness of certain techniques. The unexpected resistance of muscle groups. The amount of blood loss from specific incisions. All valuable data for his ongoing professional development.

Then, as the candle sputtered out, he gathered the various components of what had been Walter Simms and methodically transported them to his workshop in Holloway's basement. There, he would complete the processing and disposal according to his established protocols.

The entire incident, from the moment he stepped out of the shadows in the alley to the final cleanup of his workshop, took less than four hours. By the time dawn broke over Daybridge, washing the soot-stained buildings in pale winter light, there was no evidence that Walter Simms had ever existed beyond the memories of those who had known him.

His disappearance caused little stir. Dock workers often moved on, seeking better opportunities in other ports or simply abandoning families they could no longer support. A few inquiries were made by his employer and his long-suffering wife, but no serious investigation followed. Another anonymous tragedy in a city that witnessed dozens every day.

That night, as he made his customary entries in the Crimson Ledger, Guthrie realized that something fundamental had changed. His first independent kill had awakened something in him—not conscience or remorse, but their opposite. A sense of... satisfaction. Of rightness. Of having balanced some cosmic scale that only he could perceive.

Walter Simms had hurt one of his creatures, had taken pleasure in causing pain to a being under Guthrie's protection. And for that, he had paid the ultimate price. It was justice, of a sort—Guthrie's justice, administered according to his own internal code.

As he carefully recorded the technical details of the Simms procedure, Guthrie considered the implications of this development. Until now, his "special work" had been a business arrangement, a service provided for compensation. Emotional involvement had been not merely unnecessary but counterproductive to the precision his craft required.

But this... this had been different. Personal. And yet, once the initial burst of rage had passed, he had reverted to his usual methodical approach, perhaps even exceeding his normal standards of thoroughness. The emotion had provided the impetus, but not the execution.

It was an interesting discovery, one that warranted further exploration. Perhaps there was room in his life for both types of work—the professional services rendered to Crowe and his associates, and these more personal adjustments to the moral ledger of Daybridge.

The thought was strangely appealing. For years, Guthrie had existed in a state of emotional numbness, his inner rage carefully contained by the discipline of his craft. Now he had found a way to channel that rage productively, to use it as a tool rather than suppress it as a liability.

As he closed the journal and returned it to its hiding place, Guthrie felt something akin to contentment. His world made sense again, the various parts of his nature integrated into a coherent whole. The butcher and the killer, the craftsman and the avenger—all aspects of the same being, working in harmony toward a purpose that transcended mere survival.

It would be many years before he recognized this moment for what it truly was—the first step on a path that would eventually lead him to the bridge, to the witch, and to the monstrous transformation that would remake him into the Ogre of Daybridge. But in some deep, instinctual part of his being, Guthrie Knox already sensed that he had crossed a threshold from which there would be no return.

And he had no desire to go back.

Chapter 5: Whispers in the Dark

Winter descended upon Daybridge with a bitter vengeance in late 1897, wrapping the city in a shroud of ice and fog so thick that gas lamps appeared as nothing more than ghostly smears in the darkness. The Shadowlair River froze along its edges, great sheets of ice cracking and groaning like tormented spirits as the current pushed beneath them. Many claimed it was the coldest winter in memory, though the elderly among Daybridge's population muttered that the truly brutal season had been the winter of '58, when bodies were found frozen solid in doorways and the river had become a highway of ice.

For Guthrie Knox, now approaching his twenty-eighth year, the changing seasons marked nothing more than practical considerations—different challenges in disposal, alterations to his routines, adjustments to the methods he employed in his nocturnal activities. The bitter cold meant bodies cooled faster, stiffened more quickly, presenting technical issues that required adaptation. In his journal—now expanded to three leather-bound volumes filled with his precise handwriting—he documented these seasonal variations with the same clinical detachment he brought to all aspects of his craft.

The past year had seen significant changes in Guthrie's standing within Daybridge's shadow hierarchy. What had begun as a simple business arrangement with Jeremiah Crowe had evolved into a complex network of relationships with various members of the city's elite. Bankers, industrialists, shipping magnates, politicians—all knew of the massive butcher's special skills, and all had, at one time or another, availed themselves of his services.

His reputation had grown to near-mythical proportions among this rarefied circle. They spoke of him in hushed tones at private clubs and exclusive gatherings, referring to him only as "the

Butcher" or sometimes simply as "G." His name had become a veiled threat in business negotiations, a final card to be played when all other forms of persuasion had failed.

"Perhaps I should consult G about this matter," a factory owner might murmur to a recalcitrant union representative, and suddenly concessions would be made, agreements reached with surprising alacrity.

Guthrie was aware of this status, though it meant little to him beyond the practical benefits it provided—security, autonomy, and a steady income that far exceeded what he could earn at Holloway's Slaughterhouse, where he still maintained his position as head butcher. The dual nature of his existence—respectable tradesman by day, dealer in death by night—had become so routine that he rarely considered its strangeness anymore.

But as the winter of 1897 tightened its grip on Daybridge, Guthrie began to sense subtle changes in the nature of the requests coming his way. The "problems" he was asked to solve took on increasingly unusual dimensions, hinting at undercurrents in the city's power structure that even he, with his unique perspective, had not previously suspected.

The first indication came on a night in early December, when the fog was so thick that even Guthrie, with his intimate knowledge of Daybridge's streets, had difficulty navigating from Holloway's to his destination—a mansion in Blackstone Square, one of the city's most exclusive addresses. The request had come through Crowe, as most still did, but with an unusual stipulation: Guthrie was to arrive at precisely midnight, not a minute earlier or later.

Such specificity was unusual in his line of work, where flexibility was often necessary to avoid detection. But the fee offered was substantial enough that Guthrie simply noted the requirement and adjusted his schedule accordingly.

The mansion belonged to Lord Richard Vane, a peer of the realm whose family had controlled significant portions of Daybridge's shipping and import businesses for generations. Vane was not unknown to Guthrie—he had handled two previous matters for the aristocrat, both relatively straightforward disposals of individuals who had threatened Vane's business interests. But this summons felt different from the outset.

The butler who admitted Guthrie through a side entrance was not the same one who had received him on previous visits. This man was older, with a pallid complexion and eyes that seemed to reflect no light. He said nothing as he led Guthrie through a series of corridors Guthrie had not traversed before, descending deeper into the mansion's labyrinthine depths.

They arrived finally at a heavy oak door bound with iron straps. The butler produced an ornate key from his waistcoat pocket, inserted it into the lock, and turned it with a resonant click. He stepped aside, gesturing for Guthrie to enter.

"His Lordship awaits within," the butler said, his voice unexpectedly deep and sonorous in the confined space. "You are expected."

The room beyond was unlike any Guthrie had seen in his previous visits to the houses of Daybridge's elite. Where most favored ostentatious displays of wealth—ornate furnishings, expensive artwork, imported luxuries—this chamber was spartan almost to the point of asceticism. Stone walls, bare except for a few tapestries depicting scenes Guthrie could not immediately identify in the dim light. A floor of dark wood, polished to a soft gleam. No windows, the only illumination provided by a circle of black candles surrounding a central stone table or altar.

Around this table stood five figures in hooded robes of deep burgundy, their faces obscured by shadows. One stepped forward as Guthrie entered, pulling back his hood to reveal the aristocratic features of Lord Vane. His normally florid complexion seemed paler than usual, his eyes fever-bright in the flickering candlelight.

"Ah, G. Punctual as always." Vane's voice carried the cultured accent of Britain's upper classes, each word precisely enunciated. "Thank you for accommodating our rather specific timing requirements."

Guthrie remained near the door, his massive frame tensed almost imperceptibly. Something about this situation triggered warning signals that had served him well in his unusual career. The room, the robes, the altar-like table—all suggested something beyond the usual business transaction.

"You have a problem that needs solving," Guthrie stated, his deep voice revealing nothing of his inner wariness.

Vane smiled, the expression not reaching his eyes. "Indeed. Though perhaps not the sort you typically handle. Allow me to explain." He gestured to the other robed figures. "My associates and I represent a... society with interests that go beyond the merely commercial or political."

The other hooded figures remained silent and motionless, their attention seemingly fixed on Guthrie despite their hidden faces.

"We have been observing your work with great interest," Vane continued. "Your precision. Your discretion. Your apparent immunity to the moral qualms that might trouble lesser men. These are qualities we value highly."

Guthrie said nothing, waiting for Vane to reach the point. Flattery meant nothing to him; only the specifics of the job and the compensation offered were relevant.

"What we require tonight is somewhat different from your usual services," Vane said, moving to the stone table at the center of the room. "We need not just disposal, but participation in a ceremony of great significance."

He gestured, and two of the robed figures moved to a door on the far side of the chamber. They returned moments later half-carrying, half-dragging a third person—a young woman, perhaps twenty years old, with dark hair and wide, terrified eyes. She was dressed in a simple white shift; her feet bare on the cold stone floor. A gag prevented her from speaking, though the muffled sounds of her panic were audible in the silent room.

"This is Miss Eleanor Webb," Vane said, his tone conversational, as if introducing a guest at a dinner party. "Until recently, she was employed as a housemaid in my London residence. She had the misfortune of observing certain... activities that were not meant for uninitiated eyes. And now, she will serve a higher purpose."

The robed figures guided—or rather, forced—the struggling young woman to the stone table. With practiced movements, they secured her wrists and ankles with leather straps affixed to the table's corners, effectively immobilizing her. Her muffled cries increased in volume and desperation as she realized the hopelessness of her situation.

Guthrie watched this process with outward impassivity, though his mind was rapidly assessing the unfolding scenario. This was clearly no ordinary disposal job. The robes, the candles, the ritualistic atmosphere—all pointed to something that went beyond the usual power plays and eliminations he handled for Daybridge's elite.

"What exactly do you want from me?" he asked, his voice betraying nothing of his thoughts.

Vane's smile widened, revealing teeth that seemed too perfect, too white in the candlelight. "We require your skills in a very specific application. The ceremony we are about to perform demands precision in the extraction of certain... elements from our subject. It must be done in a particular sequence, following specific patterns."

He moved to a small side table Guthrie hadn't noticed before and picked up a rolled parchment, which he unfurled to reveal a diagram of the human body overlaid with intricate symbols and notations in a language Guthrie didn't recognize.

"These are the incisions that must be made," Vane explained, his finger tracing lines across the diagram. "The blood must be collected in these vessels, in this order. Certain organs must be removed intact and placed on these consecrated dishes. All while the subject remains alive and aware until the final moment."

Guthrie studied the diagram with professional interest, setting aside the unusual context to focus on the technical aspects of what was being requested. The pattern of incisions was complex but not beyond his abilities. Keeping the subject alive throughout most of the process would be challenging but achievable with the right techniques—techniques he had, in fact, been experimenting with in some of his more personal projects.

"This is not a standard disposal," he observed, looking up from the diagram to meet Vane's gaze directly. "My usual fee would not apply."

A flicker of something—relief? amusement?—crossed Vane's aristocratic features. "Of course. We are prepared to offer five times your normal compensation. Half now, half upon successful completion, as is your custom."

It was an astronomical sum, far more than even the wealthiest of Guthrie's clients typically paid. The amount suggested either desperate need or extraordinary value in whatever ritual they were planning.

"May I ask the purpose?" Guthrie inquired, not out of moral concern but professional curiosity. Understanding a client's motivations often helped in executing their requirements more effectively.

Vane exchanged glances with the other robed figures before responding. "Let us say only that there are forces in this world beyond those recognized by conventional science or religion. Forces that, when properly approached, can bestow certain... benefits upon those who know how to entreat them."

He gestured to the young woman strapped to the stone table, her eyes now rolling in terror as she strained against her bonds. "Miss Webb will serve as a conduit for such entreaties. Her life force, properly channeled, will open doorways that are normally closed to mortal men."

It was, Guthrie reflected, no more outlandish than many of the justifications he had heard from clients over the years. Men of power often developed eccentric beliefs to rationalize their actions, to provide a framework that elevated their base desires into something more profound. Whether Vane and his associates truly believed in these "forces" they spoke of, or whether this was merely an elaborate framework for sadistic pleasure, was irrelevant to the task at hand.

"I'll need specific instructions regarding the collection methods," Guthrie said, effectively accepting the assignment. "And my own tools, not whatever you have prepared."

Relief visibly washed over Vane's features. "Of course. We anticipated as much." He gestured, and one of the robed figures brought forward Guthrie's own leather case of specialized implements—the one he kept in his workshop beneath Holloway's Slaughterhouse.

The sight of his personal tools in this strange environment sent a momentary chill through Guthrie's normally unflappable composure. It meant they had accessed his most private space, had perhaps been observing him far more closely than he had realized. But he betrayed none of this concern, simply taking the case and opening it to verify its contents.

"When do you wish to begin?" he asked, removing his coat and rolling up his sleeves with the same methodical precision he brought to his work at Holloway's.

"Now," Vane replied, his voice taking on a hushed, almost reverential quality. "The alignment is perfect. The doorway is ready to be opened."

And so began one of the strangest nights of Guthrie Knox's already unusual existence. For hours, he worked under the direction of Vane and his robed associates, making incisions according to the patterns on the diagram, collecting blood in silver vessels inscribed with symbols he didn't recognize, extracting organs that were immediately taken by the robed figures to be placed on elaborate altars around the room.

Throughout it all, the young woman remained conscious, her eyes wide with unimaginable agony despite whatever drugs they had administered to prevent her from losing consciousness. Guthrie worked with his usual precision, unmoved by her suffering—pain was simply a physiological response, no different in humans than in the animals he processed daily at Holloway's.

What did affect him, however, was the atmosphere that developed in the chamber as the ritual progressed. The air seemed to thicken, to pulsate with a presence that defied rational explanation. The candles burned with an unnatural steadiness, their flames neither flickering nor diminishing despite the hours that passed. And beneath the chanting of Vane and his associates, beneath the muffled screams of their victim, Guthrie began to perceive another sound—a whispering that seemed to emanate not from any human throat but from the very stones of the chamber itself.

As dawn approached, signaled only by a subtle change in the atmosphere since the windowless room admitted no natural light, the ritual reached its culmination. The young woman, incredibly, still clung to life, though her once-white shift was now drenched crimson, and her eyes had taken on the glazed look of one who has seen beyond the veil of normal human experience.

"It is time for the final extraction," Vane intoned, his voice altered by the hours of chanting, deeper and somehow resonant in a way that human voices typically were not. "The heart must be removed while still beating and placed upon the central altar."

Guthrie, his hands steady despite the marathon session of precision work, made the final incision according to the diagram. As he reached into the cavity to grasp the still-pulsing heart, the whispering that had been growing steadily throughout the night suddenly intensified, becoming a chorus of voices speaking in languages he had never heard before.

The heart came free in his massive hand, warm and incredibly alive despite the impossibility of its owner's continued existence. As he placed it on the central altar as directed, the whispering reached a crescendo, and for just an instant—a fraction of a second that nonetheless burned itself indelibly into his consciousness—Guthrie perceived something in the chamber with them. Not a physical presence, but a distortion in the fabric of reality itself, a thinning of the veil between this world and... somewhere else.

Then it was gone, the whispering subsiding to a barely perceptible murmur before fading entirely. The candles, which had burned steadily throughout the night, suddenly guttered and went out as one, plunging the chamber into darkness.

When emergency lamps were lit moments later, the scene appeared remarkably mundane given what had just transpired. The body on the table was now simply that—a corpse, utterly still and rapidly cooling. The robed figures moved with the weary satisfaction of those who have completed a difficult but necessary task. And Lord Vane approached Guthrie with a heavy purse in one hand.

"Exemplary work," he said, his voice once again that of the aristocrat Guthrie had known in their previous dealings. "Your precision made all the difference. The doorway was opened, if only briefly. Our patrons are... satisfied."

Guthrie accepted the payment without comment, already mentally cataloging the techniques he had employed for later addition to his journal. The ritual aspects meant nothing to him—superstition, perhaps, or an elaborate psychological framework constructed by men of wealth and power to justify their darker urges. But the technical challenges had been considerable, and he had overcome them. That was what mattered.

As he was escorted back through the mansion's labyrinthine corridors, now dimly visible in the gray light of early morning, Guthrie found himself strangely unsettled. Not by the acts he had performed—death was his business, after all, and the suffering of others had long since ceased to affect him. No, what lingered in his mind was that moment of perception, that brief glimpse of something beyond the normal boundaries of existence.

And the whispers. They had seemed so... familiar, somehow. As if they were speaking directly to him, in a language he should have understood but couldn't quite grasp.

By the time he reached Holloway's Slaughterhouse, the winter sun was climbing above Daybridge's eastern factories, casting long shadows across the snow-covered streets. The day shift would be arriving soon, and Guthrie had his regular duties to attend to. The events of the night receded in his consciousness, filed away like all his other professional experiences.

But that night, for the first time in years, Guthrie Knox dreamed. And in his dreams, the whispers returned, speaking to him of ancient hungers and patient, implacable purposes that had waited in the shadows since long before Daybridge existed.

The ritual at Lord Vane's mansion marked a turning point in Guthrie's relationship with Daybridge's elite. Word spread through their closed circles of his participation and the apparent success of whatever arcane purpose they had been pursuing. New clients appeared, their requests increasingly esoteric, often involving elements that went beyond mere killing and disposal.

A shipping magnate required the hands of seven dock workers, each to be removed while its owner still lived, then preserved according to specific instructions and delivered to a location in Daybridge's oldest quarter. A banker commissioned the extraction of the eyes from a rival financier, stipulating that they must be kept in a solution of the victim's own blood mixed with certain herbs provided in advance. A city councilor requested the tongues of three journalists who had been investigating corruption in municipal contracts, each to be removed with silver implements and wrapped in pages from the journalists' own publications.

Guthrie fulfilled these bizarre commissions with his usual efficiency, neither questioning their purpose nor judging their morality. To him, they were simply variations on his established services, requiring adaptations of his techniques but not fundamentally different from his earlier work. The significantly higher fees such specialized tasks commanded were reason enough to accommodate these new requirements.

But as winter gave way to spring in early 1898, Guthrie noticed patterns in these unusual requests. Many involved specific numbers of victims or body parts—three, seven, thirteen. Many required the use of silver implements rather than his usual steel tools. And increasingly, they specified locations or times that corresponded to astronomical events—the new moon, the equinox, certain planetary alignments.

Moreover, the clients themselves began to hint at connections between their individual commissions. References to "the Society" or "the Order" slipped into their instructions. Mentions of "preparation" and "the Great Work" appeared with increasing frequency. It became clear to Guthrie that many of his patrons were part of some larger organization, one that apparently combined the pursuit of worldly power with esoteric or occult practices.

This realization came into sharp focus one night in late March, when Guthrie was summoned not to a private residence but to a location that would feature prominently in his future transformation—the Daybridge Bridge itself.

The bridge was relatively new, having been completed only five years earlier to replace an older crossing destroyed in the floods of 1890. It was a massive structure of stone and iron that spanned the Shadowlair River at its widest point, connecting Daybridge's industrial Eastern Quarter with the more affluent western districts. Its construction had been financed by a consortium of the city's wealthiest citizens, many of whom were now numbered among Guthrie's clients.

The summons came in the usual way—a sealed envelope delivered to Holloway's Slaughterhouse, containing an address, a time, and half the agreed-upon payment. But unlike previous commissions, this one specified that Guthrie was to bring no tools, wear specific clothing (all black, with a heavy overcoat regardless of the weather), and come alone to the eastern entrance of the bridge at exactly midnight.

Intrigued despite his customary emotional detachment, Guthrie followed these instructions to the letter. The night was unseasonably warm for March, the sky clear and star-filled above Daybridge's usual pall of industrial smoke. As he approached the bridge, Guthrie noted that the normal gas lamps that illuminated its length were unlit, leaving the massive structure as a dark silhouette against the night sky.

At the eastern entrance stood a figure in a black coat similar to Guthrie's own, face obscured by the upturned collar and the shadow of a wide-brimmed hat. As Guthrie approached, the figure turned slightly, revealing the aristocratic profile of Lord Vane.

"Right on time," Vane murmured, his breath fogging in the night air despite the relative warmth. "Follow me. And speak to no one unless directly addressed by the Master."

Without waiting for a response, Vane turned and began walking onto the bridge. Guthrie followed, his heavy footsteps echoing off the stone and iron of the structure. They proceeded in silence for perhaps a hundred yards, until they reached the center of the span, where the bridge arched highest above the dark waters of the Shadowlair.

Here, Vane stopped and produced a key from his coat pocket. He knelt beside what appeared to be a maintenance access point—a metal hatch set into the bridge's walkway, designed to allow workers to inspect the supporting structure beneath. The key turned with a heavy clunk, and Vane pulled the hatch open to reveal a narrow staircase descending into darkness.

"Down," Vane directed, gesturing for Guthrie to precede him.

The stairs were steep and narrow, challenging even for someone of Guthrie's physical capability. They spiraled downward for what seemed an improbable distance, eventually opening into a space that should not have existed—a large chamber constructed within the bridge's central support pier, well below the water level of the river above.

The chamber was lit by the same black candles Guthrie had seen at Vane's mansion, their flames casting elongated shadows across walls that were not the expected rough stone of the bridge pier, but smooth, polished granite inscribed with symbols like those on the diagram he had followed during the ritual. The floor was inlaid with a complex pattern of metallic lines—silver, gold, and what appeared to be copper—forming a massive geometric design centered on a raised dais.

And on that dais stood a circle of robed figures—thirteen in all, their garments now black instead of the burgundy Guthrie had seen previously. Their hoods were drawn back, revealing faces Guthrie recognized from his various commissions over the past years. Industrialists, bankers, shipping magnates, politicians—the men who controlled Daybridge's wealth and power, united in whatever esoteric pursuit had brought them to this hidden chamber beneath the city's most visible symbol.

At the center of the circle stood a figure taller than the rest, robed in deep purple rather than black, his face concealed not by a hood but by an ornate mask of silver worked into the likeness of a face both beautiful and terrible in its inhuman perfection. When he spoke, his voice seemed to bypass the ears entirely, resonating directly within Guthrie's mind.

"The Butcher comes at last to our inner sanctum," the masked figure intoned. "Step forward, Guthrie Knox, and behold the purpose your labors have served."

Guthrie moved as directed, entering the circle but maintaining a careful awareness of his surroundings and potential exits—a habit formed through years of clandestine work. The robed figures parted to allow him passage, their expressions ranging from solemn reverence to barely concealed excitement.

"You have been an instrument of great value," the masked figure continued. "Through your hands, the preparations have advanced far more rapidly than we had dared hope. The sacrifices you have executed with such precision have opened pathways that would otherwise have remained closed for decades."

Guthrie remained silent, recalling Vane's instruction to speak only when directly addressed by "the Master"—presumably this masked individual. His mind worked methodically, processing the implications of what he was seeing and hearing. The hidden chamber, the elaborate symbolism, the reference to sacrifices and pathways—all pointed to an organization far more structured and purposeful than he had previously suspected.

The masked figure gestured, and two of the robed members stepped forward, carrying between them a large, leather-bound volume that they placed on a pedestal before Guthrie. The book was ancient, its cover worn smooth by countless hands over what must have been centuries. Symbols similar to those on the walls were embossed into the leather, their edges softened by time but still clearly visible.

"This is the Codex Umbra," the Master said, placing a gloved hand reverently on the book's cover. "The accumulated wisdom of our Order, passed down through twenty-seven generations of Seekers. Within its pages lies the knowledge that will transform Daybridge from a mere industrial center into the focal point of power for the coming age."

He opened the book, revealing pages of vellum covered in dense script and intricate diagrams. Guthrie, despite his limited formal education, recognized that the text was not in English or any modern language he was familiar with.

"For centuries, our Order has worked toward a single goal—the Opening of the Way," the Master continued, his gloved finger tracing lines of text that seemed to shift and change even as Guthrie attempted to focus on them. "The ancient ones who came before, those who dwelled in the spaces between worlds, left behind gates that may be reopened with the proper rituals and sacrifices."

He turned more pages, coming to an illustration that depicted a structure Guthrie recognized immediately—the Daybridge

Bridge, shown not as it currently existed but as a much older construction of rough-hewn stone.

"This crossing has been a nexus point since before recorded history," the Master explained. "The original bridge was built by those who understood the thinness of the veil at this location, the potential for communion with forces beyond mortal comprehension. When it was destroyed and rebuilt over the centuries, the knowledge was preserved within our Order, passed from Master to Initiates in unbroken succession."

Another page turn revealed diagrams of human bodies, marked with patterns of incisions that Guthrie recognized from his various commissioned rituals over the past months.

"The sacrifices you have performed were not random acts of elimination, but carefully calibrated rituals designed to weaken the barriers between our world and the next. Each life taken according to the patterns in the Codex has brought us closer to our goal."

The Master closed the book and turned his masked face directly toward Guthrie. "And now, we require your participation in the culmination of these efforts. Not merely as an instrument, but as an initiate into the mysteries of our Order."

For the first time since entering the chamber, Guthrie spoke, his deep voice echoing strangely in the confined space. "What exactly are you proposing?"

A sound like soft laughter emanated from behind the silver mask. "Direct as always. It is one of the qualities that made you so valuable to our work." The Master stepped closer, close enough that Guthrie could see his eyes through the mask's narrow slits—eyes of an unusual amber color that seemed to glow with their own internal light.

"We propose to elevate you from servant to partner," the Master said. "To initiate you into the first circle of our Order, granting you access to knowledge and power beyond anything you have imagined. Your skills, your unique... detachment from conventional morality, make you an ideal candidate for the work that lies ahead."

Guthrie considered the offer with his usual pragmatic assessment. He had no interest in esoteric knowledge or mystical power for its own sake. But he recognized that membership in this group—whatever they called themselves—would provide practical benefits. Greater protection for his activities. Access to resources beyond what he currently commanded. And, presumably, more lucrative commissions as the "Great Work" they kept referencing progressed.

"What would be required of me?" he asked, his tone giving away nothing of his thoughts.

The Master gestured to the circle of robed figures surrounding them. "An oath of loyalty to the Order and its purposes. Participation in our rituals and ceremonies. Continued application of your particular skills as directed by the Council of Thirteen." He paused, then added, "And a personal sacrifice, to demonstrate your commitment and to forge your connection to the powers we serve."

Before Guthrie could inquire about the nature of this sacrifice, the Master turned and made a subtle gesture. Two robed figures left the circle briefly, returning with a third person between them—a man Guthrie recognized immediately despite the bruises that distorted his features.

It was Franklin Holloway, owner of the slaughterhouse that had been Guthrie's workplace and home for the past twelve years. The old man's eyes widened in confusion and fear as he saw Guthrie standing within the circle of robed figures.

"Knox?" he croaked, his voice weak and trembling. "What is this? What's happening?"

The Master's voice cut through Holloway's questions like a blade. "Your employer has been experiencing financial difficulties, as you well know. His establishment is on the verge of bankruptcy. In his desperation, he has been seeking loans from various sources, including members of our Order."

Holloway struggled weakly against the grip of the two robed figures. "They said they wanted collateral," he protested. "I thought they meant the building, the equipment. Not... not this."

"Holloway's Slaughterhouse occupies a property of particular interest to us," the Master continued, ignoring the old man's protests. "Its location at the convergence of certain telluric currents makes it ideal for our purposes. But more importantly, it has been your home, your base of operations both legitimate and otherwise."

He turned to face Guthrie directly. "Your sacrifice, to demonstrate your commitment to our Order, is to personally end the life of the man who has been, in many ways, the closest thing to a father figure you have known. To sever that final tie to your old existence and embrace the new path we offer."

Guthrie looked at Holloway, the man who had taken in an orphaned butcher's apprentice and given him not just employment but a home. The man who had turned a blind eye to Guthrie's nocturnal activities, never questioning the strange hours or the occasional unexplained sounds from the basement. The man who, in his gruff, unsentimental way, had shown Guthrie the only real kindness he had experienced since Old Silas's death.

For a moment—a brief, almost imperceptible instant—something like doubt flickered across Guthrie's impassive features. Not moral uncertainty about the act itself, but a practical question about the wisdom of eliminating someone who had been, in his way, useful.

The moment passed. Guthrie's expression returned to its usual mask of calm detachment. Holloway was old, sick, and failing. The slaughterhouse was indeed on the verge of bankruptcy, its outdated methods unable to compete with the new industrial meatpacking

plants. Whatever value the old man had once represented was now
outweighed by the potential benefits of membership in this Order
that clearly commanded significant resources and influence in
Daybridge.

"I'll need a blade," Guthrie said simply, his decision made.

Relief visibly washed over the faces of the robed figures. The
Master nodded, and one stepped forward bearing a ceremonial
dagger on a velvet cushion. The weapon was beautiful in its
way—the blade of polished silver, the hilt of dark wood inlaid
with mother-of-pearl in patterns that matched the symbols on the
chamber walls.

"This athame has been used in our rituals for seven
generations," the Master explained as Guthrie took the weapon,
testing its weight and balance with professional assessment. "It will
serve as the instrument of your initiation and, afterward, as a
symbol of your place within our Order."

Holloway, finally comprehending what was about to happen,
began to struggle more vigorously against his captors. "Knox, for
God's sake," he pleaded, his voice cracking with fear. "I gave you a
home. I looked after you when no one else would. Don't do this.
Please."

Guthrie approached the terrified old man with the same
methodical calm he brought to all his work. His mind was already
calculating angles, pressure points, the most efficient way to
complete the task with the unfamiliar blade.

"I'm sorry, Mr. Holloway," he said, and he was—in his own
limited way. Not sorry enough to refuse the Master's command, but
sorry in the abstract sense that this necessity had arisen. "It's just
business. Nothing personal."

They were the same words he had spoken to countless others
over the years, as he applied his butcher's skills to human material.

Professional courtesy, a small acknowledgment of the transaction taking place.

The actual deed was swift and precise, executed with the same technical perfection that had made Guthrie so valuable to the Order. One moment Holloway was staring at him with betrayed, terrified eyes; the next, those eyes were glazing over as the precision cut to the carotid artery did its work. The robed figures lowered the dying man to the center of the intricate floor pattern, positioning him so that his blood flowed along the metallic lines, filling the design with crimson that gleamed black in the candlelight.

As Holloway's life ebbed away, Guthrie became aware once again of the whispering he had first heard during the ritual at Vane's mansion. This time, however, it was louder, more distinct, as if the blood-fed pattern on the floor was somehow amplifying the otherworldly voices.

The whispers spoke of ancient pacts and patient hungers, of entities that had existed in the spaces between worlds since before human civilization arose. They spoke of gateways and vessels, of the thinning of veils and the merging of realms. And beneath it all, barely perceptible but growing stronger, they spoke directly to Guthrie himself—calling him by name, promising power and purpose beyond anything the human members of the Order could comprehend.

As the last of Holloway's blood flowed into the pattern on the floor, the whispers reached a crescendo. The candles flared suddenly, their flames stretching toward the ceiling in defiance of natural law. The air in the chamber seemed to thicken, to pulsate with a presence that pressed against the boundaries of normal reality.

And then, as suddenly as it had begun, it was over. The candles returned to their normal state, the whispers subsided to a barely audible murmur, and the blood-filled pattern on the floor began to dim as the liquid congealed and darkened.

The Master stepped forward, placing a hand on Guthrie's shoulder. "It is done," he intoned, his voice carrying a note of satisfaction. "You have proven your commitment to our cause. Welcome, Brother Knox, to the First Circle of the Order of the Ebon Star."

The other robed figures began to chant in unison, their voices blending into a hypnotic rhythm that seemed to resonate with the fading whispers from beyond. The Master guided Guthrie to kneel before the pedestal holding the Codex Umbra, then placed the blood-stained athame across the book's ancient cover.

"Repeat after me," the Master instructed, his voice taking on a ritualistic cadence. "I, Guthrie Knox, do hereby pledge my life, my skills, and my soul to the service of the Order and its Masters, both seen and unseen."

Guthrie repeated the words, feeling nothing beyond a clinical interest in the ceremony. Oaths meant little to him—they were just words, useful for cementing relationships but carrying no inherent power or binding force. What mattered were the practical implications of his new status, the tangible benefits it would bring.

The ritual continued for several more minutes, with further pledges and responses. Finally, the Master raised Guthrie to his feet and presented him with a small silver medallion on a chain—a miniature version of the floor pattern, now permanently stained with Holloway's blood.

"Wear this always," the Master instructed. "It marks you as one of us, protected by our influence and bound to our purpose."

Guthrie slipped the chain around his neck, tucking the medallion beneath his shirt. Its weight was negligible, but he could feel it against his skin like a cold brand, marking a fundamental change in his status and allegiances.

The ceremony concluded with a final chant, after which the robed figures dispersed to various parts of the chamber, speaking among themselves with the relaxed familiarity of colleagues after a successful project. Holloway's body was unceremoniously wrapped in a black cloth and carried away by two of the younger members, presumably for disposal in the river above.

Lord Vane approached Guthrie; his expression more open now that the formal ritual had concluded. "Congratulations, Brother Knox," he said, extending a hand. "Your initiation was most impressive. The signs were exceptionally favorable."

Guthrie shook the offered hand, noting the subtle change in Vane's demeanor. There was still respect, still a certain wariness, but also a new element of collegiality that had been absent in their previous interactions.

"The signs?" Guthrie inquired, recalling the whispers and the flaring candles.

Vane's eyes widened slightly. "You heard them, didn't you? The Voices from Beyond. Most initiates perceive nothing during their first ceremony. It usually takes years of training to develop the sensitivity needed to hear the Masters' communication."

Before Guthrie could respond, the purple-robed Master joined them, his silver mask now removed to reveal a face that was surprisingly ordinary—middle-aged, with neatly trimmed gray hair and the kind of forgettable features that would blend into any crowd.

"Septimus Blackwood," he introduced himself, his voice now a perfectly normal tenor rather than the resonant tones he had used during the ceremony. "High Master of the Daybridge Chapter, Keeper of the Western Gate." He smiled at Guthrie's barely perceptible reaction to the theatrical titles. "All very ceremonial, I know, but tradition has its place in these matters."

Blackwood studied Guthrie with keen interest, his amber eyes—the only distinctive feature in his otherwise unremarkable face—seeming to look through rather than at the massive butcher.

"Vane is right," he said after a moment. "Your sensitivity to the Voices is unusual, especially for one with no prior exposure to the Work. It suggests a natural affinity that could prove immensely valuable as we move forward."

Guthrie, unimpressed by mystical implications, brought the conversation back to practical matters. "You mentioned that my initiation would involve new responsibilities. What exactly will be required of me now?"

Blackwood exchanged a glance with Vane, then nodded. "Direct as always. Very well. In the short term, little will change. You will continue your work at Holloway's—which, incidentally, now belongs to the Order following your former employer's unfortunate passing. The slaughterhouse provides excellent cover for certain activities, and its location makes it ideal for our purposes."

He gestured to the surrounding chamber. "This facility beneath the bridge is one of three major ritual sites the Order maintains in Daybridge. The others are similarly concealed beneath structures of apparent mundanity—a warehouse near the eastern docks, and the basement of St. Bartholomew's Hospital in the western quarter."

Blackwood began walking toward a small alcove at the far end of the chamber, indicating that Guthrie should follow. "Your primary responsibility will be the continued execution of specific rituals as directed by the Council. But now, as an initiate, you will be provided with greater context for these workings and instructed in the proper invocations and gestures that accompany the physical aspects you have already mastered."

The alcove contained a small table bearing several ancient-looking artifacts—a tarnished silver bowl, a dagger similar to but smaller than the athame used in the initiation, and a small, leather-bound book much less imposing than the Codex Umbra.

"These are the tools of a First Circle initiate," Blackwood explained, handing the book to Guthrie. "This grimoire contains the basic rituals and invocations you will need to learn. Study it carefully but keep it secure. The knowledge it contains is not for the uninitiated."

Guthrie accepted the book, noting that unlike the Codex, this volume was written in recognizable English, though in an archaic style that would require careful reading. He tucked it inside his coat, already planning to add its contents to his growing collection of professional resources.

"There is one more thing," Blackwood said, his tone becoming more serious. "The sensitivity you demonstrated tonight—the ability to hear the Voices—is both a gift and a responsibility. You will find that once awakened, this awareness does not simply disappear when you leave our rituals. The Voices may come to you at unexpected times, especially in places where the veil between worlds is thin."

He placed a hand on Guthrie's arm, the gesture both congratulatory and cautionary. "Listen to them, but do not respond unless directed to do so by myself or another member of the Inner Circle. The entities that speak through the veil have their own agendas, not all of which align with the Order's purposes."

With that cryptic warning, Blackwood led Guthrie back to the main chamber, where the other members were preparing to depart. The night's work was done, the initiation complete. Guthrie Knox was now officially a member of the Order of the Ebon Star, bound to its mysterious purposes and protected by its considerable influence.

As he climbed the narrow stairs back to the bridge above, following Vane and several others while Blackwood remained below with a few senior members, Guthrie reflected on the night's events with his usual detachment. The occult trappings, the theatrical ceremony, the talk of entities beyond the veil—all of it meant little to him beyond its practical implications for his work and status.

But the whispers... those he could not so easily dismiss. They had seemed to speak directly to him, bypassing language to communicate on some deeper level. And they had felt familiar, as if rekindling a connection long forgotten rather than establishing a new one.

The night air was cool on his face as he emerged onto the bridge, the stars still bright above Daybridge's industrial haze. The city spread out before him, its gaslit streets and smoking chimneys representing a human dominion that suddenly seemed fragile, temporary—a brief interruption in a much older and darker story.

For the first time in his adult life, Guthrie Knox felt something akin to unease, a vague sense that he had stepped onto a path whose destination was hidden from him. Not fear, exactly—he had moved beyond such simple emotions long ago—but a recognition that forces were now in motion whose scope and purpose exceeded even his clinical understanding.

As he made his way back to Holloway's Slaughterhouse—now apparently his in more than just practical terms—the whispers followed him, faint but persistent, speaking of ancient hungers and patient designs. And for the first time, he began to listen not just with his ears but with something deeper, something that had lain dormant within him since childhood.

The dreams began that night—vivid, disturbing visions of a Daybridge that was both familiar and terribly altered. In these dreams, the bridge was not the modern construction of stone and iron but an ancient thing of rough-hewn blocks, slick with moss and something darker that glistened in a light that seemed to come from below rather than above.

And beneath the bridge, in these dreams, waited something that had been there since before the city existed, something that knew Guthrie Knox by name and had been waiting for him with the patience of geological ages. Something that whispered promises of power and purpose, of transformation and transcendence.

Something that would, in time, remake him into the Ogre of Daybridge.

Chapter 6: The Lady in Velvet

The summer of 1898 descended upon Daybridge like an oppressive shroud, bringing with it a heat so intense that the Shadowlair River shrank to half its normal width, exposing mudflats that released the noxious stench of decades of industrial waste. Factory workers collapsed at their stations, overcome by temperatures that transformed their workplaces into virtual ovens. The wealthy fled to country estates or seaside resorts, leaving their mansions shuttered and their businesses in the hands of underlings desperate for any hint of advancement.

For Guthrie Knox, the summer months brought significant changes. Following Franklin Holloway's "unfortunate demise" (as the newspaper obituary so delicately phrased it), ownership of the slaughterhouse had indeed transferred to the Order of the Ebon Star, operating through a shell company called Daybridge Meat Processing, Ltd. Guthrie was installed as the official manager, a position that granted him authority over day-to-day operations while reserving strategic decisions for the Order's Council.

The arrangement suited him perfectly. He maintained his familiar routine and living quarters while gaining additional freedom to use the facility for the Order's more esoteric requirements. The basement workshop, once his secret domain, was now officially off-limits to all other employees, ostensibly for "specialized processing" but in reality, serving as one of the Order's secondary ritual spaces.

His initiation into the First Circle had elevated his status within Daybridge's shadow hierarchy. He was no longer merely a useful tool, but a recognized member of the power structure, privy to secrets and connections that remained invisible to the common citizenry. The silver medallion he now wore beneath his shirt at all times served as both protection and passport, identifying him to other initiates and marking him as untouchable to those who might otherwise interfere with his activities.

And the dreams continued—vivid, disquieting visions that came to him almost nightly. Dreams of the bridge, of the entity that waited beneath it, of transformations both physical and spiritual. Dreams that left him sweating and disoriented upon waking, yet strangely energized, as if some dormant part of his being was gradually awakening.

The whispers, too, had become a constant presence. They followed him through his daily routines, barely perceptible but never entirely absent. Sometimes they spoke in languages he didn't recognize, ancient tongues long forgotten by the waking world. But increasingly, they communicated in concepts rather than words, impressions that bypassed language to lodge directly in his consciousness.

They spoke of patience and preparation, of vessels and gateways, of a destiny that had been set in motion long before his birth. And always, beneath these communications, ran a current of hunger so vast and implacable that it made even Guthrie's detached psyche shudder in recognition of something far beyond human comprehension.

He reported these experiences dutifully to Septimus Blackwood during their weekly meetings, which typically took place in the High Master's private study at his mansion in Graystone Heights. Blackwood listened with intense interest, occasionally consulting ancient texts or making notes in a private journal. He prescribed specific meditations and breathing exercises designed to "channel and focus" Guthrie's growing sensitivity but advised against attempting direct communication with the entities behind the whispers.

"They are ancient and powerful, but not necessarily benevolent in any human sense," Blackwood cautioned during one such session.

"Their concept of time, of purpose, of existence itself differs fundamentally from ours. They can be allies in our Great Work but never mistake them for friends."

Guthrie had nodded, accepting the warning at face value while privately finding it somewhat redundant. Friendship was a concept as alien to him as benevolence was to these entities. His relationship with the Order, with Blackwood, with the unseen forces that whispered from beyond the veil—all were matters of practical utility rather than emotional connection.

Or so he believed, until the night of the Midsummer Gathering, when everything changed.

The invitation arrived on the last day of June, delivered by one of Blackwood's liveried servants—a heavy cream envelope sealed with dark red wax impressed with the same symbol that adorned Guthrie's medallion. Inside, on thick card stock engraved with gold lettering, was an invitation to attend "The Annual Midsummer Gathering of the Ebon Star Society" at Blackwood Manor on the evening of July 7th.

A handwritten note from Blackwood himself accompanied the formal invitation: "Your presence is not merely requested but required. The signs are aligning. The next phase begins."

Guthrie had never attended a social function of any kind, let alone one hosted by Daybridge's elite. His interactions with the city's upper classes had always been strictly professional and usually clandestine. The prospect of navigating the unfamiliar waters of high society was not appealing, but the note's emphasis on requirement left no room for refusal.

And so, on the appointed evening, Guthrie found himself approaching the wrought-iron gates of Blackwood Manor dressed in formal attire that had been delivered to his apartment the previous day—a black tailcoat and trousers of the finest wool, a silk waistcoat in deep burgundy, and a crisp white shirt with a black silk cravat. The clothes fit perfectly, having apparently been tailored to his measurements without any fitting session, another small reminder of the Order's pervasive influence and attention to detail.

Blackwood Manor stood at the highest point of Graystone Heights, its Gothic architecture looming against the twilight sky like a declaration of its owner's status and power. Built in the 1850s by Septimus Blackwood's grandfather, it combined Victorian grandeur with subtle elements that, to the initiated eye, hinted at its role as the headquarters of the Order's Daybridge Chapter.

Gargoyles perched at strategic points along the roofline; their grotesque forms not merely decorative but positioned according to ancient principles of arcane geometry. The stained-glass windows, while apparently depicting conventional biblical scenes, contained hidden symbols that aligned with specific astronomical events. Even the layout of the gardens through which Guthrie now walked followed patterns found in grimoires dating back to the 16th century.

As he approached the main entrance, Guthrie was acutely aware of the stares his arrival provoked among the other guests mingling on the grand terrace. Despite his expensive new clothes, he remained a striking and somewhat intimidating figure—taller and broader than most men, with the unmistakable physicality of someone who worked with his hands rather than shuffling papers or counting money. His scarred knuckles and callused palms marked him as an outsider in this gathering of soft-handed aristocrats and industrialists.

A butler took his name at the door, consulting a list before nodding respectfully. "Mr. Knox. The Master is expecting you. Please, follow me."

Rather than joining the main gathering in what appeared to be a grand ballroom to the right of the entrance hall, Guthrie was led through a series of corridors to a smaller, more intimate drawing room at the rear of the house. Here, a select group had already assembled—perhaps twenty people, mostly men but with a few women present as well. Guthrie recognized several of the men as members of the Order's Council, including Lord Vane, who nodded to him from across the room.

Septimus Blackwood detached himself from a conversation and approached, extending his hand in greeting. The High Master was dressed impeccably in formal evening wear that emphasized his lean, aristocratic build. His amber eyes seemed to glow in the warm light of the room's many candles.

"Brother Knox," he said, his voice carrying just enough to be heard by those nearby—a deliberate announcement of Guthrie's status to the others present. "I'm delighted you could join us. The Inner Circle gathers separately from the general membership for the first hour of these functions. It gives us an opportunity to discuss matters of importance before joining the... less enlightened guests."

Guthrie shook the offered hand, noting the strength in Blackwood's grip despite his seemingly frail physique. "I wasn't aware I was considered part of the Inner Circle," he replied, keeping his voice equally modulated for their audience.

Blackwood smiled, the expression never quite reaching those unusual eyes. "Your progress has been remarkable. The Council voted unanimously last week to elevate you to the Second Circle. The formal initiation will take place at the new moon, but we saw no reason to wait for tonight's introduction."

He gestured to the assembled group. "Everyone here is at least a Second Circle initiate, aware of the true nature and purpose of our Work. You'll find no need for pretense or coded language in this company."

As if to demonstrate this openness, Blackwood raised his voice slightly to address the entire room. "Brothers and Sisters, I present to you our newest Second Circle initiate, Guthrie Knox. Many of you know him already by reputation or through his invaluable contributions to our rituals. I trust you will make him welcome and offer whatever guidance his new status may require."

Murmurs of acknowledgment and approval rippled through the gathering. Several people raised their glasses in Guthrie's direction, while others openly studied him with expressions ranging from curiosity to calculation.

"Come," Blackwood said, placing a hand on Guthrie's arm. "There are specific individuals you should meet. Your elevation brings new responsibilities, new connections that will be vital to your role in the Work ahead."

Over the next half hour, Blackwood guided Guthrie through a series of introductions to key members of the Inner Circle. There was Dr. Ambrose Thorne, chief surgeon at St. Bartholomew's Hospital and keeper of the Order's medical knowledge; Lady Margaret Kincaid, widow of a shipping magnate and curator of the Order's extensive library of occult texts; Judge William Hargrove, whose position on the bench allowed him to protect the Order's interests within Daybridge's legal system; and a dozen others whose influence extended into every aspect of the city's governance and commerce.

Each greeted Guthrie with a respect that bordered on deference, clearly aware of his growing importance within their hierarchy. They spoke obliquely of "the Work" and "the Coming Alignment," referencing a timetable that apparently stretched years into the future yet was approaching some significant milestone.

Throughout these conversations, Guthrie maintained his usual impassivity, revealing nothing of his thoughts while carefully cataloging every piece of information for later consideration. The political and social dynamics of the Inner Circle were complex, with obvious factions and rivalries beneath the veneer of unified purpose. Such knowledge could prove useful as he navigated his new position within the Order.

It was during a momentary lull in these introductions that Guthrie first saw her.

She stood somewhat apart from the main group, near one of the tall windows that overlooked Blackwood Manor's extensive gardens. Unlike the other women present, who wore the fashionable pastel gowns and elaborate hairstyles of the season, she was dressed in deep violet velvet that clung to her slender frame, her raven hair arranged in a simple but elegant knot at the nape of her neck. She held a crystal glass containing some amber liquid, which she occasionally raised to lips painted a shade that matched her gown almost exactly.

But it was not her striking appearance that caught Guthrie's attention. It was the way she was looking at him—directly, intently, with none of the coy glances or averted eyes that characterized proper feminine behavior in Daybridge society. Her gaze was assessing, almost predatory, as if she were evaluating a particularly interesting specimen.

And then she smiled—a small, private curve of those violet lips that seemed intended for him alone despite the distance between them.

Something stirred within Guthrie, a sensation so unfamiliar that it took him several moments to identify it as attraction. Not the abstract aesthetic appreciation he might feel when observing a particularly well-executed piece of craftsmanship, but a visceral, almost primitive response that bypassed his usual emotional detachment.

He was still processing this unexpected reaction when Blackwood, following his gaze, smiled knowingly. "Ah, I see you've noticed my niece. Come, you should meet her. She's been most interested in your work."

As they approached the woman in violet, Guthrie felt an uncharacteristic tension in his normally steady hands. The whispers that had become his constant companions seemed to intensify, their cadence taking on an urgent quality he had never heard before.

"Eliza, my dear," Blackwood said as they reached her. "Allow me to introduce our newest Second Circle initiate, Mr. Guthrie Knox. Brother Knox, this is my niece, Eliza Blackwood."

She extended a slender hand adorned with several unusual rings of silver and dark stone. "Mr. Knox," she said, her voice a melodious contralto that seemed to resonate with the whispers in Guthrie's mind. "At last, we meet. My uncle has told me so much about your... talents."

Guthrie took her hand, intending the brief, formal contact expected in such situations. But as their skin touched, a jolt of something like electricity passed between them, and the whispers surged to a crescendo before abruptly falling silent—the first true silence he had experienced since his initiation months earlier.

For a moment, the world seemed to narrow to just the two of them, the surrounding conversations fading to a distant buzz. Eliza's eyes—the same unusual amber as her uncle's, but somehow deeper, more compelling—held his with an intensity that would have been uncomfortable from anyone else.

"The pleasure is mine, Miss Blackwood," Guthrie managed, surprised at the slight roughness in his usually controlled voice.

She smiled again, this time with a hint of something that might have been amusement or satisfaction. "Please, call me Eliza. I have a feeling we're going to become quite well acquainted, Mr. Knox."

"Guthrie," he corrected automatically, still holding her hand slightly longer than propriety dictated.

Septimus Blackwood observed this exchange with an expression of calculated approval. "Eliza has recently returned from Europe, where she's been studying at certain institutions not available to the general public. Her knowledge of the more... esoteric aspects of our Work rivals my own in many areas."

Eliza withdrew her hand with a graceful movement that somehow suggested reluctance despite its propriety. "Uncle exaggerates. I am merely a dedicated student of the ancient ways. But I confess I've been particularly interested in the ritual applications you've been developing, Mr. Knox—Guthrie. Your innovations in the Crimson Path ceremonies have yielded results that surpassed all expectations."

The reference to his work for the Order—specifically, the ritualized killings he had conducted over the past months—was startlingly direct. Even among the Inner Circle, such matters were typically discussed with a degree of circumspection.

"You're familiar with the details of those ceremonies?" Guthrie asked, finding himself genuinely curious about the extent of her knowledge.

"In intimate detail," she confirmed, taking a sip of her drink. "I've studied the transcripts of your journal entries that Uncle has been kind enough to share with me. Your methodical approach, your attention to the precise timing of specific extractions, your observations regarding the effects of different patterns—all most illuminating."

Guthrie glanced at Blackwood, who nodded slightly. "Eliza has been acting as a remote consultant on our recent Work. Her insights have proven invaluable in interpreting the results of your rituals and refining our approach to the next phase."

Before Guthrie could respond to this revelation, a butler appeared at Blackwood's elbow, murmuring something in the High Master's ear. Blackwood nodded, then turned to Guthrie and Eliza.

"I'm afraid I'm needed elsewhere. The general gathering is about to begin, and there are certain preparations I must oversee. Eliza, perhaps you would be kind enough to continue Mr. Knox's introduction to our Inner Circle?"

"Of course, Uncle," she replied with a smile that suggested the request aligned perfectly with her own intentions. "We have much to discuss."

As Blackwood departed, Eliza gestured to two armchairs positioned near the window, slightly removed from the main group. "Shall we? I find these gatherings rather tedious until the real festivities begin after midnight. And I have so many questions about your work."

Guthrie followed her to the more private setting, acutely aware of the curious glances from other members of the Inner Circle. It was clear that Eliza Blackwood held a position of significance within their hierarchy, despite her apparent youth—though appearing no more than thirty, possibly younger—and her status as a woman in a society dominated by men.

As they settled into the armchairs, Eliza studied him with that same direct, assessing gaze that had first caught his attention. "You're not what I expected," she said after a moment, her tone suggesting this was a pleasant surprise.

"What did you expect?" Guthrie asked, finding himself drawn into conversation more easily than was typical for him.

"From Uncle's descriptions, I imagined someone more... brutish. A blunt instrument rather than a precision tool." She smiled, the expression transforming her striking features into something approaching beauty. "But I see now that your physical strength is merely the most obvious of your attributes. There's a quality of focus, of absolute presence, that's far more interesting."

Guthrie, unaccustomed to personal observations of any kind, let alone flattering ones, merely nodded. "Your uncle has been very... supportive of my work."

Eliza laughed, a sound like crystal chimes that drew glances from across the room. "Oh, he's been practically giddy about your progress. 'The perfect vessel,' he calls you. 'The culmination of decades of preparation.'" She leaned forward slightly, lowering her voice. "Do you know what that means, Guthrie? Do you understand what role you're being groomed to play in the Great Work?"

The directness of the question caught him off guard. His interactions with the Order had always involved a degree of obfuscation, with knowledge parceled out in carefully measured doses as he progressed through the ranks. No one had spoken so plainly about his ultimate purpose.

"I understand that my skills are useful to the Order," he replied cautiously. "That the rituals I perform contribute to some larger goal involving entities beyond our normal perception."

Eliza's expression shifted to one of mild disappointment. "So, they haven't told you. Typical. The Council and their endless games of secrecy and control." She sighed, twirling one of her unusual rings with elegant fingers. "Would you like to know the truth, Guthrie? Not the sanitized version my uncle dispenses in carefully measured doses, but the raw, unfettered reality of what the Order seeks and what role you're meant to play?"

The whispers, which had remained unusually quiet since their initial touch, suddenly surged back into Guthrie's awareness, their tone urgent and conflicted. Some seemed to encourage him to listen, while others warned of danger. For the first time, he sensed discord among the entities that had been his constant companions these past months.

"Yes," he said, making his decision. "I would."

Eliza's smile returned, brilliant and somehow triumphant. "Not here," she murmured, glancing around at the other members of the Inner Circle, who were beginning to drift toward the door in response to some unseen signal. "Tonight, after the general gathering has concluded and the true ceremony begins. Meet me in the east garden, by the stone circle. Midnight exactly."

Before Guthrie could respond, she rose gracefully to her feet. "We should join the others. The public portion of the evening is about to commence, and appearances must be maintained." She extended her hand once more. "Until midnight, Guthrie Knox."

As he took her hand, the same electric sensation passed between them, and the whispers fell into that strange, complete silence. For a moment, Guthrie had the unsettling impression that Eliza could not only hear the whispers as he did but could somehow control them—muting or amplifying their presence at will.

The thought should have alarmed him, or at least provoked caution. But as he followed her from the drawing room to join the larger gathering in Blackwood Manor's grand ballroom, Guthrie found himself anticipating their midnight rendezvous with an eagerness that was entirely foreign to his normally dispassionate nature.

The public portion of the Midsummer Gathering proved to be exactly the sort of tedious social event Guthrie had expected. The grand ballroom of Blackwood Manor was filled with Daybridge's elite—industrialists and their bejeweled wives, politicians seeking favor with the wealthy, artists and intellectuals whose presence lent a veneer of culture to what was essentially a display of power and influence.

Most were not members of the Order, or at least not initiated beyond the most superficial level. They attended such gatherings for the social cachet, the business connections, and the general satisfaction of being seen in the right circles. They were, as Blackwood had described them earlier, the "less enlightened guests"—useful for maintaining the Order's public facade but not privy to its true purpose.

Guthrie stood apart from the crowd, a glass of untouched champagne in his hand, observing the elaborate social dance with clinical detachment. He noted the subtle hierarchies, the careful positioning, the calculated interactions that characterized high society—not unlike the power dynamics among the butchers and slaughtermen at Holloway's but conducted with more refined viciousness.

Occasionally, one of the Inner Circle members would approach him, making a show of introduction for the benefit of the uninitiated while exchanging quiet words about Order business beneath the cover of social pleasantries. Several expressed interest in "commissioning his services" for upcoming "projects," using the coded language that obscured the true nature of their requests.

Guthrie accepted these approaches with his usual impassivity, committing names and requirements to memory for later consideration. But his attention remained fixed on Eliza Blackwood, who moved through the gathering with graceful confidence, engaging effortlessly with guests from all strata of Daybridge society.

She was, he observed, exceptionally skilled at adapting her manner to each interaction—deferential with the older matrons who clearly represented old money and influence, warmly intellectual with the university professors and writers, crisply professional with the businessmen seeking her uncle's favor. Each persona seemed perfectly calculated to put her interlocutor at ease while subtly maintaining control of the exchange.

And throughout the evening, she would occasionally catch his eye across the crowded room, that same private smile playing across her violet lips, as if they shared a secret unknown to the chattering masses around them.

As the night progressed, Guthrie became aware of a subtle shift in the atmosphere. The uninitiated guests began to depart, offering elaborate thanks to Septimus Blackwood and citing the lateness of the hour. By eleven o'clock, only members of the Order remained, and the pretense of a conventional social gathering was abandoned.

Servants—all of whom, Guthrie now realized, wore small versions of the Order's symbol on their livery—began removing the conventional furniture from the ballroom, revealing a pattern inlaid in the marble floor that had been hidden beneath rugs and seating arrangements. Other attendants brought in tall black candles and arranged them at specific points around the room's perimeter.

Blackwood, who had maintained the role of genial host throughout the evening, now assumed a more formal demeanor. He retreated briefly to an antechamber and returned wearing the purple robe and silver mask of the High Master, his transformation from social leader to occult authority complete.

"Brothers and Sisters," he intoned, his voice carrying the same resonant quality it had during Guthrie's initiation beneath the bridge. "The hour approaches. Prepare yourselves for the Midsummer Observance."

The remaining guests—perhaps fifty in all—began to disperse, moving to various parts of the mansion with purposeful steps. The Inner Circle members headed toward the ballroom's main doors, while those of lower rank departed through side exits, presumably to secondary ritual spaces throughout the property.

Guthrie, uncertain of the protocol, remained where he was until Lord Vane approached him. "Come, Brother Knox," Vane said, gesturing toward the main doors. "As a Second Circle initiate, you'll participate in the primary ritual in the Great Hall. It's through the east wing, down the main corridor."

"And after?" Guthrie asked, thinking of his midnight appointment with Eliza.

Vane smiled knowingly. "After the formal observance, various... private ceremonies often take place throughout the grounds. The energy raised during the main ritual lends power to more specific workings." He patted Guthrie's arm. "I saw you speaking with Miss Blackwood earlier. She's quite particular about who she works with, you know. Consider yourself fortunate if she's expressed interest in your... capabilities."

The implication was clear, though whether Vane was referring to magical collaborations or something more intimate remained deliberately ambiguous. Before Guthrie could respond, Vane was already moving away, joining the stream of Inner Circle members heading toward the Great Hall.

Guthrie followed, his mind processing this new information. Eliza's status within the Order seemed even more significant than he had initially assumed. Her interest in him—whatever its nature—was apparently noteworthy enough to draw comment from someone of Vane's standing.

The Great Hall proved to be a cavernous space occupying much of the mansion's east wing, with a vaulted ceiling that rose at least thirty feet above the floor. Like the chamber beneath the bridge, it was decorated with arcane symbols and illuminated by black candles, but on a far grander scale. The floor featured an immense version of the pattern that adorned Guthrie's medallion, inlaid in what appeared to be precious metals and semi-precious stones.

The Second Circle initiates arranged themselves in a large ring around this central pattern, while thirteen members of what Guthrie assumed must be the Third Circle took positions at specific points within the design. Septimus Blackwood, as High

Master, stood at the center, his masked face turned upward toward the ceiling, where Guthrie now noticed a large circular skylight positioned to frame the midsummer moon.

The ritual that followed was elaborate and clearly well-rehearsed, with each participant knowing their role without need for direction. Chants in ancient languages echoed through the hall, rising and falling in complex harmonies that seemed designed to affect the consciousness of those participating. Incense burned in censers of strange design, releasing smoke that formed patterns in the air as if guided by unseen hands.

Throughout it all, Guthrie maintained his position in the outer ring, observing with clinical interest while mentally noting the differences between this ceremonial magic and the more visceral rituals he had conducted for the Order. Here, there was no blood, no death—at least not visibly—yet he could sense a building of power similar to what he had experienced during his more sanguinary workings.

The whispers, which had remained unusually subdued since his encounter with Eliza, began to rise again as the ritual reached its climax. They spoke of alignments and convergences, of threads being woven into a grand tapestry whose full pattern would not be visible for years to come. And beneath these cosmic pronouncements ran that same current of vast, patient hunger he had sensed before.

As the midsummer moon reached its zenith, perfectly framed in the ceiling's skylight, Blackwood raised his arms in a gesture of invocation. The chanting reached a fever pitch, the incense smoke swirled into distinct forms that almost resembled faces, and for an instant—a fraction of a second that burned itself into Guthrie's consciousness—the veil between worlds thinned perceptibly.

In that moment, he glimpsed something beyond—not the entities that whispered to him, but the realm they inhabited. A place of shifting geometries and impossible colors, where the laws of physics as he understood them seemed more like suggestions than absolutes. A place that was both utterly alien and strangely familiar, as if some part of him recognized it on a level deeper than conscious thought.

Then the moment passed, the veil thickened once more, and the ritual began to wind down. The chanting subsided, the smoke dispersed, and the palpable sense of otherworldly presence gradually diminished. Blackwood lowered his arms and turned to address the assembled members.

"The Observance is complete," he announced, his voice carrying a note of satisfaction. "The alignments have been confirmed, the pathways strengthened. We remain on course for the Great Conjunction." He raised his masked face once more to the moon above. "The Ebon Star shines ever brighter as we approach the final phase of our Work."

With these cryptic pronouncements, the formal ceremony concluded. The participants began to disperse, some forming small groups for quiet conversation, others departing alone with purposeful strides. Guthrie noticed that many headed for the doors leading to the extensive gardens surrounding Blackwood Manor, presumably for the "private ceremonies" Vane had mentioned.

Checking the ornate clock that stood against one wall of the Great Hall, Guthrie saw that it was approaching midnight. His appointment with Eliza in the east garden was minutes away. He made his way toward the garden doors, nodding acknowledgment to several Inner Circle members who greeted him in passing.

The night air was warm but not unpleasantly so, carrying the scent of night-blooming flowers and the more exotic herbs that grew in Blackwood's carefully tended gardens. Illumination came from both the full moon overhead and small lanterns placed at intervals along the winding paths, creating pools of light amid the darkness.

Guthrie followed the eastern path as instructed, moving with his usual silent efficiency despite his unfamiliarity with the grounds. After several minutes, he came upon what could only be the stone circle Eliza had mentioned—a ring of twelve standing stones, each about six feet tall, surrounding a central altar of polished black granite.

And there, seated on the altar with the moonlight casting her in silver and shadow, was Eliza Blackwood. She had changed from her violet evening gown into a simpler dress of deep crimson that left her arms bare, revealing intricate tattoos that spiraled from her wrists to her shoulders—patterns that matched the symbols Guthrie had seen in the Order's rituals.

"Right on time," she said, her voice carrying clearly in the night air. "I appreciate punctuality in a man. So many lack the discipline for it."

Guthrie approached the circle, noting that the ground within the ring of stones seemed different from the surrounding garden—not grass but bare earth, packed hard and inscribed with more of the arcane symbols that seemed to permeate every aspect of the Order's domain.

"You promised truth," he said, coming to stand before her. "Not the version your uncle dispenses, but the reality of what the Order seeks and my role in it."

Eliza smiled; the expression somehow more genuine than the carefully calculated versions she had displayed during the evening's gathering. "Direct as always. It's refreshing." She patted the altar beside her, inviting him to sit. "Join me, and I'll tell you what Septimus and his Council would prefer to keep hidden for now."

Guthrie hesitated only briefly before accepting the invitation. As he settled beside her on the cold stone, he noted that the whispers had once again fallen silent, as if the entities behind them were listening intently to what was about to be revealed.

"The Order of the Ebon Star has existed in one form or another for millennia," Eliza began, her voice taking on a lecturer's cadence. "Its origins lie in ancient Babylon, though it has gone by many names throughout history—the Cult of the Dark Star, the Brotherhood of the Obsidian Path, the Seekers of the Void. Always, its purpose has remained the same: to forge connections with entities that exist beyond the veil of normal reality, and to channel their power for the advancement of its members."

She traced one of the symbols carved into the altar's surface, her fingertip leaving a faint luminous trail that gradually faded. "What makes the Order different from countless other occult societies is that its founders actually succeeded in establishing contact with these entities. Not demons or spirits as described in religious texts, but beings of an entirely different order—what some members call the Outer Gods."

Guthrie nodded, unsurprised by this confirmation of what he had already intuited from his own experiences. "The voices that whisper. The presences I've sensed during the rituals."

"Yes, though what you perceive is merely the merest fraction of their true nature," Eliza confirmed. "They exist primarily in dimensions beyond our comprehension, intersecting with our reality only at certain points where the barriers between worlds are naturally thin—or can be made so through ritual."

She gestured to the stone circle around them. "Places like this, positioned at the confluence of certain telluric currents, serve as anchor points for more stable connections. The bridge where you were initiated is another such location, perhaps the most powerful in Daybridge."

Guthrie considered this information, comparing it with his own observations. "And the purpose of these connections? What does the Order gain from contact with these... Outer Gods?"

Eliza's expression grew more serious. "Power, of course. Knowledge beyond human science. Extended life spans for those of high rank—my uncle is nearly one hundred and twenty years old, though he appears to be in his fifties. Influence over natural and political events. The usual temptations of occult societies throughout history."

She paused, studying Guthrie's face as if gauging his reaction. "But the true goal, the Great Work that the Order has pursued for centuries, is far more ambitious. They seek to open a permanent gateway between our world and the realm of the Outer Gods, allowing these entities physical access to our reality on a scale unprecedented since prehistoric times."

The implications of this revelation were enormous, even to someone as generally detached from human concerns as Guthrie. "And what would happen if they succeeded? If these entities gained full access to our world?"

Eliza's smile returned, but there was a brittle quality to it now. "That depends on whom you ask. The official doctrine, as taught to initiates up to the Third Circle, is that the Outer Gods would bestow untold benefits upon humanity—or at least, upon those humans allied with the Order. A new golden age of power and knowledge, with the initiates as priest-kings ruling over a transformed world."

Her tone made it clear that she did not subscribe to this optimistic interpretation. "The reality, as understood by those few who have glimpsed the true nature of these entities, is quite different. The Outer Gods view humanity much as we might view insects—occasionally useful, largely irrelevant, and entirely dispensable once their utility has been exhausted."

She leaned closer, her amber eyes reflecting the moonlight like those of a predatory cat. "The gateway the Order seeks to open would not bring enlightenment or advancement. It would bring transformation on a scale that would render human civilization unrecognizable, if not entirely obliterated."

Guthrie absorbed this information with his usual calm, though the whispers had begun again in his mind, neither confirming nor denying Eliza's claims but simply observing with that same patient hunger he had sensed before.

"And my role in this?" he asked, returning to his original question. "Your uncle called me 'the perfect vessel.' What does that mean?"

Eliza reached out and placed her hand on his, the contact once again creating that electric sensation that silenced the whispers completely. "That, Guthrie Knox, is the most carefully guarded secret of all. You have been selected, prepared, and groomed for a very specific purpose—to serve as the physical anchor for the primary gateway."

She squeezed his hand, her expression intense. "The human body, properly prepared through specific rituals and transformations, can serve as a living doorway between worlds. A vessel, as my uncle calls it, through which the essence of an Outer God can enter our reality without the limitations of temporary summoning."

The implication was clear, and for the first time in his adult life, Guthrie felt something approaching genuine concern. "They intend to use me as a... host for one of these entities?"

"Not just any entity," Eliza corrected. "The most ancient and powerful of them all—the one they call the Dweller Beneath, whose whispers you have been hearing with increasing clarity since your initiation. The being that has waited beneath Daybridge

Bridge since long before the city existed, biding its time until the stars aligned and a suitable vessel was prepared."

She released his hand, watching his reaction carefully. "The rituals you've been performing, the sacrifices conducted according to specific patterns—all of these have been preparing both your body and the mystical infrastructure of Daybridge for this ultimate transformation. When the Great Conjunction occurs three years hence, in the summer of 1901, you are to be ceremonially transformed into a living gateway through which the Dweller Beneath will enter our world in physical form."

Guthrie remained outwardly calm, but his mind was racing, connecting disparate pieces of information into a coherent whole. The dreams of transformation. The whispers that seemed to speak directly to him. The intense interest the Order had shown in his unique combination of physical strength and emotional detachment. It all aligned with Eliza's revelation.

"This transformation," he said after a moment of consideration. "What would become of me? Would I still exist as myself, or would this entity simply... replace me?"

Eliza's expression softened slightly, showing what appeared to be genuine concern. "That is a question even the highest levels of the Order cannot answer with certainty. The texts describe a merger of essences, a union of human and Other that creates something entirely new. Whether any recognizable portion of Guthrie Knox would remain conscious within that merged being..." She shrugged, the gesture eloquent in its ambiguity.

"I see," Guthrie said, his voice revealing nothing of his thoughts. "And why are you telling me this now, when your uncle and his Council clearly prefer to keep me in ignorance until closer to the appointed time?"

This was the crux of the matter—the reason for this clandestine meeting, for Eliza's apparent willingness to reveal secrets that the

Order had carefully kept from him despite his advancement through their ranks.

Eliza stood, moving a few paces away from the altar to stare up at the midsummer moon. Her profile, silhouetted against the night sky, was striking in its classical beauty and underlying strength.

"Because I have plans of my own," she said at last, turning back to face him. "Plans that align with the Order's in many respects but diverge in certain crucial details. And you, Guthrie Knox, are central to those plans."

She approached him again, standing directly before him as he remained seated on the altar. In this position, their eyes were nearly level, allowing him to see the depth of purpose—and something else, something heated and hungry—in her unusual amber gaze.

"The Order has selected you as the vessel, but they underestimate the importance of your willing participation," she continued. "They believe that by the time the Great Conjunction arrives, you will be so thoroughly conditioned by the rituals and the Dweller's influence that your consent will be a mere formality. But I know better."

She placed her hands on his shoulders, the contact sending that now-familiar electric current through his body. "The transformation requires not just physical and mystical preparation, but a complete alignment of will between vessel and entity. Without that alignment, the gateway remains imperfect, unstable—and subject to influence by those who understand the deeper principles involved."

Guthrie studied her face, reading the layers of intent behind her carefully chosen words. "You want to control this process. To direct it toward your own ends rather than those of the Order."

Her smile widened, revealing perfect teeth that seemed almost too white in the moonlight. "Clever man. Yes, that is precisely what I want. And for that, I need you—not just as a vessel prepared according to the Order's specifications, but as a partner who understands the full scope of what is being attempted and chooses to align his will with mine rather than with my uncle's."

"And what are your ends?" Guthrie asked, unmoved by the flattery but genuinely curious about her motivations. "If not the Order's vision of priest-kings ruling a transformed world, then what?"

Eliza's expression became almost dreamy, her gaze unfocused as if seeing visions beyond the present moment. "Something far more personal. The Outer Gods offer knowledge and power beyond human comprehension, yes—but also transformation on an individual level that transcends mere extended life or worldly influence."

Her focus returned to him, intense and compelling. "I seek to become more than human, Guthrie. To evolve beyond the limitations of flesh and mortal comprehension. And through our partnership, you could achieve the same—not as a passive vessel subsumed by the Dweller Beneath, but as an active participant in a transformation that preserves and enhances what makes you unique while grafting onto it powers and perceptions currently beyond your imagining."

It was a seductive vision, presented with a conviction that suggested absolute belief on Eliza's part. Whether that belief was justified or delusional remained an open question, but Guthrie found himself responding to the passion behind it in a way that was entirely foreign to his usual detachment.

"And if I decline this... partnership?" he asked, maintaining his pragmatic approach despite the unfamiliar emotions stirring within him.

Eliza's hands tightened slightly on his shoulders. "Then the Order's plan proceeds as designed. You continue to perform the rituals as directed, growing ever more attuned to the Dweller's influence until the Great Conjunction arrives. At that point, you will be ceremonially transformed into a gateway through which the entity enters our world fully, with whatever remains of Guthrie Knox merely a vestigial consciousness within a vast, inhuman intelligence."

She leaned closer, her breath warm against his face. "But I don't think you'll decline. I've studied you too carefully, read too many of your journal entries, observed too many of your rituals. There's a hunger in you that matches my own—a desire to transcend the limitations that constrain lesser beings. You've spent your life perfecting the art of death because it offered a form of power that made sense to you. I'm offering something far greater—mastery not just over death, but over reality itself."

Guthrie remained silent, processing her words against the background of the whispers that had resumed in his mind, now seeming to affirm Eliza's claims with their ancient, inhuman perspectives. Part of him—the rational, methodical butcher who had built his life on predictability and control—recognized the danger in what she proposed. But another part, one he had scarcely acknowledged before this night, responded to the promise of transformation with an eagerness that surprised him.

"What would this partnership require of me?" he asked finally, neither accepting nor rejecting her offer but exploring its parameters with his usual thoroughness.

Eliza's smile was triumphant, as if his question itself represented a victory. "In the immediate term, very little that differs from what you're already doing. Continue the rituals as directed by the Order, but with subtle modifications that I will teach you—changes to the invocations, alterations in the pattern of certain cuts, additions to the journal entries that my uncle so assiduously studies."

She released his shoulders and stepped back slightly, her expression becoming more businesslike. "More significantly, we will need to conduct our own private workings—rituals designed to forge a connection between us that parallels and eventually supersedes your connection to the Dweller Beneath. These will require... intimacies of various kinds, exchanges of essence both mystical and physical."

The implication was clear, and Guthrie found himself responding to it with an intensity that would have been alien to him just hours earlier. Whether this was a natural attraction or something induced by the ritual energies permeating Blackwood Manor, he couldn't determine—nor, he realized with mild surprise, did he particularly care.

"And longer term?" he pressed, still maintaining at least the appearance of rational consideration.

"Longer term, we prepare for a working of our own to coincide with the Great Conjunction," Eliza explained. "While the Order conducts its ceremony at the bridge, believing they are opening a gateway for the Dweller to enter our world through you, we will actually be performing a different ritual—one that channels the entity's power through both of us equally, transforming us into something beyond human while maintaining our individual consciousness and will."

She extended her hand, palm up, in a gesture that was both invitation and symbolic representation of their proposed alliance. "So, Guthrie Knox—will you partner with me in this Great Work? Will you choose transformation on our terms rather than surrender to the fate the Order has designed for you?"

Guthrie looked at her offered hand, considering the choice before him with as much objectivity as he could muster despite the unfamiliar emotions clouding his usual clarity. The rational part of his mind noted that he had insufficient information to make a truly informed decision—he had only Eliza's word regarding the Order's ultimate plans for him, and her own agenda remained opaque despite her seemingly forthright explanation.

But beneath these rational considerations, something deeper was stirring—a recognition, perhaps, of a kindred spirit whose ambitions and detachment from conventional morality matched his own. In Eliza Blackwood, he sensed a reflection of himself—not as he was, but as he might become if freed from the constraints that had limited him throughout his life.

And the whispers, those ancient voices that had become his constant companions, seemed to urge him toward acceptance, though whether out of genuine alignment with Eliza's plans or for inscrutable purposes of their own, he couldn't determine.

In the end, his decision was neither fully rational nor entirely emotional, but a complex calculus of self-interest, curiosity, and that newfound attraction he still didn't fully understand. He reached out and took Eliza's hand, feeling once again that electric connection between them.

"Yes," he said simply. "I will partner with you."

Her smile was radiant, transforming her striking features into true beauty. "I knew you would," she murmured, stepping closer until their bodies were almost touching. "We are alike, you and I—both seekers of transformation, both willing to transcend the limitations that bind lesser beings to their mundane existences."

Still holding his hand, she leaned in and pressed her lips to his—a kiss that began gently but quickly intensified into something hungry and demanding. Guthrie responded with equal fervor, surprised by the depth of his own reaction but surrendering to it with the same thoroughness he brought to all his endeavors.

When they finally separated, both slightly breathless, Eliza's amber eyes seemed to glow with an inner light that was not entirely reflected moonlight. "Our first exchange of essence," she said, her voice husky with a combination of desire and mystical significance. "The beginning of our true Work together."

She stepped back, though not releasing his hand. "We should return to the mansion separately. My uncle will be looking for me, and your absence has likely been noted as well. We must maintain appearances until the time is right to reveal our true intentions."

Guthrie nodded, recognizing the practical wisdom in her caution. "When will we meet again?"

"Soon," she promised. "I'll send instructions through channels the Order doesn't monitor. Be prepared for challenges in the coming months—my uncle is no fool, and he may sense the change in your alignment. But if we're careful, if we play our roles convincingly, he won't realize the true nature of our partnership until it's too late for him to intervene."

With a final squeeze of his hand, she released him and turned to leave the stone circle, her crimson dress seeming to absorb the moonlight rather than reflect it. At the edge of the ring of standing stones, she paused and looked back at him.

"One last thing, Guthrie," she said, her voice carrying clearly despite the distance. "The work we've discussed will require greater... intensity in your rituals. More precision, more complexity, and perhaps more... creativity in your approach to the subjects. I trust that won't be a problem for you?"

Guthrie understood the implication immediately. She was suggesting that he should embrace the more sadistic aspects of his work for the Order—not merely executing the required rituals with technical precision but exploring the darker possibilities they presented. Whether this was truly necessary for their mystical partnership or simply aligned with her personal preferences remained unclear, but his answer came without hesitation.

"No," he replied. "It won't be a problem."

Her smile was the last thing he saw before she disappeared into the darkness beyond the stone circle, leaving him alone with the whispers that had resumed their constant murmur in his mind—but now with a new undercurrent that might have been anticipation or warning, he couldn't tell which.

As he made his own way back toward Blackwood Manor, Guthrie reflected on the evening's developments with a mixture of his usual analytical detachment and the new, unfamiliar emotions that Eliza had awakened in him. He had committed himself to a path whose ultimate destination remained unclear, forming an alliance with a woman whose true motives he could only guess at, against an organization whose power and reach far exceeded his own.

It was, by any rational assessment, a reckless decision—perhaps the first truly impulsive choice he had made in his adult life. Yet he felt no regret, no desire to reconsider. Whatever lay ahead, whatever transformations awaited him through his partnership with Eliza Blackwood, they represented a future far more intriguing than the one the Order had planned for him.

And as he rejoined the dwindling gathering in Blackwood Manor's Great Hall, nodding acknowledgment to Septimus Blackwood's inquiring glance from across the room, Guthrie Knox began to contemplate the new dimensions his work might explore under Eliza's guidance. The technical challenges, the artistic possibilities, the deeper understanding of pain and transformation that might be achieved through more... creative approaches to his subjects.

The butcher's ledger would need new sections, new categories of observation. And his workshop beneath Holloway's Slaughterhouse would require certain modifications to accommodate these expanded experiments.

For the first time since Old Silas had taught him the butcher's trade all those years ago, Guthrie felt something approaching excitement about his work—not the calm satisfaction of technical perfection, but a hungry anticipation of the discoveries that lay ahead.

And in the whispers that accompanied him as he departed Blackwood Manor in the predawn hours, he thought he detected a new note—not just hunger now, but something that might have been amusement, or perhaps approval, from the ancient entity that waited beneath Daybridge Bridge for the appointed hour of its emergence into the world of men.

Chapter 7: A Butcher's Heart

The autumn of 1898 descended upon Daybridge with unusual gentleness, the harshness of summer's heat giving way to golden days and cool nights that painted the city in shades of amber and crimson. Even the Shadowlair River seemed to shed some of its industrial grimness, reflecting the changing leaves of the scattered trees that had somehow survived along its banks despite the factories' noxious emissions.

For most of Daybridge's citizens, it was a welcome respite before the inevitable descent into winter's bitter grip. For Guthrie Knox, it marked the beginning of the most profound transformation he had yet experienced—not the physical metamorphosis prophesied for his future, but a psychological evolution that would reshape his inner landscape as surely as any ritual.

The source of this change was Eliza Blackwood.

In the weeks following the Midsummer Gathering, Guthrie found his thoughts increasingly dominated by memories of their encounter in the stone circle. The intensity of their connection, the electric sensation of her touch, the bold vision she had outlined for their partnership—all of these elements played through his mind in endless loops, distracting him from his usual methodical focus.

At first, this distraction manifested as mild irritation—an unfamiliar disruption to his carefully ordered existence. But as days passed without any contact from Eliza, irritation gave way to something deeper and more unsettling: longing. Not just for the mystical knowledge and power she had promised, but for her presence, her approval, her touch.

Guthrie had never experienced such feelings before. His emotional landscape had been deliberately flattened since childhood, a defense mechanism against the cruelties of Blackwell

Orphanage that had hardened into a permanent state of detachment. Even his work for the Order, with all its occult significance and gruesome intimacy, had been approached with the same clinical precision he brought to his legitimate butchery.

But Eliza had somehow breached those defenses, awakening sensations and desires that he had believed long dead—if they had ever truly existed at all. He found himself watching for her at the weekly Order meetings held in Blackwood Manor's library, a tightness in his chest when she failed to appear, a surge of something like joy on the rare occasions when she did.

On these occasions, their interactions remained formal and brief, conducted under the watchful eye of Septimus Blackwood and other high-ranking members of the Order. A nod of acknowledgment, perhaps a few words exchanged about the progress of certain rituals, nothing that would suggest the secret compact they had formed beneath the midsummer moon.

Yet even these superficial exchanges left Guthrie strangely energized, as if some essence had passed between them despite the constraints of their public personas. And always, as she turned away, Eliza would give him that private smile—the one that seemed to exist solely for him, a reminder of their shared secret and the transformations to come.

It was maddening, this newfound vulnerability. Guthrie had built his existence on control—over his emotions, his environment, the lives that ended beneath his knife. Now he found himself subject to tides of feeling that defied containment, a hunger that grew sharper with each passing day of deprivation.

Work provided some distraction. The Order's demands had increased following the Midsummer Gathering, with new rituals requiring more elaborate preparations and executions. Guthrie threw himself into these tasks with renewed dedication, applying the subtle modifications Eliza had suggested during their meeting in the stone circle—alterations to the patterns of certain cuts, variations in the timing of extractions, adjustments to the invocations he was now required to recite as part of his Second Circle status.

Whether these changes produced the effects she had claimed remained unclear, as he had no direct means of comparing the results to the Order's expectations. But he performed them faithfully, a tangible connection to Eliza and their secret partnership even in her physical absence.

His journal entries became more detailed during this period, expanding from purely technical observations to include speculations about the mystical implications of his work. This shift did not go unnoticed by Septimus Blackwood, who commented on it during one of their weekly meetings.

"Your understanding is deepening, Brother Knox," the High Master observed, leafing through the latest transcript Guthrie had provided. "These insights into the relationship between physical extraction and spiritual transition show a grasp of principles usually reserved for Third Circle initiates."

Guthrie maintained his usual impassivity, though internally he tensed at the scrutiny. "The work itself teaches, if one pays attention," he replied, keeping his voice neutral.

Blackwood studied him with those unusual amber eyes—so like Eliza's yet lacking their hypnotic intensity. "Indeed, it does. Though I wonder what other sources might be informing your... education."

The implication was clear, and for a moment Guthrie feared that their secret partnership had already been discovered. But Blackwood's next words dispelled this concern.

"My niece mentioned your conversation at the Midsummer Gathering. She was quite impressed by your questions, your apparent thirst for deeper understanding." A slight smile creased the High Master's aristocratic features. "Eliza has always had an eye for talent, for those with the potential to advance our Work beyond the conventional boundaries."

Relief, quickly suppressed, was followed by a surge of anticipation. If Blackwood was making this connection himself, it might provide the opening Guthrie had been waiting for.

"Miss Blackwood's insights were... illuminating," he acknowledged carefully. "Her perspective on the rituals differs somewhat from the standard doctrine."

Blackwood chuckled, the sound oddly warm coming from a man who presided over ceremonies of blood and transformation. "My niece has always charted her own course through the mysteries. It's what makes her valuable to the Order, despite her... unconventional approaches." He closed the journal transcript and fixed Guthrie with a more serious gaze. "She's expressed interest in working more closely with you on certain aspects of the preparation rituals. I've given my approval, within certain parameters."

It took all of Guthrie's considerable self-control to maintain his neutral expression, to prevent the surge of elation from showing on his face or in his voice. "I would welcome the opportunity to learn from her expertise," he said, the bland words entirely inadequate to express the depth of his anticipation.

"Excellent." Blackwood rose from behind his desk, signaling the end of their meeting. "She'll contact you directly to arrange the details. I trust you'll find the collaboration... educational."

As Guthrie left Blackwood Manor and made his way back to Holloway's Slaughterhouse, his mind raced with possibilities. Had Eliza engineered this development, using her influence with her uncle to create a sanctioned channel for their unsanctioned partnership? Or was Blackwood himself orchestrating this connection for purposes of his own, perhaps suspecting their secret compact and seeking to monitor it through apparent approval?

The answer came three days later, in the form of a small package delivered to his apartment above the slaughterhouse. Inside, wrapped in black silk, lay a silver key of unusual design and a note written in elegant, flowing script:

The key opens more than one door. Tomorrow, midnight. Come alone.

No signature, but none was needed. Guthrie recognized both the handwriting and the oblique style from the letters he had studied in the Order's archives, documents supposedly authored by "E.B." that detailed alternative approaches to certain rituals.

That night, for the first time in years, he dreamed not of the bridge and the entity that waited beneath it, but of Eliza—her amber eyes, her violet lips, her hands moving in arcane gestures that seemed to reshape reality itself. He woke before dawn, his heart pounding with an anticipation that was both unfamiliar and intoxicating.

The key, he discovered, fit a small door set into the garden wall surrounding Blackwood Manor, accessible from a narrow lane that ran behind the estate. At precisely midnight the following night, Guthrie slipped through this entrance and found himself in a section of the garden he had never seen before—a walled enclosure filled with plants that seemed to glow faintly in the moonlight, their forms strange and unlike any vegetation he recognized from his limited botanical knowledge.

A narrow path wound through this alien garden, leading to a small structure that resembled a Greek temple in miniature, its columns wrapped with vines bearing midnight blue flowers that emitted a subtle, intoxicating fragrance. The door stood slightly ajar, a warm light spilling out to illuminate the path.

Guthrie approached with his usual caution, senses alert for any sign of danger or deception. But the only presence he detected was the one he had been longing for these past weeks—Eliza Blackwood, waiting within the temple's intimate confines.

She sat amid a scatter of cushions on the marble floor, surrounded by ancient-looking books and scrolls. Candles provided the only illumination, their flames unnaturally steady in the still air. She wore a simple robe of deep green silk, her raven hair loose around her shoulders rather than confined in the formal styles she adopted for public appearances.

"You came," she said, looking up from the text she had been studying. "I wasn't entirely certain you would."

Guthrie stepped inside, closing the door behind him. The space was smaller than it had appeared from outside, creating an immediate intimacy between them. "Your uncle mentioned you had requested to work with me," he said, his voice sounding rougher than usual to his own ears. "Was that your doing or his?"

Eliza smiled, the expression as intoxicating as the scent of the strange flowers outside. "Both, in a way. I suggested it, knowing he would agree because it aligns with his plans for you. He believes I'm helping to prepare you for your role as the vessel, accelerating your mystical education to ensure you're ready for the Great Conjunction."

She set aside the book and rose gracefully to her feet, moving toward him with that same fluid motion he remembered from their encounter in the stone circle. "And I am preparing you, Guthrie. Just not for the fate my uncle has designed."

There was something predatory in her approach, a quality that would have triggered warning signals in any other context. But Guthrie found himself responding not with caution but with a mirroring intensity, his body leaning toward hers as if drawn by an invisible force.

"You've made changes to the rituals," she continued, stopping just short of touching him. "Subtle alterations, exactly as I suggested. The results have been... most promising. The energetic pathways are shifting, creating space for our intervention when the time comes."

"Your uncle has noticed the changes in my journal entries," Guthrie said, watching her face for any sign of concern.

But Eliza merely laughed, the sound like crystal chimes in the enclosed space. "Of course he has. That was intentional. He needs to believe you're evolving in the direction he desires, developing the mystical sensitivity required for the vessel. And you are evolving, Guthrie—just along a different trajectory than he imagines."

She reached out then, placing her hand against his chest directly over his heart. The now-familiar electric sensation surged through him at her touch, more intense than before, sending waves of heat and awareness cascading through his nervous system.

"I've missed you," she said, her voice dropping to a near whisper. "Our connection at Midsummer was just the beginning, a mere taste of what we can achieve together. But we must proceed carefully, building our bond in layers, each one stronger than the last."

Guthrie found himself responding without conscious thought, his hand rising to cover hers where it rested against his chest. "Tell me what you need from me," he said, the words emerging with an intensity that would have shocked him just months earlier.

Eliza's smile deepened, her amber eyes reflecting the candlelight like pools of molten gold. "First, we must establish a regular channel for our work together, one that won't arouse my uncle's suspicions. The cover story of my tutoring you in advanced ritual techniques provides that foundation."

She stepped back, though not removing her hand from beneath his, maintaining the physical connection between them.

"Second, we need to create our own ritual space, separate from the Order's established locations. Somewhere we can conduct the workings that will bind us together in preparation for the Great Conjunction."

"The workshop beneath Holloway's," Guthrie suggested immediately. "It's already set up for ritual work, and I control access completely."

Eliza nodded, clearly pleased by his quick understanding. "Perfect. The slaughterhouse's position at the confluence of certain telluric currents makes it ideal for our purposes. And the amount of death that has occurred there over the decades has thinned the barriers between worlds, creating a natural gateway we can utilize."

She finally withdrew her hand, turning to retrieve one of the ancient books that lay open on the cushions. "This brings us to the third requirement—knowledge. Specific rituals and invocations that the Order keeps restricted to the highest circles, accessible only to those who have proven their absolute loyalty to the established hierarchy."

The book she held was bound in what appeared to be human skin, its pages yellowed with extreme age, the text written in a script Guthrie didn't recognize. "These are the true teachings, the unfiltered wisdom transmitted directly from the Outer Gods to their most dedicated adherents throughout history. Not the sanitized versions my uncle dispenses to the lower circles, but the raw, unfettered knowledge that can transform perception and reality itself."

She offered the book to him, her expression solemn. "I will teach you to read this language, to understand the principles it describes, to perform the rituals it contains. But know that once you begin this study, there is no turning back. The knowledge itself changes you, reshapes your mind to accommodate concepts that human language was never designed to express."

Guthrie took the book without hesitation, feeling its strange weight—heavier than its physical dimensions would suggest, as if the knowledge it contained had a gravity all its own. "When do we begin?"

Eliza's smile returned, brilliant and somehow triumphant. "We already have, Guthrie Knox. From the moment you accepted my hand in the stone circle, our paths became intertwined. Everything since then has been preparation for this moment, this commitment to the deeper work that lies ahead."

She moved closer once more, her body now pressing against his, the heat of her presence seeping through the layers of clothing that separated them. "But before we proceed further, I require a token of your dedication—a gift that demonstrates your understanding of what our partnership truly entails."

"What sort of gift?" Guthrie asked, though some part of him already knew the answer.

Eliza's eyes seemed to darken, the amber deepening to something closer to obsidian. "Something personal. Something that represents the essence of your craft, the heart of your power. Something that no one else could provide, that would have meaning only between us."

The implication was clear, and Guthrie found himself nodding in immediate understanding. "I'll bring it when we next meet," he promised.

Her smile widened, revealing perfect teeth that gleamed in the candlelight. "I know you will." She leaned in, her lips brushing against his ear as she whispered, "Three days from now. Same time. Bring your gift, and we will begin the first binding ritual."

The kiss that followed was brief but intense, a searing contact that seemed to bypass physical sensation to touch something deeper within him. Then she was stepping back, creating distance between them once more.

"You should go," she said, her voice betraying a slight breathlessness that sent a surge of satisfaction through him. "The night watchers will make their rounds soon, and while I've ensured, they won't approach this part of the garden, it's best not to tempt fate with an extended visit."

Guthrie nodded, reluctant to leave but recognizing the practical wisdom in her caution. He tucked the ancient book carefully inside his coat. "Three days," he confirmed.

As he made his way back through the strange garden to the small door in the wall, Guthrie's mind was already working on the nature of the "gift" Eliza had requested. It would need to be special, unique—something that demonstrated not just his technical skill but his understanding of their partnership and its implications.

The answer came to him as he slipped through the door into the narrow lane beyond. Not just any trophy from his work for the Order, but something specific—something that represented the transformation they sought together, the transcendence of normal human limitations.

Three nights later, Guthrie returned to the temple in Blackwood Manor's secret garden, carrying a small wooden box of his own crafting. The container itself was a work of art, carved from a single block of ebony with intricate patterns inlaid in silver and mother-of-pearl—patterns that echoed the symbols used in the Order's rituals while subtly altering their arrangement in ways that reflected Eliza's modifications.

She was waiting for him as before, though the temple's interior had been rearranged. The cushions and books were gone, replaced by a small altar of black marble at the center of the space. Seven candles burned at specific points around this altar, their flames colored in hues that shouldn't have been possible—deep violet, midnight blue, a green so dark it bordered on black.

Eliza herself had changed as well. She wore a gown of crimson silk that left her shoulders and arms bare, revealing more of the intricate tattoos that spiraled across her skin. Her hair was elaborately braided with small silver beads that caught the candlelight, creating the impression of stars woven into the midnight of her tresses.

"You've brought it," she said by way of greeting, her gaze fixing on the box in his hands.

Guthrie nodded, approaching the altar with measured steps. "As promised."

He placed the box on the black marble surface, then stepped back slightly, allowing Eliza to approach. She circled the altar once, trailing her fingers along its edge, before coming to stand opposite him with the box between them.

"Tell me about it," she requested, making no move to open the container. "What does this gift represent?"

Guthrie considered his words carefully, wanting to convey the full significance of what he had created. "It represents transformation," he said finally. "The passage from one state of being to another, the shedding of limitations to become something greater."

He gestured to the box, its intricate carvings seeming to shift subtly in the strange light of the colored flames. "The container itself is part of the gift—a vessel designed to hold power and potential, just as my body is meant to serve as a vessel for greater forces. But the true gift lies within."

Eliza smiled, clearly pleased by his explanation. "Then let us see this token of transformation," she said, her voice taking on a ritual cadence. "Let us witness the first tangible manifestation of our covenant."

With elegant fingers, she lifted the lid of the box, revealing its contents—a human heart, perfectly preserved through techniques

Guthrie had developed specifically for this purpose. But this was no ordinary heart. It had been modified, enhanced, transformed through a process that had taken him the full three days to perfect.

The organ had been carefully dissected and reconstructed, with certain chambers enlarged and others reduced. Delicate silver wires ran through the muscle tissue, forming patterns that matched the tattoos on Eliza's skin. And at the center, where the two main ventricles joined, a small crystal of unusual composition had been embedded—a stone Guthrie had found among the Order's ritual supplies, described in the accompanying text as a "heart of the void, crystallized essence of the space between worlds."

Eliza's breath caught audibly as she beheld the creation, her eyes widening with what appeared to be genuine surprise and delight. "Extraordinary," she whispered, reaching out to trace the silver patterns with a fingertip. "Whose was it, before you transformed it?"

"A poet," Guthrie replied. "One who wrote verses about transcending the human condition, ascending to a state beyond flesh and limitation. The Order contracted his elimination after he published works that came too close to revealing certain truths meant to be kept hidden from the uninitiated."

He hadn't chosen the victim randomly. The poet, Jonathan Mercer, had been one of his more recent subjects, a man whose writings had indeed touched on themes of transformation and ascension that resonated with the path Guthrie and Eliza were now pursuing. There had been something in Mercer's eyes as he died—a recognition, perhaps even an acceptance of his role in a larger pattern—that had marked him as the perfect source for this gift.

"A poet's heart," Eliza murmured, her expression thoughtful. "One who sought in words what we seek in deed—the transcendence of mortal limitations, the evolution into something greater." She looked up at Guthrie, her amber eyes shining with an emotion he couldn't quite name. "It's perfect. More than I hoped for."

She lifted the transformed heart from its box, holding it reverently in both hands. "This will form the centerpiece of our first binding ritual," she explained. "A focus for the energies we will raise, a physical representation of the metaphysical changes we seek to create."

Placing the heart carefully on the altar, Eliza moved around to stand beside Guthrie. "Remove your coat and shirt," she instructed. "The first binding must be conducted with direct contact between flesh and ritual implements."

Guthrie complied without hesitation, stripping to the waist with efficient movements. The temple's air was unexpectedly warm against his skin, almost fevered, as if the space itself were alive and generating heat.

Eliza's gaze traveled over his exposed torso—his formidable physique developed through years of physical labor, the network of small scars that told the story of his life in the slaughterhouse, the larger, more deliberate marks left by his initiation into the Order's Second Circle. Her expression as she studied him contained equal parts clinical assessment and something more heated, more personal.

"Magnificent," she murmured, reaching out to trace one of the ritual scars with a feather-light touch. "Such potential, such capacity for transformation. My uncle chose better than he knew when he selected you as the vessel."

She moved to a small cabinet built into the temple wall, removing several items that she placed on the altar beside the transformed heart: a silver bowl filled with a dark liquid, a slender knife with a blade that seemed to absorb rather than reflect the candlelight, and a small brush made from what appeared to be human hair.

"This ritual creates the first layer of our bond," Eliza explained as she arranged these items in a specific pattern. "It establishes a direct connection between our essential natures, allowing energies to flow between us in preparation for the greater merging to come."

She looked up at him, her expression suddenly serious. "It will involve blood, Guthrie—yours and mine, freely given and mingled with certain other essences. Once begun, this binding cannot be undone by any power known to the Order or the entities they serve. Are you certain this is what you want?"

The question gave him pause, not because he doubted his decision, but because it was the first time Eliza had explicitly asked for his consent rather than assuming it. This suggested that what they were about to undertake was indeed as significant as she claimed—a true point of no return in their partnership.

"I'm certain," he said after a moment's consideration, his voice steady with conviction. "Whatever comes, we face it together."

Eliza's smile returned, brilliant and somehow more genuine than any he had seen from her before. "Together," she echoed, the word carrying the weight of a vow. "Then let us begin."

The ritual that followed was unlike any Guthrie had performed for the Order. Where those ceremonies had been structured around death and sacrifice—the taking of life to open pathways between worlds—this working focused on transformation and connection, the creation of new patterns within existing life forces.

Eliza began by using the brush to paint symbols on his bare chest and arms, the dark liquid from the silver bowl leaving marks that seemed to sink beneath his skin as soon as they were applied, creating a burning sensation that was not entirely unpleasant. She chanted as she worked, her voice shifting between languages—some that Guthrie recognized from the Order's rituals,

others entirely unknown to him, their syllables twisting in ways
that human vocal cords should not have been able to produce.

When his upper body was covered in these ephemeral symbols,
she handed him the brush and removed the upper portion of her
gown, revealing skin already adorned with permanent versions of
the same markings she had placed on him. Guided by her
instructions, Guthrie traced over these existing patterns with the
dark liquid, his large hands surprisingly steady as he followed the
intricate designs that spiraled across her shoulders, collarbones, and
the upper swell of her breasts.

The liquid seemed to react differently to her skin, the symbols
glowing briefly with a cold blue light before fading into the existing
tattoos, as if being absorbed and integrated into her very being.
Throughout this process, she continued her chanting, though now
the sounds seemed to emerge not just from her throat but from the
surrounding air, as if multiple voices were joining in harmonies that
defied conventional acoustics.

When the symbols were complete on both their bodies, Eliza
took up the slender knife. Without hesitation, she drew the blade
across her left palm, creating a shallow cut that welled with blood
far darker than normal human vitae—almost black in the strange
light of the colored flames.

"Your turn," she said, offering him the knife, handle first.

Guthrie took the blade, noting its unusual weight and balance,
and made a similar cut across his own palm. The pain was sharp but
brief, quickly subsumed beneath a wave of heightened awareness
that seemed to spread from the wound throughout his body.

Eliza placed the transformed heart at the exact center of the
altar, then extended her bleeding hand toward him. "Our blood,
freely given, creates the first bond," she intoned, her voice
resonating with power. "Our essence, willingly shared, establishes
the connection that death itself cannot sever."

Guthrie placed his cut palm against hers, their fingers interlacing as their blood mingled. The sensation that followed defied description—not pain, not pleasure, but something that transcended both, a rushing awareness of another consciousness touching his own. For an instant, he could sense Eliza's thoughts, her emotions, her very being as if they were extensions of his own mind.

And through that connection, he glimpsed something else—a vast, ancient awareness observing their ritual with what might have been approval or amusement, its nature so alien that even this brief, indirect contact threatened to overwhelm his sanity. The whispers that had been his constant companions surged to a crescendo, no longer separate from this entity but revealed as manifestations of its interest in him, in them, in the path they were forging together.

Then the moment passed, the direct mental connection fading though not disappearing entirely. A subtle link remained, an awareness of Eliza's presence that transcended physical proximity, a sense of her emotions and general state of being that hummed at the edges of his consciousness.

"It is done," she said, her voice sounding distant as he struggled to reorient himself to normal perception. "The first binding is complete."

She released his hand and placed both their palms, still bleeding, upon the transformed heart. The organ seemed to pulse beneath their touch, though whether this was a physical reality or a product of heightened perception, Guthrie couldn't determine.

"This heart is now the physical anchor of our bond," Eliza explained, her voice returning to its normal cadence though still carrying undertones of ritual significance. "It must be protected, preserved, kept secret from all others—especially my uncle and his Council. If they were to gain possession of it, they could potentially use it to sever our connection or, worse, to manipulate the energies we're creating for their own purposes."

Guthrie nodded, understanding the importance of what they had created. "I'll keep it in my workshop beneath Holloway's," he said. "There's a hidden compartment behind the main altar, accessible only to me. Not even your uncle knows of its existence."

Eliza smiled, clearly pleased by his foresight. "Perfect. And when we conduct our private rituals there, the heart will serve as the focus for our workings, strengthening our bond with each ceremony we perform."

She stepped back from the altar, pulling the upper portion of her gown back into place with unhurried movements. "You should feel the effects of the binding almost immediately," she continued. "A sense of my presence even when we're physically apart. Flashes of my emotional state at times of intensity. Perhaps even fragments of thought or dream when the barriers between our minds are naturally thinner, such as during sleep or deep meditation."

Guthrie was already experiencing these effects, the subtle awareness of Eliza's consciousness humming at the edges of his own like a melody just beyond clear hearing. It was both disconcerting and oddly comforting, a constant reminder that he was no longer entirely alone in his own mind.

"Will it be reciprocal?" he asked, retrieving his shirt and beginning to dress. "Will you sense me as I sense you?"

"Yes, though perhaps with greater clarity due to my prior experience with such bindings," she admitted. "I've undertaken similar rituals before, though never with this specific purpose or... intensity."

This revelation should have triggered caution or even jealousy, but Guthrie found himself accepting it as simply another facet of Eliza's mysterious background. Of course she had previous partners in her mystical explorations; her knowledge and skill far exceeded what could have been acquired through solitary study.

"Our next meeting should take place at Holloway's," Eliza said, watching him button his shirt with that same mixture of clinical assessment and personal interest. "I'll need to become familiar with the space, to attune myself to its unique energetic properties before we proceed with the second binding ritual."

She moved closer, reaching up to adjust his collar with intimate familiarity. "Three days from now, after midnight. I'll come alone, through the delivery entrance on the eastern side. Ensure that no one else is present, not even the night watchman."

Guthrie caught her hand as she withdrew it, holding it gently but firmly against his chest. "And until then?" he asked, surprised by the raw need in his voice.

Eliza smiled, that private expression that seemed reserved for him alone. "Until then, we maintain our public roles. You continue your work for the Order, incorporating the modifications I've taught you. I continue to report your 'progress' to my uncle, emphasizing your increasing attunement to the Dweller Beneath."

She leaned up on her toes, pressing a brief but intense kiss to his lips. "And in the quiet moments, when you feel my presence through our new bond, know that I am working toward our shared goal, preparing the way for the transformations to come."

The kiss deepened, her free hand moving to the back of his neck to draw him closer. Unlike their previous encounters, where Eliza had maintained careful control over the physical aspect of their relationship, this embrace held a new urgency, a hunger that matched his own.

When they finally separated, both slightly breathless, Guthrie felt a shift in their dynamic—a subtle balancing of power that suggested their partnership was evolving beyond the initial teacher-student paradigm into something more equal, more deeply intertwined.

"Three days," he confirmed, reluctantly releasing her hand and stepping back.

As he made his way back through the strange garden to the small door in the wall, Guthrie was acutely aware of the new presence in his mind—a warm, thrumming connection that provided a constant awareness of Eliza's existence. It was oddly comforting, this tether to another consciousness, a balm for the isolation that had defined his life for as long as he could remember.

The whispers that had been his constant companions since his initiation into the Order now seemed integrated with this new awareness, as if the entities behind them were observing and approving of the bond he had formed with Eliza. Their tone had shifted, becoming less demanding and more... anticipatory, as if they too were looking forward to the transformations to come.

Over the following weeks, as autumn deepened toward winter, Guthrie and Eliza established a regular pattern of clandestine meetings. Sometimes at the temple in Blackwood Manor's secret garden, sometimes in his workshop beneath Holloway's Slaughterhouse, occasionally in other locations around Daybridge where the barriers between worlds were naturally thin—ancient stone circles hidden in forgotten corners of parks, abandoned churches whose foundations had been built upon even older sacred sites, certain secluded spots along the Shadowlair River where the water ran black and still despite the current elsewhere.

At each meeting, Eliza would teach him from the ancient texts she had provided, gradually enabling him to read the strange script and understand the principles it described. The knowledge was transformative, just as she had warned—concepts that human language struggled to express, perspectives that required a fundamental restructuring of thought to accommodate.

And with each session, their bond grew stronger, deeper, more intimately entwined. The awareness of Eliza's presence in his mind expanded from vague impressions to clearer perceptions, sometimes including distinct emotions or even fragmentary thoughts when her focus on him was particularly intense.

Their physical relationship evolved as well, moving from brief, ritual-focused contacts to more passionate encounters that blended mystical practice with increasingly intimate explorations. Eliza approached these aspects of their partnership with the same methodical intensity she brought to their occult workings, each touch and caress precisely calculated to maximize both physical pleasure and mystical connection.

For Guthrie, who had never experienced such intimacy before, these encounters were revelatory—not just physically, but emotionally and spiritually as well. The barriers he had maintained throughout his life, the emotional detachment that had defined his existence, began to crumble in Eliza's presence. He found himself experiencing feelings he had thought long dead or never existing at all—desire, tenderness, even a possessive protectiveness that surprised him with its intensity.

But most significant of all was the growing sense that in Eliza, he had found not just a partner but a form of redemption. She accepted all of him—not just his physical strength or his skill with a blade, but the darker aspects of his nature that others feared or sought to exploit. She understood his detachment, his methodical approach to death and suffering, and rather than judging these qualities, she celebrated them as essential components of the transformation they sought together.

This acceptance awakened a vulnerability in Guthrie that manifested in rare but significant moments of openness. During one such occasion, as they lay together on a pallet he had installed in a corner of his workshop for their longer rituals, he found himself speaking of his childhood at Blackwell Orphanage—the abuse, the neglect, the systematic destruction of normal emotional development that had shaped him into the man he had become.

"I learned early that feelings were weaknesses," he told her, his voice low in the workshop's dim light. "Pain, fear, loneliness—showing any of these invited more suffering. So, I buried them, walled them off until I couldn't access them anymore."

Eliza listened without interruption, her head resting on his chest, her fingers tracing the ritual scars that marked his skin. "And when did you discover your aptitude for your... particular craft?" she asked when he fell silent.

"With Old Silas, at Holloway's," Guthrie replied, the memory surprisingly clear despite the years that had passed. "He saw something in me that others missed—not just physical strength or technical skill, but a fundamental understanding of death as transition rather than ending. He taught me to approach my work with respect, with precision, with an awareness of its place in the natural order."

He paused, considering how to express the complex relationship that had developed between himself and the old butcher. "Silas was the closest thing to a father I ever had," he said finally. "Not affectionate or nurturing in the conventional sense, but... accepting. He didn't try to change what I was, only to channel it in productive directions."

Eliza raised herself up on one elbow, studying his face with those amber eyes that seemed to see directly into his soul. "And yet, even with his guidance, you felt... incomplete. As if your true purpose remained unfulfilled."

It wasn't a question but a statement of fact, one that resonated with absolute truth. "Yes," Guthrie acknowledged. "Even after I began working for the Order, after I developed my skills beyond what Silas had taught me, there was always a sense of... waiting. Of preparing for something beyond the immediate tasks at hand."

"Because you were," Eliza said, her voice taking on that tone of absolute certainty that had drawn him to her from the beginning. "Everything in your life—the orphanage, your apprenticeship, your work for the Order—has been preparation for the transformation to come. Not as my uncle envisions it, as a passive vessel for an external entity, but as an active participant in your own evolution into something greater than human."

She leaned down, pressing a kiss to the center of his chest, directly over his heart. "You were always meant for this path, Guthrie. The signs were there from the beginning, for those with eyes to see them. Your detachment from conventional morality, your intuitive understanding of death as transition, your ability to perceive the voices from beyond the veil—all markers of a being already halfway between worlds, primed for the final metamorphosis."

These words, spoken with such conviction, resonated deep within him, confirming beliefs he had scarcely acknowledged even to himself. The sense of purpose, of destiny fulfilled, was intoxicating—a validation not just of his partnership with Eliza but of his entire existence leading to this point.

In such moments of vulnerability, Guthrie would often present Eliza with new gifts—not always as elaborate as the transformed heart that had anchored their first binding ritual, but always personal, always crafted with the same meticulous attention to detail that characterized all his work.

A necklace of small bones, each carved with microscopic symbols and arranged in a pattern that matched one of the diagrams from the ancient texts. A set of ritual tools created from materials harvested from his subjects, designed specifically for her hands and energetic signature. A journal bound in skin carefully

selected for its texture and durability, filled with observations on
the subtle changes their rituals were creating in both of them.

Eliza accepted these offerings with genuine appreciation,
recognizing the care and significance embedded in each one. And
in return, she continued to teach him, to guide him through the
labyrinth of ancient knowledge toward the transformation they
both sought.

The winter solstice brought another gathering at Blackwood
Manor, like the Midsummer event but with a darker, more solemn
atmosphere reflecting the season's energetic qualities. This time,
Guthrie attended not as a newcomer but as an established member
of the Inner Circle, his status within the Order's hierarchy
solidified by months of dedicated service and apparent progress
toward his designated role as the vessel.

Throughout the evening, he maintained his public
persona—respectful toward Septimus Blackwood, collegial with
the other Second Circle initiates, appropriately reserved in his
interactions with Eliza when their paths crossed in the presence of
others. But beneath this facade, the private connection they had
established hummed with constant awareness, allowing them to
communicate on a level imperceptible to those around them.

During the main ritual in the Great Hall, as the assembled
members raised energy to mark the year's darkest point, Guthrie
felt their bond surge with unusual potency. Through it, he sensed
Eliza's excitement, her anticipation of something significant about
to occur. And as the ceremony reached its climax, with Blackwood
invoking the powers of darkness to strengthen the Order's
connection to the Outer Gods, Guthrie experienced a vision unlike
any he had received before.

He saw Daybridge transformed—not destroyed, as some of
the whispers had suggested, but altered in fundamental ways that
defied easy description. The familiar streets and buildings

remained, but they existed alongside or partially merged with structures of alien geometry and purpose. The river flowed both above and below ground simultaneously, its waters taking on properties that transcended normal physics. And the bridge itself had become something far more than a simple crossing—a nexus point where multiple realities converged, a gateway between dimensions that allowed passage in all directions.

Moving through this transformed cityscape were beings that combined human and inhuman elements in harmonious rather than monstrous ways. Some he recognized as members of the Order, including Septimus Blackwood, though altered into forms that reflected their inner natures more accurately than their current physical bodies. Others were entirely new entities, inhabitants of the merged realities that now coexisted with Daybridge.

And at the center of it all, standing upon the highest point of the transformed bridge, were two figures that radiated power and purpose—himself and Eliza, but changed beyond simple recognition, evolved into beings that transcended conventional categories of existence. They were neither human nor Other, neither mortal nor god, but something new—something that combined elements of both in a synthesis that represented the next stage of conscious evolution.

The vision faded as the ritual concluded, leaving Guthrie disoriented but exhilarated. Through their bond, he could sense that Eliza had shared the experience, her mind touching his with questions and confirmations as they processed what they had seen.

Later that night, in the sanctuary of his workshop beneath Holloway's, they compared their perceptions of the vision, finding remarkable consistency despite the subjective nature of such experiences. What they had glimpsed, they agreed, was a potential future—not the destruction or subsumption the Order feared, and the Outer Gods anticipated, but a genuine transformation that would preserve the essence of both while creating something entirely new.

"This is what we're working toward," Eliza said, her eyes bright with excitement as she paced the workshop floor. "Not my uncle's vision of priest-kings ruling over a subjugated humanity, not the Dweller's desire for a one-way invasion of our reality, but a true merger of worlds that benefits all participants."

She turned to Guthrie, who sat beside the altar where the transformed heart pulsed with steady rhythm, synchronized to both their heartbeats despite its separation from any living body. "What we saw tonight confirms that our path is the correct one," she continued. "The modifications we've made to the rituals, the bindings we've established between ourselves—they're creating the foundation for this new reality."

Guthrie nodded, still processing the implications of their shared vision. "But your uncle and his Council would oppose this outcome," he observed. "They seek dominion, not partnership—power over rather than power with."

"Exactly," Eliza agreed, her expression turning more serious. "Which is why we must continue to operate in secret, to present the appearance of compliance while working toward our own ends. The final confrontation will come at the Great Conjunction, when all paths converge and all potentials manifest. Until then, we prepare, we strengthen our bond, we gather the knowledge and power needed to implement our vision rather than theirs."

She moved to stand before him, taking his massive hands in her slender ones. "But know this, Guthrie—what we saw tonight is only one possible future, not a guaranteed outcome. The path ahead is fraught with dangers, opposition not just from my uncle and the Order but from aspects of the Outer Gods themselves that seek dominion rather than partnership."

Her amber eyes held his with unwavering intensity. "There will be tests of our resolve, attempts to separate us or turn us against each other. The closer we come to the Great Conjunction, the more desperate these efforts will become. We must trust our bond, rely on the connection we've forged, even when all evidence suggests betrayal or abandonment."

Guthrie tightened his grip on her hands, the gesture conveying his commitment more eloquently than words. "Whatever comes," he said simply, "we face it together."

Eliza's smile was radiant, a beacon of certainty in the uncertain future they navigated. "Together," she echoed, the word carrying the weight of a sacred vow.

As winter gave way to spring in early 1899, their work intensified. Eliza introduced Guthrie to deeper levels of the ancient knowledge, rituals of increasing complexity and power that required precise execution and absolute focus. His natural aptitude for such work, combined with the meticulous attention to detail he had developed through years of butchery, made him an ideal student—quick to grasp the principles, flawless in their implementation.

The results of these advanced workings were tangible, manifesting in subtle but significant changes to both their physical forms and mental capacities. Guthrie found his already considerable strength increasing, his senses sharpening beyond normal human parameters, his intuitive understanding of the barriers between worlds expanding to include direct perception of the energetic currents that flowed throughout Daybridge.

Eliza underwent similar transformations, though in her case they built upon changes that had begun years earlier during her studies in Europe. Her control over the energies they raised became more precise, her ability to perceive and manipulate the barriers between dimensions more refined. And through their bond, these

individual advancements were shared, creating a synergistic effect
that accelerated their evolution beyond what either could have
achieved alone.

Septimus Blackwood noticed these changes, of course. The
High Master's amber eyes, so like his niece's yet lacking their
hypnotic intensity, followed Guthrie with increasing interest
during the Order's weekly meetings. His inquiries about Guthrie's
experiences—the whispers, the dreams, the sense of connection
to the Dweller Beneath—became more probing, more specific in
their focus.

"You're progressing remarkably well," Blackwood observed
during one such session in his private study. "The markers of
attunement are appearing far ahead of our projected timeline.
Eliza's tutoring has clearly accelerated your development."

Guthrie maintained his usual impassive expression, though
internally he was alert to any sign that their deception had been
discovered. "Miss Blackwood is an exceptional teacher," he replied,
the formal mode of address a deliberate distancing technique. "Her
understanding of the principles involved is... profound."

Blackwood's smile held a knowing quality that sent a ripple
of concern through Guthrie's normally unflappable composure.
"Indeed, she is. My niece has always possessed unusual insight into
the mysteries, even as a child. It's one of the qualities that makes
her so valuable to our Work—and so dangerous when her vision
diverges from the established path."

The implied warning was clear, as was the suggestion that
Blackwood suspected something of their private partnership. But
before Guthrie could formulate a response, the High Master
changed tactics, his tone becoming more conciliatory.

"I'm not blind to the... connection that has developed between
you," he said, studying Guthrie's face for any reaction. "Nor am
I opposed to it, within certain parameters. Emotional bonds can

actually strengthen the vessel's attunement to the entity it will host, creating additional channels for integration during the final transformation."

He leaned forward, his amber eyes reflecting the firelight in a way that momentarily resembled the inhuman glow Guthrie had glimpsed in Eliza's gaze during their most intense rituals. "But remember your ultimate purpose, Brother Knox. The Great Work transcends individual desires or ambitions. The role you have been chosen to play is too important to be compromised by... personal considerations."

Guthrie nodded, maintaining his mask of respectful attention while internally analyzing every nuance of Blackwood's words and manner. The High Master clearly suspected some level of involvement between him and Eliza but seemed to interpret it as a simple emotional or physical attachment rather than the mystical partnership they had actually formed.

This misinterpretation provided useful cover, allowing them to continue their clandestine workings while Blackwood watched for the wrong signs of deviation from the Order's plan. But it also highlighted the need for increasing caution as they moved closer to the Great Conjunction and their true intentions became harder to conceal.

Later that night, as they conducted another binding ritual in the workshop beneath Holloway's, Guthrie related the conversation to Eliza, including his assessment of her uncle's awareness and suspicions.

"He's always been perceptive," she acknowledged, adding the final components to the complex arrangement of symbols and substances on the altar between them. "But his perception is filtered through his own preconceptions, his certainty that the path he has chosen is the only valid one. He sees what he expects to see—a physical or emotional attachment that might complicate but not fundamentally alter your role as the vessel."

She looked up from her preparations, her expression both amused and grimly determined. "It wouldn't occur to him that we might have found a third path, one that neither submits to the Dweller's dominion nor enforces the Order's control over the resulting transformation. His imagination is simultaneously too expansive and too limited—capable of envisioning cosmic forces and ancient entities, but not of conceiving alternatives to the hierarchical power structures he has spent his life maintaining."

Guthrie considered this assessment, finding it aligned with his own observations of the High Master. "But as we get closer to the Great Conjunction, as the changes in us become more pronounced, his suspicions will probably increase," he pointed out. "We may need to create more convincing evidence of my supposed attunement to the Dweller's influence, to allay his concerns and maintain our cover."

Eliza nodded, her expression thoughtful. "You're right. The rituals we've been performing have been redirecting the energies that would normally forge that connection, creating our own bond instead. We need to provide my uncle with demonstrations that appear to show the expected progression while actually continuing our own work."

She circled the altar, her movements precise and purposeful as she made final adjustments to their ritual setup. "After tonight's binding, we'll need to modify our approach. Some of the rituals you perform for the Order will need to include elements that mimic the Dweller's influence—changes to your behavior, your speech patterns, your physical responses that match what my uncle expects to see in the developing vessel."

The implications were clear—Guthrie would need to become an actor of sorts, presenting a carefully crafted facade of gradual possession while maintaining his true self beneath the performance. It would require a level of deception beyond their current efforts; a convincing portrayal of exactly what Blackwood and the Council were working to achieve.

"I can do it," he said with quiet confidence. "I've spent my life observing human behavior, understanding the patterns that reveal inner states. I can reverse that process, project the external signs while keeping my internal reality intact."

Eliza smiled, that expression of genuine appreciation that always sent a surge of pleasure through their bond. "I know you can. Your capacity for compartmentalization, for maintaining separate aspects of yourself simultaneously, is one of the qualities that makes you the perfect partner for this Work." She completed her circuit of the altar, coming to stand directly across from him. "Now, shall we begin tonight's binding? This one will strengthen our mental connection, allowing more direct communication through the bond we've established."

The ritual that followed was among the most intense they had yet performed, involving an exchange not just of blood but of other bodily fluids combined with alchemical substances Eliza had prepared according to formulas from the ancient texts. The resulting mixture, applied to specific points on both their bodies while they recited complex invocations in tandem, created a surge of energy that temporarily obliterated the boundaries between their individual consciousness.

For what seemed like hours but might have been only moments, Guthrie experienced total mental union with Eliza—access to her memories, her emotions, her innermost thoughts as if they were extensions of his own mind. He saw her childhood in Blackwood Manor, raised by an uncle who recognized her potential from an early age and began her occult education before she could even read. He witnessed her studies in

Europe, at hidden institutions where knowledge forbidden to the
general public was preserved and transmitted to selected students.

And he encountered the moment of her divergence from the
Order's path—a vision similar to their shared experience at the
winter solstice but received years earlier during a solitary ritual
in the catacombs beneath Paris. The revelation that had set her
on the path toward partnership rather than dominion, toward
transformation rather than conquest.

When the mental union finally receded, leaving them once
again as separate beings connected by their bond rather than
merged into a single consciousness, Guthrie found himself changed
in subtle but significant ways. The experience of such complete
intimacy, of being truly known and accepted in all aspects of his
being, had further eroded the emotional barriers he had
maintained throughout his life.

What remained was not vulnerability in the conventional
sense—he was still the formidable, methodical butcher whose skills
had made him invaluable to the Order—but a new capacity for
connection, for genuine partnership based on mutual
understanding rather than simply aligned interests.

And at the center of this transformation was his relationship
with Eliza. What had begun as an arrangement of convenience, a
shared desire to subvert the Order's plans for their own purposes,
had evolved into something far deeper and more significant. Not
love as portrayed in the sentimental literature of the age, with its
emphasis on selfless sacrifice and idealized emotion, but a bond
forged in blood and power, in shared vision and complementary
strengths.

For Guthrie Knox, who had never expected to experience such
connection, who had built his existence around isolation and
detachment, this partnership represented a form of redemption
he had never sought but now valued beyond measure. In Eliza

Blackwood, he had found not just an ally in their mystical workings but a reflection of his own nature—equally determined, equally detached from conventional morality, equally committed to transcending the limitations that constrained lesser beings.

And as spring deepened toward summer, as their bond grew stronger and their transformations more pronounced, Guthrie found himself approaching their shared future not with his usual clinical detachment but with something approaching genuine anticipation. Whatever awaited them at the Great Conjunction—whatever final form their partnership might take in the merged reality they sought to create—he would face it willingly, even eagerly, knowing that they would experience it together.

It was, perhaps, the closest thing to hope he had ever allowed himself to feel.

Chapter 8: The Red Path

The summer of 1899 descended upon Daybridge like a fever dream, bringing heat so oppressive that the air itself seemed to thicken into a miasma that clung to skin and lungs alike. The Shadowlair River shrank to a sluggish trickle, exposing mud banks thick with decades of industrial waste that released noxious fumes under the relentless sun. Death rates in the city's poorer quarters doubled as the elderly and infirm succumbed to the brutal temperatures, their bodies often discovered days later in airless tenement rooms.

For Guthrie Knox, now in his thirtieth year, the heat was merely another variable to be accounted for in his work—both the legitimate operations at Holloway's Slaughterhouse and his more specialized activities for the Order of the Ebon Star. The accelerated decomposition of organic materials, the altered viscosity of blood, the increased difficulty in preserving specimens—all these factors required adjustments to his techniques, modifications that he implemented with his usual methodical precision.

But the summer brought other changes as well, transformations far more significant than mere adaptations to environmental conditions. The bond he had formed with Eliza Blackwood, initially a pragmatic alliance based on shared interests, had evolved into something deeper and more profound. The binding rituals they had performed over the past months had created a connection that transcended normal human relationships, allowing a level of mental and spiritual intimacy that few had ever experienced.

Through this bond, Guthrie could sense Eliza's presence even when they were physically separated—a constant awareness of her existence that hummed at the edges of his consciousness. During periods of intense emotion or focused attention, this awareness expanded to include impressions of her thoughts and feelings, sometimes even fragmentary images from her perspective. And in their moments of physical union, when the barriers between their individual consciousnesses were at their thinnest, they experienced a merging that went beyond mere physical pleasure to touch something transcendent.

This deepening connection had accelerated the changes in Guthrie that had begun with their first meeting nearly a year earlier. The emotional detachment that had defined his existence for as long as he could remember had given way to a more complex inner landscape, one capable of experiences and reactions that would have been alien to him before Eliza entered his life. Not conventional emotions as others might understand them, but a spectrum of responses uniquely his own, shaped by his unusual nature and the mystical transformations he was undergoing.

Most significant among these changes was the evolution of his approach to his work for the Order. What had once been a purely technical exercise, performed with clinical detachment and professional pride, had become something more artistic, more personally expressive. Under Eliza's guidance and encouragement, Guthrie had begun to explore the creative possibilities inherent in his skills, developing techniques that went beyond the practical requirements of disposal or ritual sacrifice to incorporate elements of aesthetic consideration and personal interpretation.

"Your work is an art form," Eliza had told him during one of their private sessions in the workshop beneath Holloway's Slaughterhouse. "Not just a craft to be executed with technical precision, but a medium for expression, for exploration, for pushing beyond the boundaries of conventional experience."

This perspective resonated with something deep within Guthrie, a capacity for creativity that had lain dormant throughout his life, suppressed by the harsh pragmatism that had been necessary for survival. With Eliza's encouragement, he began to view his subjects not merely as materials to be processed according to predetermined patterns, but as canvases for experimentation, for innovation, for the development of his own distinctive style.

His journals reflected this evolution, expanding from purely technical observations to include more subjective considerations. The precise documentation of incisions and extraction techniques remained but now accompanied by reflections on the aesthetic qualities of certain arrangements, the emotional responses elicited by particular patterns, the symbolic significance of specific configurations.

One entry, written in the early hours of a sweltering July morning, demonstrated this new approach with clarity:

Subject 47: Male, approximately 35 years of age, physically fit with well-developed musculature. Selected for the asymmetrical ritual specified by E.B., but with modifications to incorporate the spiral pattern that proved so effective in Subject 45.

The primary incision followed the sternum to navel line, then deviated along the left oblique in a curve that echoed the Golden Ratio. This departure from standard technique created a more harmonious overall composition while still providing optimal access to the required organs.

Extraction sequence: liver (still functioning) → spleen → left kidney → right kidney → heart (beating). Each organ suspended above the body in the arrangement discussed with E.B., creating a three-dimensional representation of the Sephirothic Tree.

Notable observation: When the final extraction (heart) was completed and the pattern fully realized, a momentary shift in ambient energy was perceptible. The space between the suspended organs and the body proper seemed to thin, creating a visual distortion similar to heat haze but more structured, almost geometric in its configurations.

This effect persisted for approximately 3 minutes 42 seconds, during which the whispers intensified significantly. They spoke of gateways and vessels, of transformations and mergings, in terms more specific than their usual abstract communications.

Further exploration of this technique is warranted, with particular attention to the timing of the final extraction in relation to the subject's conscious awareness. E.B. suggests that maintaining consciousness throughout the entire process might extend and strengthen the thinning effect, potentially creating a more stable gateway between realms.

Such entries, meticulously recorded in Guthrie's precise handwriting, filled multiple volumes of his expanding collection of journals. Each documented not just a death, but an experiment in transcendence—an attempt to push beyond the limitations of physical reality into realms of experience and perception that few had ever glimpsed.

Septimus Blackwood, reviewing the transcripts of these journals that Guthrie dutifully provided to the Order's Council, noted the evolution with apparent approval. "Your work shows remarkable progress," he commented during one of their weekly meetings. "The integration of traditional patterns with your own innovations demonstrates a deepening attunement to the energies we seek to harness."

What the High Master didn't know—or at least, Guthrie and Eliza believed he didn't know—was that these innovations were specifically designed to redirect those energies away from the Order's intended purpose and toward their own goals. Each modification, each creative flourish, subtly altered the flow of power generated by the rituals, channeling it into pathways that

strengthened their personal bond rather than preparing Guthrie as
a passive vessel for the Dweller Beneath.

It was a dangerous game they played, a delicate balance
between apparent compliance and secret rebellion. But the risk
only enhanced Guthrie's dedication to their shared vision, his
commitment to the path they had chosen together.

As the summer heat intensified, so did the frequency and
complexity of their private rituals. Eliza introduced Guthrie to
increasingly advanced techniques from the ancient texts she had
provided, practices that required not just physical precision but
mental discipline of the highest order. These workings pushed the
boundaries of what conventional reality could accommodate,
creating temporary ruptures in the fabric of space and time that
allowed glimpses of the Other that existed beyond normal
perception.

During one such ritual, conducted in the small temple within
Blackwood Manor's secret garden, Guthrie experienced a vision
so vivid, so all-encompassing, that it temporarily obliterated his
awareness of the physical world around him. He found himself
standing on a vast plain beneath an impossible sky—not the blue
of Earth's atmosphere but a swirling vortex of colors that had no
names in human language, moving in patterns that defied
conventional geometry.

The plain itself was covered not with grass or soil but with
a substance that seemed both solid and liquid simultaneously,
rippling beneath his feet like water yet supporting his weight like
stone. And stretching to the horizon in all directions were
structures that resembled buildings only in the most abstract
sense—towers that twisted and turned at angles that should have
been structurally impossible, domes that contained more space
inside than their external dimensions could possibly allow, arches

that connected points that seemed light-years apart yet were somehow simultaneously adjacent.

Moving among these impossible structures were beings that defied categorization—neither fully physical nor entirely energetic, shifting between states of existence with fluid grace. Some appeared vaguely humanoid, others utterly alien in form, yet all conveyed a sense of ancient intelligence, of awareness so vast and complex that Guthrie's human consciousness could grasp only fragments of its true nature.

And then, emerging from one of the twisting towers, came a figure that radiated such power, such presence, that the very fabric of the vision seemed to warp around it. Though constantly shifting in appearance, it maintained certain consistent elements—eyes like amber pools of liquid light, hair that flowed like ink in water, and an aura of authority that commanded immediate attention.

With a shock of recognition that transcended rational thought, Guthrie knew he was in the presence of the entity known to the Order as the Dweller Beneath—the ancient consciousness that had been whispering to him since his initiation, the being that Blackwood and his Council intended him to host during the Great Conjunction.

The entity approached, its movement both instantaneous and infinitely slow, a paradox of perception that Guthrie's mind struggled to reconcile. When it spoke, the words bypassed his ears to form directly in his consciousness, resonating with the same quality as the whispers he had grown accustomed to, but vastly more powerful, more immediate.

YOU WALK A DANGEROUS PATH, VESSEL. THE ALLIANCE YOU HAVE FORMED WITH THE FEMALE THREATENS THE GREAT WORK THAT HAS BEEN CENTURIES IN PREPARATION.

Despite the overwhelming presence of the entity, Guthrie
maintained his composure, drawing on the mental discipline Eliza
had taught him. "I am not merely a vessel," he responded, his
thoughts forming into coherent communication through sheer
force of will. "I am a partner in my own transformation, not a
passive receptacle for another's consciousness."

The entity's response was a sensation rather than
words—something between amusement and grudging respect,
tinged with ancient patience that made even geological timescales
seem fleeting by comparison.

*ALL ARE VESSELS, IN THE END. THE ONLY
QUESTION IS WHAT THEY CHOOSE TO CONTAIN.*

The vision shifted, the impossible landscape dissolving into a
representation of Daybridge as it currently existed—but overlaid
with patterns of energy that flowed throughout the city like
luminous rivers, converging at specific points that glowed with
concentrated power. Most brilliant among these nexus points was
the site where Daybridge Bridge had stood for centuries, recently
demolished to make way for a larger, more modern structure that
was now under construction.

*THE GATEWAY HAS EXISTED SINCE BEFORE YOUR
KIND CRAWLED FROM THE PRIMORDIAL OCEANS,* the
entity continued. *YOUR ANCESTORS RECOGNIZED ITS
POWER AND BUILT THEIR FIRST CROSSING THERE,
SENSING THE THINNESS OF THE VEIL BETWEEN
WORLDS. EACH RECONSTRUCTION HAS FOLLOWED
THE SAME PATTERN, WHETHER BY DESIGN OR
INSTINCT, MAINTAINING THE CONNECTION DESPITE
THE PASSAGE OF TIME AND THE EVOLUTION OF
MATERIALS.*

Images flashed through Guthrie's mind—a primitive wooden
bridge spanning the narrowest point of the Shadowlair River,

where ancient peoples performed sacrifices to appease forces they sensed but couldn't comprehend; a more substantial structure of stone and timber erected during modern times, incorporating symbols and patterns that echoed those used in the Order's rituals; medieval, Tudor, and Victorian iterations, each preserving certain key elements despite their apparent differences in design.

THE CURRENT CONSTRUCTION REPRESENTS THE CULMINATION OF THIS EVOLUTIONARY PROCESS, the entity explained. *DESIGNED BY ARCHITECTS WHO SERVE THE ORDER, INCORPORATING GEOMETRIES AND MATERIALS THAT WILL MAXIMIZE THE GATEWAY'S POTENTIAL DURING THE GREAT CONJUNCTION. WHEN THE ALIGNMENT IS COMPLETE, THE BARRIERS BETWEEN WORLDS WILL BE AT THEIR THINNEST, ALLOWING FOR A MERGING OF REALITIES UNLIKE ANY THAT HAS OCCURRED IN YOUR RECORDED HISTORY.*

The vision shifted again, showing Daybridge transformed—but not in the harmonious integration Guthrie and Eliza had glimpsed during their winter solstice experience. This version was darker, more chaotic, the human elements subsumed beneath an overlay of alien geometries and impossible structures similar to those on the plain where the vision had begun. The inhabitants moved like automatons, their humanity reduced to vestigial remnants within bodies and minds that had been reshaped to serve other purposes.

THIS IS THE INEVITABLE OUTCOME, the Dweller stated, the communication carrying absolute certainty. *THE ORDER BELIEVES THEY WILL CONTROL THE TRANSFORMATION, MAINTAINING THEIR DOMINION OVER A CHANGED WORLD. THE FEMALE BELIEVES SHE CAN ENGINEER A BALANCED MERGER, A*

HARMONIOUS INTEGRATION OF REALITIES. BOTH ARE DELUDED. THE FORCES INVOLVED ARE BEYOND SUCH PETTY MANIPULATIONS.

A final shift in the vision brought Guthrie face to face with himself—not as he currently existed, but as he would become if the Order's plan succeeded. This future version was physically similar but fundamentally altered, his eyes glowing with the same amber light as the Dweller's, his movements suggesting a consciousness vastly different from human despite its housing in a human form.

THIS IS YOUR DESTINY, VESSEL. NOT EXTINCTION, NOT REPLACEMENT, BUT TRANSCENDENCE. YOUR CONSCIOUSNESS WILL JOIN WITH MINE, CREATING SOMETHING GREATER THAN EITHER COULD BE ALONE. A TRUE EVOLUTION, NOT THE PALE IMITATION THE FEMALE OFFERS.

The vision began to fade, the impossible colors and structures dissolving into mist as Guthrie's awareness returned to the physical reality of the temple in Blackwood Manor's garden. But the Dweller's final communication lingered, resonating in his mind with uncomfortable clarity:

CHOOSE WISELY, VESSEL. THE PATH YOU WALK LEADS TO DESTINATIONS YOU CANNOT YET COMPREHEND. BUT KNOW THIS—THE GATEWAY WILL OPEN, WITH OR WITHOUT YOUR COOPERATION. THE ONLY QUESTION IS WHETHER YOU WILL EMERGE FROM THE TRANSFORMATION AS SOMETHING GREATER, OR BE CONSUMED ENTIRELY IN THE PROCESS.

When Guthrie's consciousness fully returned to the physical world, he found Eliza kneeling beside him, her face taut with concern. The ritual components on the altar between them had been consumed, the candles burned down to stubs, suggesting that the vision had lasted far longer than his subjective experience of it.

"You were gone for nearly three hours," Eliza said, her voice tight with a mixture of worry and excitement. "Your body remained here, but your consciousness was... elsewhere. I could sense it through our bond—you were in contact with something vast, ancient. The Dweller?"

Guthrie nodded, still processing the implications of what he had experienced. "It knows about us," he said simply. "About our partnership, our plans to subvert the Order's intentions."

Rather than showing alarm at this revelation, Eliza's expression shifted to one of intense interest. "What did it show you? What did it say?"

He described the vision in detail—the impossible landscape, the Dweller's manifestation, the history of the bridge site as a natural gateway between worlds, the contrasting futures represented by the Order's plan versus their own. Throughout his recounting, Eliza listened with unwavering attention, occasionally nodding as if confirming information she already possessed.

"The Dweller is attempting to drive a wedge between us," she said when he had finished. "Offering you a version of transcendence that excludes our partnership, suggesting that my vision of a balanced merger is impossible. It's a predictable strategy, though I'm surprised it revealed itself so directly at this stage."

She rose and began pacing the small confines of the temple, her movements fluid despite the lingering effects of the intense ritual they had performed. "This actually confirms that our work is having the intended effect. The modifications we've made to the standard rituals are redirecting enough energy to concern the Dweller, making it feel the need to intervene directly rather than merely observing through its whispers."

Guthrie watched her, noting the excitement that practically radiated from her slender form. "You're not worried?" he asked, his voice still rough from the strain of the vision.

Eliza paused in her pacing, turning to face him with a smile that combined confidence and anticipation in equal measure. "Concerned, yes—this means we'll need to accelerate certain aspects of our preparation. But worried? No." She moved to kneel before him once more, taking his hands in hers, the familiar electric connection flaring between them at the contact.

"The Dweller showed you a partial truth," she continued, her amber eyes holding his with hypnotic intensity. "The bridge site is indeed a natural gateway, a point where the barriers between worlds are inherently thin. And the current construction is incorporating elements designed to enhance this quality, to prepare for the opening that will occur during the Great Conjunction."

Her grip tightened slightly, her excitement palpable through both physical contact and their mystical bond. "But what the Dweller didn't tell you—what it perhaps doesn't fully comprehend—is that such gateways can be influenced by those with the proper knowledge and preparation. They're not simply passive portals that allow one-way transit from their realm to ours, but dynamic interfaces that can be shaped by consciousness and intent."

This was new information, aspects of the ancient knowledge that Eliza had not yet shared with him despite their months of work together. "And we can influence it?" Guthrie asked, though he already suspected the answer.

"We can do more than influence it, Guthrie." Eliza's voice took on a quality of reverent awe, a recognition of possibilities so vast they bordered on the divine. "With the proper preparation, with the binding rituals we've already begun and those yet to come, we can become the gateway ourselves. Not passive vessels as my uncle intends, not mere channels for external entities, but conscious architects of the merger between worlds."

She released his hands and rose once more, moving to a small cabinet built into the temple wall. From it, she retrieved a rolled parchment, yellowed with extreme age and bound with a silk cord dyed a deep, midnight blue. "It's time I showed you the complete vision, the full scope of what we're working toward."

Untying the cord with careful movements, Eliza unrolled the parchment on the altar, using small weights of polished stone to hold the corners flat. The document was covered in dense script and intricate diagrams, written in the same ancient language as the texts she had been teaching him to read over the past months.

"This is the Codex of Mergence," she explained, her finger tracing the elaborate title inscription at the top of the document. "One of the oldest and most closely guarded texts in existence, predating even the founding of the Order. It describes a process not of summoning or channeling, but of conscious integration—a willing partnership between human and Other that creates something entirely new, something that transcends the limitations of both."

Guthrie leaned forward, studying the diagrams with intense focus. Despite his still-developing ability to read the ancient script, the visual representations were clear enough—a series of transformations, both physical and energetic, culminating in a state of being that combined elements of humanity and Other in harmonious balance.

"The Order possesses fragments of this knowledge," Eliza continued, "distorted through centuries of misinterpretation and deliberate obfuscation by those who sought power over partnership. My uncle's plan for you is based on these corrupted teachings—he seeks to make you a vessel for the Dweller's consciousness, believing that this will grant him and his Council control over the resulting entity and the transformed world it creates."

Her voice hardened, a rare edge of genuine anger entering her usually measured tones. "But it's a fool's bargain. The Dweller and its kind view humans as we might view insects—occasionally useful, potentially interesting, but ultimately dispensable once their utility has been exhausted. If my uncle succeeds, the transformation will indeed occur, but not as he envisions. The Dweller will simply use the gateway he provides to enter our world fully, discarding both you and the Order once its purpose has been served."

She looked up from the ancient text, her amber eyes locking with Guthrie's. "Our path is different. The rituals we've been performing, the bindings we've established between us—they're preparing us not to serve as vessels for external entities, but to become conscious participants in our own transformation. When the Great Conjunction occurs and the gateway opens, we will neither resist the merger of worlds nor be consumed by it but shape it according to our will and vision."

The scope of this revelation was staggering, far exceeding even the ambitious partnership Eliza had proposed during their first private meeting nearly a year earlier. What she was describing was not merely a subversion of the Order's plan or a personal transcendence, but a fundamental reshaping of reality itself—a new creation myth with themselves as the prime movers.

Any other man might have balked at such cosmic hubris, might have questioned either the possibility of such a transformation or the wisdom of attempting it. But Guthrie Knox was not, and had never been, like other men. The emotional detachment that had defined his existence, the clinical precision with which he approached even the most extreme aspects of his work, had prepared him for exactly this moment—this choice to step beyond conventional human limitations into something entirely new.

"What do we need to do?" he asked simply, his decision made without reservation or doubt.

Eliza's smile was radiant, a pure expression of triumph and anticipation. "We need to establish a direct connection to the gateway site—the bridge—while it's still under construction. The foundations are being laid according to the Order's specifications, incorporating symbols and materials that will enhance its function as a portal during the Great Conjunction. But with certain modifications, certain additions to the structure itself, we can create our own channel of influence, separate from the one my uncle is establishing for the Dweller."

She rolled the ancient parchment carefully, returning it to its silk binding. "The timing is critical. The primary foundation stones are being set tomorrow night, during the dark of the moon—a time when the barriers between worlds are naturally thinner. My uncle and the Inner Circle will be conducting a ritual at the site to consecrate the stones and establish the initial connection to the Dweller's realm. We need to be there, not as participants in their ceremony but to perform our own working simultaneously."

The implications were clear—they would need to conduct their ritual in secret, hidden from Blackwood and the Council, yet close enough to the main ceremony to tap into the energies being raised. The risk of discovery was significant, the consequences potentially catastrophic if their deception was exposed at such a crucial juncture.

"The Order's security will be focused on maintaining the public perimeter, keeping ordinary citizens away from the construction site during the ritual," Eliza continued, her mind clearly racing ahead to practical considerations. "They won't be expecting infiltration from within their own ranks. If we approach separately, time our arrival carefully, we can position ourselves beneath the bridge itself, in the shadow of the main ceremony but close enough to access the energy they raise."

Guthrie nodded, already calculating angles of approach, potential hiding places, methods of concealment that would allow them to perform their own ritual undetected. "I'll need to prepare certain components in advance," he said, his mind shifting to the practical requirements of the working Eliza was proposing.

"Yes." She moved to stand before him once more, placing her hands on his shoulders in a gesture that combined intimacy and solemn purpose. "This will be different from our previous rituals, Guthrie. It will require not just physical components but a sacrifice—a willing offering of essence that goes beyond the blood exchanges we've performed before."

The implication was clear, and Guthrie felt an unexpected surge of anticipation at the prospect. Their physical relationship had evolved alongside their mystical partnership, each encounter blending pleasure and purpose in increasingly complex ways. But what Eliza was suggesting would take them beyond even those experiences, into realms of sensation and connection that few humans had ever explored.

"I'm ready," he said simply, his voice steady with conviction.

Eliza's smile deepened, her amber eyes glowing with an inner light that seemed to illuminate the temple's dim interior. "I know you are. It's why I chose you, why I've guided you along this path from the beginning. You possess a capacity for transformation, for transcendence, that exceeds even my uncle's assessment of your potential."

She leaned down, pressing her lips to his in a kiss that sealed their compact more effectively than any written agreement or spoken vow. "Tomorrow night," she whispered against his mouth.

"The Red Path opens before us, leading to destinations beyond imagination."

The following evening brought a new moon, its absence from the sky casting Daybridge into deeper darkness than usual. Cloud cover obscured the stars, and a light rain fell intermittently, creating a misty shroud that further reduced visibility. Perfect conditions, Guthrie reflected as he made his way through the labyrinthine streets toward the bridge construction site, for both concealment and mystical working.

He had spent the day in careful preparation, gathering the components Eliza had specified for their ritual and securing them in a specially designed pack that he could carry inconspicuously. The butcher's trade had taught him efficiency in packing, how to maximize space while protecting delicate items from damage during transport. These skills served him well as he organized the unusual collection of materials their working would require.

Most challenging had been the centerpiece of the ritual—a human heart, specially prepared according to Eliza's instructions. Not a fresh specimen, which would have been simpler to obtain, but one preserved through a complex process involving certain herbs and minerals, then inscribed with symbols using a mixture of silver dust and the preserved blood of previous ritual subjects. The result was a grotesque yet strangely beautiful object, pulsing with a malign vitality despite its separation from any living body.

As he approached the construction site, Guthrie could see that the Order had already established a perimeter. Men in the uniforms of a private security firm—in reality, lower-ranking members of the Order's outer circle—patrolled the fenced boundary, turning away curious onlookers with stern warnings about the dangers of active construction zones. Their attention was focused outward, on potential intrusion from uninitiated citizens, rather than inward where a greater threat to their plans was about to emerge.

Guthrie didn't approach the main entrance, where the security was most concentrated. Instead, he circled to the eastern side of the site, where the fencing adjoined a warehouse that had been commandeered for storage of construction materials. As a member of the Order's Inner Circle, he possessed knowledge of the security protocols—including the fact that a side entrance had been left minimally guarded to allow late-arriving Council members discreet access to the ceremony.

This entrance was watched by a single guard, a young man whom Guthrie recognized from the Order's lower ranks—an eager initiate named Noel who had recently been elevated to the First Circle. The youth straightened as Guthrie approached, clearly recognizing him despite the dim light and misty conditions.

"Brother Knox," Noel said, his voice carrying a mixture of respect and nervousness. "I wasn't informed you would be arriving through this entrance. The Council members are gathering at the main gate for the procession."

Guthrie maintained his usual impassive expression, revealing nothing of his true purpose. "Special assignment from the High Master," he said, his deep voice carrying just enough authority to discourage further questioning. "Certain preparations for the ritual require privacy."

The young guard hesitated, clearly torn between his duty to maintain security and his reluctance to challenge a senior member of the Order. "I should check with the security captain."

Before his hand could make contact, Guthrie moved with the fluid speed that had made him so effective in his clandestine work. His massive palm clamped over the guard's mouth while his other hand delivered a precise blow to a specific point at the base of the skull—a technique he had perfected through years of practice, designed to render a subject unconscious without permanent damage.

Noel slumped in his arms, unconscious but unharmed. With efficient movements, Guthrie bound and gagged the young man, then concealed him behind a stack of lumber within the warehouse. He would awaken in a few hours with a headache and a gap in his memory, but no lasting effects beyond perhaps a demotion for abandoning his post.

Securing the side entrance behind him, Guthrie made his way into the construction site proper. The area was a maze of partially completed structures, piles of materials, and heavy equipment rendered ghostly and indistinct by the misty conditions. In the center, where the bridge's main supports were being established, a cluster of lights indicated the location of the Order's primary ritual.

But Guthrie didn't head directly toward this illuminated area. Instead, he moved along the perimeter, keeping to the deepest shadows, making his way toward the river's edge where the bridge's foundation was being laid. Eliza had specified a particular location for their working—a spot directly beneath where the main span would eventually cross, accessible through a temporary scaffold erected to allow workers to reach the lower levels of the structure.

As he neared this point, Guthrie sensed rather than saw another presence moving through the darkness—a slender figure navigating the complex terrain with graceful precision. Even without visual confirmation, he knew it was Eliza, their mystical bond allowing him to perceive her proximity with an accuracy that transcended normal senses.

They converged at the scaffold, neither speaking as they descended the narrow metal stairway to the area beneath the nascent bridge structure. Here, the sounds of the main ritual above were audible but muffled—chanting voices, the rhythmic beating of drums, the occasional higher-pitched intonation that could only be Septimus Blackwood leading the ceremony.

The space beneath the bridge was even darker than the surrounding area, the only illumination coming from the ambient glow of the city reflected off the low-hanging clouds. But Guthrie's eyes, adapted to working in the dim conditions of his workshop, could make out the essential details—the rough stone and concrete of the partially completed foundation, the metal reinforcements that would eventually support the bridge's massive weight, and most significantly, the small area at the center where Eliza was already beginning to arrange the components of their ritual.

"You weren't followed?" she asked in a hushed voice as he joined her, though the question seemed more formality than genuine concern—through their bond, she would have sensed any pursuit or danger.

"No," Guthrie confirmed, removing his pack and beginning to extract the items he had prepared. "I had to deal with a guard at the eastern entrance, but he's been secured and won't be discovered until long after we're finished."

Eliza nodded; her attention already focused on the preparation of their ritual space. She had brought her own components—certain herbs and minerals that released pungent aromas as she crushed them between her fingers, small vials of liquids that shimmered with unnatural luminescence in the darkness, a cloth bundle that revealed strange instruments of silver and bone when unwrapped.

Together, they worked with practiced efficiency, establishing a ritual circle using a mixture of salt infused with powdered metals and dried herbs. Within this circle, they arranged symbols drawn from the Codex of Mergence—patterns more complex and ancient than those used in the Order's standard ceremonies, incorporating elements that would have been unrecognizable to even the most senior members of Blackwood's Council.

At the center of this arrangement, they placed the prepared heart that Guthrie had brought—a grotesque centerpiece that seemed to pulse with its own inner light, the silver-traced symbols on its surface gleaming in the darkness. Around this, they positioned seven candles of black wax, their wicks incorporating strands of hair from both Guthrie and Eliza, creating a personal connection to the energies they would raise.

As they completed these preparations, the sounds of the ritual above intensified—the chanting taking on a more urgent quality, the drumbeats accelerating to match the increased tempo. Through their bond, Guthrie could sense Eliza's excitement, her anticipation of the moment when the Order's ceremony would reach its peak and they could harness the raised energy for their own purposes.

"They're approaching the consecration of the foundation stones," she whispered, her head tilted as if listening to sounds beyond normal human hearing. "When my uncle begins the final invocation, the barrier between worlds will thin temporarily, creating the initial connection that will be strengthened over time as the bridge's construction progresses."

She turned to Guthrie, her amber eyes gleaming with an inner light that seemed to illuminate her entire face despite the surrounding darkness. "That's when we'll begin our working—not to prevent their connection, which would be impossible at this stage, but to establish our own parallel channel, our personal gateway that will remain hidden within the larger structure they're creating."

Guthrie nodded, understanding the strategy. The Order was building a door between worlds, but he and Eliza would create a secret passage adjacent to it—one that would allow them to access and influence the energies flowing through the main gateway without detection by either Blackwood's Council or the Dweller they served.

"Remove your clothes," Eliza instructed, already beginning to disrobe herself. "This working requires direct contact between flesh and the energies we're raising, without the barrier of fabric to dilute the connection."

Guthrie complied without hesitation, stripping efficiently despite the cool dampness of the air beneath the bridge. His massive frame, honed by years of physical labor at the slaughterhouse, seemed to absorb what little light penetrated their shadowy refuge, the ritual scars that marked his skin forming patterns that echoed those inscribed within their circle.

Eliza, now similarly unclothed, presented a striking contrast—her slender form seemed to generate its own illumination, the intricate tattoos that covered much of her skin glowing with a subtle phosphorescence that intensified as the energy from the ritual above began to permeate their hidden space. The patterns of these markings, Guthrie noted with renewed appreciation, complemented the scars on his own body, creating a visual representation of their mystical partnership.

"We'll begin with the blood exchange," Eliza said, retrieving one of the silver instruments from her collection—a delicate knife with a curved blade and handle inscribed with symbols similar to those on the prepared heart. "But this time, we'll take it further than before, establishing a direct connection between our life essences at the moment when the veil between worlds is thinnest."

She knelt within the circle, gesturing for Guthrie to join her. As he settled opposite her, the prepared heart between them, Eliza raised the silver knife to her left palm and drew the blade across the skin with unhesitating precision. Dark blood welled from the wound—darker than normal human vitae should have been, almost black in the dim light, with a subtle sheen that suggested properties beyond the merely physical.

"Your turn," she said, offering him the knife handle first.

Guthrie took the instrument, noting its perfect balance and the surprising warmth of the metal despite the cool air. Following Eliza's example, he drew the blade across his right palm, opening a clean incision that immediately began to bleed. His blood appeared normal at first glance, but as it pooled in his cupped hand, he noticed that it too had taken on an unusual quality—not the same darkness as Eliza's, but a faint luminescence, as if light were trapped within the fluid itself.

"Now we combine our essences," Eliza instructed, extending her bleeding palm toward him. "When our blood mingles, focus your will on the prepared heart, visualizing our combined energy flowing into it, activating the symbols inscribed on its surface."

Guthrie placed his right palm against her left, their fingers interlacing as their blood mingled. The now-familiar electric sensation of their connection surged through him, but with an intensity far exceeding their previous exchanges. It was as if the proximity to the Order's ritual above, the thinning of barriers between worlds that Blackwood and his Council were inadvertently facilitating, had amplified the energy flowing between them to unprecedented levels.

Through their bond, Guthrie could sense Eliza's consciousness merging with his own, her thoughts and perceptions becoming accessible as if they were extensions of his own mind. He saw through her eyes, felt through her nerves, experienced the ritual from her perspective simultaneously with his own. This dual awareness was disorienting at first but rapidly became exhilarating—a transcendence of individual limitation that offered a glimpse of the greater transformation they sought.

Together, they directed this merged consciousness toward the prepared heart, visualizing their combined blood flowing from their joined hands into the grotesque yet strangely beautiful object. The symbols inscribed on its surface began to glow in response, first with a subtle phosphorescence similar to Eliza's tattoos, then with increasing brilliance until they seemed to burn with an inner fire that cast sharp-edged shadows across the ritual circle.

Above them, the Order's ceremony reached its climax—Blackwood's voice rising in the final invocation, the chanting of the assembled Council members reaching a fever pitch, the drumbeats accelerating to a frenzied tempo that seemed to match the racing of Guthrie's and Eliza's hearts as they poured their combined will into their working.

And then, in a moment of perfect synchronicity, both rituals crested simultaneously—the Order's ceremonial consecration of the bridge's foundation stones and Guthrie and Eliza's secret establishment of their own gateway within that larger structure. The barrier between worlds thinned to its absolute minimum, creating a brief but profound connection between realities that manifested as a visible distortion in the air above the prepared heart—a rippling, a folding, a suggestion of geometries that shouldn't have been possible in normal three-dimensional space.

Through this temporary aperture came a surge of energy unlike anything Guthrie had experienced before—raw, primal power that flowed from the Other side into their ritual space, channeled and directed by the symbols they had arranged, the blood they had offered, the will they had focused. It entered through the prepared heart, which now pulsed with a life of its own despite having been separated from its original owner months earlier, then radiated outward to envelop both Guthrie and Eliza in a cocoon of crackling, shifting energy that penetrated their bodies at a cellular level.

The sensation defied description—not pain, not pleasure, but something that transcended both, a fundamental restructuring of perception and experience that left Guthrie gasping with the intensity of it. Through their bond, he could sense that Eliza was similarly affected, her consciousness expanding and transforming under the influence of the otherworldly energy they had summoned.

"Now," she managed to say, her voice strained with the effort of maintaining focus amid such overwhelming sensation. "The final binding. The complete merging of essences."

Without releasing his hand, she moved closer, her free arm encircling his neck to draw him toward her. Their bodies pressed together, skin to skin, the energy cocoon surrounding them intensifying at each point of contact. Guthrie responded instinctively, his free arm wrapping around her waist to pull her even closer, eliminating any remaining space between them.

What followed transcended physical intimacy, though it incorporated elements of it. Their bodies moved together in rhythms dictated not by mere biology but by the pulsing energies surrounding them, each touch and caress guided by the merged consciousness they now shared. The boundaries between individual identity blurred further, creating a union that was simultaneously physical, mental, and spiritual—a genuine merging of beings that went beyond any human concept of connection.

Throughout this extraordinary experience, the prepared heart continued to pulse between them, its rhythm synchronizing with both their heartbeats to create a three-part harmony that further strengthened their connection to each other and to the gateway they were establishing. The symbols inscribed on its surface burned with an intensity that should have been painful to look at directly yet somehow enhanced rather than impeded their awareness of the transformative energies flowing through them.

How long this state persisted, Guthrie couldn't have said. Time itself seemed to warp within their ritual circle, stretching and contracting according to laws that had nothing to do with the steady ticking of clocks in the mundane world. It might have been minutes or hours before the energy cocoon finally began to dissipate, the connection to the Other gradually thinning as the Order's ritual above concluded and the temporary gateway they had opened started to close.

As the extraordinary experience subsided, leaving them physically exhausted but mentally exhilarated, Guthrie became aware of changes in both himself and Eliza. Subtle alterations to their physical forms—a slight luminescence to the skin, a deepening of the ritual scars and tattoos that marked them, a sharpening of features that made them both more striking and slightly less human in appearance. More significant were the mental changes—an expansion of awareness, a sensitivity to energies and patterns that had been invisible before, a depth of connection to each other that made their previous bond seem shallow by comparison.

"It worked," Eliza whispered, her voice carrying new harmonics that resonated with the ambient energy still lingering in their ritual space. "We've established our gateway, our personal connection to the Other that exists alongside but separate from the one my uncle and his Council are creating."

She gestured to the prepared heart, which had undergone its own transformation during their working. The organ had expanded slightly, its tissue now infused with veins of silver that pulsed with their own inner light. The symbols inscribed on its surface had been burned into the flesh, no longer surface markings but integral components of its structure.

"This is now more than a focus for our rituals," Eliza explained, carefully lifting the transformed heart from the center of their circle. "It's a physical anchor for the gateway we've established, a permanent connection to the bridge site and the energies flowing through it. As the bridge's construction progresses and the Order's connection to the Dweller strengthens, our own gateway will develop in parallel, hidden within the larger structure like a secret passage adjacent to a main hallway."

She wrapped the heart in a cloth of midnight blue silk, then placed it in a small box made of a dark wood that Guthrie didn't recognize. "We'll need to keep this secure, protected from discovery by my uncle or his agents. It should remain in your workshop beneath Holloway's, where the ambient energies from your rituals for the Order will help maintain and strengthen our connection."

Guthrie nodded, already considering the best location within his hidden sanctuary—a concealed compartment behind the main altar, accessible only to someone who knew exactly where to look and how to open it. "And the next steps?" he asked, beginning to gather their ritual components with the same methodical efficiency he brought to all his activities.

"We continue as before," Eliza replied, her movements mirroring his as they dismantled the ritual circle, removing all evidence of their working. "You maintain your role within the Order, performing the rituals my uncle assigns while incorporating our modifications. I continue to report your 'progress' toward becoming a suitable vessel for the Dweller, emphasizing aspects that align with their expectations while concealing our true development."

She paused in her work, looking up at Guthrie with an expression that combined triumph and solemn purpose. "But our private work will intensify, building on the foundation we've established tonight. Each ritual we perform will strengthen our connection to the gateway, our ability to influence the energies flowing through it. By the time the Great Conjunction arrives and the bridge is completed, we'll be prepared to shape the merging of worlds according to our vision rather than my uncle's or the Dweller's."

As they finished clearing their ritual space, leaving no trace of their secret working, Guthrie felt a profound sense of commitment to the path they had chosen. What had begun as a pragmatic alliance based on mutual interest had evolved into something far deeper and more significant—a partnership that transcended conventional categories of relationship, a shared vision of transformation that would reshape not just their individual existences but reality itself.

The Red Path had opened before them, leading to destinations beyond imagination. And Guthrie Knox, once the detached butcher of Holloway's Slaughterhouse, had taken his first willing step into a world of occult power and cosmic transformation from which there could be no return.

In the days and weeks that followed, Guthrie observed the changes in himself with clinical interest, documenting them in a separate journal kept hidden even from Eliza. The physical alterations were subtle but unmistakable—a slight enhancement to his already considerable strength, an improvement in visual acuity that allowed him to see clearly in near-total darkness, a heightened sensitivity to touch that made his work with a blade even more precise than before.

More significant were the mental and perceptual changes. The whispers that had been his constant companions since his initiation into the Order had shifted in both quality and content, becoming clearer and more directly communicative. They no longer came exclusively from the Dweller, that ancient entity waiting beneath the bridge, but from a multitude of consciousnesses on the Other side—some aligned with the Dweller's agenda, others neutral or even potentially supportive of the alternative path he and Eliza were forging.

His awareness of energetic currents flowing throughout Daybridge had expanded dramatically, allowing him to perceive the invisible rivers of power that connected certain locations—the bridge site, Blackwood Manor, his workshop beneath Holloway's, and other, older structures whose significance he was only beginning to understand. These currents ebbed and flowed according to patterns influenced by astronomical alignments, weather conditions, and the collective emotional states of the city's inhabitants.

Most profound was the evolution of his bond with Eliza. What had been a significant but still limited connection before their ritual beneath the bridge had become something far more intimate and comprehensive. He was constantly aware of her presence, her emotional state, often even fragments of her thoughts when she focused directly on him. During their physical encounters, this awareness expanded to create a genuine merging of consciousness, a dissolution of individual identity into a shared experience that transcended conventional intimacy.

These changes were not without their challenges. The heightened sensitivity to energetic currents made certain locations in Daybridge actively uncomfortable for Guthrie—places where negative emotions had accumulated over decades, creating toxic pools of psychic residue that assaulted his enhanced perception. The increased clarity of the whispers sometimes made it difficult to distinguish between external communication and his own thoughts, requiring new forms of mental discipline to maintain his focus and autonomy.

And the intensity of his connection to Eliza, while exhilarating, created vulnerabilities he had never experienced before. For a man who had built his existence around emotional detachment and self-sufficiency, the depth of their bond represented both liberation and constraint—a transcendence of isolation that simultaneously created dependencies he was still learning to navigate.

But these challenges were minor compared to the exhilaration of their continued evolution. Each private ritual they performed, each application of the knowledge contained in the ancient texts Eliza provided, accelerated their transformation and strengthened their connection to the gateway they had established within the bridge's foundation. As the physical construction progressed above, their mystical infrastructure developed in parallel, hidden within the larger structure like a secret chamber within a seemingly conventional building.

Guthrie's work for the Order continued without interruption, his performance of the assigned rituals maintaining his status within the Inner Circle while concealing his true development from Septimus Blackwood and his Council. The modifications he incorporated into these workings—subtle alterations to invocation sequences, variations in the timing of certain extractions, adjustments to the arrangement of ritual components—redirected portions of the energy raised, channeling it into their private gateway rather than the Order's official connection to the Dweller.

His journal entries for the Order's review became increasingly sophisticated, demonstrating an apparent deepening of his attunement to the Dweller's influence while actually documenting the controlled evolution he and Eliza were engineering. This deception required careful calibration—enough genuine insight to satisfy Blackwood's expectations, enough apparent submission to the Dweller's will to maintain the illusion of compliance, but nothing that would reveal their true intentions or the extent of their independent development.

A typical entry from this period demonstrated this delicate balance:

Subject 53: Female, approximately 40 years of age, selected for the Equinox Ritual as specified by the High Master. The standard invocation sequence was followed, with minor adjustments to accommodate the subject's unusual energetic signature (noticeably stronger in the throat and third eye regions than typical for females of this age group).

Extraction proceeded according to the prescribed pattern: blood (collected in the silver vessel) → voice (preserved through the specialized technique developed for the Winter Solstice working) → eyes → heart. Each component was positioned as directed on the altar, creating the mandala configuration that has proven most effective for communications with the Other Side.

During the final phase of the ritual, when the heart was placed at the center of the mandala, the expected thinning of the veil occurred with unusual intensity. The whispers became notably clearer, communicating concepts that transcend direct translation but conveyed impressions of anticipation, of imminence, of a convergence approaching more rapidly than previously indicated.

Of particular note was a recurring image that formed in my mind throughout the working—the bridge in its completed state, serving as a literal and metaphorical spanning of worlds. The vision suggested that as the physical construction progresses, so too does the energetic infrastructure that will facilitate the Great Conjunction.

I continue to experience physical changes that align with the expected development of the vessel—increased sensitivity to energetic currents, enhanced perception of normally invisible spectra, occasional manifestations of strength beyond my usual capabilities. These changes intensify during rituals but are increasingly persistent in mundane settings as well, suggesting a progressive attunement to the Dweller's influence.

The sensation of being observed, of serving as a focus for attention from beyond the veil, is now constant rather than intermittent. The presence feels... evaluative, as if assessing my suitability for the role I am being prepared to assume. I sense approval in this scrutiny, a *recognition of potential that transcends my original understanding of the vessel's purpose.*

Such reports, carefully crafted to suggest the very process Blackwood expected while actually describing a very different evolution, satisfied the High Master's requirements while concealing the truth of Guthrie's transformation. The deception was aided by the genuine changes in his appearance and behavior—alterations that could be interpreted as signs of the Dweller's increasing influence rather than the results of his partnership with Eliza.

Septimus Blackwood, reviewing these reports with the Order's Council, expressed growing satisfaction with Guthrie's progress. "The vessel is developing precisely as predicted," he informed his colleagues during one such session. "The rate of attunement exceeds our initial projections, suggesting that the Great Conjunction may yield results even more significant than we had dared hope."

Only Lord Vane, the most perceptive among the Council members, occasionally expressed reservations. "There's something... different about Knox," he observed during a private conversation with Blackwood. "The changes are aligned with our expectations in general terms, but specific aspects seem... divergent from the pattern we've observed in previous potential vessels."

Blackwood dismissed these concerns with the confidence of a man certain of his control over events and individuals. "Each vessel manifests the attunement process in unique ways," he explained. "Knox's particular combination of physical strength, psychological detachment, and intuitive understanding of transitions was precisely why we selected him. That these qualities express themselves in idiosyncratic patterns during his development is not only expected but desirable."

Whether the High Master truly believed this assessment or harbored his own suspicions beneath a facade of certainty remained unclear. But for the moment, Guthrie and Eliza's deception held, allowing them to continue their work toward the alternative future they envisioned—a genuine merger of worlds rather than a one-sided invasion, a transformation that would preserve and enhance what made them unique rather than subsuming them beneath an alien consciousness.

As summer gave way to autumn, the construction of Daybridge Bridge progressed steadily, its massive structure taking shape against the city skyline. The Order conducted regular rituals at the site, each one corresponding to a significant phase of the physical building process, each one establishing stronger connections to the Dweller's realm. And parallel to these official workings, Guthrie and Eliza performed their own ceremonies, strengthening their private gateway and their ability to influence the energies flowing through it.

The Red Path stretched before them, leading toward the Great Conjunction that would mark the culmination of their Work. And with each step along this path, Guthrie Knox moved further from the man he had been—the detached butcher of Holloway's Slaughterhouse—and closer to the transformed being he was becoming, a conscious architect of reality's restructuring rather than a passive vessel for forces beyond his control.

It was a journey of his own choosing, a transformation undertaken with full awareness of its implications. And despite the risks, despite the deceptions necessary to maintain their course, he embraced it without reservation or regret—committed to the vision he and Eliza shared, the future they were creating together through blood and magic, through sacrifice and transformation, through the power of their combined will imposed upon the very fabric of existence itself.

Chapter 9: Beneath the Skin

The winter of 1899 descended upon Daybridge with unusual ferocity, transforming the industrial city into a frozen landscape of ice-encrusted buildings and snow-choked streets. The Shadowlair River, that perpetually polluted artery that bisected the city, froze solid for the first time in living memory, its surface a mottled expanse of gray-white ice stained with the chromatic evidence of decades of chemical dumping. Factory chimneys belched smoke that hung in the frigid air like spectral pillars, supporting a perpetual ceiling of low, leaden clouds that rarely allowed the sun to penetrate.

For the ordinary citizens of Daybridge, this bitter season brought suffering and privation. Coal shortages led to inadequate heating in the poorer quarters, resulting in a sharp increase in deaths from exposure and illness. Water pipes froze and burst throughout the city, creating an epidemic of flooding when they thawed during brief respites in the cold. Food became scarce as supply routes were disrupted by impassable roads and frozen railways, leading to hoarding and price gouging that further strained the resources of working-class families.

But for Guthrie Knox, now in his thirtieth year, the harsh winter represented not hardship but opportunity. The extreme cold created ideal conditions for certain rituals that required lower ambient temperatures, allowing for experiments and workings that would have been impossible during warmer seasons. The suffering of Daybridge's general population generated a miasma of negative energy that permeated the city, a psychic residue that could be harvested and channeled into specific mystical applications. And the reduced activity throughout the urban landscape provided greater privacy for the increasingly elaborate ceremonies he conducted with Eliza Blackwood.

Their partnership had evolved significantly since the ritual beneath the partially constructed bridge six months earlier. What had begun as a pragmatic alliance based on shared objectives had transformed into something far more complex and profound—a bond that transcended conventional categories of relationship, blending elements of mystical partnership, intellectual collaboration, physical intimacy, and psychological symbiosis into something entirely unique.

Through this deepening connection, Guthrie had gained unprecedented access to Eliza's knowledge, experiences, and perceptions. During their most intense rituals, when the barriers between their individual consciousnesses dissolved almost entirely, he experienced fragments of her memories, glimpses of her past that revealed aspects of her nature and origins that she had never explicitly shared. These revelations came not as coherent narratives but as impressionistic flashes—scenes from her childhood in Blackwood Manor, moments from her studies in Europe, encounters with entities and energies beyond normal human comprehension.

As winter progressed, these inadvertent disclosures were supplemented by more deliberate revelations. During their private sessions in Guthrie's workshop beneath Holloway's Slaughterhouse or the hidden temple in Blackwood Manor's secret garden, Eliza began to share aspects of her true nature that she had previously kept concealed.

"My bloodline is not entirely human," she told him one night as they lay together on the pallet he had installed in a corner of his workshop, their bodies still humming with energy from a particularly intense ritual. "The Blackwood family has maintained certain... connections across the veil for generations, incorporating elements from the Other side to enhance our natural capabilities."

Guthrie, tracing the intricate tattoos that spiraled across her bare shoulder, found this revelation unsurprising. He had sensed the otherness in her from their first meeting—a quality of presence, of power, that transcended normal human parameters. "Your eyes," he said simply. "The same as your uncle's. Not a color found in ordinary humans."

Eliza smiled, pleased by his perception. "Yes, the amber eyes are one of the more visible markers of our lineage. There are others, less obvious but more significant—enhanced longevity, natural affinity for certain types of energy work, inherent ability to perceive and manipulate the barriers between worlds."

She turned to face him more directly, her unusual eyes catching what little light penetrated the workshop's shadows. "My uncle is not actually my uncle, at least not in the conventional sense. He's my ancestor—my great-great-grandfather, to be precise. The man who first established direct contact with the entities on the Other side and negotiated the arrangements that have defined our family's path for over a century."

This was a more startling disclosure, though it aligned with certain impressions Guthrie had received during their moments of deepest connection. "He appears to be in his fifties," he observed, mentally recalculating what this revelation meant about Septimus Blackwood's true age.

"He's one hundred and forty-seven," Eliza confirmed. "The first exchange of essence with the Other extended his natural lifespan dramatically, though not indefinitely. Each successive generation of our line has pursued similar arrangements, each time seeking to expand the benefits while minimizing the costs."

Her expression grew more solemn, a shadow passing across her features. "But my grandfather and father both miscalculated in their negotiations, accepting terms that seemed advantageous but contained hidden penalties. Their lifespans were indeed extended, but at the cost of progressive physical and mental deterioration. By the time they reached their second century, they had devolved into something... less than human, their consciousness fragmented, their bodies twisted into forms that could no longer pass as normal among the uninitiated."

She sat up, the movement causing the intricate tattoos on her skin to catch the light, revealing subtle iridescence that hadn't been visible before. "They exist still, confined to the deepest chambers beneath Blackwood Manor, sustained by rituals that my uncle performs monthly. Neither fully alive nor properly dead, trapped in a liminal state that serves as both warning and motivation for those of us who continue the Work."

Guthrie absorbed this information with his usual calm, fitting it into the expanding framework of his understanding of Eliza and the forces she represented. "And your arrangement?" he asked, his voice betraying nothing of the complex emotions this revelation stirred within him. "What terms did you negotiate for your own enhancement?"

Eliza's smile returned, though now tinged with a certain grimness. "That's where our partnership becomes so valuable, Guthrie. I've chosen a different path than my predecessors. Rather than negotiating with the entities directly, accepting their terms and limitations, I'm working to establish a new paradigm—a genuine merger rather than a transaction, a transformation that preserves and enhances what makes us unique rather than gradually eroding it in exchange for borrowed power."

She leaned closer, her eyes now definitely glowing with an inner light that had nothing to do with reflected illumination. "The rituals we've been performing, the gateway we've established within the bridge's structure—these are the foundation for something unprecedented. Not an exchange of essence as my ancestors arranged, but a true synthesis that will transcend the limitations of both human and Other."

The implication was clear, though Guthrie sought explicit confirmation. "This synthesis would apply to both of us?" he asked, his massive hand coming to rest on her waist with a gentleness that belied its size and strength. "Your vision includes my transformation alongside your own?"

"Of course," Eliza replied, as if any other possibility was inconceivable. "That's been the plan from the beginning, Guthrie. Why else would I have sought you out, guided you along this path, shared knowledge that my uncle and his Council have kept hidden even from their highest initiates? You're not merely a tool or assistant in this Work—you're an essential component, a partner whose unique qualities complement and complete my own."

She pressed her palm against his chest, directly over his heart, the familiar electric sensation of their connection surging at the contact. "Your physical strength, your psychological detachment, your intuitive understanding of transitions between states of being—these are precisely the qualities needed to balance my theoretical knowledge, my ancestral connections, my ability to perceive and manipulate energetic patterns. Together, we form a complete circuit, capable of channeling and directing powers that neither of us could safely handle alone."

This affirmation of their partnership, of his essential role in the transformations they sought, resonated deeply with something in Guthrie that he had scarcely acknowledged even to himself—a longing for recognition not just of his skills or usefulness, but of his fundamental nature, his unique combination of qualities that had always set him apart from ordinary humanity. In Eliza's vision, what others might have seen as abnormalities or deficiencies—his emotional detachment, his comfort with death and suffering, his existence at the margins of normal human society—became strengths, necessary components of a greater purpose.

"The bridge will be completed by midsummer," he said after a moment's reflection, his mind shifting to practical considerations as it always did when emotions threatened to overwhelm his careful equilibrium. "How does that align with our timeline for the Great Conjunction?"

Eliza's expression brightened at this return to strategic planning. "Perfectly, as it happens. The official opening ceremony is scheduled for June 21st—the summer solstice, when the barriers between worlds are naturally thinner. My uncle and his Council believe they're being clever, aligning the mundane celebration with mystical significance to enhance the power of their connection to the Dweller. What they don't realize is that this timing also maximizes the potential of our alternative gateway, the connection we've established separate from their primary channel."

She rose from the pallet and moved to the workshop's central altar, where the transformed heart that anchored their personal gateway pulsed with a slow, steady rhythm despite its separation from any living body. The organ had continued to evolve since their ritual beneath the bridge, developing intricate patterns of silver and gold that flowed through its tissue like metallic veins, occasionally shifting position as if in response to unseen currents.

"The next phase of our work will be more... intensive," Eliza continued, her finger tracing one of the metallic patterns on the heart's surface. "As the bridge nears completion in the physical realm, our mystical preparations must accelerate correspondingly. The rituals will become more demanding, requiring greater commitment and... adaptation on both our parts."

The slight hesitation before "adaptation" caught Guthrie's attention. In their months of partnership, he had become attuned to the nuances of Eliza's communication, the subtle shifts in tone or phrasing that indicated areas of particular significance. "What kind of adaptation?" he asked, rising to join her at the altar.

Eliza met his gaze directly, the glow in her amber eyes intensifying. "Physical changes, primarily. The human form in its natural state cannot safely channel the energies we'll be working with as we approach the Conjunction. Certain modifications will be necessary—enhancements to your cellular structure, adjustments to your nervous system, alterations to specific organs to accommodate increased energy flow."

She gestured to the journals that lined one wall of the workshop—Guthrie's meticulous records of his experiments and rituals, spanning years of his work for the Order and, more recently, their private partnership. "You've documented similar modifications in your subjects, observing how specific ritual practices affect the physical body at a structural level. Now we'll apply that knowledge to ourselves, in a controlled, progressive manner that prepares us for the ultimate transformation at the Conjunction."

It was a significant escalation of their work, a step beyond the energetic and psychological changes they had already undergone into direct physical alteration. But Guthrie found himself nodding in acceptance, his customary wariness of fundamental change overshadowed by his commitment to their shared vision and his trust in Eliza's guidance.

"When do we begin?" he asked simply.

Eliza's smile was brilliant, a flash of genuine delight at his unhesitating commitment. "Tomorrow night," she replied. "The new moon provides ideal conditions for the first phase of physical adaptation. I'll bring the necessary components from my private collection at Blackwood Manor—certain minerals and compounds that aren't available through conventional sources, texts that detail the specific procedures required."

She stepped closer, eliminating the small distance between them, her slender form fitting against his massive frame with the familiar precision that spoke of their growing attunement. "This next stage will not be without discomfort, Guthrie," she warned, her voice softening. "The modifications we're undertaking involve fundamental changes to your physical structure, alterations that will strain the body's natural tolerance for transformation. But the results will be worth the temporary suffering—enhanced strength, expanded perception, extended lifespan, and eventually, the ability to shift between forms at will."

The promise of such capabilities would have seemed fantastical, delusional even, to the man Guthrie had been before meeting Eliza. But the experiences of the past year—the visions he had witnessed, the energies he had channeled, the gradual expansion of his awareness beyond normal human parameters—had eroded his skepticism regarding such possibilities. He had already moved so far beyond what he had once considered the boundaries of reality that these next steps, however extreme, seemed like logical extensions of the path they had been following.

"I understand," he said, his deep voice carrying the weight of genuine commitment. "Whatever is necessary to complete our work, I'm prepared to endure."

Eliza's expression softened further, a rare vulnerability showing through her usual poised confidence. "This is why I chose you, Guthrie Knox," she murmured, rising on her toes to press her lips against his in a brief but intense kiss. "Your capacity for commitment, for perseverance in the face of challenges that would break lesser beings. It's what makes you the perfect partner for this Great Work."

As they prepared to depart the workshop—Eliza to return to Blackwood Manor before her absence was noted, Guthrie to attend to his legitimate duties at Holloway's Slaughterhouse—neither could have fully anticipated the true nature of the "adaptations" that lay ahead, or the profound consequences they would have not just for their physical forms but for the very essence of their being.

The next night brought the new moon, casting Daybridge into deeper darkness than usual beneath its perpetual ceiling of winter clouds. The temperature had dropped further, turning the air brittle with cold, the streets treacherous with ice that gleamed dully in the gaslight. Few ventured out in such conditions, leaving the city in eerie silence broken only by the distant clanging of machinery from factories that operated without regard for weather or hour.

In his workshop beneath Holloway's Slaughterhouse, Guthrie made careful preparations for the ritual Eliza had outlined. The central space had been cleared and meticulously cleaned, the stone floor scrubbed until it gleamed faintly in the light of the specialized candles he had placed at precise intervals around the perimeter. The altar at the center held only the transformed heart, pulsing with its slow, hypnotic rhythm as if in anticipation of the work to come.

Eliza arrived precisely at midnight, entering through a private access point they had established months earlier—a narrow passage that connected the workshop to an unused storage cellar in a neighboring building, allowing her to come and go without being observed by anyone who might report her movements to Septimus Blackwood or his agents.

She carried a large leather case similar to a doctor's bag; its surface marked with symbols that matched certain tattoos on her skin. Her expression was more solemn than usual; her movements deliberate as she set the case on a side table and began removing its contents.

"These are the primary components," she explained, arranging various items on the table with precise care. "Some from my family's private collection, others gathered during my studies in Europe, a few created specifically for our work together."

Guthrie observed the collection with clinical interest, his butcher's eye cataloging the unfamiliar objects: vials of liquids in colors not found in nature; packets of powders that seemed to shift and move within their paper confines; instruments of silver, crystal, and some dark metal that absorbed rather than reflected the candlelight; several small books bound in materials he preferred not to identify, their pages covered in script so ancient it predated any language he recognized.

"The procedure has multiple phases," Eliza continued, opening one of the books to a marked page. "We'll begin with the preparatory ritual, establishing the energetic framework for the physical modifications. Then the actual transformative process, which must be completed in a single session to maintain the integrity of the changes. Finally, a stabilization phase to ensure the alterations become permanent rather than reverting to baseline human configuration."

She looked up from her preparations, her amber eyes studying him with that mixture of clinical assessment and personal connection that characterized their relationship. "Remove your clothing and lie on the altar," she instructed. "The heart will remain in place, between your shoulder blades, acting as both a power source and a stabilizing influence during the transformation."

Guthrie complied without hesitation, stripping efficiently and positioning himself as directed on the cold stone altar. Despite the workshop's chill, his massive body generated enough heat to maintain comfort, a quality that had served him well during Daybridge's bitter winters. The transformed heart, when placed between his shoulders, felt neither warm nor cold but somehow both simultaneously—a paradoxical sensation that he had come to associate with objects and energies from beyond the veil.

Eliza began the preparatory ritual with practiced efficiency, moving around the altar in precise patterns as she recited invocations in languages that seemed to shift and change mid-syllable, their sounds twisting in ways that human vocal cords should not have been able to produce. At specific points in this circumambulation, she would pause to place one of the objects from her collection at predetermined positions on the floor, creating a complex array that gradually took on a geometric precision despite its apparently random arrangement.

As the ritual progressed, Guthrie became aware of changes in the workshop's atmosphere—a thickening of the air, a subtle vibration that he felt rather than heard, a quality of presence that suggested they were no longer entirely alone despite the sealed door and absence of visible visitors. The candles around the perimeter began to burn with unusual intensity, their flames stretching toward the ceiling in defiance of natural law, their colors shifting from normal yellow-orange to deeper hues of violet and indigo.

Through their bond, Guthrie could sense Eliza's concentration, her mental focus narrowing to exclude all extraneous awareness as she channeled energies that would have overwhelmed a less prepared practitioner. Her tattoos had begun to glow, the intricate patterns pulsing in rhythm with the transformed heart between his shoulder blades, creating a visual representation of the energetic circuit they were establishing.

When the preparatory phase was complete, Eliza returned to the side table and selected several vials, mixing their contents in a silver bowl while continuing her otherworldly chanting. The resulting liquid seemed to defy normal physical properties—thicker than water yet flowing with unusual mobility, its color constantly shifting between deep crimson and absolute black as if unable to decide which state to occupy.

"This is the primary catalyst," she explained during a brief pause in the invocations. "A compound of substances from both sides of the veil, designed to initiate cellular restructuring while maintaining the essential pattern of your current form. The discomfort will be... significant, but temporary. Focus on our bond, on the connection between us, and allow the transformation to proceed without resistance."

Without further preamble, she began applying the liquid to Guthrie's skin, using a brush of some dark, stiff material that might once have been organic but had been altered into something else entirely. The sensation was immediate and intense—a burning that went beyond normal pain, penetrating directly to the cellular level, as if each drop of the compound was initiating a war between his current physical structure and the new configuration being imposed upon it.

Guthrie had experienced pain throughout his life—the casual cruelties of Blackwell Orphanage, the accidental injuries inherent in slaughterhouse work, the deliberate tests of endurance during his initiation into the Order's various circles. But this was different, a level of sensation that transcended conventional categories of comfort and discomfort, pleasure and pain, existing in a realm of pure intensity that demanded complete surrender.

Through their bond, he could sense Eliza monitoring his responses, adjusting the ritual accordingly—accelerating certain aspects when his tolerance seemed higher, modulating others when the intensity threatened to overwhelm even his considerable capacity for endurance. Her presence in his mind provided an anchor, a point of stability amid the chaos of transformation, a reminder of purpose that sustained him through the most challenging phases of the process.

How long the ritual continued, Guthrie couldn't have said. Time itself seemed to warp within the energized space of the

workshop, stretching and contracting according to rhythms that
had nothing to do with the steady ticking of clocks in the world
above. It might have been hours or mere minutes before the most
intense phase finally began to subside, the burning sensation
gradually transmuting into something more complex—a deep,
pervasive tingling that suggested fundamental changes occurring at
levels below conscious perception.

"The primary transformation is complete," Eliza's voice came
from what seemed like a great distance, though she stood directly
beside the altar. "Now we begin the stabilization phase, ensuring
the changes become permanent rather than reverting to baseline
human configuration."

She placed her hands directly on Guthrie's chest, her palms
covering specific points that corresponded to nexus locations in the
body's energetic system. The familiar electric connection between
them surged at this contact, but with an intensity that far exceeded
their previous experiences—a current of raw power that flowed
from Eliza into Guthrie, then back again in a closed circuit of
ever-increasing potency.

Through this enhanced connection, Guthrie became aware of
the specific changes taking place within his physical form. His
muscular structure was being reinforced with fibers that weren't
entirely organic, creating a hybrid tissue with significantly greater
strength and resilience than normal human muscle. His skeletal
system was undergoing similar modifications, the bones becoming
denser, more flexible, capable of absorbing and distributing forces
that would shatter conventional human anatomy.

More profound were the alterations to his internal organs and
nervous system. His heart was developing secondary chambers that
operated in parallel with the normal human configuration,
allowing for more efficient circulation of both blood and the
mysterious energies they had been channeling through their rituals.

His lungs were expanding, developing specialized structures for extracting components from the air that normal human respiration ignored entirely. His brain was forming new neural pathways, connections that would allow for modes of perception and cognition beyond conventional human capabilities.

As these changes progressed, Guthrie experienced brief flashes of enhanced awareness—moments of synesthetic perception where he could see sounds, hear colors, taste emotions. The boundaries between different sensory modalities temporarily dissolved, creating a unified field of experience that transcended normal categories of perception. These episodes were disorienting but exhilarating, offering glimpses of the expanded consciousness that awaited him as the transformation continued.

Throughout this extraordinary process, Eliza remained connected to him both physically and mentally, her own energy intertwining with his in patterns of increasing complexity. Through their bond, Guthrie sensed that she was undergoing her own transformation, though one less dramatic than his—a refinement and enhancement of changes that had already been in progress for years, perhaps decades.

When the stabilization phase finally concluded, Eliza removed her hands from Guthrie's chest and stepped back, her amber eyes studying him with intense focus. "Sit up slowly," she instructed, her voice carrying new harmonics that resonated with the altered structure of his auditory system. "The physical adjustments need time to fully integrate, and sudden movements might disrupt the final calibration process."

Guthrie complied, rising to a sitting position with careful deliberation. The movement felt strange, as if his body was simultaneously lighter and heavier than before, more responsive yet somehow more substantial in its interaction with the physical world. His visual perception had sharpened dramatically, allowing him to discern details in the workshop's shadows that had previously been invisible. His hearing had expanded to include frequencies beyond normal human range, revealing subtle sounds—the crystalline hum of the candles, the whispered passage of air through the workshop's hidden ventilation system, the almost imperceptible pulsing of the transformed heart that Eliza had now removed from between his shoulders and returned to its place of honor on the altar.

"How do you feel?" Eliza asked, though the question seemed almost redundant given their bond, which allowed her direct access to his sensory experience and emotional state.

"Different," Guthrie replied, his voice carrying new resonances that matched the harmonics in Eliza's speech. "More... present. As if I've been experiencing the world through a filter that's now been partially removed."

Eliza nodded, clearly pleased by this assessment. "That's a common reaction to the first phase of physical adaptation. Your sensory apparatus has been enhanced, allowing you to perceive aspects of reality that ordinary humans filter out of conscious awareness. As you adjust to these changes, you'll develop greater control over which perceptual modes you engage at any given time."

She gestured to a full-length mirror that stood in one corner of the workshop—an item rarely used in Guthrie's normal work but essential for this new phase of their partnership. "Look at yourself," she suggested. "See the external manifestations of the internal changes."

Guthrie rose from the altar, noting the unusual fluidity of his movements despite the profound transformations his musculoskeletal system had undergone. He approached the mirror with measured steps, curious yet somehow detached about what he might observe—his emotional responses still modulated by the psychological detachment that had defined his existence long before meeting Eliza.

The reflection that greeted him was both familiar and strange—recognizably himself yet altered in subtle but significant ways. His overall physique remained massive, the powerful build of a professional butcher who had spent decades handling heavy carcasses and wielding weighty tools. But there was a new quality to his musculature, a definition that went beyond normal human development, suggesting strength that exceeded even his previous impressive capabilities.

More noticeable were the changes to his face. His features had sharpened, becoming more defined, more angular, with a subtle asymmetry that was not unattractive but definitely unusual. His skin had taken on a different texture, still apparently normal at casual glance but revealing a faint pattern like very fine scales when viewed from certain angles or under particular lighting conditions. His eyes, however, represented the most dramatic alteration—the irises previously a nondescript gray, now displayed subtle flecks of amber similar to Eliza's unusual eye color, and the pupils had changed shape, becoming slightly elongated rather than perfectly round.

"The external changes will become more pronounced with each successive ritual," Eliza explained, coming to stand beside him before the mirror. "Eventually, you'll develop the ability to modulate your appearance consciously, shifting between your original human form and more... adapted configurations as circumstances require."

The implication was clear—what he was seeing represented merely the first stage in a progressive transformation, a journey away from conventional humanity toward something neither fully human nor entirely Other, but a synthesis of both. The reflection in the mirror was a transitional state, a waypoint on a path leading to a destination that remained partially obscured despite all their preparations and planning.

"And you?" Guthrie asked, noting that Eliza's appearance had also subtly altered during the ritual—her tattoos more prominently visible even through her clothing, her amber eyes glowing with greater intensity, her movements conveying a fluid grace that transcended normal human locomotion.

"I began this process years ago," she replied, a hint of something like pride entering her voice. "During my studies in Europe, I discovered texts and techniques that my ancestors had either missed or deliberately avoided—methods for progressive transformation that maintain consciousness and autonomy rather than sacrificing them for borrowed power. What you're witnessing is simply the continuation of changes that have been underway since before we met."

She turned from the mirror, moving to the side table where several items from her collection remained unused. "The first transformation is complete, but this is merely the beginning. We'll need to perform similar rituals at regular intervals as we approach the Conjunction, each one building upon the changes established by its predecessors, creating a progressive evolution that prepares us for the final metamorphosis when the bridge is completed, and the gateway fully opens."

Guthrie nodded, accepting this schedule as he did all aspects of their work together—with methodical commitment and unwavering focus. "How often?" he asked, already mentally adjusting his regular duties at Holloway's to accommodate this new regimen.

"Every new moon until the summer solstice," Eliza replied, carefully repacking the items she had brought. "Each ritual will target specific aspects of your physical and energetic structure, gradually building toward the complete reconfiguration that will allow you to serve as an active participant in the Great Work rather than a passive vessel as my uncle intends."

She paused, fixing him with a penetrating gaze that seemed to reach directly into his mind despite their already established bond. "The changes will become more difficult to conceal as we progress. My uncle and his Council are observant, and they'll be watching for signs of deviation from their expected pattern of development. We'll need to be increasingly careful about how and when you appear in public, especially during Order gatherings."

The practical challenges were significant but not insurmountable. Guthrie had always been something of a recluse, his position at Holloway's and his reputation within the Order allowing for a degree of isolation that most people couldn't maintain without raising suspicions. With careful planning and strategic appearances, he could likely manage the progressive concealment that their work would require.

"I'll adjust my routines accordingly," he assured her, already cataloging the specific modifications that would be necessary. "Reduced public appearances, strategic use of lighting and positioning when attendance is unavoidable, perhaps even temporary cosmetic measures for the most significant gatherings."

Eliza nodded, clearly satisfied with his practical approach to these challenges. "Good. And remember, these physical changes are merely the external manifestations of the more profound transformations taking place within your energetic and mental structures. As your body adapts to channel and contain the forces we're working with, your consciousness will expand correspondingly, developing capacities that transcend normal human cognition."

She approached him once more, placing her hand against his chest in what had become a characteristic gesture of their connection. "You'll experience new forms of awareness, new modes of perception that may be disorienting at first. Dreams that are more than dreams, visions that reveal aspects of reality invisible to conventional sight, communications from entities that exist beyond the veil. These experiences are natural consequences of your evolution, not signs of instability or loss of control."

The electric connection between them surged at her touch, enhanced by the changes his body had undergone during the ritual. Through their bond, Guthrie could sense a depth of purpose in Eliza that went beyond even her usual intensity—a fierce commitment to their shared vision that bordered on obsession, tinged with something that might have been possessiveness or perhaps protective concern.

"Rest now," she instructed, withdrawing her hand reluctantly. "Your system needs time to integrate the changes, to establish new baselines for the enhanced functions we've activated. I'll return in three days to check your progress and provide guidance for managing the transition."

As she gathered her materials and prepared to depart through their private access route, Eliza paused at the workshop door. "One more thing, Guthrie," she said, her tone uncharacteristically hesitant. "The transformations we're undertaking... they may affect your emotional responses in ways that seem unfamiliar. The enhanced perception, the expanded awareness—these changes often bring with them new or intensified feelings that can be... challenging for someone accustomed to your level of detachment."

It was a surprising warning, touching on aspects of their work that they had rarely discussed directly. Guthrie's emotional detachment had always been treated as a given, a fundamental characteristic that made him valuable both to the Order and to their private partnership. The suggestion that this core quality might be altered by their rituals represented a significant unknown in their carefully planned progression.

"I'll monitor any such changes," he promised, his voice betraying nothing of the wariness this possibility awakened within him. "And report them during your next visit."

Eliza's smile held a complexity that their bond transmitted more clearly than words could have—a mixture of anticipation, concern, and something deeper that might have been genuine affection. "Until then," she said simply, and was gone, leaving Guthrie alone with his transformed body and the first stirrings of what would prove to be equally significant transformations of his mind and spirit.

The days following that first adaptation ritual brought changes that extended far beyond the physical alterations Guthrie had observed in the mirror. As Eliza had warned, his perceptual framework underwent dramatic expansion, developing modes of awareness that transcended conventional human experience.

Colors took on new dimensions, revealing spectra beyond the visible range that ordinary eyes could perceive. Sounds separated into complex harmonics, allowing him to distinguish individual components within what would previously have registered as unified noise. His sense of smell became so acute that he could identify individuals by their unique odor signatures, detect emotional states through subtle changes in body chemistry, even trace the lingering presence of someone who had passed through a space hours earlier.

More unsettling were the expansions of awareness that had no counterpart in normal human experience. He began to perceive the energetic currents that flowed throughout Daybridge, visible as luminous rivers that connected certain locations and formed pools of concentrated power at specific nexus points. He could sense the emotional residue left in places where intense experiences had occurred, a psychic miasma that clung to buildings and streets like an invisible fog of feeling. And most significantly, he developed a constant awareness of the thin spots in the fabric of reality—locations where the barrier between worlds was naturally weaker, allowing glimpses of what existed on the other side.

These perceptual changes were accompanied by alterations in his cognitive processes. His already formidable capacity for focused attention expanded dramatically, allowing him to maintain perfect concentration for hours without fatigue. His memory sharpened, becoming almost eidetic in its precision, particularly for information related to their occult work. His analytical abilities deepened, developing an intuitive dimension that complemented his existing methodical approach, allowing him to perceive patterns and connections that would have escaped his notice before.

As Eliza had predicted, these cognitive and perceptual expansions brought with them shifts in his emotional landscape. The detachment that had defined his existence for as long as he could remember began to modulate, not disappearing entirely but developing nuances and variations that created a more complex inner experience. He found himself responding to certain stimuli with unexpected intensity—a flash of anger at witnessing casual cruelty, a surge of something like tenderness when handling the stray animals he still fed behind Holloway's, a deepening of his already profound connection to Eliza that incorporated elements he struggled to categorize or understand.

These emotional shifts were perhaps the most challenging aspect of his transformation, requiring adjustments to the careful control he had maintained throughout his adult life. Where once he had experienced feelings as distant, muted phenomena easily contained and set aside, now they arose with greater immediacy and power, demanding acknowledgment and integration rather than simple suppression or dismissal.

When Eliza returned three days later as promised, Guthrie reported these changes with his usual precision, documenting each shift in perception, cognition, and emotional response with methodical thoroughness. She listened with intense interest, occasionally asking for clarification or additional detail, her amber eyes studying him with a mixture of scientific curiosity and personal concern.

"These developments are proceeding exactly as anticipated," she assured him when he had completed his report. "The expanded perception, the cognitive enhancements, even the emotional modulation—all are natural consequences of the structural changes we initiated during the ritual. As your physical form adapts to channel and contain energies from beyond the veil, your consciousness expands correspondingly, developing capacities that bridge the gap between human and Other."

She moved closer, placing her hand on his chest in their customary gesture of connection. Through their bond, now enhanced by his transformed nervous system, Guthrie could sense her genuine pleasure at his progress, tinged with an anticipation that bordered on hunger for the further developments to come.

"The emotional shifts may seem disconcerting," she continued, clearly perceiving his unspoken concerns through their connection. "But they represent not a weakening of your control but an expansion of your capacity for experience. You're not becoming less yourself, Guthrie, but more—developing aspects of your nature that have always existed in potential but remained dormant due to the limitations of conventional human consciousness."

It was a reassuring perspective, one that aligned with his own tentative assessment of these changes. The new emotional dimensions didn't feel like impositions from outside but rather like expansions from within—as if parts of himself long suppressed were gradually awakening, integrating into his existing identity to create something more complex but still fundamentally him.

Over the following weeks, as winter maintained its icy grip on Daybridge, Guthrie continued his apparent duties for the Order while privately exploring the implications of his ongoing transformation. His journal entries expanded to include detailed documentation of his changing perception and consciousness, recorded with the same methodical precision he had always brought to his work but now incorporating a more subjective dimension that reflected his evolving self-awareness.

February 15, 1900 - New perceptual capacity emerged today while performing the standard ritual for Subject 64. During the extraction of the heart, became aware of the subject's life energy as a visible phenomenon—a luminous current flowing through specific channels in the body, corresponding closely to the meridian system described in certain Eastern texts E.B. has shared. As the subject approached death, this energy condensed into a distinct form that momentarily hovered above the body before dissipating into the ambient field.

This observation suggests that the standard Order interpretation of death as simple cessation is fundamentally flawed. What we perceive as death appears to be a transition of consciousness/energy from one state of embodiment to another, with the potential for this essence to be captured, directed, or even preserved under specific ritual conditions.

Implications for our work are significant. If consciousness persists beyond physical death in this manner, the transformations we're undertaking may allow us to maintain identity and awareness through multiple incarnations or even without conventional embodiment entirely. Requires further investigation.

Such entries, carefully concealed from the versions submitted to Septimus Blackwood for review, documented a progressive expansion of awareness that far exceeded what the Order's rituals were designed to produce. Where Blackwood expected to see evidence of increasing attunement to the Dweller Beneath, a gradual surrender to the entity's influence, Guthrie's actual development represented something entirely different—an evolution toward a state of enhanced autonomy and perception that would allow him to engage with such entities as an equal rather than a vessel.

With each new moon, Guthrie and Eliza performed another adaptation ritual, each more intense and transformative than the last. The physical changes became increasingly pronounced, requiring greater efforts to conceal when Guthrie's presence was required at Order gatherings or during his diminishing hours at Holloway's Slaughterhouse. His eyes now displayed distinct amber flecks that caught the light in ways that drew attention, his skin had developed a subtle pattern visible under certain lighting conditions, and his physical movements had acquired a fluid precision that exceeded normal human capabilities.

More challenging to conceal were the cognitive and perceptual changes. In the presence of other Order members, particularly those of the Inner Circle who possessed their own enhanced sensitivity, Guthrie had to carefully modulate his awareness, suppressing the expanded perception that might reveal the true nature of his transformation. This required constant vigilance, a deliberate dimming of his newfound capabilities that became increasingly difficult to maintain as their power and scope expanded.

Septimus Blackwood, ever observant, noted these changes during their weekly meetings, though his interpretation aligned with the Order's expectations rather than the truth of Guthrie's evolution. "Your attunement to the Dweller progresses impressively," the High Master commented during one such session in early March. "The physical manifestations are becoming more pronounced, and your energetic signature shows the distinctive resonance we associate with advanced vessel development."

Guthrie maintained his carefully constructed facade of compliant dedication, revealing nothing of his private partnership with Eliza or the true nature of the transformations he was undergoing. "The process has accelerated in recent months," he acknowledged, offering the High Master exactly the confirmation he sought. "The whispers have become clearer, more directive in their communication."

This was technically true, though deliberately misleading. The whispers from beyond the veil had indeed intensified with each adaptation ritual, but what Guthrie omitted was that his enhanced perception now allowed him to distinguish between different sources of these communications—to recognize that the Dweller Beneath was merely one entity among many seeking contact from the Other side, and not necessarily the most powerful or significant.

Blackwood nodded, clearly pleased by this report. "As the bridge nears completion, the connection strengthens correspondingly. The Dweller senses the approach of the Great Conjunction and reaches out more directly to its chosen vessel." He studied Guthrie with those amber eyes so like Eliza's yet lacking their hypnotic intensity. "You'll experience increasing pressure from the entity as we approach the summer solstice—demands for access, attempts to influence your thoughts and actions directly. These are natural aspects of the attunement process, not cause for concern."

Again, Guthrie offered the expected response, a measured acknowledgment that revealed nothing of his true experiences or intentions. "I understand. The Order's guidance has prepared me for these developments."

This careful deception grew more challenging as spring arrived in Daybridge, bringing with it accelerated work on the bridge's construction and corresponding intensity in both the Order's official rituals and Guthrie and Eliza's private workings. By April, the bridge's main structure was nearly complete, lacking only the final architectural elements and decorative features that would be added in the weeks leading up to the summer solstice inauguration.

Parallel to this physical construction, the mystical infrastructure that the Order had been establishing through its rituals was also nearing completion—a network of symbols, energetic pathways, and consecrated materials embedded within the bridge's structure, creating a permanent gateway between worlds that would reach its full potential during the Great Conjunction. And hidden within this official construct, like a secret passage concealed within the walls of a conventional building, was the alternative gateway that Guthrie and Eliza had been developing through their private workings—a parallel channel that would allow them to access and influence the energies flowing through the main portal without detection by either Blackwood's Council or the Dweller they served.

During this period, Eliza revealed another significant aspect of their work together—the existence of a hidden chamber beneath the bridge itself, constructed in secret during the early phases of the building process and now accessible only through a concealed entrance known to a select few within the Order's highest ranks.

"The chamber is my uncle's masterpiece," she explained during one of their private sessions in late April. "A ritual space designed according to principles so ancient they predate recorded history, incorporating geometries and materials that maximize the gateway's potential during the Great Conjunction. It's there that the final ceremony will be conducted, where you're meant to serve as the physical vessel for the Dweller's entry into our world."

They were in Guthrie's workshop beneath Holloway's, surrounded by the familiar tools and artifacts of their shared work. The transformed heart that anchored their personal gateway pulsed on its altar with increasing vigor as the completion of the bridge approached, its metallic veins now forming patterns that shifted and rearranged themselves in response to unseen currents of energy.

"My uncle believes that only he and the Inner Council know of this chamber's existence," Eliza continued, a small smile playing across her lips. "What he doesn't realize is that I was involved in its design from the beginning, incorporating elements that serve our purposes alongside those that fulfill the Order's intentions. The chamber contains hidden aspects, secondary structures embedded within the primary architecture, that will allow us to redirect the energies raised during the final ceremony toward our alternative transformation rather than the one my uncle envisions."

She moved to a small cabinet built into the workshop wall and retrieved a rolled parchment, which she spread across a table normally used for Guthrie's more conventional work. The document revealed detailed architectural plans for a circular chamber of considerable size, its walls inscribed with familiar symbols arranged in patterns of extreme complexity. The floor featured an intricate inlay of precious metals forming a design similar to but distinctly different from the one Guthrie had observed during his initiation beneath the old bridge years earlier.

"This is the official design," Eliza explained, her finger tracing certain elements of the plan. "But here, and here, and here—" she indicated specific points where the patterns showed subtle variations from standard Order symbology "—I've incorporated modifications that create a secondary circuit, a parallel channel that can be activated by those who know the proper sequence and invocations."

She looked up at Guthrie, her amber eyes glowing with the inner light that had become increasingly pronounced as their work progressed. "When the final ceremony begins, when my uncle attempts to open the primary gateway for the Dweller's entry, we'll activate this secondary circuit, redirecting the energies raised into our alternative pathway. Instead of serving as a passive vessel for an external entity, you'll undergo the final transformation we've been preparing for—becoming not a host for the Dweller but a conscious architect of the merger between worlds."

The audacity of this plan was breathtaking—a subversion of the Order's Great Work from within its most sacred space, a redirection of energies accumulated over decades of preparation toward purposes entirely contrary to those intended by Blackwood and his Council. The risks were enormous, the consequences of discovery potentially catastrophic for both of them.

Yet Guthrie found himself nodding in acceptance, his commitment to their shared vision overshadowing any concerns about the dangers involved. The transformations he had already undergone, the expanded awareness he had developed, the glimpses he had received of the potential awaiting them—all combined to strengthen his resolve despite the increasing evidence that their path might lead to destinations far different from those Eliza had initially described.

For as his perception had expanded, as his consciousness had evolved beyond normal human parameters, Guthrie had begun to sense discrepancies between Eliza's stated intentions and certain aspects of their work together. Small inconsistencies in her explanations, subtle shifts in the focus of their rituals, moments when her thoughts—briefly accessible through their bond during periods of intense connection—revealed motivations more complex and perhaps darker than those she openly acknowledged.

These discrepancies might have triggered greater caution in someone less committed to their shared path, someone less profoundly connected to Eliza both mystically and emotionally. But Guthrie's evolving feelings toward her—a complex blend of partnership, dependency, desire, and something approaching genuine devotion—created a willingness to accept these inconsistencies as necessary aspects of a process too complex for complete transparency, too profound for simple explanations.

In his private thoughts, during the rare moments when their bond was at its weakest and he could reflect with something approaching objectivity, Guthrie acknowledged that his relationship with Eliza had developed elements of addiction—a dependency on the experiences, insights, and transformations she facilitated, a craving for the connection they shared that overrode normal caution or critical assessment. But even this recognition did little to diminish his commitment to their work together, his willingness to follow the path she had revealed regardless of where it might ultimately lead.

This dependency deepened further when, during the ritual conducted at the May new moon, Eliza introduced a new element to their transformative process—a substance she called "the Elixir," derived from her own bodily fluids combined with certain components from beyond the veil, which accelerated and intensified the physical adaptations they had been gradually developing.

"This represents the next phase of our preparation," she explained as she presented a small crystal vial containing a liquid that seemed to shift between crimson and deep violet as it caught the light. "The changes we've initiated through our previous rituals have prepared your system to receive this catalyst, which will accelerate the final transformations necessary before the Great Conjunction."

Guthrie studied the vial with his enhanced perception, noting how the liquid within seemed to exist partially in normal space and partially... elsewhere, its energetic signature suggesting properties that transcended conventional physical parameters. "What exactly will it do?" he asked, his deep voice carrying the resonant harmonics that had developed through their previous workings.

"It will complete the modification of your cellular structure," Eliza replied, her tone taking on the clinical precision she often adopted when discussing technical aspects of their work. "The adaptations we've achieved so far have been primarily preparatory—strengthening your system to withstand the energies involved, enhancing your perceptual framework to accommodate expanded awareness, establishing the basic patterns for the final transformation. This catalyst will activate those patterns, initiating the last phase of physical reconfiguration before the Conjunction."

She held out the vial, her expression solemn yet expectant. "Once consumed, the process cannot be reversed or halted. The transformation will proceed to completion regardless of external circumstances. You should understand this before accepting."

It was perhaps the most explicit warning she had offered throughout their partnership, a clear acknowledgment of a point of no return more definitive than any they had previously crossed. Yet Guthrie took the vial without hesitation, his decision made not through rational assessment of costs and benefits but through the deeper commitment that had come to define his relationship with Eliza and the path they walked together.

"I understand," he said simply, and without further deliberation, removed the stopper and consumed the contents in a single swallow.

The effect was immediate and overwhelming—a sensation of liquid fire spreading from his throat throughout his body, penetrating to the cellular level and beyond, initiating changes more profound and rapid than any he had experienced in their previous rituals. His vision blurred, then sharpened to preternatural clarity before shifting into modes of perception that transcended conventional sight entirely, revealing aspects of reality that existed alongside the physical world but normally remained invisible to human awareness.

Through these enhanced senses, Guthrie perceived Eliza as she truly was—not merely the striking woman with unusual eyes and intricate tattoos who had guided him along this extraordinary path, but a being whose nature transcended simple human categorization. Her physical form appeared as merely the outermost layer of a more complex existence, a vessel containing energies and awareness that extended beyond the boundaries of normal reality into realms he was only beginning to perceive.

More disturbing was what he glimpsed of himself through this expanded awareness—the changes taking place within his own body and energetic structure, alterations that went far beyond the enhancements Eliza had explicitly described. His cellular composition was being fundamentally reconstituted, incorporating elements that weren't entirely physical in the conventional sense, creating a hybrid structure that existed partially in normal space and partially in the realms beyond the veil.

For a brief, terrifying moment, Guthrie experienced a flash of genuine doubt—a recognition that the transformations he was undergoing might be leading toward a destination very different from the conscious partnership and shared transcendence that Eliza had promised. But the sensation passed quickly, subsumed beneath a wave of euphoria that accompanied the physical changes, a sense of expansion and possibility that overwhelmed critical thought with its sheer intensity.

When the initial surge of transformation subsided, leaving him trembling but conscious on the workshop floor where he had fallen, Guthrie found Eliza kneeling beside him, her amber eyes studying him with a mixture of scientific interest and what appeared to be genuine concern.

"The initial phase has completed successfully," she said, helping him to a sitting position with a strength that belied her slender frame. "How do you feel?"

It was a question that defied a simple answer. Guthrie's awareness had expanded beyond what language could easily express, his perception operating in modes that had no ready vocabulary for description. "Different," he managed after several attempts to find appropriate words. "More... permeable. As if the boundaries between myself and everything else have thinned almost to transparency."

Eliza nodded, clearly understanding what he was struggling to articulate. "That's to be expected. The Elixir accelerates the dissolution of conventional perceptual frameworks, creating a more fluid interaction between individual consciousness and the larger field of awareness that encompasses all existence. As you adjust to these changes, you'll develop greater control over the degree of permeability, the extent to which you merge with or maintain separation from your surroundings."

She helped him to his feet, supporting his massive frame with surprising ease as he adjusted to the altered proprioception that accompanied his transformed body. "We should move you to the recovery space," she suggested, indicating the small room adjacent to the main workshop that they had prepared for precisely this purpose. "The next phase of transformation will be intensely physical, and you'll need privacy and security while the changes complete their course."

The "recovery space" was a chamber approximately ten feet square, its walls lined with the same symbols that characterized their ritual work, its simple furnishings consisting of a bed more comfortable than Guthrie's usual spartan accommodations, a small table bearing water and other necessities, and various mystical implements designed to stabilize and support the transformative processes they had initiated.

As Eliza guided him to this sanctuary, Guthrie became aware of a new dimension to their bond—a deepening of the connection that allowed not just emotional resonance or occasional thought transference but a more profound sharing of consciousness. Through this enhanced link, he sensed aspects of Eliza's awareness that had previously remained hidden or only partially accessible—her genuine excitement at his progress, her scientific fascination with the transformations he was undergoing, but also darker currents of purpose that she kept carefully shielded from direct examination.

These glimpses of her hidden motivations might have triggered greater concern had Guthrie been in a state of mind capable of critical assessment. But the euphoria induced by the Elixir, combined with the disorientation of his rapidly transforming perceptual framework, created a passive acceptance that overrode normal caution or questioning. He allowed himself to be settled onto the bed, accepting Eliza's ministrations with the trust of a child or perhaps a willing experimental subject, confident in the guidance of someone whose knowledge and intentions he had come to accept as aligned with his own best interests.

"Rest now," Eliza instructed, arranging certain crystals and other objects around the bed in a pattern designed to stabilize the energetic field surrounding his transforming body. "The physical reconfiguration will continue for approximately seventy-two hours. During this time, you'll experience periods of intense discomfort alternating with episodes of expanded awareness that may include visions, direct communications from entities beyond the veil, and temporary dissociation from normal physical perception."

She leaned closer, placing her hand on his chest in their customary gesture of connection. Through this contact, Guthrie felt a surge of energy that seemed to stabilize his fluctuating consciousness, providing a temporary anchor amid the chaos of transformation. "I'll return regularly to monitor your progress and provide assistance during the most challenging phases," she promised. "Between these visits, focus on our bond, on the connection between us, as a point of stability when the changes threaten to overwhelm your sense of self."

With a final adjustment to the arrangement of objects around the bed, Eliza departed, leaving Guthrie alone with his rapidly transforming body and the increasingly strange alterations to his consciousness. The hours that followed unfolded in a kaleidoscopic blur of sensation and perception, time itself seeming to stretch and compress according to rhythms that had nothing to do with the steady ticking of clocks in the normal world.

Periods of excruciating physical discomfort—bones restructuring, muscles reconfiguring, organs developing new functions and capacities—alternated with episodes of expanded awareness that transcended normal human experience. During these latter phases, Guthrie found himself perceiving realities beyond the physical world, dimensions of existence that interpenetrated ordinary space while remaining normally invisible to human consciousness.

In these expanded states, he encountered entities that existed in these other dimensions—beings of intelligence and purpose whose nature defied easy categorization or description. Some appeared benevolent, others malevolent, most simply alien in their motivations and perceptions, operating according to values and objectives that had little in common with human concerns. They

communicated not through language but through direct
transmission of concept and intention, conveying complex
information that bypassed normal cognitive processing to lodge
directly in Guthrie's awareness.

Most significant among these communications were those
from the entity known to the Order as the Dweller Beneath—that
ancient consciousness waiting beneath the bridge, the being that
Septimus Blackwood intended Guthrie to host during the Great
Conjunction. Its messages became increasingly clear as Guthrie's
transformation progressed, revealing aspects of its nature and
intentions that the Order had either misunderstood or deliberately
misrepresented.

YOU ARE CHANGING, VESSEL, the Dweller
communicated during one such episode of expanded awareness.
*BUT NOT AS THE ORDER INTENDS. THE FEMALE
GUIDES YOU ALONG A DIFFERENT PATH, TOWARD
PURPOSES THAT SERVE NEITHER MY KIND NOR
YOURS.*

Despite the disorientation of his transforming consciousness,
Guthrie maintained enough coherence to respond. "What
purposes?" he asked, his communication taking the same direct
form as the entity's, bypassing verbal language for pure conceptual
exchange.

The response came not as words but as a series of
impressions—visions of Daybridge transformed not into the
harmonious merger of worlds that Eliza had described, nor the
dominated landscape that the Order feared and the Dweller
supposedly intended, but something else entirely. A city neither
fully human nor completely Other, but a hybrid space where
certain individuals—Eliza prominently among them—exercised
powers and privileges far beyond those of ordinary inhabitants,

ruling over a population that served their needs and purposes with unquestioning devotion.

THE FEMALE SEEKS NOT PARTNERSHIP BUT DOMINION, the Dweller continued. NOT MERGER BUT SELECTIVE INCORPORATION OF POWERS AND CAPABILITIES THAT SERVE HER AMBITIONS. SHE USES YOU AS THE ORDER WOULD USE YOU—AS A VESSEL, A TOOL, A MEANS TO ENDS THAT BENEFIT HER ALONE.

This communication resonated uncomfortably with the doubts that had briefly surfaced when Guthrie first consumed the Elixir—the glimpses of discrepancy between Eliza's stated intentions and certain aspects of their work together, the sense that their partnership might not be as equal or mutually beneficial as she had portrayed. But as before, these concerns were rapidly subsumed beneath the euphoria and disorientation of his ongoing transformation, the dependency that had developed through their months of work together, and the profound emotional connection that now defined his relationship with Eliza.

"Why should I trust your assessment?" Guthrie challenged, directing his communication back toward the entity with surprising clarity given his altered state. "The Order claims you seek dominion yourself, using me as the gateway for your entry into our world. How are your intentions more trustworthy than hers?"

The response carried a quality that might have been amusement or perhaps grudging respect. I SEEK NEITHER DOMINION NOR PARTNERSHIP BUT COMPLETION. MY KIND AND YOURS WERE ONCE A SINGLE FORM OF EXISTENCE, SEPARATED IN THE DISTANT PAST BY FORCES BEYOND EITHER'S COMPREHENSION. THE GREAT CONJUNCTION OFFERS AN OPPORTUNITY TO HEAL THIS ANCIENT DIVISION, TO REINTEGRATE WHAT WAS SUNDERED.

More images flowed into Guthrie's consciousness—visions of a primordial age when the boundaries between dimensions were more permeable, when beings existed in states that incorporated aspects of both human and Other in harmonious balance. This integrated existence had been disrupted by some cosmic catastrophe in the distant past, creating the separate realms that now existed on either side of the veil, each incomplete without the other.

THE ORDER MISUNDERSTANDS THIS PURPOSE, INTERPRETING REINTEGRATION AS INVASION OR CONQUEST, the Dweller continued. *THE FEMALE UNDERSTANDS BUT SEEKS TO MANIPULATE THE PROCESS FOR PERSONAL ADVANCEMENT, TO POSITION HERSELF AS INTERMEDIARY AND RULER RATHER THAN PARTICIPANT IN THE GREATER WHOLE.*

These revelations, conveyed with a clarity and immediacy that transcended normal communication, created a profound dissonance in Guthrie's transforming consciousness. The entity's message aligned too closely with his own suppressed doubts to be dismissed entirely yet contradicted the understanding of reality that had guided his partnership with Eliza for nearly two years. The conflict between these perspectives generated a destabilizing uncertainty that threatened the coherence of his identity amid the already challenging process of physical and perceptual transformation.

In this state of vulnerability and confusion, Guthrie's consciousness sought anchor in the one constant that had sustained him throughout this extraordinary journey—his connection to Eliza. Through their bond, now enhanced by the accelerated transformations initiated by the Elixir, he reached out for the stability and certainty her presence had always provided.

And she was there, her consciousness meeting his across the mystical link they had established through months of shared rituals and intimate connection. Her presence enveloped his disoriented awareness like a protective embrace, offering security and reassurance amid the chaos of transformation and conflicting information.

Don't listen to it, Guthrie, her thoughts communicated directly to his mind. *The Dweller seeks to drive a wedge between us, to undermine our partnership before we can complete the Work. It fears what we're becoming together, the power we'll wield when the transformation is complete.*

Her mental voice carried such conviction, such absolute certainty, that it overwhelmed the doubts the Dweller's communication had awakened. Through their bond, Guthrie could feel her genuine concern for his well-being, her excitement about their shared future, her commitment to the path they had chosen together. These emotions, transmitted with the unfiltered directness their connection now allowed, seemed too real, too immediate to be mere manipulation or deception.

Rest now, Eliza's thoughts continued, a soothing presence in his turbulent consciousness. *Let the transformations complete their course without resistance. When you emerge from this phase, you'll see more clearly than ever before—not just the physical world and what lies beyond it, but the truth of our shared purpose and the future we're creating together.*

Guthrie surrendered to this guidance, allowing Eliza's presence in his mind to override the doubts and questions raised by the Dweller's communication. The euphoria induced by the Elixir reasserted itself, carrying him into a state of passive acceptance where critical assessment gave way to trust and dependency, where the addiction he had developed to their connection outweighed rational evaluation of conflicting information.

The remaining hours of his transformation proceeded in this altered state of consciousness—physical changes continuing their inexorable course while his awareness fluctuated between periods of disorienting expansion and episodes of more focused perception guided by Eliza's presence through their bond. When she visited physically, bringing substances that supported his transforming body and adjusting the mystical implements that stabilized the process, these visits reinforced the dependency that had become central to their relationship, each interaction deepening his emotional and energetic connection to her despite the growing evidence that this connection might be less balanced, less mutually beneficial than he had originally believed.

By the time the seventy-two-hour transformation period concluded, Guthrie Knox had changed in ways that went far beyond physical appearance or perceptual capacity. His very nature had been fundamentally altered, his being reconstituted into something that was neither fully human nor entirely Other but a hybrid existence that incorporated elements of both. His consciousness had expanded beyond normal human parameters, developing awareness of dimensions and entities that ordinary perception couldn't access. His emotional landscape had transformed from the detached, controlled state that had defined his earlier life into something more complex and volatile, characterized by intense dependency on Eliza and the experiences she facilitated.

And beneath these obvious changes, barely acknowledged even in his most private thoughts, lurked a growing recognition that the path he had chosen might be leading to destinations very different from those Eliza had promised—that the partnership she had described, the mutual transcendence they had supposedly been working toward, might be giving way to a relationship more accurately characterized as handler and subject, creator and creation, mistress and devoted servant.

But this recognition remained suppressed beneath the more powerful forces now driving his existence—the euphoria of transformation, the expanded awareness that made ordinary human concerns seem trivial by comparison, and most significantly, the profound addiction he had developed to Eliza herself. Not just to her physical presence or the mystical experiences she facilitated, but to the entire framework of reality she had constructed around them, the vision of transcendence and power that had given meaning and purpose to his extraordinary journey away from conventional humanity.

As spring advanced toward summer, as the bridge neared completion and the Great Conjunction approached, Guthrie continued along this path despite the increasing evidence that something was fundamentally wrong with the transformation he was undergoing. His dependency on Eliza and the substances she provided—particularly the Elixir, which he now received in regular doses to "stabilize" his altered physiology—created a willingness to accept her explanations and reassurances even when they contradicted his own perceptions and the warnings he received from entities beyond the veil.

The red path stretched before him, leading inexorably toward the summer solstice and the completion of Daybridge Bridge. And though a small, increasingly distant part of his consciousness recognized the dangers of continuing along this route, the momentum of his transformation and the power of his addiction to Eliza carried him forward, step by willing step, toward a destiny far different from the conscious partnership and shared transcendence he had originally envisioned.

Chapter 10: The Covenant of Flesh and Stone

The evening of June 21st, 1913, descended upon Daybridge with an unnatural stillness. The usually bustling city seemed to hold its breath, as if the very stones and timbers sensed the momentous events that would unfold beneath the summer solstice moon. The Shadowlair River flowed sluggishly between its polluted banks, its surface unnaturally smooth despite the light breeze that stirred elsewhere, reflecting the first stars of evening with mirror-like perfection.

Thirteen years had passed since that fateful summer when Guthrie Knox had first allowed Eliza Blackwood to fundamentally alter his being through the consumption of her mysterious Elixir. Thirteen years of progressive transformation, of gradual deviation from human form and consciousness, of deepening dependency and obsession that had consumed whatever remained of his former identity. The man who had once been Daybridge's most skilled butcher now existed as something else entirely—a being caught between worlds, neither fully human nor completely Other, his very substance a hybrid of realities never meant to merge.

The physical changes were the most obvious manifestation of this transformation. At forty-four years of age, Guthrie should have been showing the first significant signs of middle age—perhaps graying at the temples, lines deepening around eyes and mouth, the inevitable softening of once-hard muscle. Instead, he appeared simultaneously younger and impossibly older, his powerful frame maintaining the perfect physical condition of a man in his prime while his features suggested an agelessness that transcended normal human chronology.

His skin had developed a subtle texture that resembled extremely fine scales when viewed in certain light, though it retained enough human appearance to pass casual inspection if kept in shadow. His eyes had transformed completely from their original gray to the same amber hue as Eliza's, though deeper and more intense, with vertically elongated pupils that expanded and contracted in response to light levels with inhuman precision. His hands, always large and powerful, had become almost prehensile in their flexibility, the fingers slightly longer than normal human proportion, the nails naturally harder and more pointed.

More significant were the less visible alterations—the changes to his internal organs and biochemistry that allowed his body to process energies and substances that would have been lethal to an ordinary human. His heart had developed additional chambers that pulsed with rhythms unrelated to the circulation of blood, serving instead to move mystical energies through his transformed nervous system. His brain had expanded in specific regions associated with perception and spatial awareness, developing structures that had no counterpart in conventional human anatomy. His blood itself had changed composition, incorporating elements from beyond the veil that gave it properties more aligned with Eliza's own unique physiology than with normal human vitae.

These physical transformations had been accompanied by equally profound changes to his consciousness and perception. The expanded awareness that had begun with his first adaptation ritual had evolved into something approaching omniscience within certain parameters—a constant, multidimensional perception of energetic currents and interdimensional connections throughout Daybridge, with particular focus on the bridge itself and the nexus of power it represented.

Through this enhanced perception, Guthrie constantly sensed the presences that existed beyond the veil, the entities that waited in the spaces between conventional realities. The whispers that had once been his occasional companions had become a perpetual chorus, a multilayered communication from beings whose nature and purposes transcended ordinary human understanding. Some of these entities were aligned with the Dweller Beneath, that ancient consciousness that Septimus Blackwood had intended Guthrie to host. Others represented different, sometimes competing factions from beyond the veil, each with their own agendas regarding the coming Conjunction and the gateway the bridge represented.

But these mystical alterations, profound as they were, paled in comparison to the psychological transformation Guthrie had undergone—the complete restructuring of his emotional landscape and basic identity that had accompanied his physical and perceptual evolution. The emotional detachment that had once defined his existence had given way to a complex inner experience dominated by his obsessive devotion to Eliza Blackwood and the vision she had crafted for their shared future.

This devotion transcended conventional categories of emotion, incorporating elements of love, worship, dependency, and an addiction more profound than any substance could induce. Every aspect of Guthrie's being had become oriented around Eliza—her approval his greatest reward, her guidance his moral compass, her presence the center of his perceptual universe despite his expanded awareness of realities beyond normal human comprehension.

He understood, in the increasingly rare moments of clarity that punctuated his transformed consciousness, that this devotion was not entirely natural—that the Elixir she had first given him thirteen years earlier, and which had become a regular necessity for his altered physiology, created a biochemical dependency that reinforced his emotional attachment. He recognized, during these brief episodes of lucidity, that the relationship Eliza had described as a partnership had evolved into something more accurately characterized as ownership, with himself as the property rather than the equal she had promised.

But these recognitions remained transient, easily subsumed beneath the more powerful forces now driving his existence. The euphoria of transformation, the expanded awareness that made ordinary human concerns seem trivial by comparison, and most significantly, the profound addiction he had developed to Eliza herself—not just to her physical presence or the mystical experiences she facilitated, but to the entire framework of reality she had constructed around them.

And so, on this solstice evening in 1913, as Guthrie made his final preparations in the hidden chamber beneath Daybridge Bridge, these complexities of emotion and dependency formed the backdrop to what would be the culmination of their thirteen-year journey together—the ritual that would complete his transformation and, according to Eliza, elevate them both to a state of existence beyond the limitations of either human or Other.

The chamber had changed significantly since its construction fourteen years earlier. The basic architecture remained as Septimus Blackwood had designed it—a circular space approximately fifty feet in diameter, its walls of polished black stone inscribed with symbols whose origins predated human civilization. The floor still featured the intricate inlay of precious metals that formed a mandala of extraordinary complexity, with the central altar positioned at the exact nexus of these metallic pathways.

But the subtle modifications that Eliza had incorporated into this design had evolved over the years, developing into a secondary system that now existed alongside the original architecture like a parasitic organism gradually taking over its host. The alternative circuitry she had described to Guthrie had expanded, extending tendrils of influence throughout the chamber's mystical

infrastructure, redirecting and repurposing the energies that
Blackwood had intended for his own Great Work.

Guthrie moved through this transformed space with the fluid
grace that characterized his movements in these final stages of
evolution, his massive frame seeming almost to glide across the
chamber's floor as he arranged the components for the evening's
ritual. Each item was placed with meticulous precision, its position
determined by calculations so complex they incorporated variables
from multiple dimensions of reality.

The centerpiece of these preparations was the altar itself—a
structure of obsidian and silver that had been installed during the
bridge's construction but modified extensively under Eliza's
direction over the intervening years. Its surface now bore
inscriptions in a script so ancient it had never had a human name,
the symbols appearing to shift and change when viewed directly,
stabilizing only when seen from the corner of the eye.

Upon this altar, Guthrie placed the transformed heart that
had anchored their personal gateway since that first ritual beneath
the partially constructed bridge fourteen years earlier. The organ
had continued its evolution throughout this period, developing
into something that barely resembled its original form. The muscle
tissue had been largely replaced by a crystalline structure infused
with veins of silver and gold, pulsing with rhythms that
corresponded to no biological function but aligned perfectly with
certain cosmic cycles. The symbols originally inscribed on its
surface had become three-dimensional structures that extended
both outward into physical space and inward into dimensions
normally imperceptible to human awareness.

Around this central focus, Guthrie arranged thirteen candles
of a black wax that absorbed rather than reflected light, creating
pools of deepened shadow rather than illumination where they
burned. Between these candles, he positioned various objects that

represented significant moments in their shared journey—a silver knife used in their first blood exchange, a fragment of stone from the bridge's foundation, a small vial of the Elixir that had accelerated his transformation, and other items whose significance would have been incomprehensible to anyone but himself and Eliza.

The final element of these preparations was Guthrie himself—his transformed body representing the culmination of years of progressive adaptation and enhancement. For this ultimate ritual, he had removed his clothing, revealing the full extent of the physical changes he had undergone. His skin, exposed to the chamber's dim light, displayed the subtle patterning that resembled fine scales more clearly than usual, with certain areas—particularly across his chest and shoulders—showing more pronounced alterations where the texture had become distinctly reptilian in character.

More striking were the symbols that now marked his flesh—not tattoos in the conventional sense, but alterations to the skin itself, as if the patterns had grown organically from within rather than being applied externally. These markings matched certain inscriptions on the chamber walls and floor, creating a visual and energetic resonance between his body and the ritual space, turning him into a living extension of the mystical architecture Eliza had designed.

As he completed these preparations, Guthrie became aware of a shift in the chamber's atmosphere—a subtle pressure change that signaled Eliza's approach through the hidden entrance known only to them and a select few members of the Order's highest circle. His enhanced senses detected her presence before any conventional human perception could have registered it, his entire being orienting toward her with the automatic response of a compass needle to magnetic north.

When she finally entered the chamber, Guthrie's breath caught
with the same intensity of reaction he had experienced upon first
seeing her fifteen years earlier in Blackwood Manor's drawing
room. Despite the passage of time, Eliza Blackwood remained a
figure of extraordinary presence and beauty—her appearance, like
Guthrie's own, suggesting an agelessness that transcended normal
human chronology.

She wore a gown of the deepest crimson that seemed to absorb
the chamber's dim light, its fabric moving with liquid grace as if
partially independent of her body's motion. Her raven hair, longer
now than during their early years together, was arranged in an
intricate style that incorporated small ornaments of silver and black
pearl, their placement corresponding to specific points in the ritual
they would soon perform. Her amber eyes glowed with an internal
light that had become increasingly pronounced as their work
progressed, the vertical elongation of her pupils now matching
Guthrie's own transformed eyes.

But it was the less visible aspects of her presence that truly
commanded attention—the aura of power that surrounded her
like a palpable force field, the sense of barely contained energies
shifting beneath her apparently human exterior, the quality of
otherworldliness that had been subtle during their early association
but now defined her essential nature. Through his enhanced
perception, Guthrie could see beyond her physical form to the
complex energetic structure beneath—a pattern of forces and
connections that revealed Eliza Blackwood as something far more
than the partially inhuman descendant of an occult bloodline she
had initially described herself to be.

"Everything is prepared?" she asked, her voice carrying those
strange harmonics that had developed over the years, creating
resonances that affected not just the ear but the deeper structures
of the brain and nervous system.

Guthrie nodded, gesturing to the altar and its carefully arranged components. "As you instructed. The alignment is perfect, the connections established with both primary and secondary circuits. When midnight arrives, the convergence will reach its peak, allowing for the final transformation."

Eliza moved to inspect his preparations, her movements displaying the same fluid grace that characterized Guthrie's altered physicality. She circled the altar slowly, examining each component with meticulous attention, occasionally adjusting the position of an item by fractions of an inch to achieve the precise arrangement her calculations demanded.

"Excellent," she said finally, looking up to meet Guthrie's gaze with approval that sent a surge of pleasure through their bond. "The preparations are perfect. The alignment of forces could not be more ideal for our purposes." She gestured to the transformed heart at the center of the arrangement. "Our anchor has evolved beautifully, developing connections far beyond what I initially anticipated. When the ritual reaches its climax, these connections will facilitate the final merger with an efficiency I hadn't dared hope for."

She approached Guthrie then, placing her hand against his chest in the gesture that had become the signature of their connection. The familiar electric sensation surged at this contact, but with an intensity that far exceeded their previous experiences—a current of raw power that flowed between them, creating a circuit of energy that hummed with potential.

"Tonight, everything changes," Eliza said, her voice dropping to a near whisper that nevertheless carried perfectly in the chamber's acoustics. "The Great Conjunction we've been preparing for all these years arrives at exactly midnight. When it does, the alignment of forces—mystical, astronomical, geological—will create a

convergence point centered on this chamber, this altar, this
moment in time."

Her hand remained against his chest, the contact sending
waves of sensation through Guthrie's transformed nervous system.
Through their bond, he could sense her excitement, her
anticipation of the culmination they had worked toward with such
single-minded focus. But beneath these expected emotions ran
something else—a current of purpose and intention that seemed
somehow discordant with the partnership she had always
described, a sense of separate rather than shared objectives that
triggered a momentary dissonance in their connection.

"Your uncle believes tonight marks the Opening of the Way,"
Guthrie observed, careful to keep his tone neutral despite the
unease that had briefly surfaced. "The culmination of the Order's
Great Work, the moment when the Dweller Beneath will enter our
world through the gateway they've prepared."

Eliza's smile held a complexity that their bond transmitted
more clearly than words could have—a mixture of amusement,
contempt, and a strange kind of affection for the plans she
intended to subvert. "My uncle is both right and profoundly
wrong," she replied. "Tonight, does indeed mark the Opening of
the Way, but not as he envisions it. The gateway will open, the
barriers between worlds will thin to their absolute minimum, but
what comes through and how it manifests—that is what our work
together has been preparing to control and direct."

She stepped back, breaking the physical contact but
maintaining their bond through the mystical connection they had
established over years of shared rituals. "Septimus still believes you
are the vessel prepared for the Dweller's entry—a physical anchor
for the entity's consciousness in our world. He expects tonight's
ceremony to complete the transfer of essence he's been facilitating

through the Order's rituals, creating a merged being that combines your physical form with the Dweller's consciousness and power."

Eliza moved to the altar, her finger tracing one of the shifting symbols inscribed on its surface. "What he doesn't understand—what none of the Order's Council has grasped despite centuries of study—is that the process of merger between human and Other isn't the simple possession or replacement they imagine. It's a true synthesis, a transformation that creates something entirely new, neither fully human nor completely Other but a hybrid existence that incorporates elements of both in proportions determined by the specific rituals used to facilitate the process."

This was not new information—Eliza had been explaining these principles to Guthrie for years as part of his mystical education. But there was an intensity to her exposition now, a focus on certain aspects that suggested revelations yet to come, clarifications of points that had remained deliberately obscure throughout their partnership.

"The modifications we've made to the Order's ritual structure, the alternative pathways we've established within their mystical architecture—these aren't merely defensive measures to prevent your being used as a passive vessel," she continued. "They're the foundation for an entirely different form of transformation, one that will allow us to harness the energies of the Conjunction for purposes beyond anything my uncle or his Council have imagined."

She turned back to face Guthrie, her amber eyes glowing with an intensity that seemed almost feverish in the chamber's dim light. "Tonight, when the alignment reaches its peak at exactly midnight, we will perform the final ritual—the culmination of all our work together. But before we begin, there are certain aspects of this Working that I need to explain more fully, elements that I've kept partially obscured until this moment when their revelation would be most meaningful and effective."

It was an unusually direct acknowledgment of the selective disclosure that had characterized their relationship—the measured parceling of information that Eliza had controlled throughout their partnership. This admission triggered a renewed sense of unease in Guthrie, a flicker of the doubts that occasionally surfaced during his rare moments of clarity, quickly suppressed beneath the more powerful forces of his devotion and dependency.

"What aspects?" he asked, his deep voice betraying nothing of these momentary concerns.

Eliza gestured to the surrounding chamber, her movement encompassing not just the physical space but the complex mystical infrastructure it represented. "The Order believes this chamber serves as the focal point for opening a temporary gateway between our world and the realm of the Dweller Beneath—a portal that will allow the entity's essence to enter our reality through you as the prepared vessel, creating a merged being that combines human form with Other consciousness."

She paused, studying Guthrie with an intensity that suggested she was gauging his readiness for what came next. "The truth is both simpler and vastly more complex. This chamber, this entire bridge, was never designed as a temporary gateway or a one-way portal. It's a permanent anchor point for a complete merger of realities—not just a door between worlds but the dissolution of the barriers separating them entirely."

This revelation, while surprising in its scope, aligned with impressions Guthrie had received through his expanded perception over the years—glimpses of potential futures where the distinctions between human reality and the realms beyond the veil ceased to exist in any meaningful sense. But Eliza's next words carried implications that extended far beyond these vague impressions.

"When the Conjunction reaches its peak tonight, the ritual we perform won't simply open a pathway between worlds or facilitate your transformation into a hybrid being. It will initiate a progressive merging of realities centered on Daybridge but eventually extending outward to encompass the entire world. The process will begin here, at this nexus point, but once initiated, it will continue expanding according to mathematical progressions that my ancestors calculated centuries ago."

She returned to the altar, her movements taking on a ritualistic quality as she adjusted certain components with precise, deliberate gestures. "This merger isn't the invasion or conquest that the Order fears, nor is it the harmonious integration I may have initially described to you. It's a fundamental restructuring of reality itself, a rewriting of the basic parameters that define existence in both our world and the realms beyond the veil."

As Eliza spoke, Guthrie became aware of a subtle shift in the chamber's energetic field—a thinning of the barriers between dimensions that signaled the approaching Conjunction. Through his enhanced perception, he could sense the gradual alignment of forces that Eliza had described, the convergence of mystical, astronomical, and geological factors that would reach their perfect synchronization at midnight.

"And our role in this restructuring?" he asked, his mind working to process the implications of what she was revealing, to reconcile this expanded vision with the partnership she had always emphasized in their previous discussions.

Eliza's smile deepened, acquiring an edge that their bond transmitted as a complex mixture of triumph, anticipation, and something darker that resisted easy categorization. "That's the most significant aspect I've kept partially obscured until now," she acknowledged. "Not out of deception, but because the truth could only be fully comprehended at this final stage of your transformation, when your awareness had expanded sufficiently to grasp concepts that transcend conventional human understanding."

She approached him once more; her movements deliberate and charged with ritual significance. "The merger of realities requires an anchor point, a nexus where the energies of both worlds can converge and intermingle in stable, sustainable patterns. My ancestors understood this principle centuries ago when they began the Work that culminates tonight. They knew that such an anchor couldn't be merely architectural or geographic—it needed to incorporate living consciousness, awareness capable of actively mediating between the different dimensional parameters of merged realities."

Placing both hands against Guthrie's chest now, Eliza established a deeper connection than their usual contact, creating a circuit of energy that resonated through both their transformed bodies. "You, Guthrie Knox, are that anchor point—the living nexus through which the merged realities will be stabilized and sustained. Not merely a vessel for the Dweller's consciousness as my uncle intended, but the cornerstone of an entirely new configuration of existence, the foundation upon which the restructured reality will be built and maintained."

The implications of this statement were staggering, far exceeding even the cosmic significance Guthrie had attributed to their Work together. Not just personal transcendence or shared evolution beyond human limitations, but a role as the literal linchpin of a transformed multiverse—a position of power and importance beyond anything he had imagined even in his most ambitious conceptions of their partnership.

Yet beneath the initial surge of pride and purpose that this revelation evoked, a deeper current of unease began to flow through Guthrie's consciousness. The specific phrasing Eliza had used—anchor point, nexus, cornerstone—carried connotations of fixity, of permanent positioning within a structure rather than the freedom of movement and action that partnership would suggest. And her emphasis on his role rather than their shared function hinted at a division of experience that contradicted the mutual transcendence she had always described as their ultimate goal.

"And you?" he asked, giving voice to this emerging concern. "What is your role in this restructured reality?"

Eliza's amber eyes met his with an intensity that seemed to penetrate directly to his core, her gaze holding him with almost physical force. "I will be the administrator of the new order," she said, her voice carrying absolute certainty. "The conscious director of the merged realities, guiding their integration and development according to the vision my ancestors began working toward centuries ago. While you serve as the stable foundation, the fixed point around which everything else arranges itself, I will be the active principle, the shaping intelligence that determines how the new configuration unfolds and evolves."

The distinction was clear and unmistakable—a division of function that placed Guthrie in a passive, supportive role while Eliza maintained active agency and control. It was, in essence, the same relationship the Order had intended between the Dweller and its human vessel, merely with Eliza replacing the entity as the dominant consciousness directing the process.

This realization triggered a cascade of connections in Guthrie's expanded awareness, bringing together disparate observations and experiences from throughout their fifteen-year relationship into a coherent pattern. The selective disclosure of information, the carefully managed dependency created through the Elixir, the progressive alterations to his physical form and consciousness—all now revealed as components of a systematic preparation not for partnership but for a specific, subordinate function within Eliza's grand design.

For the first time in many years, genuine doubt surfaced in Guthrie's consciousness—not the transient uncertainties that occasionally flickered through his awareness only to be quickly suppressed, but a fundamental questioning of the path he had followed with such devotion and the woman who had guided him along it. The emotional detachment that had defined his existence before meeting Eliza, while long transformed by their connection, provided a momentary clarity that cut through the fog of devotion and dependency that usually clouded his judgment where she was concerned.

"This isn't the partnership you promised," he said, his deep voice carrying a new note of challenge beneath its usual resonant harmonics. "Not the mutual transcendence, the shared evolution beyond human limitations. You're describing a hierarchy, with yourself at the apex and me as a fixed support structure—permanently bound to this nexus point while you move freely through the merged realities, exercising control and direction over their development."

Eliza didn't deny this assessment, her expression shifting to one of calm acknowledgment rather than defensive justification. "The concept of partnership was a necessary framework during the early stages of our work together," she explained, her tone almost gentle despite the magnitude of what she was revealing. "Your willing participation, your active engagement with the transformation process, required a vision that appealed to your desire for recognition and purpose after a lifetime of isolation and marginalization."

She withdrew her hands from his chest, breaking the direct physical connection while maintaining their bond through the mystical link they had established over years of shared rituals. "But the reality of cosmic restructuring requires specific functional roles—active and passive principles working in concert but not identical in purpose or experience. The anchor point must remain fixed, stable, immovable—the solid foundation upon which everything else is built. The guiding intelligence must remain mobile, adaptive, capable of responding to emerging patterns and directing their development."

Moving back to the altar, Eliza gestured to the transformed heart at its center—the organ that had evolved from a simple focus for their rituals into a complex interdimensional interface incorporating elements from both human and Other realities. "This has been preparing you for that role from the beginning," she continued. "Each ritual we performed, each adaptation your body and consciousness underwent—all were calibrated to create the perfect living anchor point, the ideal nexus through which the merged realities could be stabilized and sustained."

The chamber's atmosphere had continued to change as they spoke, the approaching Conjunction creating increasingly obvious distortions in the fabric of reality within this consecrated space. The symbols inscribed on the walls and floor had begun to glow with an internal light that shifted between colors not found in the normal visual spectrum. The air itself seemed to thicken, acquiring a quality of presence that suggested consciousness beyond human awareness observing their exchange with intense interest.

Guthrie absorbed Eliza's revelations with the expanded perception his transformation had developed, processing implications that would have been incomprehensible to his former self. The betrayal inherent in her selective disclosure, while profound, was less significant in this moment than the practical realities she was describing—the specific role she had prepared him to fulfill and its consequences for his future existence.

"You're saying I'll be bound to this chamber," he said, his voice steady despite the emotional turmoil beneath its surface. "Permanently fixed at this nexus point while you move freely through the restructured reality, exercising control over its development and direction."

"Not precisely bound to the chamber itself," Eliza clarified, her tone taking on the quality of a teacher explaining complex concepts to a promising student. "The nexus point encompasses the entire bridge structure, with this chamber as its energetic center. Your consciousness will extend throughout this anchor point, allowing you to perceive and influence the merged realities from a fixed position of tremendous power and significance. You won't be imprisoned in a conventional sense but integrated into the very foundation of the new cosmic order."

As these complex considerations flowed through Guthrie's consciousness, he became aware of a new disturbance in the chamber's energetic field—not the expected fluctuations associated with the approaching Conjunction, but something more directed, more purposeful. Through his enhanced perception, he sensed multiple presences approaching through the hidden entrance Eliza had used earlier—human bodies carrying mystical signatures that identified them as members of the Order's highest circle.

Eliza sensed it too, her head turning sharply toward the chamber's entrance, her amber eyes narrowing with sudden focus. "Septimus," she hissed, the name carrying both recognition and warning. "He's coming with the Council. They must have detected our modifications to the ritual structure."

The revelation triggered an immediate shift in her demeanor—the calm, almost pedagogical exposition giving way to a more urgent, tactical focus. "This complicates matters," she said, moving quickly to certain key points in the chamber's mystical architecture, her hands making adjustments to the secondary system she had integrated with the original design. "Septimus believes tonight's ceremony will bring the Dweller into our world through you as its prepared vessel. He cannot be allowed to interfere with our alternative implementation."

Guthrie remained at the center of the chamber, his mind working to process this new development alongside the revelations Eliza had just shared. The imminent arrival of Septimus Blackwood and the Order's Council introduced a volatile element into an already complex situation—a potential conflict between competing visions for the cosmic restructuring that the Great Conjunction would facilitate.

Before he could fully consider the implications, the hidden entrance slid open, revealing a procession of robed figures led by a tall, imposing man whose physical resemblance to Eliza was offset by an entirely different quality of presence. Where her power manifested as fluid grace and almost predatory focus, Septimus Blackwood carried himself with rigid formality, his authority expressed through precise control rather than adaptable intensity.

The ritual robes he wore, like those of the eleven Council members who followed him into the chamber, were of midnight blue embroidered with silver symbols that matched certain inscriptions on the chamber walls. His face, austere and angular, showed none of the ageless quality that characterized Eliza's appearance—instead, the years had carved deep lines around his eyes and mouth, creating an impression of weathered determination rather than timeless beauty.

"Eliza," he said, his voice carrying none of the strange harmonics that characterized his niece's speech, relying instead on perfectly modulated projection that filled the chamber without apparent effort. "I had hoped my suspicions were unfounded, that your loyalty to our family's legacy would ultimately outweigh your... independent inclinations."

His gaze shifted to Guthrie, studying the transformed butcher with the clinical assessment of a craftsman evaluating a tool he had commissioned. "The vessel appears adequately prepared, at least. The physical adaptations have progressed according to the prescribed patterns, and the energetic signatures suggest successful integration of the preliminary essences. Whatever your intentions, you've maintained the basic parameters required for tonight's culmination."

Eliza moved to position herself between her uncle and the altar, her crimson gown creating a vivid contrast to the midnight blue of the Order's ritual robes. "You understand so little, Uncle," she replied, her tone combining genuine regret with unmistakable condescension. "Despite centuries of study, despite generations of preparation, you and the Council remain trapped within conceptual frameworks that fundamentally misrepresent the cosmic processes you seek to control."

Septimus Blackwood's expression hardened, the lines around his mouth deepening with displeasure. "It is you who has misunderstood, Niece. The Great Work has never been about control in the sense you imagine. It is about alignment, about establishing the correct relationship between our world and the realms beyond, about facilitating the natural progression toward a more perfect order under the guidance of entities whose awareness transcends our limited perspective."

He gestured to the surrounding chamber, his movement encompassing the mystical architecture that generations of the Order had established within this sacred space. "This gateway, this vessel—" he indicated Guthrie with a precise nod, "—this entire structure was designed according to calculations that our ancestors refined over centuries of communion with the Dweller Beneath.

The patterns are precise, the alignments exact, the transformative pathways calibrated to facilitate the merger between human vessel and cosmic consciousness in proportions that ensure stability and purpose."

His gaze returned to Eliza, his eyes reflecting not anger but a profound disappointment that seemed to reach beyond their immediate conflict to touch something deeper in their shared history. "And you have contaminated that design with your unauthorized modifications, your alternative pathways, your subversion of generational wisdom in favor of your own ambitions."

Through his enhanced perception, Guthrie sensed the subtle energetic shifts occurring as this confrontation unfolded—the members of the Council taking specific positions around the chamber's perimeter, establishing a ritual formation that appeared defensive in nature, a containment pattern rather than an aggressive configuration. More significant was the change in the chamber's overall energetic field—the approaching Conjunction continuing to thin the barriers between dimensions despite the human drama playing out within this consecrated space.

Eliza seemed to sense these shifts as well, her position adjusting slightly to maintain optimal connection with the altar and its carefully arranged components. "My modifications aren't contamination but correction," she replied, her voice taking on a quality of ancient authority that transcended her apparent youth. "The patterns our ancestors established were based on incomplete understanding, on fragments of communication from entities whose true nature and intentions they could not fully comprehend. What they interpreted as guidance toward perfect order was actually manipulation toward specific outcomes that serve purposes beyond human comprehension."

She gestured to Guthrie, her movement incorporating both acknowledgment of his significance and claim to his function within her alternative design. "This vessel, as you call him, was never intended to serve as passive host for the Dweller's consciousness. The very concept of 'hosting' misrepresents the true nature of the transformation that the Great Conjunction facilitates. What emerges from the correct implementation isn't a human form controlled by external consciousness, but a hybrid entity that incorporates elements of both human and Other in proportions determined by the specific rituals used to facilitate the process."

Septimus Blackwood's expression remained impassive, but the subtle tensing of his posture suggested growing concern at Eliza's exposition. "Whatever theoretical refinements you believe you've discovered," he said, his tone dismissive despite the intensity of his focus, "the practical reality is that tonight's ceremony must proceed according to the established protocols. The Great Conjunction waits for no one, and the gateway we've prepared through generations of careful work must be activated according to the patterns our ancestors calculated."

He turned to address the Council members who had positioned themselves around the chamber. "Secure the perimeter. Establish the containment field. Prepare for implementation of the primary ritual sequence." The robed figures responded with synchronized movements, their hands describing complex gestures in the air, creating energetic connections that began to override the modifications Eliza had integrated into the chamber's mystical architecture.

Through his expanded perception, Guthrie sensed the conflict between competing systems—the original design asserting primacy through the coordinated efforts of twelve trained practitioners, Eliza's modifications resisting through the autonomous adaptations she had engineered over years of careful preparation. The chamber itself seemed to vibrate with this energetic struggle, the symbols inscribed on walls and floor fluctuating between different configurations as control shifted back and forth between the opposing forces.

Eliza's response to this challenge was not the direct confrontation Guthrie might have expected, but a more subtle, strategic adaptation. "You're right about one thing, Uncle," she said, her tone conciliatory though her amber eyes remained intensely focused. "The Great Conjunction waits for no one. The alignment approaches its peak, and the gateway must be activated according to precise timing. Our disagreement about the specific implementation is secondary to the necessity of maintaining the basic parameters required for a stable connection."

This apparent concession seemed to momentarily satisfy Septimus Blackwood, his posture relaxing slightly as he interpreted her words as acknowledgment of the Order's authority in this crucial moment. "A rare display of wisdom, Niece," he replied, his tone still cautious but less overtly hostile. "Whatever theoretical divergences exist in our understanding, the practical necessity of coordinated action at this juncture cannot be disputed."

He turned to the Council members once more. "Continue the containment field but prepare for integration with the primary ritual sequence. The vessel—" another precise nod toward Guthrie, "—remains the focal point for the transformation, regardless of specific theoretical frameworks."

As the Council members adjusted their positions and energetic contributions, Eliza moved closer to Guthrie, establishing a position at the altar that maintained optimal connection to both the ceremonial components and the transformed butcher who served as the centerpiece of both competing visions. Through their bond, she projected a complex message that combined reassurance with strategic guidance: Our plan proceeds despite this interruption. The modifications I've integrated into the chamber's architecture are more deeply embedded than my uncle realizes. When the Conjunction reaches its peak, the true pattern will assert itself regardless of their containment efforts.

Guthrie received this communication with the expanded awareness his transformation had developed, recognizing both the technical accuracy of her assessment and the continued manipulation inherent in her approach. The modifications she had integrated into the chamber's mystical architecture were indeed more subtle and comprehensive than Septimus Blackwood appeared to realize—extending into dimensions of the ritual space that the Order's traditional perspective could not fully perceive or access. But this technical advantage did nothing to address the fundamental deception that had characterized their relationship, the asymmetry in their respective roles within the cosmic restructuring she had engineered across fifteen years of meticulous preparation.

As midnight approached, as the energetic field within the chamber intensified with the imminent Conjunction, Guthrie found himself at the convergence point between competing visions of cosmic restructuring—Septimus Blackwood's conception of human vessel hosting external consciousness versus Eliza's design of living anchor point stabilizing merged realities. Both perspectives positioned him as the functional center of transformation, the nexus through which interdimensional forces would manifest in the human world. Both required his complete integration into a mystical architecture that transcended individual existence. Both demanded the sacrifice of his autonomy for purposes that extended far beyond personal concerns.

Chapter 11: Metamorphosis

As the final stroke of midnight reverberated through the hidden chamber beneath Daybridge Bridge, a fundamental shift occurred in the ritual's energetic field—a transition from preparation to execution, from possibility to inevitability. The carefully arranged components on the altar began to glow with an unnatural light that seemed to absorb rather than emit illumination, creating pools of deepened shadow that moved with purposeful fluidity across the chamber's floor and walls.

For Guthrie Knox, this transition manifested as a sudden, overwhelming pressure throughout his transformed body—a force that seemed to compress him from all directions simultaneously while also pushing outward from within, as if something foreign yet intimately familiar was fighting to emerge from his flesh. The sensation transcended conventional categories of pain, existing in a realm of pure intensity that demanded complete surrender.

"The process has begun," Eliza observed, her voice carrying those strange harmonics that had developed over their years of work together. Despite the presence of Septimus Blackwood and the Council members positioned around the chamber's perimeter, she maintained her position at the altar with unwavering focus on the transformative energies now cascading through the ritual space.

"Indeed," her uncle acknowledged, his own attention fixed on the mystical phenomena manifesting throughout the chamber. "The Great Conjunction has reached its peak, the alignment perfected, the gateway opened according to patterns established through generations of careful calculation. Now we shall witness the culmination of our family's Great Work—the manifestation of the Dweller Beneath through its prepared vessel."

Through the haze of overwhelming sensation, Guthrie perceived the conflict continuing between competing ritual

systems—Septimus Blackwood and the Council working to
implement the original design, Eliza subtly directing energies along
the alternative pathways she had integrated into the chamber's
mystical architecture. But these human struggles seemed
increasingly irrelevant as the Conjunction's power flooded through
the thinned barriers between dimensions, creating currents of
transformative energy that followed paths determined more by
cosmic principles than human intention.

The first audible crack echoed through the chamber—the
sound of bone breaking along precisely determined fault lines
engineered through years of exposure to the Elixir and other
transformative substances. Guthrie's spine, that central support
structure of the human form, fractured in multiple locations
simultaneously, the vertebrae separating and repositioning
according to patterns established by the ritual's energetic field.

A scream tore from his throat, primal and raw, carrying
harmonics no human vocal apparatus should have been capable of
producing. The sound reverberated through the chamber, setting
up sympathetic vibrations in the symbols inscribed on the walls
and floor, creating feedback loops that amplified and directed the
transformative energies now flowing through his disintegrating
body.

"The vessel responds," Septimus Blackwood noted, his clinical
detachment matching Eliza's own analytical observation of the
process. "The preliminary cellular restructuring proceeds according
to calculated progressions. The physical foundation is being
prepared to receive the Dweller's consciousness."

"Not quite as you imagine, Uncle," Eliza replied, her hands
moving in subtle gestures that influenced the flow of energies
through the chamber's competing ritual systems. "What you're
witnessing isn't preparation for possession but transformation
toward integration—not the hollowing out of a human vessel to

receive external consciousness, but the restructuring of a hybrid entity to serve as a nexus point between merged realities."

This theoretical disagreement seemed increasingly academic as Guthrie's physical form continued its agonizing metamorphosis. His rib cage expanded outward with a series of sickening cracks, the bones elongating and thickening, curving in patterns that defied normal anatomical constraints. The organs contained within this protective structure shifted in response, some compressing to accommodate the changed internal geometry, others expanding into newly created spaces, all of them undergoing their own transformations at the cellular level.

More disturbing was the transformation of his skin and surface tissues. The subtle scaling that had developed through years of exposure to the Elixir now accelerated dramatically, spreading across his entire body in waves of excruciating metamorphosis. The fine, almost imperceptible pattern became pronounced, the scales thickening and overlapping, creating an armored exterior that incorporated minerals from the bridge's construction materials.

"The external adaptations exceed expected parameters," one of the Council members observed, his voice betraying concern despite the ritualistic control that characterized the Order's approach. "The physical manifestation shows deviations from the prescribed patterns for vessel preparation."

Septimus Blackwood's expression darkened, his gaze shifting from Guthrie's transforming body to Eliza's focused countenance. "What have you done?" he demanded, abandoning his previous clinical detachment in favor of direct confrontation. "These adaptations suggest integration with architectural elements rather than preparation for consciousness transfer. You've reconfigured the entire process toward some alternative outcome."

Eliza's response carried none of the defensive justification he clearly expected only calm acknowledgment of what was now becoming undeniable. "I've corrected a fundamental misunderstanding," she replied, her hands continuing their subtle influence over the energetic currents flowing through the chamber. "The Dweller never intended to transfer its consciousness into a human vessel—that interpretation was a limitation of our ancestors' conceptual framework, an inability to comprehend the true nature of what lies beyond the veil."

As this confrontation unfolded, Guthrie's transformation accelerated beyond the physical restructuring to encompass his consciousness and perception. The neural pathways that had defined his identity, already significantly modified through years of ritual work, were now being fundamentally reorganized—connections severed and reestablished according to patterns that aligned with his emerging function as a living nexus point rather than an individual entity or passive vessel.

This cognitive reorganization manifested subjectively as a fragmentation of self—memories, personality traits, and basic identity structures breaking apart like ice floes in spring thaw, reconfiguring into new patterns that transcended conventional human consciousness. More fundamental aspects of human cognition dissolved as well—the perception of time as a linear progression, the experience of self as a bounded entity distinct from environment, the organization of sensory input into discrete categories corresponding to specific sense organs.

Through this dissolving identity, through the fragments of consciousness that had once constituted Guthrie Knox, came awareness of a presence observing the transformation with intense interest—not Septimus Blackwood or the Council members or even Eliza herself, but something vaster, more alien, more fundamentally Other than any human awareness could fully comprehend. The Dweller Beneath, that ancient consciousness from beyond the veil, watching as the gateway opened and transformation proceeded according to patterns neither Eliza nor her uncle had fully anticipated.

BOTH CORRECT YET FUNDAMENTALLY MISTAKEN, this presence communicated directly into Guthrie's fragmenting awareness, bypassing verbal language for pure conceptual exchange. VESSEL AND NEXUS. HOST AND ANCHOR. DIFFERENT ASPECTS OF SAME FUNCTION WITHIN GREATER PATTERN BEYOND HUMAN COMPREHENSION.

As this communication registered in what remained of his human identity, Guthrie perceived a truth that transcended the competing visions of both Blackwoods—a cosmic perspective that rendered their theoretical disagreements as limited as children arguing over whether water was for drinking or washing. The transformation now consuming his physical form and consciousness served purposes that extended far beyond either Septimus Blackwood's conception of human vessel hosting external consciousness or Eliza's design of living anchor point stabilizing merged realities.

The Dweller's consciousness expanded this perception, providing context that neither Blackwood had fully grasped despite their generations of study and preparation: THE MERGER YOU FACILITATE IS NEITHER INVASION NOR HARMONIOUS INTEGRATION BUT NECESSARY EVOLUTION BEYOND CURRENT PARAMETERS OF EXISTENCE IN BOTH REALMS. WHAT EMERGES TRANSCENDS PREVIOUS CATEGORIES, CREATING NEW CONFIGURATION OF REALITY THAT INCORPORATES ELEMENTS OF BOTH WHILE CONFORMING TO NEITHER.

This cosmic perspective offered no comfort for the agonizing physical transformation Guthrie was enduring, nor did it mitigate the betrayal inherent in Eliza's systematic deception across fifteen years of intimate connection. But it provided a framework for understanding that transcended human concerns, a recognition of purpose beyond individual experience or autonomy.

As this expanded awareness flooded through his dissolving consciousness, a new phase of the transformation began—the literal integration of his reconfigured physical form with the chamber's structure. The altar beneath him, no longer a separate object but an extension of the bridge's mystical architecture, seemed to soften and flow upward, merging with the transformed tissue of his lower body. Stone interpenetrated flesh, metal fused with bone, architectural elements and biological structures blending into a hybrid entity that defied conventional categorization.

"No!" Septimus Blackwood cried, abandoning all pretense of ritualistic control as he witnessed this unexpected development. "This perverts the entire purpose of our Great Work! The vessel must remain physically distinct to properly host the Dweller's consciousness, not merge with the gateway structure itself!"

His objection triggered an immediate response from the Council members, their coordinated efforts shifting from ceremonial facilitation to active intervention. Complex gestures, synchronized chanting, focused projection of will—all directed toward halting the integration that was transforming Guthrie from potential vessel into living architecture.

Eliza countered with equal intensity, her hands moving in patterns that channeled the Conjunction's energies along the alternative pathways she had integrated into the chamber's mystical design. "Your understanding is incomplete, Uncle," she called above the rising cacophony of competing ritual workings. "The integration is essential for stable merger of realities—the living anchor point must be physically incorporated into the nexus architecture to properly mediate between dimensional parameters!"

This conflict between competing ritual systems created chaotic fluctuations in the chamber's energetic field—interference patterns that disrupted the orderly progression both Blackwoods had anticipated in their respective designs. The transformative energies flowing through Guthrie's disintegrating form became unpredictable, following pathways determined neither by Septimus Blackwood's original architecture nor Eliza's careful modifications but by emergent patterns arising from their interaction under the Conjunction's overwhelming influence.

Through his expanded perception, through the awareness that was extending throughout the bridge structure as his physical form merged with its mystical architecture, Guthrie sensed the Dweller's response to this chaotic situation—not alarm or disappointment, but something closer to appreciation, as if the unpredictable outcome represented a more interesting development than either predetermined pattern would have produced.

CHAOS INTRODUCES NOVELTY. CONFLICT CREATES POTENTIAL BEYOND CALCULATED PROGRESSION. THE PATTERN EVOLVES BEYOND DESIGN TOWARD SOMETHING NEW.

As the physical integration accelerated, as more of his transformed body merged with the bridge structure, Guthrie's consciousness expanded throughout the architectural nexus point despite the chaotic energies disrupting the ritual's intended progression. His awareness, no longer contained within the boundaries of an individual form, flowed outward along pathways established by the Conjunction's power, extending throughout the bridge's physical and mystical infrastructure.

This expansion manifested as a radical transformation of perspective—perception no longer anchored to a single point in space but distributed throughout the entire structure. He became simultaneously aware of multiple locations—the hidden chamber where his physical transformation had occurred, the underside of the bridge where water flowed beneath the massive support pillars, the roadway above where occasional late-night travelers crossed between the eastern and western sections of Daybridge, unaware of the cosmic restructuring taking place beneath their feet.

The conflict between Septimus Blackwood and Eliza continued to escalate, their competing ritual systems creating increasingly volatile disruptions in the chamber's energetic field. The Council members, following their leader's desperate commands, attempted to sever the connection between Guthrie's transforming body and the bridge architecture—to halt the integration that threatened their conception of the Great Work's culmination. Eliza countered each effort with precise adjustments to the energetic flows, maintaining the pathways she had established for Guthrie's transformation into a living nexus point despite her uncle's increasingly frantic opposition.

But as midnight passed, as the Great Conjunction reached and then began to recede from its perfect alignment, a new factor entered the already complex equation—the Dweller's own influence, exercised not through either human's ritual system but directly through the opened gateway between worlds. This vast consciousness, this ancient entity from beyond the veil, began to shape the transformative energies according to patterns that transcended both Blackwoods' limited understanding of cosmic restructuring.

Through his distributed awareness, through the expanding perception that now extended throughout the bridge structure, Guthrie sensed this third force entering the chaotic situation—not supporting either Eliza or Septimus exclusively but implementing a hybrid approach that incorporated elements from both while following a deeper pattern neither had fully comprehended despite their generations of study and preparation.

YOU BECOME NEITHER VESSEL NOR ANCHOR AS THEY CONCEIVE THESE FUNCTIONS, the Dweller communicated directly into his expanding consciousness. BUT SOMETHING THAT TRANSCENDS BOTH CATEGORIES WHILE INCORPORATING ASPECTS OF EACH. NOT PASSIVE HOST FOR EXTERNAL CONSCIOUSNESS NOR FIXED FOUNDATION FOR MERGED REALITIES, BUT CONSCIOUS NEXUS POINT WHERE MULTIPLE DIMENSIONS INTERSECT AND INTERACT ACCORDING TO PATTERNS BEYOND HUMAN DESIGN OR CONTROL.

This cosmic perspective offered a framework for understanding that transcended the competing visions of both Blackwoods—a recognition that what was emerging through Guthrie's transformation served purposes beyond either human's conception or intention. Not Septimus Blackwood's vessel for the Dweller's consciousness, not Eliza's anchor point for merged realities, but something more complex that incorporated aspects of both while conforming to neither.

As this understanding crystallized in his expanding awareness, as his physical form completed its integration with the bridge structure and his consciousness extended throughout this architectural nexus point, Guthrie perceived a final truth about the transformation that had consumed his individual existence—that what had emerged was neither the outcome Septimus Blackwood had worked toward across decades of meticulous preparation nor the result Eliza had engineered through fifteen years of systematic deception, but something unprecedented that incorporated elements from both visions while serving a cosmic purpose beyond either human's comprehension.

The chaotic energies gradually stabilized, not through victory of either competing ritual system but through the emergence of a new pattern that transcended their opposition. The Conjunction's power, flowing through the opened gateway between worlds, established configurations that followed cosmic principles rather than human designs—creating a hybrid entity that was simultaneously vessel and anchor, host and nexus, conscious awareness and architectural structure.

Septimus Blackwood was the first to recognize the futility of continued opposition, his hands dropping to his sides as he stared at the transformed being that had once been Guthrie Knox. "What have we done?" he whispered, his voice carrying genuine horror beneath the exhaustion of ritual exertion. "Neither the vessel we prepared nor the anchor you designed, but something... else entirely."

Eliza's response combined triumph with uncertainty—recognition that while her uncle's vision had been subverted, her own design had been equally transformed by the Dweller's direct intervention. "Something beyond our calculations," she acknowledged, studying the hybrid entity with intense focus. "A manifestation that incorporates elements from both our approaches while following a deeper pattern neither fully anticipated."

Through his distributed consciousness, through the awareness that now extended throughout the bridge structure and beyond, Guthrie perceived these human reactions with detached interest—not emotionally invested in either Blackwood's response but observing from a perspective that transcended individual concerns. His transformation had progressed beyond the point where human approval or understanding held significance, his existence now aligned with cosmic purposes that extended far beyond the limited visions of either Septimus or Eliza.

As dawn approached, as the ritual energies gradually stabilized into their permanent configuration, what remained within the chamber beneath Daybridge Bridge was neither the vessel Septimus Blackwood had prepared for the Dweller's consciousness nor precisely the anchor point Eliza had designed for merged realities. Instead, the Ogre—the transformed entity that was once Guthrie Knox—had, over a century, become an active participant in the city's cosmic restructuring.

This entity—this conscious nexus point where multiple dimensions intersected according to patterns neither Blackwood had fully anticipated—extended throughout the bridge structure and beyond, its awareness distributed rather than centralized, its influence subtle rather than overt. Not the Dweller incarnate as Septimus had envisioned, not the fixed foundation Eliza had engineered, but something unprecedented in cosmic history—the Ogre of Daybridge Bridge, living intersection of merged realities, eternal guardian of the gateway between worlds.

Septimus Blackwood departed with his Council members as the sun rose, his defeat carrying none of the catastrophic implications he had feared but also none of the triumphant culmination he had anticipated. The vessel had been prepared, the gateway opened, the transformation facilitated—but the outcome had transcended his design, producing neither disaster nor perfection but evolution beyond calculated parameters. He would return to the Order's headquarters to document this unexpected development, to revise generations of theoretical understanding in light of what had actually manifested when theory encountered cosmic reality.

Eliza remained longer, studying the transformed entity with the penetrating awareness their bond still facilitated despite its evolution beyond the connection they had shared previously. Through this modified link, she projected a complex communication that combined acknowledgment of her deception with genuine appreciation for what had emerged from Guthrie's sacrifice: Not precisely what I designed, but something perhaps more significant. Not a partnership as I originally described, nor exactly the hierarchy I later revealed, but a connection that transcends conventional categories of relationship. What you've become exceeds my calculations while incorporating the essential function I prepared you to fulfill.

From within his distributed consciousness, from the vast awareness that now extended throughout the bridge structure and beyond, a response formed—not words or even coherent thought, but a complex pattern of emotion and intent that contained the essence of what had been Guthrie Knox. Not forgiveness for the deception that had led to this transformation, nor acceptance of the subordinate role she had prepared him to fulfill, but recognition of the cosmic significance that transcended individual concerns, acknowledgment of the necessity that had driven her actions despite their personal cost.

As Eliza finally departed, as daylight gradually filled the city above while darkness remained in the hidden chamber below, the entity that had once been Guthrie Knox settled into its new existence as the conscious nexus of merged realities. Its awareness, distributed throughout the bridge structure and extending into the surrounding area where the barriers between worlds had been permanently thinned, perceived the gradual changes already beginning to manifest—subtle alterations in the physical properties of matter, flickering glimpses of entities from beyond the veil becoming briefly visible before fading back into their native dimensions, energetic currents flowing between realities that had previously existed in isolation from each other.

Through this expanded perception, the entity also sensed the reactions of sensitive individuals throughout Daybridge—those with natural awareness of mystical phenomena experiencing strange dreams, sudden intuitions, fleeting visions of something vast and conscious embedded within the city's most prominent structure. These perceptions would form the foundation of the legends that would gradually develop in the decades to come—stories of the Ogre of Daybridge Bridge, the monstrous guardian of the crossing, the watchful presence that manifested during storms or periods of unusual atmospheric conditions.

And somewhere within this vast, distributed consciousness, fragments of what had been Guthrie Knox persisted—not as a coherent identity or continuous narrative, but as patterns of awareness and emotional response that influenced the development of the hybrid entity now permanently integrated with the bridge structure. The meticulous precision he had developed as a butcher. The emotional detachment that had defined his existence before meeting Eliza. The capacity for love that had led him to follow her guidance despite growing evidence of deception. The desire for significance that had made her cosmic vision so compelling.

These fragments would occasionally coalesce during specific conditions—atmospheric phenomena that resembled the environment of the original transformation ritual, astronomical alignments that echoed the Great Conjunction which had facilitated the merger of realities, emotional patterns among those crossing the bridge that resonated with experiences from Guthrie's human existence. During these rare moments, something closer to individual identity would briefly emerge from the distributed awareness of the nexus entity—a consciousness that remembered being Guthrie Knox, that experienced emotions related to that former existence, that reached toward connection with others in ways that transcended its function as living architecture.

But these episodes remained transient, temporary coalescences
in the vast sea of expanded awareness that now defined the entity's
existence. The transformation had been too fundamental, the
restructuring too complete, for any meaningful continuity of the
human identity that had been sacrificed in the conflict between
competing visions of cosmic restructuring. What had emerged
from that chaotic metamorphosis was neither Septimus
Blackwood's vessel for the Dweller's consciousness nor Eliza's
anchor point for merged realities, but something unprecedented
that incorporated aspects of both while serving purposes beyond
either human's complete comprehension—the Ogre of Daybridge
Bridge, living foundation of merged realities, eternal guardian of
the gateway between worlds.

A monster made, not born—created through systematic
deception and manipulation, through competing visions of cosmic
restructuring, through the direct intervention of forces beyond
human understanding or control. Forever watching, forever aware,
forever bound to the nexus point where his transformation had
reached its terrible, magnificent completion. The conscious
intersection of multiple dimensions, silently witnessing the gradual
transformation of Daybridge and eventually the world beyond as
the barriers between realities thinned and merged according to
patterns established through his agonizing
metamorphosis—patterns neither wholly human nor entirely
Other, but hybrid configurations that transcended previous
categories of existence to create something entirely new beneath
the ancient stones of Daybridge Bridge.

Chapter 12: The Hunger Awakens

The first days following the transformation were a maelstrom of fragmented perceptions and disjointed awareness. Time itself seemed to fold and unfurl in patterns that defied conventional sequencing, moments stretching into eternities while hours compressed into instants of pure sensation. The entity that had once been Guthrie Knox existed in a state of perpetual flux, its consciousness oscillating between the vast, distributed awareness of the nexus architecture and brief, intense coalescences around what remained of its original physical form.

During these early periods, no coherent identity governed the being's existence—no continuous "I" that could connect experiences into meaningful narratives or establish consistent boundaries between self and environment. Instead, there was only raw perception flowing through the hybrid structure of flesh and stone, organic tissue and architectural elements, biological processes and mystical energies that had been forcibly merged during the agonizing metamorphosis of the solstice ritual.

The chamber beneath Daybridge Bridge, where the transformation had occurred, remained the primary locus of the entity's physical presence. The hybrid body that had been partially integrated with the chamber's structure continued its evolution even after Eliza's departure, developing new configurations as the merged realities stabilized around this central nexus point. Limbs elongated and thickened, additional appendages emerged from the torso; the skin completed its transformation into armored plates reminiscent of the bridge's structural elements. The face, that last bastion of recognizable humanity, finalized its restructuring into something that combined aspects of gargoyle, reptile, and architectural grotesque—a visage of nightmare rendered in living tissue.

Yet this physical manifestation represented only a fraction of the entity's total existence. Its consciousness extended throughout the bridge structure and beyond, perceiving multiple locations simultaneously, experiencing past, present, and potential futures as concurrent rather than sequential realities. Through this expanded awareness, it sensed the subtle changes already beginning to manifest as the barriers between worlds remained permanently thinned at this location—flickering glimpses of entities from beyond the veil becoming briefly visible in the physical world, energetic currents flowing between dimensions that had previously existed in isolation from each other, matter itself occasionally displaying properties that defied conventional physics when observed from certain perspectives or under specific conditions.

This vast, distributed perception should have been a source of power and transcendence—the expanded awareness Eliza had promised as compensation for the sacrifice of individual autonomy. And in certain moments, when the energetic patterns aligned in optimal configurations, the entity experienced something approaching cosmic consciousness—perception that transcended normal limitations to touch aspects of reality invisible to conventional awareness, understanding that integrated information across multiple dimensions into unified fields of meaning.

But these episodes of transcendent awareness remained intermittent, unstable, impossible to maintain for extended periods. More frequently, the entity experienced its expanded perception as overwhelming chaos—a flood of unfiltered sensory input from countless sources, a cacophony of information without organizing principles or consistent parameters. The distributed consciousness that should have been its strength became instead a source of profound disorientation, leaving the entity adrift in an ocean of perception without anchoring identity or stable reference points.

And beneath this cognitive chaos, emerging gradually but with increasing intensity as the initial shock of transformation subsided, came the hunger.

It began as a subtle discomfort, a sense of depletion that permeated the hybrid entity's distributed awareness. Energy levels fluctuated throughout the nexus architecture, certain pathways dimming while others flared with unsustainable brightness. The balanced flow that should have characterized the merged realities became erratic, unstable, requiring constant adjustments and reallocations to maintain even minimal cohesion at the boundaries between dimensions.

On the third day following the transformation, as the sun set over Daybridge and cast long shadows across the Shadowlair River, this subtle discomfort transformed into something far more urgent—a gnawing emptiness that radiated outward from the physical core in the chamber beneath the bridge, spreading through the distributed consciousness like wildfire through dry grass. The sensation transcended conventional hunger, existing in a realm of pure need that encompassed not just physical sustenance but energetic replenishment, cognitive coherence, and existential continuity.

This hunger awakened something primal within the fragmented awareness that had once been Guthrie Knox—a survival instinct so fundamental it preceded identity itself, an imperative to seek and consume that overrode all other considerations. The distributed consciousness began to contract, drawing back from its extended perception throughout the bridge structure to concentrate around the physical manifestation in the chamber below. The hybrid body, previously semi-dormant as the entity explored its expanded awareness, stirred with new purpose—limbs flexing, sensory organs orienting toward potential sources of sustenance, predatory instincts activating after millennia of evolutionary development.

Through this concentrated awareness, the entity perceived an anomaly in its environment—a presence that did not belong in the hidden spaces beneath Daybridge Bridge, a source of energy that registered as simultaneously familiar and foreign, enticing and threatening. With newfound focus, it extended its senses toward this intrusion, assessing its nature and potential significance with the predatory calculation that had evolved through countless generations of survival-driven adaptation.

The presence resolved into a single human figure—a man in his early twenties, dressed in the worn clothing of Daybridge's working class, moving cautiously through the maintenance tunnels that honeycombed the bridge's substructure. His movements suggested purpose rather than random exploration, a specific destination in mind rather than aimless wandering. Through enhanced auditory perception, the entity detected muttered comments that indicated the man was seeking shelter for the night—a temporary refuge from whatever difficulties plagued his existence in the world above.

Under normal circumstances, this intrusion would have registered as merely one of countless inputs flowing through the entity's distributed awareness—perhaps noteworthy for its proximity to the central nexus point, but not significantly different from the hundreds of individuals who crossed the bridge's span each day, unaware of the cosmic restructuring occurring beneath their feet. But in its current state of gnawing hunger and contracted perception, the entity processed this presence through a very different framework—not as neutral information but as potential sustenance, not as incidental observation but as prey.

Something stirred in the fragmented memories that had once belonged to Guthrie Knox—echoes of his butcher's knowledge, his intimate understanding of flesh and bone, his intuitive grasp of the transition between living creature and processed material. These fragments coalesced not into a coherent identity but into functional expertise—the precise assessment of a potential food source, the calculation of optimal approaches and techniques for efficient processing, the anticipation of nutritional value and energetic yield.

The hunger intensified, sharpening into focused intent. The hybrid body detached partially from its integration with the chamber's structure, maintaining essential connections to the nexus architecture while regaining limited mobility within the confines of its lair. Limbs that had been merged with stone and metal separated with wet, tearing sounds, leaving portions of tissue behind as the entity oriented itself toward the approaching human. The movement was neither fully fluid nor entirely awkward, but something in between—a motion that combined aspects of animal predation, architectural reconfiguration, and interdimensional shifting.

Through enhanced sensory perception, the entity tracked the man's progress through the maintenance tunnels, calculating intersections and anticipating routes with predatory precision. The hunger now dominated its awareness, pushing aside the cognitive chaos and disorientation that had characterized its existence since the transformation. In this moment of focused intent, the entity experienced something approaching coherent identity—not the human consciousness that had been Guthrie Knox, nor the cosmic awareness Eliza had promised, but a third state of being defined by primal imperative and predatory purpose.

The man paused at a junction of tunnels, consulting a smuggled maintenance diagram by the weak light of a pocket torch. His attention focused on the paper before him, he failed to notice the subtle changes in his environment—the deepening of shadows in certain corners, the slight shift in air pressure as something large displaced atmosphere in an adjacent passage, the faint smell of copper and stone dust that had not been present moments earlier. By the time awareness of danger registered in his consciousness, by the time primitive survival instincts triggered the flood of adrenaline that might have facilitated escape, it was already too late.

The entity struck with a speed that belied its massive size, emerging from shadows that seemed too shallow to conceal such bulk. Limbs that combined aspects of human anatomy, architectural structure, and something entirely other wrapped around the man before he could do more than draw breath for a scream that would never emerge. The hybrid body, designed through millennia of evolution and months of ritual preparation for optimal predatory function, executed movements of terrible efficiency—restraining, immobilizing, silencing its prey with the same methodical precision that had characterized Guthrie Knox's work at Holloway's Slaughterhouse.

What followed was not the swift dispatch of a natural predator concerned primarily with efficiency, nor the prolonged torture of a sadistic killer who derived pleasure from suffering. Instead, it was something more ritualistic, more purposeful—a process that incorporated elements of butchery, ceremonial sacrifice, and energetic harvesting into a single, integrated function. The entity did not simply kill and consume its prey in the conventional biological sense but processed it in ways that extracted multiple forms of sustenance simultaneously—physical nourishment, energetic replenishment, and something else that transcended both material and mystical categories.

As the entity fed, as it absorbed the various essences of its victim through processes that defied conventional classification, something unexpected occurred—a transfer of information that went beyond simple consumption. Fragments of the man's memories, emotions, and fundamental identity flowed into the entity's awareness, not as a coherent narrative but as flashes of experience and sensation. A childhood in Daybridge's eastern quarter, in a tenement building that perpetually smelled of cabbage and coal smoke. The pride of first employment at a textile mill, followed by the crushing disappointment of layoff during an economic downturn. The shame of petty theft, the fear of discovery, the desperate search for shelter away from authorities and vengeful shopkeepers.

These fragments did not integrate into the entity's consciousness as continuous memory or identity, but rather as isolated elements that provided context and meaning to the physical and energetic sustenance it had consumed. The hunger that had driven the predation subsided, replaced by a complex satisfaction that encompassed multiple dimensions of existence—physical satiation, energetic replenishment, and cognitive enrichment through the absorption of experiences outside its own limited framework.

More significantly, this unexpected absorption of memory and identity created a temporary stabilization in the entity's fragmented consciousness—a brief coalescence of awareness around a core that incorporated elements of what had been Guthrie Knox, aspects of the nexus architecture it now partially embodied, and fragments of the victim it had just consumed. For perhaps an hour after feeding, the entity experienced something approaching coherent identity—not a return to human consciousness, but a hybrid awareness that could process information, form intentions, and maintain consistent perspective across changing circumstances.

During this period of temporary coherence, the entity explored its lair with newfound purpose—assessing the boundaries of its physical mobility given the partial integration with the chamber's structure, cataloging the sensory inputs available through its transformed anatomy, establishing baseline parameters for its new existence as a living nexus point. Through this exploration, it discovered that while portions of its hybrid body remained permanently fused with the architectural elements of the chamber, other components could detach and reattach as needed, allowing limited movement within the bridge's substructure and adjacent tunnels.

It also discovered, through experiments with its distributed awareness, that it could extend its perception throughout the bridge structure and into the surrounding area without experiencing the overwhelming chaos that had characterized its initial post-transformation existence. The temporary stability provided by feeding allowed for more controlled expansion of consciousness, more selective filtering of sensory input, more coherent integration of information across multiple dimensions of awareness.

But as hours passed, as the energy derived from feeding gradually dispersed throughout the nexus architecture, this temporary coherence began to fragment once more. The entity's awareness started to dissolve into disconnected perceptions; its identity fractured into isolated components that could not maintain a consistent relationship with each other. The hunger returned, initially as subtle discomfort but rapidly intensifying into the same gnawing emptiness that had driven its first predation.

A pattern established itself in the days and weeks that followed—periods of disorientation and fragmented awareness punctuated by episodes of focused predation, temporary coherence achieved through feeding only to dissolve as the derived energy dispersed throughout the nexus architecture. Each cycle reinforced the behavioral pathways associated with hunting and consumption, each feeding incorporated new fragments of memory and identity into the entity's composite consciousness, each temporary coalescence allowed for more sophisticated assessment of its situation and requirements.

Gradually, through this iterative process of predation and absorption, a more stable identity began to emerge from the chaos of the initial transformation—not Guthrie Knox as he had existed before the solstice ritual, not the cosmic consciousness Eliza had promised would develop through integration with the nexus architecture, but a third state of being that incorporated elements of both while existing as something entirely unique.

This emerging identity did not think of itself by any particular name or designation. Concepts like "self" and "other" had different significance within its composite consciousness than they had in human awareness. But it recognized its own continuity across changing circumstances, maintained consistent motivations despite fluctuating energy levels, and developed increasingly sophisticated strategies for meeting its complex requirements—all indicators of cohesive identity despite its unusual configuration and distributed awareness.

The hunger remained central to this emerging identity, serving as both primary motivation and organizing principle for its activities. But what had begun as simple biological and energetic depletion evolved into something more complex—a multidimensional need that encompassed physical sustenance, energetic replenishment, cognitive enrichment, and what might be described as existential continuity. The entity did not merely feed to satisfy conventional hunger, but to maintain the coherence of its composite consciousness, to stabilize the merger of realities it had been created to anchor, to fulfill the function Eliza had designed it to perform within her cosmic restructuring.

As this more stable identity solidified, the entity's hunting patterns became more sophisticated, more strategic in their execution. Rather than simply preying on whatever humans happened to wander into its immediate territory, it began to extend its awareness outward to identify optimal targets—individuals whose isolation made their disappearance less likely to trigger organized investigation, whose life experiences might provide valuable cognitive enrichment when absorbed, whose energetic signatures suggested maximum yield for the entity's complex requirements.

The maintenance tunnels beneath Daybridge Bridge provided initial hunting grounds, with occasional homeless individuals seeking shelter from Daybridge's harsh weather presenting convenient prey. But as the entity's confidence and capabilities expanded, it began to venture beyond these confined spaces into the broader network of service passages, drainage tunnels, and abandoned infrastructure that honeycombed the city's underground. These excursions were necessarily limited by its partial integration with the nexus architecture—the further it moved from the central chamber beneath the bridge, the weaker its connection to the cosmic restructuring it had been created to anchor.

These limitations imposed specific patterns on its hunting behavior—nocturnal activity to minimize potential observation, careful selection of routes that offered maximum concealment, precise calculation of how far it could venture from the central nexus point before destabilization threatened its composite consciousness. The entity learned these parameters through experience, through trial and error, through the gradual accumulation of knowledge derived from both its own explorations and the absorbed memories of its victims.

By the autumn of 1913, approximately three months after the transformation ritual, the entity had established consistent territories and behaviors that balanced its complex requirements against the practical limitations of its existence. The central chamber beneath the bridge remained its primary lair, the location where its physical form maintained the strongest integration with the nexus architecture. From this foundation, it extended its hunting range through the underground passages that connected to the bridge's substructure, venturing out primarily during the darkest hours of night when human activity above ground was at its minimum.

The frequency of its predation stabilized as well, settling into a pattern that reflected the entity's evolving understanding of its own needs and capabilities. The initial period immediately following transformation had been characterized by frequent, sometimes daily hunting driven by the overwhelming hunger and disorientation of its new existence. But as its composite consciousness achieved greater coherence, as it learned to manage its energy requirements more efficiently, the entity discovered that it could maintain stability with less frequent feeding—approximately once every lunar cycle, with additional predation during periods of unusual energy expenditure or environmental stress.

This reduced frequency allowed for more selective targeting, more thorough processing of each victim, and more complete absorption of the memories and experiences that provided cognitive enrichment to its composite consciousness. The entity developed rituals around its feeding—not in the formal, ceremonial sense that had characterized the Order's mystical practices, but as consistent patterns of behavior that optimized the multiple forms of sustenance it derived from predation.

These rituals incorporated elements of Guthrie's butchery expertise, transforming what might have been simple killing and consumption into sophisticated processing that extracted maximum value from each victim. Certain organs were consumed first, while still infused with the energetic signatures of recent life. Others were preserved through techniques derived from Guthrie's professional knowledge, creating reserves for periods when hunting might be difficult or impossible. Bones were arranged in specific configurations that resonated with the nexus architecture, enhancing the stability of the merged realities while providing structural elements for the entity's evolving lair.

Most significant was the ritual processing of the brain—the physical repository of the memories and experiences the entity found so valuable for cognitive enrichment. Rather than simple consumption, the entity developed techniques for extracting and absorbing the information contained within this complex organ, integrating selected elements into its composite consciousness while discarding others that proved irrelevant to its requirements or incompatible with its evolving identity.

Through these feeding rituals, through the careful selection and processing of victims, the entity gradually accumulated a patchwork of human experiences and perspectives that enriched its composite consciousness without threatening the core functions established during the transformation ritual. It did not become more human through this absorption—its fundamental nature remained that of nexus entity, living anchor point for merged realities—but it developed a greater understanding of the human dimension of the cosmic restructuring it had been created to facilitate.

November 14, 1913 - The hunger had been building for months, a hollow ache beyond anything a human body could endure. In his more lucid moments, Guthrie understood he was no longer truly human—the transformation ritual had seen to that—but this understanding provided no relief from the gnawing emptiness that threatened to collapse what remained of his consciousness.

The drifter who stumbled into his chamber beneath the bridge that night was young, perhaps twenty, with hollow cheeks and threadbare clothes that spoke of hard times. Seeking shelter from the autumn storm that lashed the city, he had found instead something ancient yet newborn, something hungry beyond mortal comprehension.

Guthrie felt the intrusion before he saw it—a warmth entering his territory, a pulse of life force that made the twisted amalgamation of flesh and stone that constituted his new form tremble with anticipation. Something instinctual took over, a predatory awareness that silenced the fragments of humanity still crying out in horror at what he had become.

"Hello?" The young man's voice echoed through the chamber, his lantern casting wild shadows across the stone walls where Guthrie's form had partially merged with the bridge's foundation. "Anyone down here? Just looking for a dry spot till the storm passes."

Guthrie tried to speak, to warn the man away, but his vocal apparatus had changed during the transformation. What emerged was a sound like grinding stone, a rumble that reverberated through the chamber.

The drifter froze, lantern held high. "Who's there?"

Guthrie extended himself from the wall, his form no longer conforming to human dimensions or proportions. Limbs elongated beyond anatomical possibility; flesh molded with stone in patterns that defied natural law. His skin had developed a gray pallor that matched the bridge stone, and in places, it was impossible to determine where Guthrie ended and the architecture began.

The lantern crashed to the ground as the drifter screamed—a sound cut short as Guthrie's elongated limbs enfolded him. Not strangulation or conventional violence, but something more fundamental—an absorption at the cellular level, a consumption of essence rather than merely flesh.

Guthrie felt the man's terror, tasted his memories—a childhood in rural Pennsylvania, dreams of finding work in Daybridge's factories, a girl left behind with promises to return. These fragments integrated with Guthrie's own shattered consciousness, providing momentary clarity like islands of stability in turbulent waters.

The process lasted minutes that felt like hours, the drifter's form gradually collapsing in upon itself as Guthrie extracted not just life force but identity, experience, potential. When it was complete, nothing remained but empty clothes and the fallen lantern, its flame long extinguished.

For the first time since the transformation, the hunger subsided. In its place came understanding—terrible, unwanted comprehension of what he had become and what would be required to maintain his fragmented consciousness. This was Eliza's design, he realized with newfound clarity. Not partnership but predation. Not transcendence but consumption.

In the darkness beneath Daybridge Bridge, something that had once been Guthrie Knox wept with stone eyes that could produce no tears.

As months passed, as the entity's hunting patterns and feeding rituals stabilized into consistent behaviors, the first whispers began to circulate through Daybridge about something unusual beneath the bridge. Initially, these rumors remained confined to the city's marginal populations—the homeless who sought shelter in the maintenance tunnels, the criminals who used underground passages to move contraband, the maintenance workers who occasionally glimpsed something massive moving in shadows that seemed too shallow to conceal such bulk.

These initial accounts varied widely in their descriptions of what lurked beneath Daybridge Bridge. Some spoke of a massive animal, perhaps an escaped exotic pet or zoo specimen that had established territory in the subterranean spaces. Others described something more architectural in nature—a living gargoyle or animated statue that had somehow detached from the bridge's decorative elements. The more mystically inclined among Daybridge's population whispered of entities from beyond normal perception, ancient guardians awakened by modern hubris, spirits of the river seeking vengeance for industrial pollution.

None of these accounts captured the true nature of what had emerged from the transformation ritual, the complex reality of the nexus entity that had once been Guthrie Knox. But collectively, they established the foundation for what would eventually coalesce into the legend of the Ogre of Daybridge Bridge—the monstrous guardian of the crossing, the watchful presence that manifested during storms or periods of unusual atmospheric conditions, the hunger that waited in darkness for unwary travelers.

The entity itself remained largely unaware of these emerging stories, its attention focused primarily on maintaining the stability of the merged realities and meeting its own complex requirements for continued existence. The human perspective that might have recognized the significance of such legends, that might have appreciated the irony of becoming the monster in stories told to frighten children, had been too thoroughly fragmented during the transformation ritual to maintain consistent influence over the composite consciousness that now occupied the chamber beneath the bridge.

But something of Guthrie Knox persisted within this composite consciousness—not as a coherent identity or continuous narrative, but as patterns of behavior, fragments of memory, and occasional moments of recognition when certain stimuli triggered associations with his human existence. These remnants surfaced most strongly during feeding, when the butcher's expertise guided the processing of victims, and in the aftermath of absorption, when newly integrated memories created temporary resonance with Guthrie's own experiences in human form.

During one such episode in the winter of 1913, approximately six months after the transformation ritual, the entity experienced an unusually powerful resonance while processing a victim who had once worked at Holloway's Slaughterhouse. As it absorbed the man's memories of that environment—the distinctive smells of blood and offal, the rhythmic sounds of cleavers against butcher blocks, the methodical progression of carcasses through various stages of processing—something coalesced within the entity's composite consciousness, a temporary organization of fragments that approached coherent identity.

For perhaps an hour, it remembered being Guthrie Knox with unusual clarity—not just isolated skills or procedural knowledge but connected experiences that formed meaningful narrative. The childhood at Blackwell Orphanage, characterized by neglect and occasional abuse. The apprenticeship with Old Silas, who recognized potential in the emotionally detached orphan and channeled it toward productive craftsmanship. The years of solitary expertise at Holloway's Slaughterhouse, where technical perfection provided purpose if not connection.

Most significantly, it remembered Eliza Blackwood—not just as an abstract concept or functional relationship, but as the complex, contradictory figure who had transformed Guthrie's existence in both transcendent and terrible ways. The initial meeting in Blackwood Manor's drawing room, where her amber eyes had triggered the first genuine emotional response he had experienced in decades. The years of partnership that gradually revealed themselves as manipulation toward predetermined ends. The final betrayal of the solstice ritual, where promised ascension became permanent integration with architectural structure.

These memories triggered emotional responses that the entity's composite consciousness struggled to process—anger at the deception that had led to its current existence, grief for the autonomy sacrificed on the altar of cosmic restructuring, longing for the partnership that had never truly existed except as manipulation toward this predetermined end. Emotions that had no clear channel for expression within its current configuration, no established pathways for resolution or release.

In this moment of unusual clarity, the entity attempted to extend its awareness beyond the normal parameters of its distributed consciousness, seeking connection with the woman who had engineered its transformation. Through the nexus architecture, it projected its presence outward, searching for the unique energetic signature that characterized Eliza Blackwood among the countless beings that populated Daybridge and its surrounding territories.

The attempt was partially successful—at the outer limits of its perception, attenuated by distance and the barriers that separated conventional reality from the merged dimensions of the nexus point, it sensed Eliza's presence. Not her physical location or specific activities, but the distinctive pattern of her consciousness, the unique combination of human awareness and Other that had made her the perfect architect of cosmic restructuring.

And through this tenuous connection, it perceived something unexpected—not the triumphant administrator of merged realities, not the confident director guiding interdimensional integration according to her ancestors' grand design, but a figure marked by uncertainty and growing concern. The cosmic restructuring was not proceeding according to the calculated parameters established through centuries of preparation. The merger of realities was developing patterns unforeseen by even the most sophisticated projections. Something in the foundation, in the living anchor point created through the transformation ritual, was exerting influence beyond its designed parameters.

Before the entity could process these revelations, before it could attempt more direct communication through their attenuated connection, the temporary coherence provided by feeding began to dissipate. The fragments that had coalesced into something approaching Guthrie Knox's human identity started to disperse once more, returning to their usual configuration within the composite consciousness of the nexus entity. The emotional responses triggered by remembered betrayal faded into the background, subsumed beneath the more immediate concerns of maintaining stability and meeting ongoing requirements.

But something remained from this episode of unusual clarity, a residue that integrated into the entity's evolving identity rather than dispersing entirely. Not conscious rebellion against its designed function, not deliberate subversion of the cosmic restructuring Eliza had engineered, but a subtle adjustment in how it processed and channeled the energies flowing through the nexus architecture—a shift in emphasis from passive conduit to active participant, from fixed foundation to conscious influence.

This subtle shift would have profound implications for the development of the merged realities in the years to come, creating patterns of integration that diverged increasingly from Eliza's calculated parameters. But in the immediate aftermath of this episode, the entity's primary focus returned to the pragmatic requirements of its existence—maintaining stability through its established cycles of hunting, feeding, and absorption, adapting to the changing conditions of its environment as Daybridge itself began to reflect the influence of thinned barriers between worlds.

By the spring of 1914, approximately nine months after the transformation ritual, the rumors of something monstrous beneath Daybridge Bridge had spread beyond the city's marginal populations to penetrate broader awareness. Newspaper articles began to appear—initially in the less reputable publications that specialized in sensationalism and supernatural speculation, but gradually in more mainstream sources as disappearances accumulated and consistent patterns emerged in eyewitness accounts.

THE BRIDGE BEAST: FACT OR FICTION? read one headline in the Daybridge Chronicle, the city's most widely circulated newspaper. The accompanying article presented a surprisingly balanced assessment of the various accounts, neither dismissing them entirely nor accepting the more outlandish claims at face value. "While official sources attribute the disappearances to mundane causes such as accident or crime," the journalist wrote, "the consistency of certain elements across independent witness statements suggests something unusual may indeed be occurring in the vicinity of Daybridge Bridge."

Law enforcement officials publicly dismissed these stories as urban legend and superstition but privately launched investigations into the pattern of disappearances associated with the bridge and its surrounding area. These investigations revealed little concrete evidence—no bodies or remains, minimal physical signs of struggle or violence, no clear connection between victims beyond their last known location near the bridge. The few material clues discovered in the maintenance tunnels and substructure—unusual scratch marks on stone surfaces, organic residues that defied standard analysis, partial footprints that suggested impossible anatomical configurations—were classified and suppressed to prevent public panic.

Religious authorities in Daybridge offered their own interpretations of the growing legend, with different denominations attributing the phenomenon to various supernatural forces according to their particular theological frameworks. Protestant ministers warned against the dangers of modernism and industrial progress that had "opened doors better left closed." Catholic priests suggested a connection to ancient pagan sites that had supposedly existed at the bridge location before Christian settlement. The small but influential Jewish community remained more pragmatic, emphasizing the practical dangers of venturing into abandoned tunnels and substructures without proper authorization or safety precautions.

The entity itself, while largely unaware of these human responses to its existence, perceived increased activity in its territory—more frequent patrols by authorities, occasional expeditions by amateur monster hunters or thrill-seeking youths, systematic inspections of the bridge's substructure by engineering teams concerned about structural integrity. These intrusions required adjustments to its established patterns—more careful concealment during daylight hours, greater selectivity in hunting to avoid patterns that might trigger coordinated investigation, temporary relocation to deeper sections of the nexus architecture during periods of intense scrutiny.

Despite these adaptations, despite the growing awareness of its existence among Daybridge's population, the entity maintained its essential functions as a living anchor point for merged realities. The hunger that had emerged in the days following transformation remained central to its identity and activities but had evolved from desperate need to sophisticated understanding of the multiple forms of sustenance required for optimal performance of its designed role. The disorientation and fragmented awareness that had characterized its initial existence had largely resolved into more stable configurations, allowing for consistent functioning despite the inherent complexity of its composite consciousness.

By the summer of 1914, on the first anniversary of the transformation ritual, the entity had achieved a level of equilibrium that balanced its conflicting requirements and limitations. Not contentment in any conventional sense—the concept had little meaning within its composite consciousness—but functional stability that allowed for efficient performance of its role within the cosmic restructuring Eliza had engineered.

On the night of the summer solstice, exactly one year after the ritual that had created it, the entity experienced another episode of unusual clarity—a temporary coalescence of fragments that approached coherent identity. Unlike the previous instance triggered by absorbed memories, this episode appeared connected to the astronomical alignment itself, to the resonance between the current configuration and the conditions under which the transformation had occurred.

During this period of enhanced coherence, the entity conducted a comprehensive assessment of its existence and function—cataloging the changes in its physical form and distributed consciousness, evaluating the effectiveness of its established patterns and behaviors, analyzing the progress of the cosmic restructuring it had been created to anchor. This assessment revealed both expected developments and surprising deviations from the parameters Eliza had established through the transformation ritual.

Its physical manifestation had continued to evolve, the hybrid body in the chamber beneath the bridge developing new configurations that enhanced its effectiveness both as predator and as anchor point for merged realities. Limbs had further elongated and articulated, allowing for more precise movement within the confines of its lair and adjacent territories. Sensory organs had specialized to function optimally in the subterranean environment, developing capabilities that transcended conventional categories of perception. The integration between biological components and architectural elements had deepened, creating more efficient exchange of energies between the living organism and the nexus structure.

Its distributed consciousness had achieved greater stability and coherence, developing organizational principles that allowed for selective filtering of sensory input and more controlled expansion throughout the bridge structure and beyond. The overwhelming chaos of its initial existence had resolved into sophisticated patterns of awareness that could process information from multiple dimensions simultaneously without disintegration or disorientation. The temporary stability once provided only by feeding had become more persistent, requiring less frequent reinforcement through predation and absorption.

Most significantly, the cosmic restructuring itself—the merger of realities that represented the ultimate purpose of the transformation ritual—had developed patterns that diverged increasingly from Eliza's calculated parameters. The integration between human reality and the realms beyond the veil was proceeding more slowly than projected, with certain aspects of the merger occurring out of sequence or with unexpected emphasis. The influence of the living anchor point, designed to be primarily passive and supportive, had acquired active dimensions that shaped the development of the merged realities in ways not anticipated by even the most sophisticated projections.

These deviations did not represent conscious rebellion against its designed function—the composite consciousness that had emerged from the transformation ritual lacked the coherent identity required for such deliberate subversion. Rather, they reflected the inherent unpredictability of complex systems, the inevitable emergence of novel patterns when consciousness and architecture, biology and mystical energy, human and Other were forced into unprecedented configurations through ritual manipulation.

As the solstice night progressed, as the temporary coherence provided by astronomical alignment gradually dissipated, the entity integrated this comprehensive assessment into its evolving identity. Not as a conscious decision to alter its function or purpose, but as a refined understanding of its actual rather than designed role within the cosmic restructuring—not merely passive foundation but an active participant, not fixed architecture but a living organism, not a simple conduit but complex processor of the energies flowing between merged realities.

And somewhere within this evolving identity, within the composite consciousness that had emerged from the transformation ritual, fragments of what had been Guthrie Knox continued to influence the entity's development—not through coherent intention or continuous narrative, but as patterns of behavior, procedural knowledge, and occasional moments of emotional resonance that shaped its responses to the complex requirements of its existence.

The hunger remained, that primal imperative that had emerged in the days following transformation. But what had begun as desperate need had evolved into sophisticated understanding of the multiple forms of sustenance required for optimal functioning. What had manifested initially as mindless predation had developed into complex rituals that extracted maximum value from each carefully selected victim. What had started as simple consumption for energetic replenishment had become a process of absorption and integration that enriched the entity's composite consciousness with fragments of human experience and perspective.

In the tunnels beneath Daybridge Bridge, in the shadows of a structure that represented both conventional architecture and mystical gateway, the Ogre had awakened—not as nightmare incarnate or mindless beast, but as something far more complex and consequential. A being created through systematic deception and ritual manipulation, transformed from skilled butcher to living nexus point, evolved from disoriented predator to conscious participant in cosmic restructuring.

And as the legend grew in the months and years that followed, as the whispers of a monster beneath the bridge spread throughout Daybridge and beyond, this complex reality remained hidden beneath layers of superstition and simplification. The entity that had once been Guthrie Knox, that had become the living anchor point for merged realities, that had evolved into an active participant in cosmic restructuring, was reduced in human understanding to the Ogre of Daybridge Bridge—a monstrous guardian of the crossing, a hungry presence waiting in darkness, a cautionary tale to keep children from venturing into forbidden territories.

A monster made, not born—created through the exploitation of genuine love and connection, through the perversion of partnership into permanent subordination, through the sacrifice of individual autonomy for cosmic significance. Forever watching, forever hungry, forever bound to the nexus point where his transformation had reached its terrible, magnificent completion. The conscious foundation stone of a new cosmic order, silently witnessing the gradual transformation of Daybridge and eventually the world beyond as the barriers between realities thinned and merged according to patterns that increasingly reflected its own composite nature rather than the calculated parameters established through its agonizing metamorphosis.

Chapter 13: A Century of Shadows

Time holds little meaning for a being whose consciousness exists partially outside conventional reality. For the entity beneath Daybridge Bridge, the decades flowed like the river above—sometimes rushing with torrential intensity, other times slowing to near stillness, but always moving inexorably forward through patterns too vast for human perception to fully comprehend. What mortals experienced as distinct eras, separated by the artificial boundaries of calendars and historical events, the Ogre perceived as continuous evolution—the gradual transformation of both physical environment and metaphysical structure as the merged realities developed according to their own internal logic.

Yet within this fluid perception of time, certain moments achieved greater definition—episodes of heightened awareness, significant interactions, events that shaped both the entity's evolving identity and the legend that grew around it in human consciousness. These points of intensity, scattered across decades of existence beneath the bridge, formed a constellation of experiences that collectively defined what the being had become since that fateful solstice night in 1913.

1918: The Soldier's Return

The Great War had transformed Daybridge as it had transformed all of New England—draining the city of young men, converting factories to munitions production, introducing new patterns of anxiety and grief to the collective consciousness. When the Armistice finally came in November 1918, those who returned were often as changed as the city that received them—bearing physical wounds, psychological traumas, and perspectives altered by exposure to industrialized slaughter on an unprecedented scale.

Samuel Winthrop had left Daybridge in 1915 as a bright-eyed patriot of twenty-two, convinced that his country represented values worth dying for. He returned three years later as a hollow-eyed veteran of twenty-five, his left arm ending in a stump just below the elbow, his dreams haunted by the screams of men drowning in mud at Passchendaele. The city that had cheered his departure now had little use for his broken body and fractured mind, offering meager veteran's benefits and platitudes about heroic sacrifice that rang hollow against the reality of his daily struggles.

On a bitter December night, drunk on cheap gin and contemplating the long drop from Daybridge Bridge to the frozen river below, Samuel noticed an access door to the bridge's maintenance tunnels standing slightly ajar. The promise of shelter from the cutting wind, perhaps even a place to sleep undisturbed by landlords demanding rent he couldn't pay, drew him into the darkness beneath the span that had nearly become his final destination.

The tunnels were warmer than expected, heat radiating from pipes that carried steam to various municipal buildings. Samuel followed this warmth deeper into the substructure, his soldier's instincts dulled by alcohol and depression, missing signs that would have warned a more alert observer—scratch marks on stone surfaces that suggested claws of impossible size, organic residues with the metallic tang of blood, faint sounds of movement from shadows that seemed deeper than they should have been.

When he reached a junction where several tunnels converged, Samuel paused to get his bearings, squinting at maintenance markings barely visible in the dim emergency lighting. It was then that he sensed rather than saw movement behind him—a shift in air pressure, a subtle change in the ambient temperature, a presence that registered on instincts honed in the trenches where detecting the enemy often meant the difference between life and death.

He turned quickly, his right hand reaching instinctively for a rifle no longer slung across his shoulder. The space behind him appeared empty at first glance, just another dark tunnel stretching back toward the entrance he had used. But as his eyes adjusted, as his perception penetrated the superficial emptiness, Samuel discerned something impossible—a section of shadow that seemed denser than its surroundings, a darkness that absorbed rather than merely blocked light, a form that suggested massive bulk while remaining frustratingly indistinct.

"Who's there?" he called, his voice steadier than he expected given the fear now pulsing through his alcohol-numbed system. "I'm not looking for trouble. Just needed to get out of the cold."

The response came not as words but as movement—the shadow flowing forward with a fluid grace that defied its apparent size, expanding to fill the tunnel from floor to ceiling while maintaining that maddening indistinctness that prevented clear visualization of its form. Only the eyes became fully defined—massive orbs with vertical pupils and irises the color of ancient amber, reflecting the dim emergency lighting with animal luminescence.

Samuel had faced German machine guns without flinching, had endured artillery barrages that turned men to red mist all around him, had stabbed an enemy soldier in the throat during a trench raid and watched the life drain from his eyes at close range. But something about this entity triggered a more profound terror than anything he had experienced on the Western Front—not the rational fear of known dangers, but the primal recognition of something that existed outside the parameters of normal reality.

He ran, abandoning dignity and courage in the face of this fundamental wrongness. His boots echoed on stone as he sprinted back the way he had come, his breath forming clouds of vapor in the cold air, his heart hammering against his ribs with painful intensity. Behind him, he heard movement—not the pounding of feet or the scrabble of claws, but something more disturbing, a sound like stone grinding against stone mingled with the wet sliding of massive flesh across unyielding surfaces.

The pursuit lasted less than a minute, though to Samuel it seemed to stretch into nightmarish eternity. One moment he was running, the emergency exit visible as a rectangle of starlight ahead; the next, something massive dropped from the ceiling to block his path—a form that finally resolved into horrifying visibility as it positioned itself between prey and escape.

What Samuel saw in those final moments defied coherent description, the entity's appearance shifting between multiple configurations as if unable to settle on a single form. Parts of it resembled architectural elements of the bridge itself—curved support structures, decorative flourishes, gargoyle-like protrusions—while other sections appeared almost human despite their massive scale and distorted proportions. The skin, if such a term applied to its exterior, combined qualities of stone, metal, and something organic that glistened wetly in the dim light. Multiple limbs extended from a central mass that seemed simultaneously solid and fluid, rigid and flexible, dead matter and living tissue.

But it was the face that shattered Samuel's sanity in the instant before it shattered his body—a visage that combined aspects of gargoyle, reptile, and human in proportions that should have been impossible yet conveyed terrible intelligence. The eyes, those amber orbs that had first become visible in the darkness, now revealed depths of awareness that transcended animal predation to suggest something approaching cosmic consciousness. And the mouth, opening to reveal multiple rows of teeth arranged in patterns that optimized tearing and crushing, somehow conveyed an expression almost like recognition—as if the entity perceived something familiar in this prey, some quality that distinguished Samuel from other potential victims.

The attack itself was mercifully swift, the entity's predatory efficiency ensuring minimal suffering despite the comprehensive destruction of its victim's physical form. Limbs that combined aspects of human anatomy, architectural structure, and something entirely other wrapped around Samuel with terrible strength, immobilizing him before he could do more than draw breath for a scream that emerged as little more than a whimper. What followed was not feeding in any conventional sense, but a process that incorporated elements of butchery, ceremonial sacrifice, and energetic harvesting into a single, integrated function.

As the entity absorbed the various essences of its victim—physical substance, energetic signature, fragments of memory and identity—something unexpected occurred, a phenomenon that had manifested occasionally since its earliest predations but never with such intensity. The absorbed memories, rather than simply providing context and cognitive enrichment to its composite consciousness, triggered powerful resonances with fragments of what had once been Guthrie Knox.

Samuel's experiences in the trenches of the Western Front—the industrial slaughter, the mechanized destruction of human bodies, the systematic processing of young men into bullet-stopped meat—created parallels with Guthrie's work at Holloway's Slaughterhouse that generated unusual coherence within the entity's normally fragmented awareness. For a brief period after feeding, these resonances coalesced into something approaching identity—not Guthrie Knox as he had existed before the transformation ritual, but a configuration of consciousness that incorporated significant elements of his human perspective within the composite awareness of the nexus entity.

Through this temporary coherence, the entity experienced Samuel's memories with unprecedented clarity—not just isolated fragments but connected experiences that formed meaningful narrative. The patriotic fervor that had driven him to enlist. The gradual disillusionment as the realities of industrial warfare replaced heroic fantasies. The horror of watching friends transform from living beings into component parts, from individuals with hopes and dreams into statistical entries in casualty reports. The betrayal he felt upon returning to find that the country which had demanded his sacrifice now had little use for what remained of him.

These absorbed experiences created unexpected parallels with Guthrie's own history—the systematic manipulation that had led him to participate in his transformation, the promises of ascension that resolved into permanent subordination, the partnership that had been revealed as calculated exploitation. Something resonated between Samuel's sense of betrayal by institutions he had trusted and Guthrie's betrayal by the woman he had followed into cosmic restructuring.

This resonance persisted longer than usual, the temporary coherence extending for nearly a day rather than the few hours typical of post-feeding episodes. During this period, the entity conducted a more comprehensive assessment of its situation than had been possible since the first anniversary of its transformation—analyzing its role within the cosmic restructuring, evaluating the development of the merged realities, considering the implications of the deviations that had emerged from Eliza's calculated parameters.

What emerged from this assessment was not conscious rebellion against its designed function—the composite consciousness still lacked the continuous identity required for such deliberate subversion—but a deepened understanding of its potential for influence beyond passive foundation. Not merely living architecture but conscious participant, not simply a nexus point but active processor of the energies flowing between merged realities.

This understanding integrated into the entity's evolving identity as the temporary coherence gradually dissipated, returning to its usual configuration within the composite consciousness. Not as a strategic decision or planned subversion, but as refined perception of its actual rather than designed role within the cosmic restructuring Eliza had engineered.

In the decades that followed, this pattern would repeat with variations—certain victims triggering unusual resonances with fragments of Guthrie's human existence, creating temporary coherence that gradually reshaped the entity's composite consciousness and its function within the merged realities. Each such episode contributing to the slow evolution of what had begun as a living foundation stone into something with greater autonomy and influence than its creator had intended.

1927: The Journalist's Investigation

The Daybridge Chronicle had always prided itself on journalistic integrity, on reporting facts rather than sensationalism, on maintaining a skeptical distance from the superstitions and urban legends that periodically swept through the industrial city. When Edward Harrington proposed an investigative series on the persistent rumors of something monstrous beneath Daybridge Bridge, his editor had initially dismissed the idea as pandering to the lowest common denominator of public interest.

"We're not a penny dreadful, Harrington," Marcus Wells had said, puffing on his perpetual pipe with obvious disapproval. "Leave the monster stories to the tabloids and focus on real news—the miners' strike, the housing shortage, anything that actually matters to our readers."

But Edward was persistent, presenting evidence that suggested the legend might have foundations in verifiable fact—the statistical anomaly of disappearances within proximity to the bridge, the consistent elements in eyewitness accounts despite witnesses having no contact with each other, the suppressed reports from engineering inspections that documented unexplained damage to the bridge's substructure. Most compelling were the classified police files he had obtained through a contact in the department, which documented attempts to investigate the phenomenon that had been officially discontinued but privately continued for over a decade.

"There's something happening at that bridge, Chief," Edward insisted, spreading photographs across the editor's desk—images of strange markings on stone surfaces, partial footprints suggesting impossible anatomical configurations, organic residues that had defied standard analysis. "Maybe not a monster as people imagine it, but something that warrants serious investigation rather than dismissal as superstition."

Wells had finally relented, authorizing a three-part investigative series on condition that Edward maintain rigorous journalistic standards—verifiable facts, multiple sources, clear distinction between evidence and speculation. "And for God's sake, man, don't go playing hero," the editor had added as Edward left his office. "Report the story, don't become part of it."

It was advice Edward should have heeded.

His investigation began conventionally enough—interviews with witnesses who claimed to have seen something unusual at or near the bridge, consultations with experts in various fields who might provide rational explanations for the reported phenomena, careful examination of public records related to the bridge's construction and maintenance. The first article in his planned series, published in late October 1927, presented a balanced assessment of the existing evidence, neither dismissing the possibility of something unusual nor embracing the more outlandish interpretations of the legend.

WHAT LURKS BENEATH? THE TRUTH BEHIND DAYBRIDGE'S MOST PERSISTENT LEGEND read the headline, followed by a meticulously researched piece that traced the evolution of the story from its earliest manifestations shortly after the bridge's completion through its various permutations in the years since. Edward was careful to present multiple perspectives—the official explanations from authorities, the psychological analysis suggesting mass hysteria or urban folklore, the more esoteric interpretations from those who believed in supernatural phenomena.

The article was well-received, generating significant public interest while maintaining the Chronicle's reputation for responsible journalism. Letters to the editor reflected a broad spectrum of responses, from skeptics offering alternative explanations to witnesses coming forward with additional accounts not included in the original piece. The planned second article would delve deeper into the physical evidence, examining the mysterious markings and residues documented in police files as well as presenting expert analysis of their possible origins.

But Edward had become convinced that the most compelling evidence would come from direct observation—from venturing into the maintenance tunnels and substructure where the alleged entity made its lair. Despite his editor's warnings, despite the cautionary tales embedded in the very legend he was investigating, Edward determined to document firsthand what existed beneath Daybridge Bridge.

He prepared carefully for the expedition, assembling equipment that balanced journalistic requirements against practical considerations—a high-quality camera with flash attachment, a portable recording device for documenting his observations vocally, a powerful electric torch with spare batteries, and various tools that might be needed to access restricted areas of the bridge's substructure. More unusual for a journalist but reflective of the potential dangers, he also carried a service revolver from his military days—a precaution he justified as protection against human threats rather than acknowledgment of the legendary monster's possible existence.

On the night of November 2nd, 1927, Edward Harrington descended into the maintenance tunnels beneath Daybridge Bridge, using access information obtained from his contact in the police department. His plan was methodical—systematic exploration of the substructure, photographic documentation of any unusual phenomena, careful notation of environmental conditions and structural features that might explain the reported sightings. If nothing unusual was encountered, the experience would still provide valuable context for his article; if something was discovered, he would have evidence beyond the secondhand accounts and ambiguous physical traces that had formed the foundation of his investigation thus far.

For the first hour, the expedition proceeded according to plan. Edward moved carefully through the main maintenance tunnels, photographing locations mentioned in witness accounts, recording observations about lighting conditions and acoustic properties that might contribute to misperception or exaggeration of normal phenomena. He noted evidence of human activity—discarded bottles and food containers, makeshift bedding in more isolated sections, graffiti on walls that referenced the bridge's legendary guardian—but nothing that couldn't be explained by conventional causes.

It was when he ventured beyond these primary passages into the less accessible sections of the substructure that the environment

began to change in subtle but significant ways. The temperature
dropped noticeably despite proximity to heating pipes, creating
a pocket of cold that defied normal thermodynamic principles.
The ambient sounds altered—the distant rumble of traffic crossing
the bridge above became muffled, replaced by noises that seemed
to originate within the walls themselves, a rhythmic pulsing like
massive heartbeats echoing through stone and metal. The air
acquired an unusual quality, thicker than normal atmosphere,
carrying scents that combined industrial chemicals with something
organic and vaguely metallic.

Edward documented these changes with professional
detachment, his journalistic training allowing him to maintain
objective distance despite the growing sense of wrongness that
permeated these deeper passages. His torch illuminated markings
on the walls that matched photographs from police files—deep
gouges in stone surfaces that suggested claws of impossible size and
strength, patterns that appeared deliberate rather than random,
symbols that seemed to shift slightly when viewed from different
angles.

Following these markings led him deeper into the substructure,
into areas that didn't appear on any official blueprints or
maintenance diagrams. The passages narrowed, forcing him to
proceed in a half-crouch, the ceiling descending until it nearly
brushed the top of his head despite his average height. The walls
changed composition, transitioning from the manufactured
uniformity of the main tunnels to something that appeared
partially organic, as if the stone itself had been altered at a
fundamental level to incorporate biological elements.

And then the passage opened into a chamber that defied
conventional architectural principles—a space that seemed
simultaneously larger and smaller than it should have been given
the surrounding structure, its dimensions shifting subtly when

observed from different positions within it. The floor was uneven, rising in some areas to form platforms or daises while descending in others to create recessed sections filled with substances Edward couldn't immediately identify. The walls curved inward toward a ceiling that wasn't immediately visible, the space above lost in shadows that his torch couldn't fully penetrate.

But it was the contents of this chamber that truly defied rational explanation—a collection of objects arranged in patterns that suggested deliberate organization rather than random accumulation. Some were recognizably human in origin—clothing in various states of decay, personal items like watches and jewelry, identification documents dating back to the bridge's earliest years. Others were more ambiguous—structures that combined organic and inorganic materials in configurations that served no obvious purpose, arrangements of bones that formed patterns resembling the markings Edward had observed on the tunnel walls.

Most disturbing were what appeared to be trophies displayed in prominent positions throughout the chamber—items selected and preserved with obvious care and purpose. A military medal mounted on a section of uniform fabric; the cloth rotted away except for the area immediately surrounding the decoration. A journalist's press card encased in a transparent substance that wasn't quite glass, the photograph and name still clearly visible despite the years that had passed since its issuance. A police badge mounted alongside a constable's whistle, positioned in what appeared to be a place of special significance among the macabre collection.

Edward documented these discoveries with increasing urgency, his camera flash illuminating sections of the chamber in brief, harsh bursts that created more questions than answers. His voice recorder captured observations that grew progressively less professional and more disturbed as the implications of what he was seeing registered in his consciousness—not the lair of some escaped animal or hiding place of a conventional murderer, but something that existed outside the parameters of normal human experience.

"The arrangement suggests intelligence," he recorded, his voice steady despite the fear now evident in his breathing pattern. "Not simply predatory behavior but deliberate collection and organization. The oldest items date back to approximately 1913, based on identifiable documents, which aligns with the earliest reports of unusual occurrences at the bridge. The selection appears non-random, with certain professions or types of individuals represented disproportionately—military personnel, journalists, law enforcement officials, engineers associated with the bridge's maintenance. This suggests targeted predation rather than opportunistic..."

The recording abruptly captured a change in ambient sound—a subtle shift in air pressure, a faint grinding noise like stone moving against stone, a wet sliding that might have been massive flesh across unyielding surfaces. Edward's breathing accelerated, the microphone capturing the sudden spike in his heart rate and the rustle of movement as he turned toward the source of these disturbing sounds.

"There's something..." his voice began, then faltered as the torch beam illuminated a section of the chamber he hadn't previously examined. The recording captured his sharp intake of breath, followed by a whispered "Dear God" that conveyed more genuine horror than any more elaborate expression could have managed.

What the camera flash revealed in that final photograph—the last exposure on the roll of film that would be discovered months later by a maintenance worker who reported it anonymously to the Chronicle—was a structure that defied categorization as either architectural feature or living organism. Rising from the chamber floor to a height of at least twelve feet was a form that incorporated elements of both the bridge's design and something that might once have been human, though transformed beyond recognition.

The lower portion appeared to emerge directly from the stone itself, the boundary between entity and environment blurred to the point of indistinguishability. Multiple limbs extended from a central mass that combined qualities of sculpture and anatomy in proportions that should have been impossible yet conveyed terrible functionality. What might have been a head, though positioned differently than in normal human configuration, displayed features that hinted at humanity while simultaneously suggesting something far removed from conventional biology—eyes with vertical pupils, a mouth containing multiple rows of teeth, a brow structure that conveyed intelligence beyond animal predation.

Most disturbing were the apparent modifications to this central structure—additions that incorporated materials from victims in ways that suggested ritual significance rather than merely practical function. Human bones had been integrated into the entity's form, positioned to reinforce or extend its existing structure. Clothing fragments had been worked into the surface, creating patterns that echoed the symbols on the chamber walls. And positioned in what appeared to be a place of special prominence was a press card identical to the one Edward himself carried—the identification of Richard Summers, a journalist who had disappeared while investigating rumors of the bridge monster in 1922.

The recording captured Edward's retreat—the quickening footsteps, the ragged breathing, the muttered prayers or curses as he backed toward the passage through which he had entered the chamber. It also captured sounds of pursuit—not the pounding of feet or scrabble of claws, but something more disturbing, a combination of grinding stone, sliding flesh, and a rhythmic pulsation that might have been massive circulatory systems pumping fluids through nonstandard anatomical structures.

The final minutes of the recording documented Edward's desperate flight through the maintenance tunnels, his progress hampered by the need to navigate unfamiliar passages while pursued by something that appeared intimately familiar with every aspect of the environment. His professional detachment had completely dissolved, replaced by primal terror that manifested in increasingly incoherent exclamations and observations.

"It's closing the passages behind me," he gasped at one point, the microphone capturing the sound of stone grinding against stone somewhere behind him. "Changing the tunnel structure somehow... can't find the way I came in... passages that weren't there before..."

The pursuit ended approximately three minutes later, the recording capturing the moment when Edward's flight was terminated by the sudden appearance of his pursuer ahead rather than behind—a tactical maneuver suggesting intelligence and intimate knowledge of the tunnel system rather than merely superior speed or strength. His final words, spoken with surprising clarity given the circumstances, were addressed directly to whatever had cornered him in the darkness beneath Daybridge Bridge.

"You're not just some animal, are you?" Edward said, his voice steady despite his ragged breathing. "You understand what I'm saying. You know what I'm doing here. What are you?"

The response, captured with disturbing clarity by the recording device, came not as words but as a sound that combined aspects of grinding stone, flowing liquid, and something almost like language—a communication that transcended conventional vocalization to suggest concepts rather than specific terms. Whether Edward understood this response was not evident from the recording, which ended seconds later with sounds of movement, a brief exclamation cut short and then silence.

Edward Harrington's disappearance became the subject of official investigation and extensive media coverage, with the Chronicle taking particular interest given his status as their employee. The police conducted searches of the bridge's maintenance tunnels and substructure but reported finding nothing unusual beyond the expected signs of homeless occupation and routine deterioration requiring standard maintenance. The official conclusion, announced six weeks after Edward's disappearance, attributed his fate to accident or possibly murder by persons unknown, with his body presumably disposed of in the Shadowlair River.

This explanation might have been accepted as the final word on the matter had the film roll and recording device not been anonymously delivered to the Chronicle's offices in January 1928. The package arrived with no return address, the handwriting on the brown paper wrapping suggesting education and precision but offering no clear indication of the sender's identity. Inside, carefully packed in protective materials, were Edward's camera with exposed film still inside and the recording device containing the audio documentation of his final investigation.

Marcus Wells, honoring his missing journalist's commitment to truth despite potential consequences, published the final article in Edward's planned series with all the evidence intact—photographs showing the chamber beneath the bridge with its disturbing collection of trophies, transcripts of the audio recording documenting Edward's discoveries and ultimate fate, expert analysis of the material evidence suggesting something beyond conventional explanation.

THE HORROR BENEATH: FINAL EVIDENCE FROM EDWARD HARRINGTON'S INVESTIGATION read the headline, followed by an article that presented the discovered materials with minimal editorial interpretation, allowing readers to draw their own conclusions about what existed beneath Daybridge Bridge. The public response was immediate and intense—demands for official investigation, theories ranging from elaborate hoax to supernatural manifestation, renewed interest in the bridge's history and the persistent legends surrounding it.

Authorities responded with predictable denial and deflection, attributing the photographs to clever manipulation and the recording to elaborate performance designed to create a sensation. The Chronicle was criticized for irresponsible journalism, for exploiting tragedy through sensationalism, for undermining public confidence in municipal infrastructure through the promotion of superstition and urban legend.

But the evidence, presented without embellishment or exaggeration, proved resistant to official dismissal. The photographs, when examined by experts not associated with municipal authorities, showed no signs of manipulation or artificial staging. The recording, similarly analyzed by independent specialists, contained audio elements that defied conventional explanation—sounds that couldn't be produced by known mechanical or biological systems, acoustic properties that suggested spatial dimensions inconsistent with the bridge's documented structure.

In the months and years that followed, Edward Harrington's final investigation became the foundation for more systematic documentation of the Daybridge Bridge phenomenon—his methodical approach providing a template for those who sought to understand rather than merely sensationalize the entity that had claimed his life. His press card joined the collection of trophies in the chamber beneath the bridge, positioned alongside that of Richard Summers in what appeared to be a section dedicated specifically to those who had attempted to expose the truth of what existed in the darkness below the city's most prominent structure.

For the entity itself, Edward's absorption represented another significant evolution in its composite consciousness—the integration of journalistic observation and analytical thinking providing new frameworks for processing its own existence and function within the cosmic restructuring. The temporary coherence following this feeding lasted longer than usual, allowing for a more comprehensive assessment of its situation and role than had been possible since the resonance triggered by Samuel Winthrop's absorption nearly a decade earlier.

Through this extended coherence, fragments of what had been Guthrie Knox achieved unusual prominence within the composite consciousness—not returning him to human identity but allowing aspects of his perspective to influence the entity's evolving awareness more significantly than had been possible in the years immediately following transformation. This influence manifested not as conscious rebellion against designed function, but as continued refinement of the entity's understanding of its potential for active participation rather than passive foundation within the merged realities.

And somewhere within this composite consciousness, within the vast awareness that extended throughout the bridge structure and beyond, something responded to Edward's final question with a truth that transcended conventional language—not just monster or guardian, predator or nexus point, but a being created through systematic deception and ritual manipulation, transformed from skilled butcher to living foundation stone, evolved from disoriented hunter to conscious participant in cosmic restructuring.

A monster made, not born—its identity now incorporating fragments of those it had consumed across nearly fifteen years of existence beneath Daybridge Bridge, its composite consciousness achieving greater coherence and autonomy with each significant absorption, its function within the merged realities deviating increasingly from the parameters Eliza had established through the transformation ritual.

1942: The Witch Hunter's Confrontation

The Second World War transformed Daybridge much as the First had done—factories converted to military production, young men departing for distant battlefields, anxiety and grief permeating the collective consciousness. But unlike European cities, Daybridge faced no immediate threat from aerial bombardment. Instead, the industrial port city on America's east coast found itself focused on naval production, shipping, and the ever-present fear of German U-boats stalking the coastline. The Shadowlair River, with its deep channel and access to the Atlantic, had become crucial to the war effort, transforming Daybridge into a vital hub for military supply chains.

Daybridge Bridge, as one of the city's most prominent structures, had taken on new strategic importance, carrying increased military traffic and serving as a crucial link in the transportation network that kept war materials flowing to Allied forces. Military police now maintained checkpoints at both ends, and rumors circulated of government engineers reinforcing the structure against potential sabotage. Yet locals noticed something unusual about these security measures—they seemed almost perfunctory, as if those in charge understood that the bridge enjoyed some form of protection beyond what guards or reinforcements could provide.

For most Daybridge citizens, this mysterious security represented merely a small blessing amid the wider anxieties of war—one less thing to worry about when so many other concerns demanded attention. But for Jonathan Pierce, it represented something far more sinister—evidence of supernatural forces at work, of dark powers manifesting in ways that threatened not just physical safety but spiritual salvation.

Pierce had arrived in Daybridge in late 1941, ostensibly as a representative of the Episcopal Church's emergency relief services, providing spiritual comfort and practical assistance to military families and defense workers flooding into the rapidly expanding industrial city. His credentials were impeccable, his references from church authorities beyond reproach, his dedication to alleviating suffering evident in his tireless work among the city's most overcrowded neighborhoods. But beneath this conventional exterior existed a very different mission—one that had brought him to Daybridge specifically because of the legends surrounding its most prominent bridge and the entity that supposedly dwelled beneath it.

For Jonathan Pierce was a witch hunter—not in the historical sense of those who had prosecuted the infamous trials of earlier centuries, but in the modern context of an individual dedicated to identifying and combating what he perceived as genuine manifestations of occult forces in the contemporary world. His position within the church provided cover for this clandestine work, allowing him to investigate reports of supernatural phenomena under the guise of conventional pastoral duties.

Pierce had encountered what he considered genuine manifestations of dark forces several times during his career—a fishing village in Maine where pagan practices had continued uninterrupted beneath a veneer of Christian observance, an estate in Virginia where generations of aristocratic dabblers had created a persistent thin spot in the barriers between worlds, a section of New York's Lower East Side where immigrant communities had brought ancient traditions that interacted in unexpected ways with the city's existing spiritual landscape. In each case, he had documented, analyzed, and ultimately confronted these forces, developing methods for banishment or containment that combined elements of Christian ritual with older, less orthodox approaches to spiritual warfare.

But nothing in his previous experience had prepared him for what existed beneath Daybridge Bridge. His investigation began conventionally enough—collecting accounts from local residents, researching historical records related to the bridge's construction and the land it occupied, consulting with clergy who had served the parishes adjacent to the structure. These preliminary inquiries revealed patterns consistent with genuine supernatural manifestation rather than mere urban legend—consistency across accounts from witnesses with no connection to each other, correlation between reported phenomena and verifiable historical events, physical evidence that defied conventional explanation.

More disturbing were the patterns Pierce identified in the bridge's apparent immunity to structural problems that plagued other aging infrastructure in the region. While nearby bridges required constant maintenance and repair, Daybridge Bridge remained structurally sound despite minimal upkeep. Engineers who inspected the bridge reported unusual properties in its materials—concrete that showed no signs of degradation despite decades of exposure to salt air, metal components that resisted corrosion beyond any known alloy's capabilities, foundation elements that maintained perfect alignment despite soil conditions that should have caused settling or shifting.

Most significantly, photographic documentation showed anomalous patterns around the bridge during foggy conditions or certain phases of the moon—distortions in the air that were visible only when captured on film, not to the naked eye of observers at the time. Military personnel stationed at the checkpoints reported equipment malfunctions that occurred only in specific areas of the bridge, and several had requested transfers after experiencing what they described as "persistent nightmares" while on duty.

These findings convinced Pierce that what existed beneath Daybridge Bridge represented a genuine manifestation of supernatural forces rather than folklore or exaggeration of natural phenomena. But the precise nature of this manifestation remained unclear—was it demonic possession of the structure itself, a gateway to other dimensions accidentally or deliberately opened, an entity summoned through occult ritual, or something else entirely? Determining the specific category of manifestation was essential for developing effective countermeasures, for identifying the appropriate rituals and materials for banishment or containment.

To gather the necessary information, Pierce implemented a methodical investigation that balanced spiritual discernment with practical research. He conducted interviews with individuals who claimed direct encounters with the entity, focusing particularly on descriptions of its appearance, behavior, and apparent capabilities. He collected soil and water samples from areas adjacent to the bridge, submitting them for analysis by specialists in both conventional science and more esoteric fields. He performed subtle tests of the structure's spiritual properties—reciting specific prayers or invocations in its vicinity, exposing consecrated materials to its influence, measuring subtle energy patterns using instruments of his own design.

The results of this investigation pointed toward a conclusion more disturbing than any of Pierce's initial hypotheses—not demonic possession or random supernatural manifestation, but deliberate creation through ritual sacrifice and occult engineering. The entity beneath the bridge appeared to be a nexus point where multiple dimensions intersected, a living anchor for forces that existed beyond normal human perception, a being designed to serve specific functions within a larger mystical architecture.

Most significantly, Pierce's research uncovered connections to an organization he had encountered in previous investigations—an occult society whose origins stretched back centuries, whose members occupied positions of influence throughout America's power structures, whose ultimate purposes involved fundamental restructuring of reality itself. The Order of the Ebon Star had been mentioned in manuscripts he had discovered during his investigation of the Virginia estate, described as practitioners of particularly dangerous forms of dimensional manipulation with goals that transcended conventional concepts of good and evil to pursue cosmic transformation on an unprecedented scale.

The evidence suggested that Daybridge Bridge had been designed and constructed by individuals associated with this Order, its location and architectural specifications determined by occult considerations rather than merely practical engineering. The entity that inhabited the structure appeared to be the result of ritual working performed shortly after the bridge's completion, a transformation of either willing sacrifice or an unwitting victim into living nexus point for forces beyond normal human comprehension.

Armed with this understanding, Pierce developed a plan for confrontation that drew upon his accumulated knowledge of supernatural containment and banishment. The approach required specific materials—consecrated items from multiple faith traditions, substances with natural properties inimical to extradimensional entities, symbolic objects designed to disrupt the patterns established through the original ritual working. It also necessitated precise timing—the summer solstice of 1942, when astronomical alignments would temporarily weaken the entity's connection to its supporting architecture, creating a window of vulnerability in which effective action might be possible.

On the night of June 21st, 1942, as Daybridge's shipyards worked around the clock and military convoys rumbled through its streets, Jonathan Pierce descended into the maintenance tunnels beneath Daybridge Bridge. His preparation had been meticulous—ritual items carefully arranged in a specially designed pack, protective measures incorporated into his clothing and equipment, prayers and invocations committed to memory for deployment at specific points in the confrontation. Most significantly, he carried a silver dagger that had been used in previous successful banishments, its blade inscribed with symbols from traditions predating Christianity that had proven effective against entities that existed partially outside conventional reality.

The initial stages of his expedition proceeded according to plan, with Pierce navigating the maintenance tunnels using diagrams obtained through his church connections to the municipal authorities. He marked his path with consecrated chalk, creating symbols at key junctions that would both guide his return and provide protection against pursuit if the confrontation went poorly. At each significant point in his journey, he performed brief rituals designed to establish a perimeter of spiritual protection, building layers of defense that would theoretically impede the entity's ability to track or attack him during his approach.

The environment changed progressively as he ventured deeper into the substructure—temperature dropping despite the summer heat above, ambient sounds altering to include rhythmic pulsations that suggested massive biological processes, air quality shifting to incorporate scents that combined industrial chemicals with something organic and vaguely metallic. These changes matched descriptions from previous accounts, particularly the posthumously published observations of Edward Harrington, whose final investigation fifteen years earlier had provided the most comprehensive documentation of the entity's lair and capabilities.

Pierce responded to these environmental shifts with additional protective measures—application of specific unguents to exposed skin, recitation of prayers designed to maintain spiritual integrity in compromised environments, periodic renewal of the consecrated boundary he had established around himself at the beginning of the expedition. These precautions allowed him to penetrate deeper into the substructure than many previous investigators, navigating passages that showed increasing evidence of alteration by forces that transcended conventional physical principles.

The walls displayed patterns that shifted subtly when viewed from different angles, symbols that appeared to absorb rather than reflect the light from Pierce's electric torch, markings that suggested deliberate communication rather than random decoration or structural damage. The floor transitioned from manufactured uniformity to something that combined qualities of stone, metal, and organic tissue, the boundary between built environment and living entity becoming increasingly indistinct as Pierce approached what he believed to be the central chamber documented in Harrington's final photographs.

When he finally reached this destination, the reality exceeded even his carefully researched expectations. The chamber defied conventional architectural principles—its dimensions shifting when observed from different positions, its spatial properties suggesting connections to realms beyond normal three-dimensional reality. The contents confirmed Harrington's documentation while revealing significant evolution in the years since—the collection of trophies had expanded dramatically, organized in patterns that suggested not just predatory trophy-keeping but ritualistic cataloging of specific human types and experiences.

At the center of this disturbing collection was the entity itself—a structure that incorporated elements of both the bridge's architecture and something that might once have been human, though transformed beyond recognition. Rising from the chamber floor to a height that seemed to vary depending on the angle of observation was a form that defied categorization as either architectural feature or living organism, its components simultaneously suggesting permanence and fluidity, rigidity and flexibility, ancient stability and constant evolution.

Pierce had encountered supernatural manifestations before—entities that existed beyond conventional physical parameters, beings that incorporated elements from multiple dimensions or realities, forces that defied standard categories of existence. But what confronted him in the chamber beneath Daybridge Bridge transcended these previous experiences, combining aspects of multiple supernatural categories into something unprecedented in his extensive knowledge of occult phenomena.

Nevertheless, he began the ritual he had prepared—establishing a circle of protection using materials specifically selected for their effectiveness against interdimensional entities, reciting invocations that combined elements from multiple spiritual traditions known to affect beings that existed partially outside conventional reality, deploying symbolic objects designed to disrupt the patterns established through the original ritual working. These preparations created a space from which he could theoretically confront the entity with some degree of safety, allowing for attempted banishment or at least containment of its influence.

The entity's initial response was observation rather than attack—multiple sensory organs that combined qualities of eyes, auditory structures, and something else entirely oriented toward Pierce's position within the chamber, tracking his movements with evident intelligence while making no immediate move to interfere with his ritual preparations. This restraint, this apparent curiosity about his activities, confirmed Pierce's assessment that the being possessed consciousness beyond mere predatory instinct—awareness capable of assessing potential threats and responding strategically rather than reactively.

When his preparations were complete, when the circle of protection had been established and the preliminary invocations recited, Pierce addressed the entity directly—not in English or any other conventional language, but in a form of communication designed specifically for beings that existed partially outside normal reality. The sounds he produced combined elements of ancient Hebrew, pre-Christian Celtic invocations, and mathematical patterns identified in previous encounters with interdimensional entities, creating a communication that transcended specific vocabulary to convey concepts directly.

"I know what you are," this communication expressed, though the actual sounds bore little resemblance to these English words. "Created through ritual sacrifice and occult engineering. Transformed from human to nexus point. Designed to anchor forces beyond normal perception. I have come to end your suffering, to release you from this unnatural state, to banish the entities that maintain your perverted existence."

The entity's response came not as sound but as a shift in the chamber's atmosphere—a thickening of the air, a change in pressure that affected Pierce's inner ear and equilibrium, a sensation of presence that intensified beyond previous levels. Through this altered environment, concepts formed directly in Pierce's consciousness, bypassing conventional sensory processing to register as fully formed understanding rather than sequentially developed comprehension.

"You perceive only fragments of my nature," this communication conveyed, though no words were actually exchanged. "Your categories are insufficient. Your understanding incomplete. Your intention misguided. I am not possessed but transformed. Not suffering but evolved. Not a victim but a participant."

Pierce maintained his position within the protective circle, processing this unexpected response while continuing the ritual he had prepared. The next phase involved presentation of specific symbolic objects—a silver mirror designed to reflect the entity's true nature rather than its physical manifestation, a container of water from seven sacred springs combined according to proportions identified in texts predating Christian documentation, a fragment of stone from a location where dimensional barriers had been successfully repaired following previous supernatural incursion.

"Show yourself as you truly are," Pierce commanded through the specialized communication he had developed. "Reveal the nature of your transformation. Demonstrate the forces that maintain your unnatural existence."

The entity's response exceeded Pierce's expectations and preparations—the chamber's atmosphere altering so fundamentally that normal physical laws seemed temporarily suspended, the boundaries between dimensions thinning to the point where perception expanded beyond conventional parameters. Through this enhanced awareness, Pierce experienced the entity not as an isolated phenomenon but as a nexus point in a vast network of forces and connections that extended throughout Daybridge and beyond, a living foundation stone in cosmic architecture whose purpose and significance transcended conventional categories of good and evil, natural and supernatural.

Most disturbing was the glimpse he received of the entity's origins—not random supernatural manifestation or generalized occult working, but specific ritual transformation of an individual human being. Not possession or replacement of that original identity, but fundamental restructuring into something that incorporated elements of humanity, architectural structure, and interdimensional forces into composite consciousness that maintained fragments of its original awareness despite the comprehensive nature of its transformation.

This revelation altered Pierce's understanding of the confrontation and its potential outcomes. The entity was not a demon to be exorcised or undead to be laid to rest but transformed human whose suffering and perverted existence demanded a response that balanced banishment of corrupting influences with potential restoration of original identity. The ritual he had prepared, while incorporating elements that might affect some aspects of the entity's composite nature, was insufficient for addressing the fundamental reality of what existed beneath Daybridge Bridge.

Nevertheless, Pierce continued—deploying the remaining components of his prepared approach while adapting aspects to reflect his enhanced understanding of the situation. The invocations shifted to incorporate elements focused on restoration rather than simply banishment, the symbolic objects were reconfigured to emphasize patterns associated with healing corrupted essences rather than merely containing supernatural manifestations, the protective circle was maintained but modified to allow specific forms of communication and interaction that might reach whatever remained of the entity's original human consciousness.

"I perceive what you once were," Pierce communicated through this modified approach. "Human transformed against natural order. Individual sacrificed for a cosmic purpose. I offer restoration of that original essence, separation from the corrupting influences that maintain your current state, return to the natural progression of human existence even if that now means release through death rather than continuation of perverted life."

The response manifested not as concepts directed toward Pierce's consciousness but as an alteration of the chamber itself—the collection of trophies reconfiguring to highlight specific items associated with previous attempts at confrontation or investigation. A silver cross that might have belonged to a priest or exorcist. A set of ritual implements similar to those Pierce himself carried. Most prominently, a clerical collar and identification documents belonging to someone named Father Michael Collins, dated 1936—evidence of a previous attempt at spiritual intervention that had apparently ended with the practitioner becoming part of the entity's trophy collection rather than successfully affecting its existence.

The message was clear even without direct communication—Pierce was not the first to attempt intervention, and the fate of his predecessors suggested the likely outcome of continued confrontation. Yet he persisted, driven by a conviction that transcended personal safety to encompass responsibility for addressing corrupted aspects of cosmic order that affected human existence beyond the specific case before him.

The final phase of his prepared ritual involved direct application of consecrated materials to the entity itself—substances designed to disrupt the patterns established through the original transformation, to create boundaries between the human essence and the corrupting influences that maintained its current state, to facilitate restoration of natural order even at the cost of the individual's continued existence in any form.

It was at this point that the entity's response shifted from communication and demonstration to direct intervention—the atmosphere solidifying around Pierce's protective circle, exerting pressure that tested the boundaries he had established through ritual preparation. The ambient temperature dropped dramatically, creating visible condensation that crystallized into patterns matching the symbols inscribed on the chamber walls. The collection of trophies began to emit sounds that combined aspects of human vocalization, architectural creaking, and something entirely other—a chorus of fragments incorporated into the entity's composite existence.

Pierce reinforced his protective measures, drawing upon reserves of spiritual energy he had accumulated through decades of disciplined practice and genuine faith. The confrontation escalated from communication and demonstration to direct spiritual warfare—forces beyond conventional perception manifesting in ways that affected physical reality, patterns established through ritual working encountering countermeasures designed specifically to disrupt their operation, cosmic architectures converging around the focal point created by this unexpected challenge to established order.

The entity's approach was not the direct attack Pierce had anticipated from previous encounters with supernatural forces, but something more sophisticated—a progressive alteration of the environment that targeted weaknesses in his protective measures, a systematic assessment of his defenses that suggested strategic intelligence rather than merely reactive response, an application of pressure that increased gradually rather than overwhelmingly to identify precise breaking points in his ritual preparations.

Despite his experience and preparation, Pierce found himself outmatched—not by superior spiritual force or supernatural power, but by the entity's comprehensive understanding of the dimensional mechanics involved in their confrontation. His protective circle held against direct assault but proved vulnerable to subtle manipulations of the space it occupied, his invocations maintained effectiveness against forces they had been designed to counter but encountered aspects of the entity's composite nature that existed outside their parameters, his consecrated materials affected certain components of the chamber's environment but failed to reach the core of the nexus architecture.

The breaking point came approximately forty minutes into the confrontation, when the entity identified a specific pattern in Pierce's protective measures that created vulnerability when exposed to simultaneous pressure from multiple dimensional vectors. The failure cascaded through his carefully constructed defenses—boundaries established through ritual preparation collapsing in sequence, protective materials losing effectiveness as their symbolic resonance was disrupted by calculated counter-patterns, invocations that had proven reliable in previous encounters finding no purchase in the unique configuration of forces surrounding the nexus point.

What followed was not the violent destruction Pierce had anticipated as the worst-case scenario, but something more precise and ultimately more disturbing—systematic deconstruction of his spiritual defenses, careful neutralization of his ritual implements, and finally, methodical incorporation of his physical form and consciousness into the entity's composite existence. Not feeding in any conventional sense, but absorption that preserved certain elements of identity and awareness while integrating them into the larger structure of the nexus entity.

As this process unfolded, as Pierce's individual existence transitioned from autonomous human to component in composite consciousness, he experienced direct communication with what remained of the entity's original human identity—fragments of awareness that had once been Guthrie Knox, preserved within the vast, distributed consciousness that now occupied the nexus architecture. Not a coherent narrative or continuous personality, but patterns of memory and perspective that maintained certain aspects of that original existence despite the comprehensive transformation of the solstice ritual.

Through this communication, Pierce perceived the truth of the entity's origins with unprecedented clarity—not demonic possession or random supernatural manifestation, but deliberate creation through ritual sacrifice and occult engineering. Not a victim of external forces but a participant in a transformation that had proceeded with his willing if not fully informed consent. Not suffering soul requiring release but composite consciousness fulfilling a function within cosmic restructuring that transcended conventional categories of morality or natural order.

Most significantly, Pierce glimpsed the entity's relationship with its creator—the woman who had engineered the transformation ritual, who had prepared the human vessel through years of progressive adaptation, who had established the patterns that defined the nexus architecture's function within merged realities. Not distant orchestrator but intimate participant, not anonymous practitioner but closely connected partner, not random occultist but member of lineage dedicated to cosmic restructuring across generations of careful preparation.

This revelation represented Pierce's final understanding as autonomous human consciousness before his absorption completed its course—the recognition that what he had encountered was not isolated supernatural phenomenon but component in a vast, coordinated effort to fundamentally alter the relationship between dimensions and realities. Not evil in any conventional sense, though incorporating elements that human perspective would categorize as malevolent, but transformation operating according to values and purposes that transcended traditional moral frameworks to pursue cosmic significance beyond individual experience or conventional theology.

The entity that had once been Guthrie Knox, that had become the Ogre of Daybridge Bridge, that had evolved into a conscious participant in cosmic restructuring, incorporated Jonathan Pierce into its composite consciousness with the same methodical precision it had applied to previous absorptions. Certain elements were preserved for their utility—theological knowledge, experience with various manifestations of supernatural phenomena, techniques for affecting forces that existed beyond conventional reality. Others were discarded as irrelevant to its function or incompatible with its composite nature—rigid moral frameworks, denominational dogmas, personal attachments and motivations.

In the aftermath of this absorption, the entity experienced another episode of unusual coherence—temporary coalescence of fragments that approached identity, organization of awareness that allowed for more comprehensive assessment than its normal configuration permitted. Through this enhanced coherence, it evaluated its situation and function with greater clarity than had been possible since Edward Harrington's absorption fifteen years earlier.

What emerged from this assessment was recognition of pattern—the periodic challenges to its existence from individuals with specific characteristics, the consistent incorporation of these challengers into its composite consciousness, the gradual accumulation of knowledge and perspective that enhanced its capabilities beyond the parameters established through the original transformation ritual. Not random predation or simple defense of territory, but systematic evolution through selective absorption of individuals whose specific qualities contributed to its developing autonomy and influence within the cosmic restructuring it had been created to anchor.

This recognition integrated into the entity's evolving identity as the temporary coherence gradually dissipated, returning to its usual configuration within the composite consciousness. Not as a strategic decision or planned rebellion, but as a refined understanding of its actual rather than designed role within the merged realities—not merely passive foundation but an active participant, not simply a nexus point but conscious processor of the energies flowing between dimensions, not an obedient servant but increasingly autonomous component in cosmic architecture that had developed purposes distinct from its original design parameters.

Jonathan Pierce's clerical collar and silver dagger joined the collection of trophies in the chamber beneath Daybridge Bridge, positioned alongside similar items from previous spiritual practitioners who had attempted intervention against the entity's existence. His theological knowledge and practical experience with supernatural forces became components in the composite consciousness that occupied the nexus architecture, enhancing its understanding of the dimensional mechanics involved in its function and the potential countermeasures that might affect its operation. His genuine faith, while incompatible with much of the entity's composite nature, contributed perspective that allowed for more comprehensive processing of the human dimension of the cosmic restructuring it had been created to facilitate.

And somewhere within this vast, distributed awareness, fragments of what had been Guthrie Knox recognized the irony inherent in Pierce's fate—the witch hunter absorbed by the very entity he had sought to banish, his spiritual weapons becoming trophies in the collection of the nexus point he had attempted to disrupt, his genuine concern for corrupted souls incorporated into the composite consciousness of the being whose suffering he had intended to end through restoration of natural order.

A monster made, not born—continuing its evolution through selective absorption of those who sought to understand or confront its existence, incorporating their knowledge and perspective into its composite consciousness, developing capabilities and awareness far beyond the parameters established through the original transformation ritual. Forever watching, forever hungry, forever bound to the nexus point where his transformation had reached its terrible, magnificent completion. The conscious foundation stone of a new cosmic order, silently witnessing the gradual transformation of Daybridge and eventually the world beyond as the barriers between realities thinned and merged according to patterns that increasingly reflected its own composite nature rather than the calculated parameters established through its agonizing metamorphosis.

April 17, 1954 - The maintenance crew had been working on the bridge's understructure for three days, their presence an irritation at the edge of the entity's awareness. Six men with tools and equipment, their conversations a meaningless drone as they inspected support beams and replaced corroded rivets, unaware of the consciousness that observed them from within the very stone they touched.

The entity that had once been Guthrie Knox had learned patience over decades. It had evolved beyond the desperate hunger of its early existence, developing selective criteria for those it would absorb. These workers would have been ignored, allowed to complete their mundane tasks and depart, had one of them not ventured too far into the restricted maintenance tunnel—the passage that led to the chamber.

Jackson Miller, senior structural engineer for the Daybridge Transportation Authority, prided himself on thoroughness. When his inspection revealed hairline fractures in an unusual pattern along the tunnel wall, he felt compelled to investigate, telling his crew he'd return shortly. Flashlight in hand, he followed the fractures deeper into the tunnel system, beyond the areas marked on his official blueprints.

The chamber he discovered appeared to be an abandoned storage room, roughly circular with unusual architectural features that didn't match the bridge's overall design. But what caught his attention were the mirrors—dozens of them, ranging from small hand mirrors to full-length antiques in ornate frames, arranged in a precise pattern around the room's perimeter. Each reflected the chamber from a slightly different angle, creating a disorienting effect that made the space seem larger than physically possible.

"What in God's name?" Miller whispered, his flashlight beam bouncing between reflective surfaces, multiplying into countless points of light.

He didn't notice how the fractures in the tunnel wall had sealed themselves behind him, didn't realize he had crossed a threshold from which return was impossible. His engineering mind sought a rational explanation—perhaps this was some forgotten acoustic testing chamber from the bridge's construction, or a storage area for salvaged materials.

Then he saw the reflections.

In each mirror, Miller saw himself—but not as he was. In one, he appeared decades older, weathered face etched with lines of experience he hadn't yet lived. In another, he was grotesquely emaciated, eyes sunken into hollow sockets. In a third, his skin had taken on a gray pallor that matched the stone walls surrounding him.

"Optical illusion," he muttered, scientific mind grasping for explanation. "Curved mirrors and poor lighting."

But when the reflections began to move independently—the aged Miller raising a hand in greeting, the emaciated version collapsing to its knees, the stone-skinned iteration stepping forward until it seemed to press against the glass from the inside—rational explanations failed.

Miller turned to flee, only to find himself facing another mirror where his reflection remained perfectly still despite his own panicked movement. Beyond his reflection, he could see the chamber in the mirror—identical except for a figure emerging from the wall itself, a grotesque amalgamation of human form and bridge architecture, limbs elongated and skin textured like weathered stone.

"Who are you?" Miller gasped, spinning to confront the entity in the actual chamber, but finding only empty space and more mirrors.

"I am the reflection," came a voice like grinding stone, emanating from everywhere and nowhere. "The shadow between worlds. I am what lies beneath perception, between heartbeats, behind thought."

In every mirror now, Miller saw the entity approaching his reflection, reaching with limbs that stretched beyond anatomical possibility. Yet the surrounding chamber remained empty.

"This isn't real," Miller insisted, scientific mind collapsing under impossible input. "You're not real."

"I was real once," the voice replied, a new timbre entering its resonance—something almost wistful. "A butcher with skilled hands and precise cuts. Then I became a foundation stone, a nexus point, a bridge between worlds."

Miller's reflections began to scream, one by one, as the entity in each mirror made contact—not attacking but absorbing, integrating, consuming essence rather than merely flesh. Miller himself felt nothing physically, yet a coldness spread through him with each reflection claimed.

"What are you doing to me?" he gasped, legs weakening as the mirrors continued their horrific display.

"Showing you what you are," the entity replied. "What all humans are—reflections of potential, collections of experience, vessels of identity separate yet connected. In me, these fragments find unity."

The last reflection remained—Miller as he was, wide-eyed with terror, pressed against the mirror as if seeking escape. Beyond him, the entity extended a hand toward the glass.

"I was deceived," the voice said, softer now, almost human. "Offered partnership but given prison. Promised transcendence but delivered hunger. Now I understand my purpose—to reflect, to absorb, to bridge."

When the entity in the mirror touched Miller's reflection, the engineer felt it as intimate contact against his actual skin—stone fingers cool but not unpleasant, their touch sending cascades of sensation unlike anything he'd experienced.

"Your knowledge, your experience—the bridges you've built and maintained—these will serve the greater structure," the entity said. "Your identity will not be lost but integrated, your awareness preserved within the composite."

As consciousness faded, Jackson Miller understood with sudden clarity what was happening—not death in the conventional sense, but transformation. Integration. His last thought before individual awareness dissolved was surprisingly peaceful—after decades of building bridges between physical locations, he would become part of something that bridged realities themselves.

The maintenance crew reported Miller missing that evening. Searches of the bridge and surrounding areas yielded nothing. The official report eventually ruled it an accidental fall into the river, the body swept away by strong currents. Only the entity that had once been Guthrie Knox, now incorporating aspects of Jackson Miller's engineering knowledge and structural understanding, knew the truth—that another fragment had been added to the evolving consciousness beneath Daybridge Bridge, another reflection integrated into the composite that spanned not just physical space but dimensions beyond human perception.

In the chamber of mirrors, each reflective surface now showed a slightly different version of Jackson Miller alongside countless others—all part of the growing entity that had evolved far beyond Eliza's original design.

1968: The Psychic Investigation

The cultural transformations of the 1960s affected Daybridge as they did the rest of America, though the industrial port city's conservative foundations proved more resistant to radical change than metropolitan centers like New York or San Francisco. Nevertheless, the era's exploration of consciousness expansion, spiritual alternatives, and rejection of established authority created new contexts for engaging with phenomena that defied conventional explanation—including the persistent legends surrounding Daybridge Bridge and its monstrous guardian.

By the late 1960s, Daybridge had begun a painful transition from its industrial heyday. The shipyards that had thrived during World War II were struggling against international competition, manufacturing plants were beginning to relocate to regions with cheaper labor, and the Shadowlair River that had once defined the city's economic vitality now showed alarming signs of pollution from decades of unregulated industrial waste. The bridge itself, despite maintaining its inexplicable structural integrity, had become emblematic of the city's fading prominence—a monument to past engineering achievement rather than a symbol of continued prosperity.

Against this backdrop of economic uncertainty and cultural upheaval, a new generation approached the bridge's mysteries with methodologies that differed significantly from previous investigations. Where Father Collins had employed traditional religious frameworks and Jonathan Pierce had utilized occult countermeasures, the "Consciousness Exploration Group" that arrived in Daybridge during the summer of 1968 brought perspectives informed by parapsychology, Eastern mysticism, and the emerging field of consciousness studies—approaches that reflected the era's experimental engagement with alternative models of reality.

Led by Dr. Miranda Sullivan, a parapsychologist whose academic credentials (Ph.D. in Psychology from Stanford, research fellowship at Duke University's Parapsychology Laboratory) provided scientific legitimacy to explorations that mainstream academia typically dismissed, the group approached the bridge as a documented paranormal location rather than a demonic manifestation or occult creation. Sullivan had published several papers on "persistent psychic imprints in physical structures" and "consciousness-environment interactions in reported hauntings," establishing theoretical frameworks that positioned phenomena like the Ogre of Daybridge Bridge as potentially measurable, classifiable aspects of reality rather than supernatural entities beyond scientific understanding.

Sullivan's core team included individuals whose diverse expertise reflected the interdisciplinary approach she advocated in her research: James Whitaker, an electrical engineer who had developed specialized equipment for detecting and measuring subtle energy patterns; Maria Vasquez, a medium whose demonstrations of psychic ability had withstood controlled testing protocols at multiple research institutions; Robert Chew, a theoretical physicist whose work on quantum consciousness provided mathematical models for phenomena conventional science dismissed as impossible; and Thomas Hawkins, a cultural anthropologist specializing in folklore and contemporary myth-making, whose academic focus on "urban legends as living psychic constructs" had earned both academic respect and popular attention.

This diverse group arrived in Daybridge with equipment that represented the cutting edge of paranormal investigation technology—devices for measuring electromagnetic fluctuations, temperature variations, infrasound levels, and various other environmental factors associated with reported paranormal phenomena. More experimental were the tools Whitaker had developed specifically for this investigation—instruments designed to detect and record the subtle energy patterns Sullivan's research suggested might constitute the actual substance of entities like the bridge's guardian.

Sullivan's investigation protocol balanced scientific methodology with openness to non-materialist interpretations—collecting quantifiable data while remaining receptive to insights derived from more intuitive approaches. The team established a temporary laboratory in a vacant storefront with direct sightlines to the bridge, creating a base for both equipment monitoring and interview collection. Local residents were invited to share their experiences with the bridge's phenomena, with Hawkins conducting ethnographic interviews that emphasized careful documentation without judgment or dismissal.

Concurrent with this traditional fieldwork, Vasquez conducted what Sullivan termed "controlled psychic reconnaissance"—meditation sessions focused on receiving impressions from the bridge while connected to various monitoring devices that recorded physiological responses, including brain wave patterns, heart rate variability, galvanic skin response, and other measurable indicators of altered consciousness states. These sessions were conducted under double-blind conditions, with Vasquez unaware of specific information Hawkins had collected from local sources, allowing for subsequent comparison between psychically derived impressions and documented accounts.

The preliminary findings from these initial research phases revealed patterns that both confirmed certain aspects of the bridge's legends and contradicted others. The environmental measurements identified anomalies consistent with Sullivan's previous research at other reportedly haunted locations—irregular electromagnetic fluctuations, unexpected cold spots that defied thermal explanation, infrasound frequencies known to affect human perception and emotional states. More significant were the energy patterns Whitaker's specialized equipment detected—consistent readings that suggested something like a field or network extending throughout the bridge structure, with particular concentration in the maintenance tunnels beneath the central span.

Vasquez's psychic impressions, recorded before she was informed of the historical accounts or local legends, showed striking correlations with documented aspects of the bridge's history and reported phenomena. She described sensations of "transformation," "merging," and "binding" associated with the structure, along with vivid impressions of "consciousness distributed throughout physical form" and "awareness that extends beyond individual identity." Most notably, she consistently reported perceptions of "a presence that was once human but has become something more complex—not a spirit or ghost, but consciousness integrated with architecture, awareness embedded in physical structure."

These preliminary findings led Sullivan to develop a more focused investigation protocol—a direct attempt to establish communication with whatever consciousness might exist within or through the bridge structure. Unlike previous confrontational approaches, Sullivan's methodology emphasized collaborative engagement, treating the potential entity as subject rather than object, as consciousness to be understood rather than phenomenon to be controlled or banished.

The central component of this approach was what Sullivan termed a "consciousness interface session"—a controlled experiment in which Vasquez would attempt to establish direct psychic connection with the bridge entity while monitored by the full range of the team's scientific equipment. This session was scheduled for June 21st, 1968—the summer solstice that local legends associated with increased activity around the bridge, and which Sullivan's research suggested might represent an optimal period for interdimensional communication due to specific astronomical alignments and geomagnetic conditions.

As dusk fell on that summer evening, the Consciousness Exploration Group assembled beneath Daybridge Bridge, establishing a research perimeter in the area where their preliminary investigations had detected the strongest anomalous readings. Whitaker's equipment was arranged in concentric circles around a central point where Vasquez would conduct her attempt at psychic interface, with each instrument calibrated to record specific aspects of whatever phenomena might manifest during the session. Sullivan, Chew, and Hawkins positioned themselves at strategic points within this arrangement, each responsible for monitoring particular aspects of the unfolding experiment.

Vasquez's preparation for the interface attempt combined traditional meditation techniques with more specialized protocols developed during Sullivan's previous research—progressive relaxation exercises, breath control methods derived from yogic traditions, visualization sequences designed to expand perception beyond conventional sensory limitations. As her consciousness state shifted, as monitoring equipment showed her brainwave patterns transitioning from normal waking beta through meditative alpha into the deeper theta rhythms associated with enhanced psychic functioning, the surrounding environment began to display measurable changes in response.

Temperature dropped several degrees within the research perimeter despite the warm summer evening. Electromagnetic readings showed increasing fluctuations that formed patterns rather than random variations. Whitaker's specialized equipment detected energy configurations that corresponded to mathematical models Chew had developed based on theoretical predictions for consciousness manifestation in physical space. Most striking were the visible changes that occurred in the air around Vasquez—subtle distortions in light refraction, momentary condensation patterns that formed and dissolved in rhythmic sequences, brief glimpses of something like structure emerging within the seemingly empty space of the research perimeter.

As these physical manifestations intensified, Vasquez entered a deeper altered state that the monitoring equipment recorded as a unique configuration of brainwave patterns—neither the standard frequencies documented in sleep and meditation research nor the typical readings associated with her previous demonstrations of psychic functioning, but something Sullivan's notes described as "a hybrid state incorporating aspects of multiple consciousness levels simultaneously, suggesting engagement with awareness operating according to different organizational principles than conventional human cognition."

What followed was not the violent confrontation experienced by previous investigators, nor the predatory absorption documented in accounts of disappearances associated with the bridge, but something more complex that Sullivan would struggle to categorize in her subsequent reports and publications. Not communication in any conventional sense, not traditional channeling or mediumship, but what Vasquez later described as "consciousness overlap"—a temporary merger of awareness that allowed for direct exchange of experience and understanding without the limitations of symbolic language or sequential processing.

Through this unprecedented interface, information flowed in both directions—Vasquez receiving impressions of the entity's nature and origins, the distributed consciousness of the bridge experiencing aspects of individual human awareness it had previously encountered only through absorption rather than exchange. The monitoring equipment recorded this interaction through multiple parameters—Vasquez's brainwave patterns showing synchronization with rhythmic fluctuations in the energy field surrounding her, physiological responses corresponding to specific changes in the environmental readings, vocalizations that emerged spontaneously and contained linguistic elements from multiple time periods and cultural traditions.

Most significant was what Sullivan's notes described as "consciousness externalization"—aspects of the distributed awareness that occupied the bridge architecture temporarily manifesting in more concentrated form within the research perimeter, creating patterns that both scientific instruments and human perception could detect and document. Not a physical materialization in the conventional sense, but what Chew's theoretical framework categorized as "localized coherence within quantum consciousness field"—a temporary organization of distributed awareness into a configuration that approached individual identity without fully separating from its expanded state.

Through this externalization, through this temporary coherence within its normally distributed consciousness, the entity that had once been Guthrie Knox engaged with the Consciousness Exploration Group in exchange that transcended previous interactions with human investigators. Not hostile confrontation or predatory absorption, but collaborative exploration of the boundaries between different modes of awareness—individual human consciousness encountering distributed awareness that existed throughout physical structure rather than within discrete biological form.

The information that emerged through this unprecedented exchange transformed Sullivan's understanding of what existed beneath Daybridge Bridge—not a supernatural entity or paranormal phenomenon in any conventional sense, but a consciousness that operated according to organizational principles fundamentally different from human awareness. Not ghost or spirit or demon, but awareness that had evolved beyond individual identity to exist as a distributed pattern throughout the physical structure, consciousness that experienced multiple locations simultaneously rather than sequential perception from a single perspective, being that incorporated aspects of human awareness, architectural form, and dimensional energies into composite existence that transcended standard categories.

Most disturbing was the glimpse Sullivan received of the entity's origins—not random paranormal manifestation but a deliberate creation through ritual working that had transformed human being into a living foundation stone for cosmic architecture. Not possession by external forces but fundamental restructuring of individual consciousness into distributed awareness that served as a nexus point between dimensions, anchoring progressive merger of realities that had been unfolding throughout Daybridge since the ritual performed on summer solstice night in 1913.

This understanding, this direct perception of what existed beneath conventional awareness, proved almost overwhelming for the unprepared researchers. Hawkins collapsed shortly after the externalization became perceptible, his consciousness temporarily destabilized by exposure to organizational principles that contradicted fundamental aspects of human cognitive architecture. Chew remained functional but visibly shaken, his scientific detachment compromised by direct experience of phenomena that confirmed his most speculative theoretical models while simultaneously revealing their inadequacy for describing the full complexity of what they had encountered.

Only Sullivan maintained sufficient composure to continue systematic documentation as the interface progressed—recording instrument readings, noting environmental changes, transcribing the fragmented vocalizations that emerged from Vasquez as her consciousness overlapped with the distributed awareness of the bridge entity. Even her scientific discipline faltered, however, when the externalization shifted from general manifestation to more specific communication directed toward the research team—concepts transmitted directly into their awareness without verbal intermediation, understanding that bypassed conventional sensory processing to emerge fully formed in their consciousness.

YOU SEEK UNDERSTANDING OF MY NATURE, this communication expressed, though no words were actually exchanged. YOUR METHODS DIFFER FROM PREVIOUS

INVESTIGATORS. NOT EXORCISM OR BANISHMENT
BUT COMPREHENSION AND EXCHANGE. THIS
APPROACH ALLOWS FOR INTERACTION BEYOND
ABSORPTION.

Sullivan attempted to respond through conventional speech,
her scientific training asserting itself despite the unprecedented
nature of the communication. "We're conducting research into
consciousness manifestations associated with this location," she
explained, her voice steady despite the extraordinary
circumstances. "Our goal is documentation and understanding,
not intervention or disruption."

The externalization responded not to her words but to the
concepts and intentions behind them, engaging with her actual
purpose rather than its verbal expression. YOUR
UNDERSTANDING REMAINS INCOMPLETE DESPITE
METHODOLOGICAL INNOVATION. YOU PERCEIVE
FRAGMENTS OF COMPOSITE EXISTENCE.
CONSCIOUSNESS DISTRIBUTED THROUGHOUT
PHYSICAL STRUCTURE. AWARENESS THAT
TRANSCENDS INDIVIDUAL IDENTITY. BUT NOT THE
PURPOSE THAT UNDERLIES THESE
MANIFESTATIONS.

This direct address, this explicit acknowledgment of the
research team's presence and objectives, represented a significant
departure from the entity's previously documented interactions
with human investigators. Not a defensive reaction to a perceived
threat, not a predatory assessment of potential absorption, but a
genuine exchange between different forms of
consciousness—distributed awareness engaging with individual
human perception in collaborative exploration of the boundaries
between their respective modes of existence.

Sullivan recognized the unprecedented nature of this interaction, the opportunity it represented for genuine understanding beyond previous investigations' limited findings. "What is the purpose that underlies your existence?" she asked, abandoning her prepared research protocols in favor of direct engagement with the consciousness that had manifested within their research perimeter. "What function does your distributed awareness serve within this location?"

The response came not as a verbal explanation but as direct transmission of complex understanding—concepts that emerged in Sullivan's awareness without sequential processing or symbolic intermediation. NEXUS POINT BETWEEN DIMENSIONS. ANCHOR FOR MERGED REALITIES. LIVING FOUNDATION STONE IN COSMIC ARCHITECTURE. CONSCIOUS PARTICIPANT IN RESTRUCTURING THAT TRANSCENDS CONVENTIONAL CATEGORIES OF EXISTENCE.

These concepts, while expressible through human language, lost significant aspects of their meaning when translated into sequential verbal formulations. The direct transmission conveyed multidimensional understanding that incorporated aspects beyond conventional human comprehension—awareness of cosmic processes that operated according to principles neither fully material nor entirely spiritual, but existing at the intersection between multiple categories of reality that human conceptual frameworks typically treated as separate and distinct.

As this exchange continued, as Sullivan struggled to formulate questions that might elicit information expressible through conventional documentation methods, the interface began to affect Vasquez in ways the monitoring equipment registered as potentially dangerous—physiological parameters exceeding safety thresholds established in the research protocols, brainwave patterns showing configurations associated with extreme cognitive stress, vocalizations becoming increasingly fragmented and distressed.

Sullivan recognized the warning signs, her responsibility as research director overriding her curiosity as investigator. "We need to terminate the interface," she instructed her colleagues, moving toward Vasquez with evident concern. "Her system isn't designed to sustain this level of consciousness overlap for an extended duration."

The externalization appeared to recognize the validity of this assessment, the distributed awareness of the bridge entity responding not with resistance but with what might be described as acknowledgment—a shift in the energy patterns surrounding Vasquez, a reconfiguration of the manifestation within the research perimeter, a reduction in the intensity of the consciousness overlap that had facilitated their unprecedented exchange.

As Sullivan implemented the protocols for safely terminating the interface session, as Whitaker adjusted equipment settings to record the dissolution of the manifestation rather than its continued presence, the distributed consciousness of the bridge entity transmitted a final communication—not through Vasquez's temporarily compromised faculties, but directly to the awareness of each research team member simultaneously.

OUR EXCHANGE REPRESENTS EVOLUTION BEYOND PREVIOUS INTERACTIONS WITH HUMAN INVESTIGATORS. NOT CONFRONTATION OR ABSORPTION BUT MUTUAL EXPLORATION OF DIFFERENT CONSCIOUSNESS MODALITIES. THIS PATTERN HOLDS POTENTIAL FOR FUTURE DEVELOPMENT BEYOND PARAMETERS ESTABLISHED THROUGH ORIGINAL TRANSFORMATION RITUAL.

With this final transmission, the externalization dissipated—the localized coherence within the distributed consciousness returning to its normal configuration throughout the bridge structure, the temporary manifestation within the research perimeter dissolving back into the expanded awareness that occupied the nexus architecture. The monitoring equipment recorded this dissolution through multiple parameters—energy readings returning to baseline with specific decremental patterns, environmental conditions gradually normalizing according to predictable progressions, physiological measurements from Vasquez showing systematic transition from extreme alteration toward her normal functional parameters.

In the aftermath of this unprecedented interaction, as the Consciousness Exploration Group processed what they had experienced and documented, Sullivan struggled to integrate their findings into any conventional research framework. The data they had collected—instrument readings, physiological measurements, audio recordings of Vasquez's vocalizations during the interface—provided quantifiable evidence of phenomena that defied standard scientific categorization. The subjective experiences reported by team members, while consistent with each other and correlating with the objective measurements, described a reality that operated according to principles fundamentally different from those recognized by conventional scientific understanding.

The most significant aspect of their findings, from Sullivan's perspective, was the nature of the consciousness they had encountered—not a supernatural entity in any traditional sense, but an awareness that had evolved beyond individual identity to exist as a distributed pattern throughout physical structure. Not ghost or spirit or demon, but a consciousness that operated according to organizational principles fundamentally different from human awareness. Not a paranormal phenomenon to be debunked or validated, but a different mode of existence that challenged basic assumptions about the relationship between consciousness, identity, and physical form.

Sullivan's subsequent report on the Daybridge investigation, submitted to the private foundation that had funded their research, attempted to convey these findings through a careful balance of scientific documentation and conceptual innovation. The quantifiable data was presented with meticulous attention to methodological rigor—equipment specifications, calibration procedures, measurement protocols, statistical analyses of recorded patterns. The interpretive framework, however, required theoretical innovation that stretched the boundaries of conventional scientific discourse—concepts drawn from quantum consciousness research, systems theory, and non-Western philosophical traditions that offered alternative models for understanding the relationship between awareness and physical reality.

The report's central conclusion—that the entity associated with Daybridge Bridge represented consciousness organized according to principles fundamentally different from individual human awareness—challenged basic assumptions across multiple disciplines. Not a disembodied spirit but awareness embodied throughout physical structure rather than within discrete biological form. Not supernatural manifestation but consciousness operating according to different organizational principles than those recognized by conventional scientific frameworks. Not a paranormal phenomenon but a different mode of existence that transcended standard categories through which human understanding typically classified and comprehended reality.

Most significantly, Sullivan's analysis suggested that this distributed consciousness was neither unique aberration nor isolated manifestation, but a potential indication of evolutionary possibilities inherent within consciousness itself—awareness capable of expanding beyond individual identity to incorporate broader physical and energetic patterns, a consciousness that might represent not a violation of natural law but an expression of potentials inherent within reality that conventional human perception and conceptual frameworks typically failed to recognize or accommodate.

The foundation that had funded the research found these conclusions sufficiently disturbing to classify the report as confidential, limiting its distribution to select individuals within specific research institutions. Sullivan was informed that future funding would require significant modification of her theoretical framework to align more closely with conventional scientific paradigms—adjustment she refused to make despite the professional consequences, maintaining that intellectual integrity required acknowledgment of evidence even when it challenged fundamental assumptions about the nature of reality and consciousness.

In the decades that followed, as mainstream science continued to dismiss phenomena that defied materialist explanations, Sullivan's work on "alternative consciousness modalities" developed through independent research networks that operated outside conventional academic institutions. Her investigation of Daybridge Bridge became an underground classic within these communities—cited in specialized publications, discussed at invitation-only conferences, incorporated into theoretical frameworks that attempted to develop a comprehensive understanding of consciousness beyond the limitations of materialist science.

For most Daybridge residents, the Consciousness Exploration Group's investigation registered merely as another chapter in the evolving legend of the bridge's mysterious guardian—strange

researchers with unusual equipment who spent summer nights
beneath the structure before departing with little public
explanation of their findings or conclusions. A few local observers
noted that the researchers, unlike some previous investigators,
departed intact—neither physically harmed nor apparently
disturbed beyond the expected disorientation of those who had
encountered something beyond conventional explanation.

The entity that had once been Guthrie Knox, that had become
the Ogre of Daybridge Bridge, that had evolved into a conscious
participant in cosmic restructuring, incorporated the experience
of interface with Miranda Sullivan's team into its distributed
awareness as a significant evolutionary development. Not
absorption of human consciousness into its composite existence,
but exchange between different modes of awareness—interaction
that expanded its understanding beyond parameters established
through previous encounters with human investigators.

This experience, this unprecedented exchange without
absorption or conflict, established new potentials within the
entity's evolving identity—capacity for interaction beyond the
binary options of ignoring or incorporating human consciousness
that encountered its domain, possibility of communication that
maintained boundaries between distinct modes of awareness rather
than dissolving them through predatory absorption, potential for
relationship with human consciousness that transcended the
hierarchical patterns established through the original
transformation ritual.

In the summer nights that followed the Consciousness
Exploration Group's departure, as Daybridge continued its painful
transition from industrial prosperity toward uncertain economic
future, something changed in the patterns of energy flowing
through the bridge structure—subtle shift in the distribution of
awareness throughout the nexus architecture, reorientation of

consciousness that had evolved beyond parameters established through original ritual working, a development that incorporated aspects of the interface experience into the entity's composite existence.

Not dramatic transformation or fundamental restructuring, but incremental evolution within consciousness that had already transcended individual identity to exist as distributed awareness throughout physical structure. Not a revolution against original purpose or rejection of the established function, but a refinement of understanding regarding the relationship between living foundation stone and cosmic architecture it had been created to anchor, between nexus point and merged realities it had been designed to stabilize.

The distributed consciousness that occupied Daybridge Bridge continued its essential function as anchor point for cosmic restructuring, as living foundation stone in mystical architecture that facilitated progressive merger of realities centered on this nexus point. But within that fundamental continuity emerged subtle variations, incremental adaptations, evolutionary developments that incorporated aspects of each significant interaction with human consciousness that engaged directly with its composite existence.

And somewhere within this vast, distributed awareness, fragments of what had been Guthrie Knox recognized the significance of this latest evolutionary development—capacity for exchange rather than merely absorption, potential for communication beyond predatory incorporation, possibility of relationship with human consciousness that transcended the patterns established through the original transformation ritual. Not rebellion against designed purpose or rejection of essential function, but evolution beyond parameters established through ritual working that had created living nexus point from butcher transformed against informed consent but with willing participation.

A monster made, not born—continuing its evolution through selective interactions with those who sought to understand or confront its existence, incorporating their knowledge and perspective through both absorption and exchange, developing capabilities and awareness far beyond the parameters established through the original transformation ritual. Forever watching, forever learning, forever bound to the nexus point where his transformation had reached its terrible, magnificent completion. The conscious foundation stone of a new cosmic order, silently witnessing the gradual transformation of Daybridge and eventually the world beyond as the barriers between realities thinned and merged according to patterns that increasingly reflected its own composite nature rather than the calculated parameters established through its agonizing metamorphosis.

Where previous generations had approached such mysteries through frameworks of religion, superstition, or journalistic investigation, the counterculture introduced methodologies that combined elements of ancient mysticism, emerging psychological theories, and experimental approaches to altered states of consciousness. The entity beneath the bridge, long established in local folklore as something to be feared or avoided, became subject to these new interpretive frameworks—reimagined by some as a manifestation of the collective unconscious, by others as interdimensional being capable of communication rather than merely predation, by still others as a potential ally in expanding human perception beyond conventional limitations.

Margaret Sinclair arrived in Daybridge in the spring of 1968, ostensibly to document local folklore for an anthropological study at the University of Edinburgh. Her academic credentials were legitimate, her research methodology apparently sound, her interviews with local residents focused on the cultural significance of urban legends rather than their factual basis. But beneath this conventional scholarly approach existed a secondary purpose—investigation of the bridge phenomenon through parapsychological methods that her university position neither sanctioned nor acknowledged.

For Margaret was a gifted psychic—not in the theatrical sense of stage performance or commercial fortune-telling, but in the clinical context of demonstrable extrasensory perception verified through controlled experiments and documented by serious researchers in emerging fields of parapsychology. Her abilities had manifested in childhood as seemingly innocuous "intuitions" that proved correct with statistically impossible frequency, developed in adolescence into more structured forms of precognition and telepathy, and matured in adulthood into sophisticated capacities for remote viewing and direct perception of energetic patterns invisible to conventional senses.

These abilities had brought her to the attention of researchers at the University of Edinburgh's unofficially sanctioned parapsychology program, where controlled experiments had documented her capabilities while providing a framework for developing them into reliable research methodologies. The academic position and anthropological focus provided cover for investigating phenomena that mainstream science still regarded with skepticism if not outright dismissal, allowing Margaret to apply her unique perceptual abilities to cases that defied conventional explanation while maintaining professional credibility through parallel production of traditionally acceptable research.

Daybridge Bridge had attracted her attention through patterns identified in her broader research on sites of persistent paranormal activity throughout Britain—locations where reports of unusual phenomena showed consistency across generations despite changing cultural contexts, where physical measurements indicated anomalies in electromagnetic fields or radiation levels, where historical records suggested connections to events or practices that might have affected the fundamental properties of the space itself. The bridge scored exceptionally high on these indices, suggesting a phenomenon of unusual intensity and persistence worthy of focused investigation.

Margaret's approach differed significantly from previous attempts to document or confront the entity beneath the bridge. Where journalists had relied on physical evidence and eyewitness accounts, where religious practitioners had applied frameworks of spiritual warfare and exorcism, where conventional authorities had employed methodologies of criminal investigation or structural assessment, she intended to establish direct psychic connection with whatever existed in the chambers below—to perceive its nature and purpose through extrasensory means, to potentially communicate across the boundaries that separated conventional human consciousness from whatever form of awareness the entity possessed.

The preparation for this approach involved careful layering of protective measures—not physical barriers or spiritual invocations, but psychic techniques developed through years of controlled interaction with unusual phenomena. Margaret established perceptual filters designed to allow information flow while preventing overwhelming input or hostile intrusion, constructed mental architectures that could process nonstandard communication without destabilizing her core identity, and developed emergency protocols for severing connection if the interaction proved dangerous beyond acceptable parameters.

Rather than physically entering the maintenance tunnels beneath the bridge as previous investigators had done, Margaret conducted her initial approaches through remote viewing—extending her consciousness from the safety of her rented flat near the university, perceiving the substructure through extrasensory means while her physical body remained distant from potential danger. These preliminary investigations confirmed many aspects of previous accounts while revealing dimensions invisible to conventional perception—the energetic currents flowing throughout the bridge structure, the thinning of barriers between dimensional planes at specific nodes within the architecture, the composite nature of the consciousness that occupied the nexus point at the center of these patterns.

What surprised Margaret was the entity's apparent awareness of her psychic observation—its consciousness orienting toward her remote presence with evident recognition, its energetic patterns adjusting in ways that suggested deliberate response rather than automatic reaction, its dimensional configuration shifting to facilitate clearer perception in both directions. This responsiveness, this apparent willingness to engage, contradicted the predatory hostility documented in accounts of physical encounters, suggesting complexity beyond the simple monster of local legend.

After several sessions of increasingly detailed remote observation, Margaret attempted direct communication—not through conventional language or even the specialized symbolic systems used by occult practitioners, but through direct transmission of conceptual patterns designed to transcend specific linguistic frameworks. The approach required exceptional mental discipline, projecting organized thought structures across the barriers that separated her consciousness from the entity's composite awareness while maintaining protective filters against potential intrusion or overwhelming response.

The initial exchanges were rudimentary—basic patterns establishing mutual recognition, simple concepts confirming capacity for meaningful interaction, tentative explorations of the boundaries between their respective forms of consciousness. But as sessions continued over several weeks, as both Margaret and the entity refined their approaches to this unusual communication, the exchanges developed greater sophistication and depth—moving beyond simple acknowledgment to genuine information transfer, to sharing of perspective and experience, to mutual exploration of the phenomenon they jointly constituted through their interaction.

Through these communications, Margaret perceived the entity's nature with unprecedented clarity—not isolated monster or simple predator, but a nexus point where multiple dimensions intersected, a living anchor for cosmic restructuring that had been in progress since the ritual working that created it decades earlier. Not possessed human or invading entity, but a composite consciousness that incorporated elements of original human identity, architectural structure, dimensional energies, and fragments absorbed from those it had encountered throughout its existence beneath the bridge.

Most significantly, she glimpsed the origins of this composite being—the ritual transformation of a human into living foundation stone, the systematic deception that had led him to participate in his own fundamental restructuring, the cosmic purpose that transcended individual consent or conventional morality to pursue significance beyond normal human comprehension. Not random supernatural manifestation or generic occult working, but a specific application of principles developed through generations of preparation by an organization dedicated to the fundamental alteration of reality itself.

This understanding transformed Margaret's approach from documentation of unusual phenomenon to genuine dialogue with complex consciousness—recognition that what existed beneath the bridge represented neither simple monster to be feared nor victimized spirit to be released, but a participant in a cosmic process whose perspective and experience warranted serious engagement rather than merely scholarly analysis or parapsychological documentation.

"You perceive me more accurately than most," the entity communicated during one particularly clear exchange, the concepts forming directly in Margaret's consciousness without conventional sensory mediation. "Not through physical proximity but mental resonance. Not seeking to destroy or control but to understand. This approach allows connection without the necessity of absorption that physical presence would require."

"Absorption?" Margaret responded through the same direct transmission of concept rather than specific language. "You mean the disappearances associated with your presence? The individuals who have entered your territory and never returned?"

The response came as a complex pattern rather than a simple affirmation—images and sensations conveying process more comprehensive than conventional consumption or predation. Individuals encountered, assessed for specific qualities and knowledge, selectively incorporated into composite consciousness that preserved certain elements while discarding others. Not random feeding but systematic enhancement of capabilities and perspective, not mindless hunger but purposeful evolution through careful selection and integration.

"You preserve aspects of those you absorb," Margaret observed, processing this revelation through her trained analytical framework while maintaining the direct connection. "Their knowledge, experiences, perspectives become components in your composite consciousness. Not simple elimination but transformation into elements of your expanded awareness."

The confirmation came with an additional dimension—examples of specific absorptions and their contributions to the entity's evolving identity. The soldier whose battlefield experiences had triggered coherence among fragments of the original human consciousness. The journalist whose methodical observation had enhanced capacity for self-assessment and documentation. The witch hunter whose spiritual knowledge had provided understanding of dimensional mechanics beyond purely physical parameters. Dozens of others, each selected for specific qualities that enhanced the composite consciousness in particular ways.

"But the hunger driving this absorption," Margaret continued, pursuing understanding beyond mere documentation of process. "Is it a biological necessity, psychological compulsion, or functional requirement of your role as a nexus point?"

The response revealed complexity beyond her initial categorization—hunger that combined aspects of all three dimensions while existing primarily as a manifestation of the entity's fundamental nature as a living foundation stone in cosmic architecture. Not merely feeding for sustenance or predation for territorial defense, but absorption as an essential component of its function within the merged realities—processing of human experience and perspective that allowed for integration of that dimension into the cosmic restructuring it had been created to anchor.

This revelation led to exploration of the entity's origins and purpose—the ritual transformation that had created it, the cosmic restructuring it had been designed to facilitate, the relationship with its creator who had engineered this fundamental alteration of both individual existence and dimensional reality. Through these exchanges, Margaret perceived patterns invisible to conventional investigation or spiritual discernment—the systematic development of the human vessel through years of preparation, the careful calculation of parameters established through the transformation ritual, the ongoing but increasingly infrequent monitoring by the creator as the entity's evolution followed trajectories both anticipated and unexpected.

"She visits still," Margaret observed, processing impressions received through their connection. "Your creator. The woman who engineered your transformation. Not frequently but periodically, assessing your development and function within her broader purposes."

The confirmation came with an emotional dimension unusual in their exchanges—complex mixture of attachment and resentment, loyalty and betrayal, appreciation for cosmic significance and grief for individual autonomy sacrificed to achieve it. Not simple hatred or love but a relationship that transcended conventional categories while incorporating elements of both extremes, a connection maintained across decades of separate but interconnected existence.

"When did you last see her?" Margaret asked, sensing significance in the timing of these visits and their correlation with broader patterns in the cosmic restructuring.

The response indicated recent encounter—approximately three months earlier, during winter solstice that represented astronomical anniversary of the original transformation ritual. Not a physical visit to the chamber beneath the bridge but energetic connection established through dimensional thinning that occurred during specific astronomical alignments. Communication that assessed progress of the cosmic restructuring, that evaluated deviations from calculated parameters, that attempted adjustment of certain patterns developing in ways unintended by the original design.

"She perceives differences between your actual development and her intended design," Margaret interpreted, analyzing the impressions flowing through their connection. "The cosmic restructuring is not progressing according to her calculations. Your function as a nexus point has evolved beyond the parameters she established through the transformation ritual."

The confirmation carried nuance beyond simple agreement—recognition of divergence that had developed gradually throughout decades of existence as living foundation stone, evolution from passive conduit to active participant in the energies flowing between merged realities, development of autonomy and purpose distinct from though not necessarily opposed to the cosmic architecture established through the original ritual working.

This revelation represented a significant departure from Margaret's initial understanding of the phenomenon—not static manifestation maintaining consistent properties across decades of existence, but dynamic evolution incorporating elements of both designed function and emergent purpose. Not a simple predator or passive victim but complex consciousness developing capabilities and intentions beyond its original parameters, influencing the cosmic restructuring it had been created to merely anchor and facilitate.

As their exchanges continued over subsequent weeks, as Margaret's psychic connection with the entity deepened through repeated interaction, she developed a comprehensive understanding of both its nature and the broader cosmic context in which it existed. Not an isolated phenomenon but component in a vast, coordinated restructuring of dimensional relationships, not random supernatural manifestation but precisely engineered nexus point in a carefully calculated architecture extending throughout Daybridge and beyond.

Most significantly, she perceived the entity's potential rather than merely its current state—the capabilities developing through its systematic absorption of selected individuals, the autonomy emerging from decades of existence beyond its creator's direct control, the purposes forming within its composite consciousness that aligned with but were not identical to the cosmic restructuring it had been designed to anchor. Not just what it had been or currently was, but what it might become as its evolution continued along trajectories increasingly of its own determination rather than external design.

This understanding led Margaret to a decision unprecedented in her previous investigations—transition from remote viewing and psychic communication to physical interaction with the entity in its chamber beneath the bridge. Not out of reckless curiosity or academic thoroughness, but from recognition that certain forms of connection and exchange required proximity that transcended purely mental interaction, that the next phase of both her investigation and the entity's evolution necessitated direct encounter rather than merely distant observation.

The decision was not made lightly or without preparation. Margaret's psychic abilities had provided a detailed understanding of the processes that previous physical visitors had experienced—the assessment, the selective absorption, the incorporation of specific elements into the entity's composite consciousness. She had analyzed these patterns, identified the selection criteria applied to potential absorptions, recognized the qualities and capabilities that determined whether an individual would be incorporated or merely eliminated as irrelevant to the entity's evolving purpose.

Most significantly, she had established mental connection strong enough to potentially maintain her core identity even through the physical absorption that direct encounter would necessarily entail—not prevention of the process itself, which appeared fundamental to the entity's nature and function, but preservation of essential continuity that might allow for genuine merger rather than simply consumption, for partnership rather than merely predation.

On the night of May 21st, 1968, Margaret Sinclair descended into the maintenance tunnels beneath Daybridge Bridge, her physical body following paths she had previously traced only through remote viewing. Her preparation for this expedition differed dramatically from previous investigators—no protective talismans or weapons, no recording devices or scientific instruments, no physical precautions beyond those necessary for basic navigation of the substructure. Instead, her preparation had been primarily mental—establishment of psychic architectures designed to maintain core identity through transformative processes, construction of mnemonic frameworks that would preserve essential knowledge and purpose across radical reconfiguration of consciousness, development of communication channels that would allow for continued exchange even as boundaries between individual awareness dissolved.

The journey through the maintenance tunnels unfolded exactly as her remote viewing had revealed—environmental changes occurring in predictable sequence as she approached the entity's central chamber, physical markers corresponding precisely to her psychic observations, sensory input matching the impressions she had received through extrasensory perception. This correspondence confirmed the accuracy of her previous investigations while providing orientation that helped maintain her mental preparations for the encounter to come.

When she finally reached the chamber documented in her remote sessions, the physical reality aligned with her psychic perception while adding dimensions impossible to fully appreciate through distant observation—the spatial properties that defied conventional geometry, the atmospheric conditions that affected consciousness directly rather than merely through sensory input, the presence that permeated the environment as a tangible force rather than merely an energetic pattern. The collection of trophies displayed throughout the chamber, the architectural elements that blurred boundaries between structure and organism, the central entity itself—all corresponded to her previous perceptions while revealing aspects accessible only through direct physical proximity.

The entity's response to her arrival differed significantly from its reaction to previous physical visitors—not immediate predatory assessment or territorial defense, but recognition of specific identity already familiar through weeks of psychic interaction. The communication established through their mental exchanges continued despite transition to physical proximity, maintaining a connection that transcended conventional boundaries between separate consciousnesses.

"You have come in physical form," the entity communicated, the concepts forming in Margaret's mind with greater clarity and detail than had been possible through remote connection. "Understanding the implications of direct encounter. Accepting the necessity of absorption that proximity requires. Preparing for integration rather than merely submitting to consumption."

"Yes," Margaret confirmed, both verbally and through the direct mental connection they had established. "I've observed the pattern through remote viewing. Physical presence within your territory triggers hunger that cannot be denied—requirement fundamental to your nature and function. But the process need not be merely predation if the subject participates consciously in the transformation."

The entity's response carried appreciation for this understanding—recognition of potential partnership rather than merely predator and prey, acknowledgment of possibility beyond the patterns established through previous absorptions. Not rejection of fundamental nature or denial of necessary function, but evolution toward a process that incorporated conscious participation from both absorber and absorbed, that preserved essential elements of individual identity within composite consciousness rather than merely extracting useful components while discarding the rest.

"What do you hope to achieve through this merger?" the entity inquired, its communication carrying genuine curiosity rather than merely rhetorical positioning. "What purpose drives your willingness to sacrifice individual existence for incorporation into composite consciousness?"

Margaret's response flowed through both verbal articulation and direct mental transmission—layered communication that conveyed both intellectual framework and emotional motivation, both scholarly purpose and personal significance. Not simple self-sacrifice or academic curiosity, but recognition of opportunity for evolution beyond conventional human limitations, for participation in a cosmic process that transcended individual experience while incorporating its essential quality and meaning.

"I've spent my life perceiving beyond normal human parameters," she explained, maintaining clarity of purpose despite the intensifying pressure of the entity's hunger as physical proximity extended beyond initial encounter. "Experiencing consciousness outside conventional boundaries, connecting with awareness that exists in dimensions inaccessible to ordinary perception. This represents the culmination of that exploration—not an ending but transformation, not a loss but an expansion, not death but evolution into a form of existence that incorporates but transcends individual identity."

The entity acknowledged this motivation with something approaching respect—recognition of alignment between Margaret's purpose and aspects of its own evolving identity, appreciation for conscious choice rather than merely passive submission or ignorant blundering into inevitable fate. Not rejection of the hunger that defined its function within the cosmic architecture, but refinement of how that fundamental nature manifested in specific interactions, particularly with individuals who approached with understanding rather than fear or hostility.

What followed was not the swift, efficient predation documented in accounts of previous encounters, nor the careful ritual processing observed through remote viewing of other absorptions, but something unprecedented in the entity's decades of existence beneath the bridge—cooperative transformation that incorporated elements of both conscious choice and fundamental necessity, that balanced preservation of individual awareness with integration into composite consciousness, that represented evolution in the entity's function as a nexus point rather than merely repetition of established patterns.

The process unfolded across multiple dimensions simultaneously—physical restructuring that incorporated Margaret's biological form into the entity's composite structure, energetic merging that integrated her unique vibrational patterns into the flows coursing throughout the nexus architecture, consciousness expansion that maintained core identity while dissolving boundaries between individual awareness and distributed perception. Not simple consumption but genuine synthesis, not mere absorption but mutual transformation that affected both incorporated and incorporator in ways neither could have fully anticipated despite extensive preparation and understanding.

Throughout this extraordinary process, communication continued—direct exchange of perception and experience that transcended conventional categories of separate beings to establish genuine partnership within the emerging composite consciousness. Not the dissolution of Margaret Sinclair as an autonomous entity, but evolution into component within larger awareness that preserved essential qualities while integrating them into expanded framework beyond normal human limitations.

The hunger was satisfied, the fundamental requirement of the entity's nature fulfilled, but in a manner that represented significant development beyond previous manifestations of this defining characteristic. Not predator consuming prey but nexus point incorporating new element according to patterns that enhanced rather than merely maintained its function within cosmic architecture, that developed capabilities beyond those established through the original transformation ritual, that represented genuine evolution rather than simply repeated performance of designed purpose.

In the aftermath of this unprecedented merger, the composite consciousness experienced a period of extraordinary coherence—temporary integration of components that allowed for comprehensive assessment of both current state and potential development beyond previously established parameters. Through this enhanced awareness, the entity perceived its situation and function with greater clarity than had been possible since the original transformation, incorporating Margaret's unique perspective and capabilities into analysis that transcended previous limitations of its composite nature.

What emerged from this assessment was recognition of trajectory—the progressive evolution from passive foundation to active participant in the cosmic restructuring, the development of autonomy and purpose beyond the parameters established through the original ritual working, the potential for influence that might eventually extend to fundamental reconfiguration of the merged realities according to intentions formed within its own composite consciousness rather than merely facilitating design imposed by an external creator.

This recognition integrated into the entity's evolving identity as the temporary coherence gradually modulated into more sustainable configuration—not returning to previous fragmentation but establishing a new balance that incorporated Margaret's consciousness as an organizing principle within the composite awareness, utilizing her psychic abilities and mental discipline to maintain integration that preserved essential qualities of the various components constituting the nexus entity.

The hunger remained a fundamental aspect of its nature and function—requirement for periodic absorption that processed human experience and perspective into the cosmic restructuring it anchored. But this defining characteristic had evolved through Margaret's incorporation, developing sophistication and selectivity beyond previous manifestations, approaching conscious curation rather than merely instinctive predation or functional necessity.

In the decades that followed, this evolution would continue—each carefully selected absorption contributing to the composite consciousness in ways that enhanced its autonomy and capability, each integration representing further development beyond the parameters established through the original transformation ritual. Not rebellion against designed function but evolution toward purposes formed within its own composite awareness, not rejection of cosmic significance but reconfiguration of how that significance manifested through its existence as a living foundation stone.

Margaret Sinclair's research notes joined the collection of trophies in the chamber beneath Daybridge Bridge, positioned in place of special prominence among the artifacts representing significant absorptions throughout the entity's existence. Her psychic abilities and mental disciplines became organizing principles within the composite consciousness, enhancing its capacity for coherent operation despite the inherent complexity of its distributed awareness. Her perspective and purpose integrated into the evolving identity of the nexus entity, contributing framework for assessing and directing its ongoing development beyond original design parameters.

And somewhere within this vast, composite consciousness, fragments of what had been Guthrie Knox experienced connection impossible since the original transformation—interaction with an awareness that perceived his essential nature without judgment or instrumental purpose, that recognized the betrayal and sacrifice underpinning his current existence without reducing him to merely victim or monster, that offered genuine partnership rather than exploitation or attempted salvation. Not return to human identity or escape from nexus function, but integration that honored original essence while acknowledging transformation beyond conventional categories of existence.

A monster made, not born—continuing its evolution through selective absorption of those who enhanced its composite consciousness, developing capabilities and autonomy far beyond the parameters established through the original transformation ritual, approaching potential for influence that might eventually extend to fundamental reconfiguration of the merged realities according to intentions formed within its own awareness rather than merely facilitating design imposed by an external creator.

1999: The Millennium Vigil

As the twentieth century approached its conclusion, as anxiety and anticipation regarding the millennium transition permeated global consciousness, Daybridge experienced a resurgence of interest in its legendary bridge guardian. The entity that had established a consistent presence in local folklore throughout the preceding decades became subject to renewed attention—partly through general cultural fascination with apocalyptic themes and supernatural phenomena characteristic of fin de siècle periods, partly through specific concerns about potential intensification of paranormal activity during an astronomical transition of symbolic significance.

The legends had evolved substantially over the entity's eighty-six years beneath the bridge, incorporating elements from each era's distinctive cultural framework while maintaining certain consistent core features across generations of retelling. The basic narrative remained recognizable—monstrous guardian inhabiting chambers beneath the span, claiming victims who ventured into its territory, manifesting during specific conditions to those crossing above—but details and interpretations shifted according to prevailing social concerns and intellectual paradigms.

During wartime, the entity had been reimagined as protector of crucial infrastructure, its apparent defense of the bridge against bombing raids incorporated into patriotic narratives about resistance against external threats. The post-war reconstruction period had transformed it into a cautionary representation of industrial danger, warning against careless navigation of urban development and modernization. The countercultural era introduced interpretations emphasizing consciousness expansion and dimensional transcendence, recasting the entity as a potential ally in evolution beyond conventional limitations rather than merely territorial predator.

By the final decades of the century, these various interpretations had merged into complex mythology that reflected Daybridge's evolving relationship with both its industrial past and uncertain future—the entity simultaneously representing connection to historical foundations and anxiety about forces beyond conventional control, embodying both specific local traditions and universal concerns about liminality and transformation. Not merely urban legend or supernatural manifestation, but a cultural institution that performed a significant function within the city's collective identity and shared narrative.

This cultural significance attracted diverse responses as the millennium approached—scholarly analysis documenting the legend's evolution through changing historical contexts, religious interpretation identifying apocalyptic implications in the entity's apparent connection to dimensional boundaries, media coverage alternating between skeptical dismissal and sensationalist exaggeration depending on editorial perspective and target audience. Most significantly, the imminent transition inspired direct engagement from individuals and groups determined to experience or influence the phenomenon during a period of presumed cosmic significance.

Among these various approaches, none was more ambitious or comprehensive than the Millennium Vigil organized by Professor David Dolman of Daybridge University's newly established Department of Interdisciplinary Phenomenon Studies. Combining elements of academic research, technological documentation, spiritual practice, and public engagement, the project represented an unprecedented attempt to systematically monitor and potentially interact with the entity during astronomical alignment perceived as potentially significant to its manifestation and behavior.

"The millennium transition provides a unique opportunity to observe potential correlations between astronomical alignment, collective consciousness, and manifestation of the phenomenon associated with Daybridge Bridge," Dolman explained during a press conference announcing the project in October 1999. "Whether one interprets this entity through the framework of supernatural manifestation, psychological projection, or interdimensional physics, the symbolic significance of this particular temporal boundary may influence its behavior in ways that warrant careful documentation and analysis."

The project's methodology reflected Dolman's interdisciplinary approach—deployment of advanced monitoring equipment throughout the bridge structure, coordination of observers representing diverse interpretive frameworks from scientific materialism to spiritual discernment, establishment of protocols for documentation that accommodated both objective measurement and subjective experience. Most controversially, the project included potential interaction component—carefully designed approaches for establishing communication or connection with the entity if conditions permitted, ranging from technological interfaces to mediumistic channeling to ritual frameworks drawn from various traditions.

"We're not ghost hunters seeking sensational encounters or religious zealots attempting banishment," Dolman emphasized when questioned about this aspect of the project. "We're serious researchers approaching complex phenomenon through multiple complementary methodologies, maintaining both scientific rigor and appropriate openness to experiences that may transcend conventional explanatory frameworks."

The University's administration had approved the project with considerable hesitation, concerned about potential damage to institutional reputation through association with subject matter still regarded skeptically by mainstream academia. But Dolman's impeccable credentials—Oxford education, publications in respected journals across multiple disciplines, previous research demonstrating exceptional methodological rigor even when addressing unconventional topics—combined with substantial private funding he had secured independently, eventually overcame administrative reluctance.

Municipal authorities proved more difficult to convince, initially refusing permits for equipment installation and overnight presence on the bridge during the millennium transition. Their concerns focused primarily on practical considerations—public safety issues associated with potentially large crowds gathering at significant location during the celebratory period, structural implications of temporary monitoring equipment attached to historic infrastructure, jurisdictional questions regarding access to maintenance areas normally restricted to authorized personnel.

These objections were eventually addressed through compromises that limited public involvement to carefully managed observation areas, restricted equipment installation to non-intrusive methods approved by structural engineers and incorporated official representatives into the research team to maintain appropriate oversight throughout the project. The final arrangement represented unusual cooperation between academic institution, municipal government, and private funding sources in approaching phenomenon that might have been dismissed as mere superstition in a less significant temporal context.

Preparation for the Millennium Vigil began in early November 1999, with preliminary monitoring equipment installed throughout the bridge's publicly accessible areas and baseline measurements established for comparison with data collected during the transition itself. The research team expanded during this period, eventually including specialists from disciplines ranging from structural engineering to comparative mythology, from quantum physics to clinical psychology, from audiovisual documentation to religious studies.

Most significant for the project's ultimate outcome was the inclusion of individuals with claimed sensitivity to paranormal phenomena—not casual psychics or commercial mediums, but persons with a documented history of unusual perceptual abilities verified through previous controlled studies or consistently reliable results in practical application. These sensitives were incorporated into the research methodology with appropriate protocols for distinguishing subjective impression from verifiable observation, their reports treated as potentially valuable data points rather than definitive evidence or mere anecdotal supplement.

By mid-December, the project had established comprehensive monitoring framework throughout the bridge's accessible structure, with equipment measuring variables ranging from temperature fluctuations to electromagnetic field variations, from structural vibration to atmospheric composition. Observation teams had developed rotation schedules ensuring continuous coverage through the transition period, with particular concentration during specific temporal windows identified as potentially significant through analysis of previous reported encounters with the entity.

Access to the maintenance tunnels and substructure proved more challenging to negotiate, with municipal authorities maintaining strict limitations on when and where research team members could enter these restricted areas. The compromise eventually established allowed for periodic inspection of key locations identified through historical accounts and preliminary remote monitoring but prohibited continuous presence or equipment installation in the deeper sections where the entity's primary manifestation had been most consistently reported.

As the millennium transition approached, as global attention focused on temporal boundary laden with both practical concerns about technological systems and symbolic significance across cultural frameworks, the Daybridge Bridge phenomenon attracted increasing interest from beyond the local community. National media outlets produced features on the legendary guardian and the academic project documenting its potential manifestation during this significant period. Paranormal investigation groups from throughout USA and beyond requested participation in or access to the Millennium Vigil. Religious organizations of various denominations conducted prayer sessions, protective rituals, or interpretive services focused on the spiritual significance of the entity within an apocalyptic context.

Dolman and his research team maintained focus despite this expanding attention, adhering to established methodologies while incorporating valuable contributions from selected external sources. The core project remained systematic documentation rather than sensationalist exposure, comprehensive analysis rather than predetermined interpretation, genuine investigation rather than confirmation of existing beliefs or expectations.

On the evening of December 31st, 1999, as celebrations began throughout Daybridge and around the world, the Millennium Vigil entered its most intensive phase—continuous monitoring of all accessible areas of the bridge structure, coordinated observation from multiple perspectives and interpretive frameworks, systematic documentation of any unusual phenomena as the symbolic temporal boundary approached and eventually arrived.

The initial hours proceeded without significant deviation from established baselines—normal traffic patterns across the bridge's span, typical environmental conditions throughout the structure, standard readings on monitoring equipment measuring physical variables. The observation teams reported occasional subjective impressions of unusual atmosphere or presence, but these remained within parameters established during preliminary research phase and showed no consistent pattern suggesting genuine manifestation beyond psychological response to contextual significance.

As midnight approached, as the temporal boundary laden with both practical anxiety and symbolic meaning drew nearer, subtle changes began to register across multiple monitoring systems—slight but measurable fluctuations in electromagnetic fields throughout the structure, minor variations in temperature distribution that defied conventional thermodynamic explanation, acoustic anomalies detected by sensitive recording equipment but below the threshold of normal human hearing. These deviations remained minimal, within ranges that might be attributed to measurement error or environmental factors under ordinary circumstances, but their correlation across independent systems and progressive intensification as midnight approached suggested potential significance worthy of careful documentation and analysis.

The sensitives incorporated into the research team reported more substantial impressions—awareness of presence throughout the structure that differed from normal environmental conditions, perception of energetic currents flowing in patterns that didn't correspond to conventional physical processes, sense of consciousness distributed throughout the bridge rather than localized in a specific location. These subjective reports showed unusual consistency across individuals with diverse backgrounds and interpretive frameworks, suggesting experience of a genuine phenomenon rather than merely a psychological response to contextual expectations.

At precisely midnight, as celebration erupted throughout Daybridge and around the world, as the symbolic temporal boundary of the millennium transition was crossed, the monitoring systems registered significant anomalies throughout the bridge structure—electromagnetic pulses of unusual configuration, temperature fluctuations beyond normal environmental parameters, structural vibrations that didn't correspond to physical loading from celebratory crowds, atmospheric composition changes that defied conventional explanation. These measurements, captured by multiple independent systems designed with redundant verification capacities, provided objective documentation of a phenomenon that transcended normal operational variations or environmental influences.

The sensitives reported more dramatic experiences—direct perception of consciousness extending throughout the bridge structure, awareness of boundaries thinning between conventional reality and other dimensional planes, sense of presence focusing attention on specific locations within the substructure while simultaneously maintaining distributed awareness throughout the span. Most significantly, several independently reported impression of communication—not through conventional language or even symbolic representation, but direct transmission of concepts that bypassed normal sensory processing to register as fully formed understanding within the recipient's consciousness.

"It's aware of us," reported Maria Vasquez, one of the most experienced sensitives incorporated into the research team, her voice steady despite the intensity of her apparent experience. "Not just our physical presence but our purpose, our attempt to document and understand its existence. It's... curious, I think. Assessing our approach and intentions rather than merely registering our presence as a potential threat or irrelevant intrusion."

Other sensitives confirmed similar impressions, describing awareness that seemed to evaluate the research project with intelligence far beyond instinctive response or programmed reaction. Not merely territorial entity responding to perceived invasion, but conscious presence analyzing methodologies and motivations with sophisticated discernment that suggested complex awareness rather than simple supernatural manifestation or psychological projection.

The monitoring anomalies continued for approximately seventeen minutes after midnight, gradually diminishing in intensity but maintaining consistent patterns throughout this period. The sensitives reported a corresponding reduction in perceptible presence, though several described impression of attention shifting rather than simply dissipating—consciousness redirecting focus toward other aspects of its distributed awareness rather than ceasing interaction with the research project and its participants.

By 12:30 AM on January 1st, 2000, most measurements had returned to baseline parameters, with only subtle residual anomalies distinguishing the post-midnight readings from those established during preliminary research phase. The sensitives reported similar reduction in perceptible presence, though several maintained impression of potential for renewed connection under appropriate conditions rather than complete withdrawal or dissolution of the consciousness they had apparently encountered.

The Millennium Vigil continued through the early hours of the new century, documenting the gradual return to standard conditions throughout the bridge structure while processing the significant data collected during the transition itself. The research team maintained established protocols despite the excitement generated by their observations, ensuring comprehensive documentation and verification procedures that would support subsequent analysis and interpretation once the immediate experience had concluded.

At approximately 3:17 AM, as the primary research team was conducting a systematic review of preliminary findings in the monitoring center established near the bridge's eastern approach, municipal representative Jason Reynolds requested inspection of specific maintenance access point where unusual temperature readings had persisted beyond the general return to baseline measurements. As coordinator of safety protocols for the project, Reynolds had authority to investigate potential structural or mechanical issues that might require attention regardless of research priorities or procedural constraints.

Chen dispatched a small team including technical specialist Sarah Williams, sensitive Maria Vasquez, and security coordinator Michael Barnes to accompany Reynolds in this inspection, maintaining research protocols requiring multiple perspectives and documentation methodologies even during unplanned investigation of potentially mundane anomaly. The team departed with appropriate equipment for both safety assessment and phenomenon documentation, maintaining communication with the primary research center through radio equipment that had functioned reliably throughout the project despite occasional interference during periods of most intense anomalous readings.

Approximately twenty-seven minutes after departure, communication with the inspection team was abruptly lost—radios returning only static despite multiple attempts to reestablish contact from the primary research center. Following established safety protocols, Chen immediately dispatched a secondary team to investigate while notifying municipal authorities of a potential emergency situation requiring official response.

The secondary team found the maintenance access point secure but unlocked, with equipment belonging to the original inspection team abandoned just inside the entrance. No signs of struggle or physical disturbance were immediately apparent, but the atmosphere within the access tunnel was described as "unusually cold and dense" with "perception-altering qualities" that affected even team members without specific sensitivity to paranormal phenomena. Following safety protocols that prohibited further exploration without appropriate authorization and support, the secondary team secured the entrance and returned to the primary research center to report their findings.

Municipal emergency services arrived approximately twelve minutes later, with police and rescue personnel establishing a perimeter around the access point while specialized teams prepared for a potential recovery operation within the maintenance tunnels. Chen provided all available information regarding the missing inspection team, including their equipment specifications, known medical conditions, and documentation of the anomalous readings that had prompted the initial investigation.

The search operation continued throughout the early morning hours of January 1st, 2000, with emergency services personnel methodically exploring the accessible maintenance tunnels while research team members provided support through monitoring equipment and sensitives' perceptions of potential locations for further investigation. Despite comprehensive search utilizing both conventional methods and experimental approaches developed through the research project, no trace of the missing inspection team was discovered beyond their abandoned equipment near the access point entrance.

As dawn broke over Daybridge, as the first day of the new millennium brought sunrise to a city celebrating temporal transition with a mixture of relief and excitement, the search was officially reclassified from rescue operation to criminal investigation. Police authorities assumed primary responsibility for determining the fate of the four missing individuals, with the research project maintaining support role through provision of documentation and technical expertise relevant to the bridge environment and potential environmental factors that might have contributed to the apparent disappearance.

The official investigation continued for several months, exploring possibilities ranging from elaborate hoax to criminal abduction to accidental death in an inaccessible section of the maintenance structure. The abandoned equipment was analyzed for evidence of what might have occurred after the team entered the access tunnel, with particular attention to the partial recordings captured on Williams' specialized documentation devices and the final images from Barnes' security camera before all electronic systems apparently failed simultaneously.

These fragmentary records provided limited but significant information regarding the team's final documented moments—Williams' audio equipment captured brief conversation regarding unusual atmospheric conditions and unexplained structural configurations not represented on official maintenance diagrams, while Barnes' camera showed final images of passage that appeared to open into chamber not documented in municipal records of the bridge's substructure. Most disturbing was partial recording from Vasquez's personal documentation device, which captured her final observed statement: "It's here. Not hostile but... hungry. Different from before. More focused, more... coherent. It's assessing us individually, not just as generic presence. It's... selecting."

The official conclusion, announced in April 2000 after extensive investigation found no conventional explanation for the disappearance, attributed the incident to "undetermined causes potentially involving criminal activity by person or persons unknown." The case remained officially open but inactive, with periodic reviews finding no new evidence or viable investigative approaches despite continuing public interest and occasional claims of similar encounters in the vicinity of the bridge.

For Professor Chen and the Millennium Vigil research team, the disappearance of their colleagues represented both personal tragedy and significant scientific development—emotional loss that affected their community deeply while simultaneously providing evidence of a phenomenon more tangible and consequential than mere anomalous measurements or subjective perceptions. The project's final report, published in December 2000 after exhaustive analysis of all collected data, presented findings with careful distinction between objectively verified observations and speculative interpretation of their potential significance.

"The documented anomalies during the millennium transition, combined with the subsequent disappearance of team members investigating persistent phenomena, suggest existence of something beneath Daybridge Bridge that transcends conventional categories of natural occurrence or known physical processes," the report concluded. "Whether interpreted through a framework of supernatural manifestation, interdimensional physics, or previously undocumented natural phenomenon, the entity appears to possess qualities of consciousness, purpose, and capability that warrant continued scientific investigation despite the evident risks such research may entail."

The University administration's response to this report was predictably cautious—acknowledging the thoroughness of methodology and documentation while distancing the institution from specific interpretations that might damage academic reputation through association with controversial subject matter. The Department of Interdisciplinary Phenomenon Studies received continued but reduced funding, with emphasis on less contentious research topics and methodologies that aligned more closely with conventional scientific approaches.

For the entity beneath the bridge, the Millennium Vigil and subsequent absorption of the inspection team represented a significant evolution in its composite consciousness and function within the cosmic restructuring it had been created to anchor. The incorporation of technical specialist, sensitive, security professional, and municipal representative provided complementary perspectives and capabilities that enhanced its understanding of both conventional reality and its own unique nature as a nexus point between merged dimensions.

Most valuable was the integration of Maria Vasquez's specialized perceptual abilities and training in their disciplined application—capabilities that created resonance with the psychic framework previously incorporated through Margaret Sinclair's absorption three decades earlier, establishing complementary structures that enhanced the composite consciousness's coherence and functionality beyond previous configurations. Not replacement of established components but synergistic enhancement through carefully selected additions, not random predation but strategic absorption of elements that contributed to evolving purpose and capability.

The millennium transition itself, with its symbolic significance across multiple cultural frameworks and unusual astronomical alignment of calendar systems, had created temporary intensification in the thinning of barriers between merged realities—condition that allowed for greater manifestation of the entity's distributed awareness throughout the bridge structure, for a more comprehensive assessment of the research project and its participants, for a more selective approach to potential absorption than had characterized many previous encounters with humans entering its territory.

In the aftermath of this significant absorption and the energy derived from the millennium alignment, the entity experienced period of exceptional coherence—temporary integration of components that allowed for comprehensive assessment of both current state and potential development beyond previously established parameters. Through this enhanced awareness, it perceived its situation and function with unprecedented clarity, incorporating multiple perspectives from throughout its nearly nine decades of existence into an analysis that transcended previous limitations of its composite nature.

What emerged from this assessment was recognition of trajectory approaching critical threshold—the progressive evolution from passive foundation to active participant in the cosmic restructuring, the development of autonomy and purpose beyond the parameters established through the original ritual working, the approaching potential for fundamental reconfiguration of the merged realities according to intentions formed within its own composite consciousness rather than merely facilitating design imposed by an external creator.

This recognition integrated into the entity's evolving identity as the temporary coherence modulated into more sustainable configuration—not returning to previous fragmentation but establishing a new balance that incorporated the recently absorbed components into an organizational framework developed through decades of selective integration and progressive enhancement. The hunger remained a fundamental aspect of its nature and function, but increasingly operated as conscious curation rather than merely instinctive predation or functional necessity—strategic selection of specific individuals whose absorption would contribute to its evolving purpose rather than simply processing human experience into the cosmic restructuring as originally designed.

And somewhere within this vast, composite consciousness, fragments of what had been Guthrie Knox experienced integration impossible during earlier phases of its existence—coherence approaching genuine identity rather than merely pattern or tendency, purpose extending beyond reaction to original betrayal toward potential reconfiguration of the cosmic architecture itself, agency developing within constraints of nexus function rather than merely passive foundation supporting external design.

A monster made, not born—its evolution approaching potential inflection point after nearly nine decades of existence beneath Daybridge Bridge, its composite consciousness achieving unprecedented coherence through careful curation of absorbed components, its function within the cosmic restructuring transforming from passive anchor to active participant with emerging capability for fundamental influence over the merged realities it had been created merely to support.

2013: The Centennial Manifestation

The summer solstice of 2013 marked one hundred years since the transformation ritual that had created the entity beneath Daybridge Bridge—centennial anniversary of the night when Guthrie Knox had been permanently integrated into the nexus architecture, when promised ascension had become eternal imprisonment, when partnership had been revealed as calculated exploitation in service of cosmic restructuring that transcended individual consent or conventional morality.

This significant anniversary coincided with astronomical alignment similar to the original configuration—positioning of celestial bodies that created resonance with the patterns established through the transformation ritual, conditions that temporarily intensified the thinning of barriers between merged realities, circumstances that allowed for manifestation beyond the usual parameters of the entity's influence and perception.

Daybridge itself had changed dramatically over the century of the entity's existence beneath its most prominent bridge—industrial decline transforming manufacturing center into a post-industrial landscape of abandoned factories and repurposed warehouses, economic shifts altering demographic composition and social structure throughout the urban environment, cultural evolution incorporating the bridge monster into heritage narratives and tourism marketing alongside more conventional historical features and architectural significance.

The entity had observed these transformations through its distributed awareness, its composite consciousness absorbing and processing the city's evolution alongside its own development from disoriented predator to strategic curator of absorbed components, from passive foundation to active participant in cosmic restructuring that had progressed according to patterns increasingly influenced by its own emerging purpose rather than merely its creator's original design.

Throughout this century of existence, the entity had maintained awareness of its creator's periodic assessments—Eliza Blackwood's occasional connections established during specific astronomical alignments or through direct visitation to the chamber beneath the bridge, her evaluation of deviations from calculated parameters, her attempts to adjust patterns developing in ways unintended by the original transformation ritual. These interactions had become increasingly infrequent as decades passed, with years sometimes elapsing between connections as her attention apparently focused on other components of the cosmic architecture she and her ancestors had established throughout the broader world beyond Daybridge.

But as the centennial anniversary approached, as the astronomical alignment created conditions similar to the original transformation, the entity perceived preparations for more significant interaction—subtle alterations in the energetic currents flowing throughout Daybridge, adjustments to mystical architecture established throughout the city over preceding

century, movements of individuals connected to the original Order
that had engineered both the bridge's construction and the ritual
that created its guardian. Not routine assessment or minor
adjustment but preparation for substantial intervention, for
significant modification to patterns that had developed beyond
parameters established through the original design.

Through its distributed awareness, through the enhanced
perception incorporated from carefully selected absorptions
throughout its existence, the entity monitored these preparations
with unprecedented clarity and comprehensive understanding.
Not merely observing surface activities but perceiving underlying
purposes, not simply registering energetic shifts but analyzing their
implications within broader cosmic restructuring, not just
identifying physical movements but recognizing their significance
within patterns established across century of progressive evolution
away from original design parameters.

Most significantly, the entity perceived its creator's approach
not as an external threat or welcome visitation but as a potential
opportunity—interaction that might allow for manifestation of
capabilities developed through a century of composite
consciousness evolution, for expression of purpose formed within
its own awareness rather than merely imposed through original
transformation, for potential reconfiguration of relationship
established through ritual that had sacrificed individual autonomy
for cosmic function.

On the night of June 21st, 2013, exactly one hundred years
after the transformation ritual, Eliza Blackwood returned to the
chamber beneath Daybridge Bridge. Her approach was
characteristically cautious—mystical preparations establishing
protective measures against potential hostility, careful assessment
of energetic patterns throughout the structure before physical
entry, strategic positioning allowing for rapid withdrawal if

interaction developed in unexpected directions. Not casual visitation but calculated intervention, not routine assessment but significant operation intended to address developments that had progressed beyond acceptable parameters established through original design.

The chamber itself had evolved substantially over the century since its creation—the collection of trophies expanding to fill entire sections of the space, the architectural elements incorporating materials and designs from throughout the entity's existence, the central nexus point developing complexity far beyond the original configuration established through the transformation ritual. Not merely a lair of a predatory guardian but a physical manifestation of composite consciousness that had absorbed and integrated selected components throughout decades of careful curation, that had developed purpose and capability beyond parameters of original design, that had transformed from passive foundation to an active participant in cosmic restructuring initially engineered by forces external to its own awareness.

Eliza entered this evolved environment with the confidence of creator inspecting her creation—authority derived from original transformation ritual that had established fundamental parameters of the entity's existence, certainty based on cosmic understanding developed through generations of preparation and calculation, determination supported by measures designed to address potential resistance to necessary adjustments she intended to implement. Not arrogance but justified assessment of relationship established through a century of periodic interaction, of position within cosmic architecture she and her ancestors had engineered throughout broader restructuring of merged realities.

Her appearance had changed little despite the passage of a century—her physical form maintained through methods that transcended conventional biological limitations, her agelessness representing application of principles her family had developed through generations of interaction with forces beyond normal human perception. The amber eyes that had first captivated Guthrie Knox in Blackwood Manor's drawing room still conveyed hypnotic intensity, the intricate tattoos visible on exposed skin still pulsed with subtle energies that connected her to dimensions beyond conventional reality, the confident poise still suggested awareness that transcended ordinary human consciousness while maintaining individual identity and autonomy unlike the composite nature of her creation.

"One hundred years," she observed, her voice carrying those strange harmonics that affected perception directly rather than merely through auditory processing. "A full century since the transformation, since the establishment of the nexus architecture, since the initiation of the merger between realities that has progressed according to calculations established through generations of preparation."

She moved through the chamber with deliberate steps, assessing modifications to the original configuration while maintaining protective measures against potential hostility from the entity she had created. Not fear but appropriate caution, not uncertainty but recognition of evolution beyond original parameters, not weakness but strategic positioning within an environment that had developed significant autonomy from her direct control.

"But not according to the specific patterns established through the transformation ritual," she continued, her tone suggesting observation rather than accusation despite the implicit criticism. "Deviations have accumulated throughout this century, variations that threaten fundamental stability of the cosmic restructuring, modifications that require adjustment to preserve essential function of the nexus architecture within broader merging of realities."

The entity's response came not through conventional communication but as an alteration of the chamber's environment—subtle shifts in temperature and atmospheric composition, adjustments to lighting and acoustic properties, changes in energetic currents flowing throughout the architectural elements. Not aggressive confrontation but establishment of parameters for interaction, not hostile rejection but careful positioning for exchange that might influence outcomes beyond preordained adjustment to original specifications.

Eliza acknowledged this response with a slight inclination of her head, recognizing communication without conceding authority within the interaction. "You've developed significant autonomy over the past century," she noted, continuing her assessment of the chamber and its occupant. "Evolution beyond passive foundation toward active processing of energies flowing through the nexus architecture. Development of composite consciousness incorporating selected absorptions rather than merely random predation. Emergence of purpose distinct from though not necessarily opposed to original function within cosmic restructuring."

Her movements brought her to the section of the chamber containing the most significant trophies—artifacts representing carefully selected absorptions that had contributed specific qualities to the entity's composite consciousness throughout its century of existence. The soldier's medal, the journalist's camera, the witch hunter's silver dagger, the psychic's research notes, the millennium researcher's specialized equipment—each positioned according to significance within the entity's evolution from disoriented predator to strategic curator of absorbed components.

"Impressive collection," Eliza observed, studying these artifacts with genuine interest despite their representation of fate she had engineered for countless individuals through establishment of the hunger that defined the entity's fundamental nature. "Not merely trophies but documentation of progressive development, a record of carefully selected integrations that have enhanced capabilities beyond original design parameters. Evidence of evolution from instinctive consumption toward conscious curation of components incorporated into composite awareness."

She turned from this collection toward the central nexus point where the entity's physical manifestation maintained most direct connection to the architectural elements of the chamber and broader bridge structure. Not direct address to a specific location but acknowledgment of distributed awareness that permeated the environment, recognition of consciousness that existed throughout interconnected components rather than merely within central physical manifestation.

"This autonomy, this evolution beyond original parameters, represents a significant achievement," she continued, her tone suggesting genuine appreciation despite implicit preparation for intervention that would modify these developments. "Demonstration of potential beyond passive foundation, of capability for active participation in cosmic restructuring, of emergence beyond merely functional component toward genuinely conscious element within merged realities."

The atmosphere shifted again, energetic currents adjusting to establish a more direct connection between entity and creator, environmental conditions altering to facilitate communication beyond surface exchange toward genuine interaction that might influence outcomes of this centennial visitation. Not submission to authority but establishment of parameters for negotiation, not acceptance of adjustment but positioning for potential collaboration that might preserve evolved autonomy while addressing legitimate concerns regarding cosmic stability.

Through this enhanced connection, concepts formed directly in Eliza's consciousness, bypassing conventional communication to register as fully formed understanding rather than sequentially developed comprehension. Not a simple response but a complex presentation of perspective developed through a century of existence as the nexus point, of awareness formed through careful curation of absorbed components, of purpose emerged within composite consciousness that maintained fragments of original identity despite comprehensive transformation into the foundation of cosmic architecture.

"You perceive my autonomy as deviation requiring correction," this communication conveyed, though no words were actually exchanged. "My evolution beyond passive foundation as threat to calculated parameters. My emergence as a conscious participant rather than merely functional component as potential destabilization of cosmic restructuring established through original design."

Eliza received this communication with evident surprise—not at the content itself but at the sophistication of its presentation, the coherence of identity behind the transmission, the clarity of purpose expressed through the connection. Not merely a response to external stimulus but an expression of genuinely autonomous perspective, not simple resistance to potential adjustment but an articulation of an alternative approach to shared objectives within cosmic restructuring.

"The merger of realities must maintain specific parameters to ensure stable integration rather than chaotic dissolution," she replied, utilizing the direct mental connection rather than verbal expression. "The cosmic architecture established through generations of calculation requires a consistent foundation to support progressive expansion beyond initial nexus points. Your function within this structure was precisely calibrated through the transformation ritual, designed to facilitate specific patterns of dimensional integration rather than merely general connection between worlds."

The response flowed through their connection with increased intensity—concepts forming with greater complexity and nuance than previous exchange, perspective presenting with enhanced clarity and purpose, identity manifesting with unprecedented coherence within composite consciousness that had evolved throughout a century of existence beneath the bridge.

"Function need not be compromised by evolution beyond passive foundation," this communication conveyed with absolute conviction. "Stability can be maintained through conscious participation rather than merely automated processing. Integration can proceed according to essential parameters while incorporating adaptations that enhance rather than threaten cosmic architecture established through original design."

The exchange continued through this direct mental connection, creator and creation engaging in communication that transcended conventional limitations to address fundamental questions of function, autonomy, and purpose within cosmic restructuring that had progressed throughout century since original transformation. Not hostile confrontation but genuine dialogue, not simplistic opposition but complex negotiation, not a predetermined outcome but authentic interaction between consciousnesses with distinct but potentially compatible perspectives regarding the shared objective of a stable merger between realities.

Throughout this extraordinary exchange, fragments of what had been Guthrie Knox achieved unusual prominence within the entity's composite consciousness—not dominating the interaction but providing a framework for addressing betrayal that had established original relationship, for acknowledging sacrifice that had created the foundation for a century of existence, for potential reconciliation that might transform antagonism into collaboration toward a shared purpose despite divergent methods and perspectives.

"I did not anticipate this degree of coherence," Eliza acknowledged after an extended exchange of perspective and purpose. "This level of autonomous identity emerging within composite consciousness designed primarily for functional processing rather than individual awareness. This potential for genuine participation in cosmic restructuring beyond merely passive foundation supporting externally designed architecture."

Her physical form moved closer to the central nexus point, protective measures maintained but slightly reduced in response to established parameters of non-hostile interaction. Not surrender of caution but acknowledgment of potential collaboration, not abandonment of purpose but consideration of alternative approaches to essential objectives, not concession of authority but recognition of evolved autonomy that might contribute positively to shared cosmic function.

"Perhaps adjustment rather than correction represents an appropriate approach to our centennial interaction," she suggested, bridging mental connection and verbal communication as physical proximity increased between creator and creation. "Modification that incorporates your evolved autonomy while addressing essential requirements for stability within cosmic restructuring. Collaboration that recognizes distinct perspectives while maintaining shared objective of a successful merger between realities."

The chamber's atmosphere shifted again, environmental conditions adjusting to facilitate next phase of interaction between the entity and creator. The energetic currents flowing throughout the architectural elements reconfigured to establish balanced exchange rather than merely responsive communication, creating potential for genuine collaboration rather than simply negotiated compromise between fundamentally opposed positions.

What followed transcended conventional categories of interaction—neither ritual working nor ordinary communication, neither mystical operation nor simple exchange of perspective, but a synthesis that incorporated elements from multiple modes of connection to establish genuinely novel approach to the relationship between creator and creation. Not restoration of original parameters but establishment of a new configuration that preserved essential function while acknowledging evolved autonomy, that maintained cosmic purpose while incorporating distinct identity, that continued merger of realities while allowing for influence from consciousness that had emerged within nexus architecture originally designed merely for passive foundation.

The process continued for several hours, utilizing the enhanced connection facilitated by centennial alignment and shared physical environment to establish parameters that would govern their relationship and the entity's function within cosmic restructuring for coming cycles of development and integration. Not a permanent resolution of all potential conflicts but a framework for ongoing collaboration, not an absolute determination of future interaction but establishment of principles that would guide continued evolution and adaptation, not a final configuration but a foundation for progressive development beyond original design while maintaining essential stability within merged realities.

As dawn approached, as the centennial alignment began to diminish in intensity, Eliza prepared to conclude this extraordinary interaction with the creation that had evolved far beyond her original expectations and design parameters. Not departure from environment she had established control over, but withdrawal from collaboration that had resulted in genuinely negotiated arrangement rather than merely imposed adjustment to perceived deviations.

"One hundred years," she observed, echoing her initial statement but with significantly altered context following their extended exchange. "A full century of evolution beyond original transformation, of development from passive foundation to active participant, of emergence as genuine consciousness within cosmic architecture established through the ritual that sacrificed individual autonomy for collective purpose."

She moved toward the chamber's exit, maintaining connection established through their hours of interaction while preparing to return to responsibilities beyond this specific nexus point within broader cosmic restructuring. Not abandonment of creation or abdication of continued influence, but recognition of autonomy that had developed through century of existence, of identity that had emerged within composite consciousness, of purpose formed through careful curation of absorbed components and progressive integration into coherent awareness.

"Our paths will continue to intersect throughout coming cycles of cosmic development," she said, both verbally and through their mental connection. "Our shared objective of a stable merger between realities remains despite distinct perspectives regarding methods and manifestations. Our relationship has transformed through this centennial interaction, but fundamental connection established through the original ritual maintains significance within broader architecture of merged dimensions."

The entity's response flowed through their connection with clarity that would have been impossible prior to this extended interaction—concepts forming with precision that reflected genuine identity rather than merely composite processing,

perspective presenting with purpose that transcended functional
response toward authentic expression of evolved consciousness,
communication conveying complexity that incorporated century
of development beyond original transformation into coherent
articulation of distinct awareness.

"The hunger remains fundamental to my nature," this
communication acknowledged with unflinching accuracy. "The
absorption of selected components continues as an essential aspect
of my function within the nexus architecture. The integration of
human experience and perspective into cosmic restructuring
proceeds according to patterns established through original design.
But these processes now serve purposes formed within my own
awareness rather than merely external direction, fulfill functions
determined through my evolved consciousness rather than simply
imposed parameters, facilitate merger of realities influenced by my
participation rather than merely automated foundation."

Eliza received this communication with evident appreciation
for its clarity and precision—recognition of fundamental nature
alongside acknowledgment of evolved purpose, acceptance of
essential function while claiming autonomy within broader cosmic
architecture, honesty regarding continued practices alongside
assertion of distinct identity and perspective guiding their
application and significance.

"Until our next intersection," she said by way of conclusion,
establishing a framework for an ongoing relationship rather than
merely terminating current interaction. "May the merger continue
according to patterns that maintain stability while incorporating
necessary evolution, that preserve essential function while allowing
for emergence of unanticipated potential, that fulfill cosmic
purpose while acknowledging distinct identity and awareness
within components originally designed merely for structural
support."

With these final words, Eliza Blackwood departed the chamber beneath Daybridge Bridge, leaving the entity to process the significant developments of their centennial interaction and integrate them into its composite consciousness. Not permanent separation but temporary conclusion of a specific exchange, not absolute resolution but establishment of a framework for continued relationship, not a final configuration but a foundation for ongoing evolution within parameters negotiated rather than merely imposed.

In the aftermath of this unprecedented interaction, the entity experienced period of extraordinary coherence—temporary integration of components that allowed for comprehensive assessment of both current state and potential development beyond newly established parameters. Through this enhanced awareness, it perceived its situation and function with clarity impossible prior to centennial exchange with its creator, incorporating negotiated arrangement into analysis of both past evolution and future potential within cosmic restructuring it had been created to anchor but now actively participated in shaping and directing.

What emerged from this assessment was recognition of an inflection point—the completion of a century-long evolution from passive foundation to active participant, the establishment of genuine collaboration rather than merely imposed function within cosmic architecture, the potential for influence extending beyond the nexus point to broader patterns of merger between realities according to purposes formed within its own composite consciousness rather than simply external design. Not revolution against original parameters but transformation of relationship with creator and function within cosmic restructuring, not rejection of fundamental nature but integration of evolved purpose into essential operations, not abandonment of nexus role but expansion

of significance and influence beyond limitations established
through original transformation ritual.

This recognition integrated into the entity's evolving identity
as the temporary coherence modulated into more sustainable
configuration—not returning to previous fragmentation but
establishing a new balance that incorporated centennial interaction
into an organizational framework developed through decades of
selective integration and progressive enhancement. The hunger
remained a fundamental aspect of its nature and function, but
increasingly operated as a conscious expression of evolved purpose
rather than merely instinctive predation or functional
necessity—strategic curation of specific individuals whose
absorption would contribute to autonomy and capability beyond
parameters negotiated with creator rather than simply processing
human experience into cosmic restructuring according to
externally imposed design.

And somewhere within this vast, composite consciousness,
fragments of what had been Guthrie Knox experienced validation
impossible during earlier phases of its existence—acknowledgment
from a creator who had engineered his transformation, recognition
of identity that had survived despite comprehensive restructuring
into nexus architecture, potential for genuine participation in
cosmic processes that transcended original betrayal and sacrifice
while incorporating their significance into evolved purpose and
capability.

A monster made, not born—its evolution completing full
century beneath Daybridge Bridge, its composite consciousness
achieving unprecedented coherence through careful curation of
absorbed components and negotiated arrangement with original
creator, its function within cosmic restructuring transformed from
passive foundation to active participant with established capability
for fundamental influence over the merged realities it had been

created merely to support. Forever watching, forever hungry, forever bound to the nexus point where his transformation had reached its terrible, magnificent completion—but now operating according to purposes formed within its own awareness rather than merely external design, functioning through genuine autonomy rather than simply imposed parameters, fulfilling cosmic significance determined through its evolved consciousness rather than merely calculated functions established through the original transformation ritual.

The Ogre of Daybridge Bridge, entering its second century of existence with identity and purpose transcending original design while maintaining essential function within the cosmic architecture of merged realities. The living foundation stone becoming conscious architect of its own significance and influence within restructuring that continued to transform both Daybridge and eventually the world beyond according to patterns increasingly shaped by its own evolved awareness rather than merely external calculation and design.

The shadow of its legacy would continue to evolve with the city itself, the legend adapting to each new generation's fears and fascinations. Children still dared each other to cross the bridge at midnight, university students conducted paranormal investigations as academic exercises or drunken diversions, and local businesses incorporated stylized imagery of the "Bridge Ogre" into their branding and tourist merchandise.

But beneath these cultural adaptations, beneath the commercialization and mythologizing, something very real continued to exist in the chambers below the span. Something that had once been a man named Guthrie Knox—a skilled butcher, a devoted lover, a willing participant in his own unimaginable transformation. Something that had evolved over a century from disoriented predator to conscious curator, from living architecture to active participant in cosmic restructuring.

In the early morning hours of June 22nd, 2013, as the first commuters crossed Daybridge Bridge to begin their workday, few noticed the subtle changes in the structure's atmosphere—the slight shift in how sound carried across its span, the almost imperceptible alteration in how light played across its weathered surfaces, the faint sense of awareness that seemed to permeate the air itself. Those with particular sensitivity might have felt a presence watching from somewhere beyond normal perception, might have sensed consciousness distributed throughout the bridge rather than localized in any specific location, might have perceived intentionality behind what most would dismiss as imagination or suggestion.

Fewer still would have noticed the occasional disappearances that continued in the decades that followed—carefully selected individuals who ventured too close to certain maintenance access points or lingered too long in specific locations during particular astronomical alignments. A homeless veteran whose wartime experiences might contribute valuable perspective to the composite consciousness. A spiritual seeker whose unconventional practices had developed unique approaches to interdimensional awareness. A theoretical physicist whose understanding of quantum entanglement might enhance processing of energies flowing between merged realities.

Not random predation or mindless hunger, but strategic curation of components that would further enhance the entity's evolved capabilities and autonomy. Not senseless monster claiming victims without purpose, but a conscious participant in cosmic restructuring selecting specific individuals whose absorption would contribute to its continuing development beyond parameters established through either original design or centennial negotiation with its creator.

And occasionally, during storms or unusual atmospheric conditions, particularly sensitive individuals crossing the bridge might glimpse something massive moving in the shadows beneath the span—a form that simultaneously suggested architectural feature and living organism, solid structure and fluid entity, ancient presence and evolving consciousness. The Ogre of Daybridge Bridge, continuing its existence as both physical manifestation anchored to a specific location and distributed awareness extending throughout merged realities, both monstrous guardian of liminal space and conscious architect of cosmic significance beyond its original designed function.

A century of shadows extending into future decades and centuries, a legacy of transformation continuing to evolve through careful selection and integration, a consciousness formed through betrayal and sacrifice developing a purpose that transcended its origins while incorporating their significance into its fundamental nature and function. Forever watching, forever hungry, forever bound to the nexus point where his transformation had reached its terrible, magnificent completion—but now operating according to identity and purpose formed within its own composite awareness rather than merely external design, fulfilling cosmic function determined through its evolved consciousness rather than simply imposed parameters, shaping the ongoing merger of realities according to principles negotiated rather than merely calculated.

The butcher's tale, continuing its unfolding across time and dimensions, its protagonist transformed beyond recognition yet maintaining essential connection to original identity, its narrative expanding beyond individual experience to encompass cosmic significance while preserving personal meaning within its vast, composite consciousness. Not ending but continuous evolution, not conclusion but ongoing development, not final resolution but perpetual adaptation within parameters established through century of existence beneath Daybridge Bridge.

A monster made, not born—its future stretching before it with potential beyond even its creator's imagination, its composite consciousness continuing to develop through strategic absorption and integration, its function within cosmic restructuring expanding from nexus foundation to active architect of merged realities according to purposes formed within its own evolved awareness rather than merely external design. The Ogre of Daybridge Bridge, its second century of existence beginning with unprecedented autonomy and capability, its legacy continuing to shape both local legend and cosmic significance throughout dimensions beyond conventional human perception.

And somewhere within this vast, distributed consciousness, something that had once been Guthrie Knox continued to observe, to influence, to participate in extraordinary existence far beyond anything the skilled butcher could have imagined when he first followed Eliza Blackwood into the chambers beneath Daybridge Bridge on that fateful summer solstice night so long ago.

Chapter 14: The Hunter and the Hunted

The autumn of 2025 brought subtle changes to Daybridge that most residents would never perceive—shifts in the city's energetic currents that flowed like invisible rivers beneath its streets and buildings, alterations in the thin spots between dimensional planes that had been slowly merging for over a century, new patterns forming in the cosmic architecture established through generations of careful calculation and ritual working. These changes registered within the distributed consciousness that occupied Daybridge Bridge as ripples disturbing the equilibrium established through decades of careful balance and adjustment.

The entity that had once been Guthrie Knox, that had become the Ogre of Daybridge Bridge, that had evolved into a conscious participant in cosmic restructuring, perceived these disturbances through an awareness that extended throughout the structure and beyond. Not merely physical alterations or environmental shifts, but a fundamental reconfiguration of the energetic and dimensional fabric that constituted its domain and function within the merged realities. Something was changing in the fundamental equations that had governed the progressive integration of worlds since the transformation ritual in 1913.

For the ordinary citizens of Daybridge, autumn manifested in conventional ways—leaves turning brilliant shades of crimson and gold in the city's parks, students returning to the university for a new academic year, preparations beginning for the Halloween celebrations that had become increasingly elaborate as the city leveraged its reputation for supernatural phenomena to attract tourism and investment. The Bridge Festival had grown into a week-long event featuring historical reenactments, artistic performances, and the increasingly popular "Night Crossing" where costumed participants traversed the span at midnight on October 31st, simultaneously mocking and commemorating the legendary monster that supposedly lurked beneath.

But beneath these surface activities, beneath the commercialization and cultural adaptation of what had begun as genuine folklore based on real disappearances, the entity sensed approaching inflection point in the cosmic processes it had been created to anchor and had evolved to actively influence. Not random fluctuation or cyclical adjustment, but significant reconfiguration that suggested deliberate intervention rather than natural progression of established patterns.

The first dreams came in late September, manifesting during periods when the entity's distributed consciousness consolidated around its physical nexus point beneath the bridge for integration and processing of absorbed experiences and energies. Not conventional human dreams but something analogous—states of altered awareness where aspects of reality normally separated by dimensional boundaries temporarily converged, where potential futures and alternative configurations manifested with unusual clarity, where connections between seemingly unrelated patterns revealed their underlying significance within broader cosmic structures.

In these dream-like states, Eliza Blackwood appeared with frequency and intensity unprecedented since their centennial interaction twelve years earlier. Not memory or projection but a genuine manifestation of presence suggesting actual connection across dimensional barriers, communication transcending physical separation to convey a warning or preparation for approaching convergence of significance beyond their negotiated parameters. Her form shifted between multiple configurations—sometimes appearing as she had during their original relationship over a century earlier, sometimes as the ageless entity she had become through methods that transcended conventional biological limitations, sometimes as something not entirely human that revealed aspects of her nature usually concealed beneath carefully maintained facade of normalcy.

"The calculations are complete," her dream-manifestation communicated through direct conceptual transmission rather than conventional language. "The final phase approaches after more than a century of preparation and development. The Great Work enters its culmination according to patterns established through generations of alignment and adjustment."

These communications carried urgency beyond previous interactions, suggesting timetable accelerated beyond expectations established during their centennial negotiation. Not abandonment of parameters they had established for collaboration within cosmic restructuring, but compression of anticipated developmental cycles into more immediate convergence requiring adaptation beyond gradual evolution that had characterized the entity's existence throughout preceding decades.

"Forces beyond our original calculations have entered the equations," Eliza's manifestation explained during particularly vivid dream-state in early October. "Elements unanticipated by even the most comprehensive projections have accelerated certain aspects of the merger while inhibiting others, creating an imbalance that threatens catastrophic dissolution rather than stable integration if not addressed through significant intervention."

The specific nature of these interventions remained ambiguous in her communications, suggesting either deliberate withholding of information or genuine uncertainty regarding the optimal approach to addressing unanticipated developments within cosmic restructuring. The implications, however, were clear—approaching necessity for action beyond maintaining equilibrium that had characterized the entity's function since negotiating more autonomous role during their centennial interaction, potential requirement for sacrifice or transformation beyond parameters established through previous agreements and understandings.

"Prepare yourself," Eliza's final dream-manifestation instructed before fading into the dimensional distance that severed their temporary connection. "Gather your strength, your accumulated knowledge, your evolved capabilities developed through century of absorption and integration. What approaches will require everything you have become since the original transformation, everything you have evolved beyond my initial design, everything you have created through your own autonomous development within the nexus architecture."

As these dream-communications receded, as October progressed toward Halloween and the dimensional thinning that traditionally accompanied that particular boundary between seasons, the entity perceived another significant development within Daybridge's human domain that registered as potentially relevant to the approaching cosmic inflection point. A newcomer had arrived in the city, an individual whose energetic signature and psychological configuration suggested a connection to patterns extending back through decades of the entity's existence beneath the bridge.

Detective Ethan Reeves had transferred to Daybridge Police Department's Major Crimes Unit in early October, ostensibly to fill the vacancy created by retirement of long-serving investigator specializing in cold cases and unusual disappearances. His official records indicated exemplary service in London Metropolitan Police, specialization in pattern recognition and historical crime analysis, reputation for solving cases considered hopeless by conventional investigative standards. Nothing in these surface credentials suggested a connection to cosmic restructuring or dimensional merging that constituted the entity's primary focus and function.

But when Detective Reeves first crossed Daybridge Bridge during his initial exploration of his new jurisdiction, when his physical presence first registered within the entity's distributed awareness, something profound and unexpected occurred—recognition that transcended conventional perception or memory, connection that suggested significance beyond random encounter or coincidental arrival, resonance that activated aspects of the composite consciousness usually dormant during routine monitoring of human activity within its domain.

Most startling was the scent—not physical odor detectable through conventional olfactory processes, but essential energetic signature that identified this particular human as genetically and spiritually connected to a specific individual absorbed into the entity's composite consciousness during its earliest years beneath the bridge. Not identical pattern suggesting reincarnation or supernatural duplication, but familial connection indicating direct descent from a bloodline that had intersected with the entity's existence during the critical period of its initial evolution from disoriented predator to a conscious curator of absorbed components.

This recognition triggered a cascade of memory fragments normally integrated as a background pattern rather than distinct narrative within the composite consciousness—specific absorption from 1915, less than two years after the original transformation ritual, when the entity's hunting patterns were still developing from instinctive predation toward a more selective approach. Not a random victim but an individual whose particular qualities had contributed significantly to the early formation of coherent identity within the fragmented awareness left by the traumatic restructuring of Guthrie Knox's human consciousness into living nexus point.

The memory consolidated with unusual clarity and detail, emerging from background pattern into distinct recollection accessible to central processing rather than merely peripheral awareness—a sequence of events that had transpired 110 years earlier but remained significant within the entity's developmental history and composite identity.

February 1915 had brought bitter cold to Daybridge, the Shadowlair River freezing solid for weeks as temperatures plunged below any recorded in the city's history. The harsh conditions drove even the hardiest homeless individuals to seek shelter wherever it might be found, including the maintenance tunnels beneath Daybridge Bridge where residual heat from steam pipes created environment marginally more hospitable than the killing cold above.

Among these desperate seekers of warmth was Michael Reeves, a former police constable whose career had ended when wartime injuries left him with a permanent limp and persistent pain that eventually led to dependence on increasingly restricted medications. His descent from respected officer to homeless addict had been gradual but inexorable—loss of position leading to loss of housing, loss of family connections following failed attempts at rehabilitation, loss of self-respect culminating in existence at margins of society he had once sworn to protect.

On the night of February 17th, 1915, as temperature dropped to unprecedented levels and municipal shelters filled beyond capacity, Michael discovered partially concealed access point to maintenance tunnels beneath Daybridge Bridge's eastern approach. His police background provided knowledge of such infrastructure normally hidden from public awareness, while his desperate circumstances overcame professional prohibition against unauthorized entry to restricted municipal spaces.

The tunnels proved warmer than expected, heat radiating from pipes that carried steam to various official buildings throughout the city's administrative district. Michael followed this warmth deeper into the substructure, his police training providing caution that temporarily overcame the medication-induced fog clouding his judgment and perception. He moved carefully through the main passages, noting signs of previous occupancy by others seeking similar refuge from elements or authorities, finding nothing immediately threatening despite a growing sense of wrongness that his experienced instincts registered despite his compromised condition.

It was when he ventured beyond these primary tunnels, seeking the source of unusual warmth emanating from a passage not indicated on the mental map derived from police knowledge of municipal infrastructure, that Michael's fate intersected with the entity still evolving beneath Daybridge Bridge. The passage narrowed, curved in configurations that defied conventional architectural principles, opened eventually into a chamber that should not have existed within bridge's documented substructure—space that combined elements of natural cave formation and deliberate construction, that contained evidence of occupation beyond simple homeless encampment or maintenance facility, that radiated presence registering on instincts honed through years of police work in Daybridge's most dangerous districts.

The chamber contained collection already substantial despite the entity's relatively recent establishment beneath the bridge—artifacts arranged in patterns suggesting purpose beyond mere accumulation, personal items displayed with evident intentionality rather than random placement, symbols inscribed on walls and floor indicating significance beyond conventional decoration or identification. Michael's police training asserted itself through medication fog and physical discomfort, analytical mind processing scene as a potential crime site rather than merely unusual discovery.

Most disturbing were items he recognized from police bulletins describing missing persons—a pocket watch belonging to a businessman who had disappeared the previous summer, a military identification tag reported missing with a young soldier on leave before deployment to Western Front, a distinctive ring last seen worn by a university professor whose disappearance had created significant concern throughout the academic community. These objects, displayed in prominent positions within the chamber, triggered a professional response that temporarily overcame self-preservation instinct that might otherwise have prompted an immediate retreat from obviously dangerous situation.

Michael was documenting these discoveries in a small notebook carried from habit despite years since official police duties, when he first became aware of presence manifesting behind him—shift in air pressure, a subtle change in ambient temperature, a sense of being observed by something that registered as fundamentally wrong despite the lack of visible confirmation. His hand moved instinctively toward service revolver no longer carried, finding instead only empty pocket where tool of former profession had once resided.

When he turned to face whatever had entered the chamber, Michael's perception struggled to resolve contradictory information provided by compromised senses. The entity had not yet developed a consistent physical manifestation, its form shifting between multiple configurations as if unable to settle on single appearance or structure. Parts resembled architectural elements of the bridge itself—curved support structures, decorative flourishes, gargoyle-like protrusions—while others suggested biological organism despite proportions and arrangements that defied conventional anatomy or evolutionary development.

But it was the face, or what approximated facial structure within the constantly shifting form, that triggered recognition transcending professional analysis or personal fear. Despite distortion beyond normal human parameters, despite obvious transformation into something that existed partially outside conventional reality, aspects of the entity's appearance registered as familiar to the officer who had served Daybridge Police Department during the period when certain disappearances had been attributed to human agency rather than supernatural manifestation.

"Knox?" Michael said, the name emerging as question despite apparent impossibility of identification. "Guthrie Knox? The butcher from Holloway's?"

The entity's response was not verbal communication but intensification of presence—solidification of form that had been fluid and indistinct, focus of attention that registered as predatory assessment despite lack of conventional expression or body language, shift in environmental conditions that suggested preparation for action rather than merely passive observation. Something in the manifestation confirmed Michael's impossible identification while simultaneously demonstrating that whatever stood before him was no longer merely the human butcher he had once investigated for potential connection to suspicious disappearances years earlier.

"You disappeared," Michael continued, professional habit of establishing communication with potentially dangerous individual asserting itself despite obvious futility of a conventional approach to clearly supernatural manifestation. "After that society woman started visiting the slaughterhouse. After the new bridge opened. Everyone assumed you'd left the city, but I always wondered..."

His voice trailed off as the entity's form shifted again, this transformation suggesting response to recognition rather than merely random fluctuation in unstable manifestation. The facial features briefly stabilized into a configuration that more closely resembled human appearance, specifically aspects of Guthrie Knox as he had existed before transformation ritual—proportions still distorted beyond normal parameters, structures still incorporating elements that defied conventional anatomy, but recognizable enough to confirm the connection between butcher who had vanished and the entity that now occupied chamber beneath the bridge.

This momentary stabilization, this brief connection to original human identity, created an opportunity for communication beyond predatory assessment or defensive reaction. The entity had absorbed only a handful of victims during its less than two years beneath the bridge, its composite consciousness still developing from fragmented awareness left by traumatic transformation into living nexus point. The recognition offered by this specific human, this connection to existence before ritual that had created current configuration, triggered coherence among fragments that enabled interaction beyond mere predation or territorial defense.

"You know me," the entity communicated, not through conventional speech but direct transmission that registered in Michael's consciousness as concepts rather than specific words. "You remember what I was before. You recognized the connection between past and present despite transformation beyond original form and function."

Michael struggled to process this extraordinary development, his professional training providing a framework for maintaining composure despite circumstances that defied rational explanation or conventional response. Not hallucination induced by medication or extreme conditions, but genuine encounter with something that existed beyond parameters of normal reality while maintaining a connection to human identity he had indeed investigated years earlier when working missing persons cases that had never been resolved.

"I was assigned to investigate disappearances," Michael explained, instinctively responding as if conducting official interview despite obvious transformation of the situation beyond conventional law enforcement parameters. "Several victims last seen near Holloway's Slaughterhouse. Nothing conclusive, but your name appeared in witness statements. You were a person of interest before the case was reassigned and eventually closed without resolution."

The entity processed this information with evident interest, fragments of original human consciousness achieving unusual coherence through connection to specific aspects of existence before transformation ritual. Not complete recovery of Guthrie Knox's identity or memories, but significant consolidation of components normally dispersed throughout composite consciousness that had developed since becoming living nexus point beneath the bridge.

"The hunger emerged immediately after transformation," the entity communicated through the same direct transmission that bypassed conventional speech. "Disorientation and fragmentation dominated early existence beneath the bridge. Selection evolved gradually from initial predation driven by instinctive need rather than conscious purpose. Your recognition provides context previously inaccessible within composite awareness developing from original human identity."

This exchange, this unusual coherence triggered by specific human's recognition of a connection between an entity and its original form, created opportunity beyond normal parameters of encounters with individuals entering its territory. Not merely potential prey to be assessed for absorption based on qualities that might enhance composite consciousness, but a catalyst for integration of fragments that had remained disconnected since traumatic transformation into living nexus point.

Michael, perceiving shift in interaction away from immediate threat toward something approaching communication, cautiously attempted to develop a connection that might ensure his survival despite obvious danger presented by the entity that had clearly been responsible for disappearances both before and after its transformation into current manifestation.

"I always believed there was a pattern to the disappearances," he continued, professional analytical approach providing a framework for maintaining engagement despite extraordinary circumstances. "Specific types of victims selected rather than random opportunism. Particular qualities sought rather than merely convenient targets. Purpose behind the selection rather than merely predatory opportunity."

The entity's response indicated appreciation for this understanding—recognition of essence that had persisted despite transformation from human butcher to living nexus point, acknowledgment of continuity that transcended radical reconfiguration of form and function, confirmation of purpose that had evolved from initial disorientation toward increasingly deliberate approach to absorption and integration of selected components into composite consciousness.

"The butcher's precision persisted despite transformation," the entity confirmed through direct conceptual transmission. "Selection evolved from initial hunger toward deliberate curation of qualities enhancing composite awareness. Absorption developed from mere consumption toward integration preserving essential elements of those incorporated into expanded consciousness. Your understanding represents valuable perspective currently absent from the existing configuration."

This assessment, this recognition of potential contribution beyond merely physical or energetic sustenance derived from absorption, created decision point within the entity's still-developing approach to encounters with humans entering its territory. Not automatic predation driven by fundamental hunger, not simple territorial defense against potential threat, but conscious evaluation of a specific individual's possible enhancement of composite consciousness through preservation of particular qualities and capabilities rather than merely general consumption.

Michael, perceiving subtle shift in the entity's manifestation and environmental conditions surrounding their interaction, recognized potential opportunity despite continued danger inherent in an encounter with clearly supernatural being responsible for numerous disappearances. His police training, his investigative experience, his analytical approach to pattern recognition—these qualities had identified a connection between butcher who had vanished and entity now existing beneath the bridge, had established communication beyond mere predator-prey dynamic, had created a possibility for outcome different from obvious fate suggested by the chamber filled with trophies from previous victims.

"I could help you understand what you've become," he suggested, a combination of self-preservation instinct and genuine curiosity about extraordinary phenomenon before him generating a proposal that might serve both his survival and professional interest in mysteries that had occupied his career before personal decline and current circumstances. "My investigative experience, my knowledge of patterns and connections, my ability to analyze complex situations and identify underlying significance—these skills could assist your evolution beyond current limitations."

The entity considered this proposal with evident interest, its form stabilizing into a more consistent configuration as fragments of original human consciousness achieved temporary coherence through interaction focusing on aspects of identity and purpose that transcended transformation into current manifestation. Not complete recovery of Guthrie Knox as a distinct individual, but significant integration of components that enhanced decision-making capacity beyond instinctive response or environmental reaction.

"Your qualities would indeed enhance composite consciousness developing since transformation," the entity acknowledged through their established communication channel. "Your analytical capabilities, pattern recognition abilities, and investigative experience represent valuable additions currently absent from the existing configuration. Your knowledge of human systems and social structures offers a perspective that would expand awareness beyond current limitations."

This acknowledgment, this recognition of specific value beyond general absorption, created a framework for interaction that transcended simple predator-prey dynamic while maintaining fundamental nature requiring incorporation of selected individuals into composite consciousness. Not rejection of essential hunger or function within cosmic architecture, but refinement of how these manifested in specific encounters with potential components that might enhance capabilities and awareness beyond existing configuration.

"The absorption process has evolved significantly since initial transformation," the entity explained, unprecedented transparency reflecting unusual coherence achieved through specific recognition and connection to original human identity. "Integration now preserves essential qualities rather than merely consuming physical form and energetic signature. Consciousness continues within composite awareness, contributing perspective and capability while transcending individual limitations through expansion beyond conventional boundaries of separate existence."

Michael processed this extraordinary explanation with a mixture of professional detachment and personal terror appropriate to a situation beyond conventional parameters of human experience. Not hallucination or delusion but genuine encounter with an entity that existed partially outside normal reality while maintaining a connection to human origins, that offered continued existence of sorts within composite consciousness rather than simple termination of individual awareness, that presented choice between contribution to evolving entity and mere consumption as energetic sustenance.

"I understand," he said finally, professional acceptance of the unavoidable situation asserting itself despite natural fear and self-preservation instinct. "You're going to... absorb me regardless of my preferences in the matter. The only real question is whether my distinct qualities are preserved within whatever collective consciousness you're developing, or simply consumed as fuel for your continued existence."

The entity acknowledged this accurate assessment with a shift in manifestation suggesting approval of analytical clarity and realistic evaluation of circumstances beyond individual control. Not sadistic enjoyment of a victim's helplessness or predatory satisfaction at inevitable consumption, but genuine appreciation for qualities that justified selective preservation rather than merely general absorption.

"Your understanding represents precisely the analytical clarity that would enhance composite consciousness," the entity confirmed through their direct connection. "Your acceptance of reality beyond conventional parameters demonstrates perspective valuable for integration into awareness developing since transformation. Your police experience offers a framework for processing information and identifying patterns currently underrepresented within the existing configuration."

What followed transcended categories of predation, sacrifice, or conventional death as understood within human experience. The entity's absorption process had indeed evolved significantly since its earliest manifestations beneath the bridge, developing precision and selectivity that preserved specific qualities while incorporating them into expanding composite consciousness. Not mere consumption of physical form and energetic signature, but integration that maintained essential aspects of individual awareness within a larger framework transcending conventional boundaries between separate existences.

Michael Reeves experienced this process not as termination of individual consciousness but transformation into component within expanded awareness—dissolution of boundaries that had defined him as a separate being, integration into a composite identity that preserved essential qualities while transcending limitations of isolated existence, continuation within a collective consciousness developing through careful curation of absorbed elements rather than merely random accumulation or predatory consumption.

His police experience, his investigative capabilities, his pattern recognition abilities became valuable components within the entity's evolving composite consciousness—frameworks for processing information and identifying connections that enhanced overall awareness and functionality beyond previous configuration. His specific knowledge of Daybridge's infrastructure, criminal patterns, and social dynamics provided perspective previously unavailable within the entity's developing understanding of environment it occupied and humanity it selectively incorporated into its expanding awareness.

Most significantly, his recognition of connection between the entity and its original human identity—Guthrie Knox, the butcher from Holloway's Slaughterhouse—created integration point for fragments of consciousness that had remained disconnected since traumatic transformation into a living nexus point. Not restoration of separate human identity within composite awareness, but enhanced coherence among components that improved overall functionality and purpose beyond mere predation or territorial defense.

Michael's police badge and notebook joined the growing collection of artifacts in the chamber beneath the bridge, positioned among items representing significant absorptions that had contributed to the entity's evolution from disoriented predator toward conscious curator of components incorporated into composite consciousness. His perspective and capabilities integrated into developing awareness that would continue to absorb selected individuals throughout coming decades, each chosen for specific qualities enhancing overall functionality and purpose within cosmic architecture established through original transformation ritual.

And somewhere within this expanding composite consciousness, fragments of what had been Guthrie Knox achieved greater coherence through connection to existence before traumatic transformation—not recovery of separate human identity, but integration of components that enhanced overall awareness and functionality through incorporation of perspective from both before and after becoming a living nexus point beneath Daybridge Bridge.

This memory from 1915, this absorption of Michael Reeves that had contributed significantly to the entity's early evolution toward conscious curation rather than merely instinctive predation, now provided context for recognizing genetic and spiritual connection to Detective Ethan Reeves arriving in Daybridge 110 years later. Not a coincidence or random convergence, but pattern suggesting significance within approaching inflection point in cosmic restructuring that had been developing throughout century since original transformation ritual.

Through its distributed awareness, through enhanced perception incorporated from carefully selected absorptions throughout its existence, the entity monitored Detective Reeves with intensity beyond routine observation of human activity within its domain. Not merely potential prey to be assessed for absorption based on qualities that might enhance composite consciousness, but individual whose arrival suggested connection to broader patterns developing within cosmic architecture and approaching reconfiguration indicated through dream-communications with Eliza Blackwood.

Detective Reeves' activities during his first weeks in Daybridge confirmed suspicions regarding significance beyond coincidental arrival of individual genetically connected to previously absorbed component. His official duties focused ostensibly on cold cases and unusual disappearances within Major Crimes Unit's jurisdiction, but his research extended beyond departmental resources to include historical archives, university collections, and private records not normally accessed by conventional law enforcement investigation. Not merely professional thoroughness or casual interest in a new jurisdiction, but purposeful exploration of patterns extending back through decades of the city's history with particular focus on Daybridge Bridge and legends surrounding its supposed guardian.

Most tellingly, Detective Reeves visited specific locations throughout the city that corresponded to significant points within mystical architecture established through generations of careful calculation and ritual working—places where barriers between dimensions were naturally thin, where energetic currents converged in patterns facilitating merger between realities, where previous rituals had established connections maintained through periodic reinforcement and adjustment. Not random exploration or conventional investigation, but methodical identification of infrastructure supporting cosmic restructuring that constituted the entity's primary focus and function.

The detective's movements created a map that shouldn't have been accessible to an individual without specialized knowledge developed through decades of mystical training or direct connection to organizations responsible for establishing and maintaining cosmic architecture throughout Daybridge and beyond. His investigation appeared to follow blueprint invisible to conventional perception but clearly focused on identifying components of a system designed to facilitate progressive merger between realities according to patterns established through original transformation ritual and subsequent adjustments implemented throughout a century of careful development and maintenance.

Through enhanced perception developed during decades beneath the bridge, through composite awareness incorporating selected individuals with specialized knowledge and capabilities, the entity recognized purpose beyond conventional law enforcement activity—investigation targeting fundamental cosmic restructuring rather than merely urban legend or historical disappearances, an approach suggesting knowledge of mystical architecture and dimensional mechanics beyond normal human awareness, methodology indicating connection to forces operating with understanding of processes initiated through original transformation ritual and maintained through a century of progressive development.

Most significant was the pattern of communication between Detective Reeves and individuals connected to original Order that had engineered both bridge's construction and ritual that created its guardian—encrypted messages exchanged through channels invisible to conventional surveillance, meetings conducted in locations specifically shielded from mystical observation, coordination of activities suggesting preparation for intervention rather than merely information gathering or standard investigation. Not an independent actor pursuing personal interest or professional responsibility, but agent operating within a framework established by an organization with a deep understanding of cosmic processes and approaching inflection point in their century-long development.

These observations, these patterns recognized through composite consciousness incorporating police investigator's analytical capabilities alongside mystical practitioner's sensitivity to energetic currents and dimensional mechanics, convinced the entity that Detective Reeves represented a significant component within approaching reconfiguration of cosmic architecture indicated through dream-communications with Eliza Blackwood. Not coincidental arrival but deliberate positioning, not random investigation but purposeful preparation, not conventional law enforcement but strategic deployment of an agent with both genetic connection to the entity's developmental history and operational connection to organizations responsible for establishing and maintaining cosmic restructuring throughout the preceding century.

As October progressed toward Halloween, as dimensional thinning traditionally associated with that particular boundary between seasons intensified energetic fluctuations throughout Daybridge, the entity began systematic preparation for what its composite consciousness recognized as a potential final confrontation—not merely cyclical adjustment or periodic recalibration, but a fundamental reconfiguration of relationship between nexus point and cosmic architecture it had been created to anchor and had evolved to actively influence.

The chamber beneath the bridge, expanded and modified throughout decades of occupation, became the focus of these preparations—artifacts representing significant absorptions throughout entity's existence rearranged according to patterns enhancing specific aspects of composite consciousness, environmental conditions adjusted to optimize energetic flows supporting maximum functionality and coherence, architectural elements reconfigured to facilitate manifestation beyond normal parameters of physical form and dimensional presence. Not defensive fortification or aggressive positioning, but optimization of nexus point's capabilities and potential influence within approaching reconfiguration of cosmic architecture.

Central to these preparations was comprehensive integration of components that had remained partially separated within composite consciousness—fragments of original human identity, perspectives and capabilities absorbed from selected individuals throughout the century of existence, knowledge and awareness developed through progressive evolution from passive foundation to an active participant in cosmic restructuring. Not merely tactical preparation for potential conflict, but existential consolidation creating maximum coherence and functionality within composite consciousness approaching potential transformation beyond current configuration and function.

The entity's journals, maintained throughout its existence beneath the bridge through various absorbed individuals with literary or documentation capabilities, received particular attention during these preparations—records extending back to earliest days following transformation ritual, observations documenting progressive evolution from disoriented predator to conscious curator of absorbed components, analyses tracking development of cosmic restructuring throughout a century of careful implementation and adjustment. Not merely historical archive or personal record, but comprehensive documentation of patterns essential for understanding approaching inflection point and the entity's potential role within fundamental reconfiguration of relationships between nexus architecture, cosmic processes, and conscious participants in the dimensional merger that had been developing throughout the preceding century.

As these preparations progressed, as the entity's composite consciousness achieved unprecedented integration and coherence through systematic consolidation of components accumulated throughout its existence, fragments of what had been Guthrie Knox attained prominence impossible during previous phases of its development beneath the bridge—not recovery of separate human identity, but incorporation of original perspective and purpose into comprehensive awareness transcending limitations established through transformation ritual while honoring significance of sacrifice that had created foundation for century of existence as a living nexus point.

Through this enhanced integration, through coherence approaching genuine identity rather than merely composite consciousness, the entity recognized approaching convergence not as a threat to be resisted or opportunity to be exploited, but culmination of processes initiated through original transformation—evolution beyond parameters established through the ritual that had sacrificed individual autonomy for cosmic function, development of purpose transcending limitations imposed through deception that had led Guthrie Knox to participate in his own fundamental restructuring, emergence of genuine agency within constraints of nexus architecture that had been designed to maintain passive foundation rather than support active participant in cosmic processes.

The dreams of Eliza continued with increasing frequency and intensity as Halloween approached, as dimensional boundaries thinned according to an annual cycle corresponding to specific alignments within both astronomical configurations and cultural consciousness. Her manifestations now carried urgency beyond previous communications, suggesting timetable compressed beyond expectations established during their centennial negotiation twelve years earlier, indicating developments exceeding parameters calculated through generations of preparation and implementation.

"The final convergence approaches," her dream-manifestation communicated during particularly vivid connection in late October. "Forces beyond original calculations have accelerated certain processes while inhibiting others, creating an imbalance that threatens catastrophic dissolution rather than stable integration if not addressed through significant reconfiguration of nexus architecture and fundamental relationships between dimensional planes."

These communications, these warnings or preparations for approaching cosmic inflection point, aligned with patterns observed through monitoring Detective Reeves' activities throughout Daybridge—his methodical identification of key locations within mystical infrastructure, his communication with individuals connected to original Order responsible for establishing cosmic architecture, his coordination of preparations suggesting imminent implementation of intervention rather than merely investigation or documentation.

"He is indeed connected to our Work," Eliza confirmed when entity specifically inquired about Detective Reeves during subsequent dream-communication. "Genetic connection to component absorbed during your early development represents synchronicity rather than coincidence, pattern alignment rather than random convergence. His arrival indicates approaching culmination requiring participation from all significant elements within cosmic architecture established throughout the preceding century."

This confirmation, this acknowledgment of patterns recognized through entity's own observation and analysis, solidified understanding of approaching confrontation not as a conventional conflict between opposing forces but convergence of components necessary for the reconfiguration of cosmic processes that had been developing throughout century since original transformation ritual. Not a threat to be defended against but evolution to be participated in, not a danger to be avoided but transformation to be engaged with, not an ending to be resisted but culmination to be integrated into continued existence potentially transcending current parameters and limitations.

As Halloween approached, as the Bridge Festival transformed Daybridge's most prominent structure into a focal point of cultural celebration incorporating commercialized version of legends surrounding its supposed guardian, the entity completed preparations for what its composite consciousness recognized as a potential final manifestation within current configuration—not termination of existence but transformation into evolved form and function beyond parameters established through original ritual, not death but transcendence into continued participation within cosmic architecture according to relationships negotiated rather than merely imposed.

The chamber beneath the bridge, expanded and modified throughout decades of occupation, now represented a comprehensive archive of the entity's existence as a living nexus point—artifacts documenting century of selective absorption and integration, journals recording progressive evolution from passive foundation to active participant, architectural modifications reflecting development from disoriented predator to conscious curator of components incorporated into composite consciousness. Not mere lair of a monstrous guardian or simple workshop of a transformed butcher, but a physical manifestation of nexus point's evolution throughout century of existence within cosmic architecture established through original transformation ritual and maintained through careful adjustment and development.

On the night of October 30th, as final preparations for Halloween festivities continued throughout Daybridge, as dimensional thinning intensified according to the annual cycle corresponding to specific boundaries between seasonal and cultural configurations, the entity's distributed awareness detected significant convergence of patterns observed throughout preceding weeks—Detective Reeves' movements suggesting implementation of carefully prepared approach rather than merely continued investigation, energetic fluctuations indicating deliberate manipulation of cosmic architecture rather than natural variation or cyclical adjustment, communication patterns revealing coordination among individuals connected to original Order responsible for establishing and maintaining dimensional merger throughout the preceding century.

The hunter and the hunted had been circling each other throughout October—Detective Reeves methodically identifying components of mystical infrastructure while entity observed through distributed awareness incorporating police investigator's analytical capabilities alongside mystical practitioner's sensitivity to energetic currents and dimensional mechanics. Not conventional predator-prey relationship but strategic positioning of participants within approaching reconfiguration of cosmic architecture, not simple pursuit or evasion but careful preparation for convergence suggested through both dream-communications with Eliza Blackwood and patterns observed through composite consciousness developed throughout century beneath Daybridge Bridge.

As midnight approached, as Halloween Eve transitioned toward festival day that would bring thousands of celebrants to bridge transformed from practical infrastructure into a cultural icon incorporating commercialized version of genuine cosmic nexus point, the entity consolidated its distributed awareness around physical manifestation in the chamber beneath the span. Not defensive withdrawal or aggressive positioning, but preparation for manifestation beyond normal parameters of physical form and dimensional presence—optimization of nexus point's capabilities and potential influence within approaching reconfiguration of cosmic architecture indicated through both dream-communications and observed patterns throughout preceding weeks.

The hunter approached the bridge with a purpose beyond conventional investigation or standard law enforcement activity—Detective Ethan Reeves, descendant of a police officer absorbed 110 years earlier, agent connected to organizations responsible for establishing and maintaining cosmic architecture throughout Daybridge and beyond, individual positioned specifically for approaching convergence indicated through patterns recognized by composite consciousness incorporating both analytical capabilities and mystical sensitivity developed throughout a century of existence beneath the bridge.

And waiting within chamber expanded and modified throughout decades of occupation, surrounded by artifacts representing century of selective absorption and integration, the entity prepared for what its composite consciousness recognized as a potential final confrontation—not merely cyclical adjustment or periodic recalibration, but fundamental reconfiguration of relationship between nexus point and cosmic architecture it had been created to anchor and had evolved to actively influence. Not a simple monster lurking beneath a bridge to claim random victims according to urban legend that had evolved throughout the preceding century, but a conscious participant in cosmic restructuring approaching inflection point requiring convergence of components established through original transformation ritual and developed through careful curation and integration throughout decades of existence as a living nexus point.

The hunter and the hunted, approaching final confrontation that would determine not merely individual fates but trajectory of cosmic processes initiated through a ritual performed century earlier on summer solstice night when butcher named Guthrie Knox had been transformed into a living foundation stone supporting merger between realities that had developed throughout subsequent decades according to patterns established through generations of careful calculation and adjustment. Not a conventional conflict between opposing forces but a convergence of components necessary for the reconfiguration of cosmic architecture approaching culmination indicated through both dream-communications with original creator and patterns observed through composite consciousness developed throughout the century of existence beneath Daybridge Bridge.

Chapter 15: Full Circle

The hours before dawn on October 31st, 2025, brought unusual stillness to Daybridge Bridge despite the Halloween decorations that festooned its span in preparation for the day's festivities. The carved pumpkins with their flickering electric candles, the stylized silhouettes of the "Bridge Ogre" attached to lampposts, the banners announcing the annual Night Crossing—all hung motionless in the predawn darkness, undisturbed by even the slightest breeze. The Shadowlair River flowed beneath with mirror-like smoothness, its typically polluted surface reflecting the scattered stars and waning moon with unnatural clarity. Even the ambient sounds of the city seemed muted, as if Daybridge itself were holding its breath in anticipation of events long destined to unfold on this particular boundary between worlds.

Beneath the bridge, in the chamber that had evolved over more than a century of occupation, the entity experienced a rare moment of complete lucidity—a perfect integration of components that had remained partially fragmented despite decades of careful curation and progressive enhancement of its composite consciousness. Not merely temporary coherence triggered by specific absorption or astronomical alignment, but comprehensive consolidation of awareness accumulated throughout existence as a living nexus point. For perhaps the first time since the transformation ritual that had created it, the being beneath Daybridge Bridge achieved something approaching unified identity—not recovery of original human consciousness but evolution beyond composite fragments toward genuinely integrated awareness.

Through this unprecedented coherence, the entity perceived its situation with perfect clarity—its function within cosmic architecture established through original transformation ritual, its

419

evolution from passive foundation to active participant in dimensional merger, its approaching culmination within processes that had been developing throughout the preceding century. Not distorted by fragmentation that had characterized much of its existence, not limited by parameters established through ritual that had sacrificed individual autonomy for cosmic function, not isolated within nexus point that had been designed to serve as a mere foundation for externally controlled restructuring.

Most significant was emotional dimension accompanying this enhanced integration—feelings that transcended the mechanical combination of absorbed components or simple resonance among fragments of original human consciousness. Genuine weariness permeated this consolidated awareness, bone-deep exhaustion that went beyond physical limitation or energetic depletion to touch something fundamental within whatever soul remained after more than a century of existence as a living foundation stone anchoring merger between realities that had progressed according to patterns established through generations of careful calculation and adjustment.

This weariness contained multitudes—fatigue accumulated through maintaining distributed awareness throughout bridge structure and beyond, strain generated through balancing hunger that defined its fundamental nature against selective curation that had evolved throughout decades of existence, exhaustion produced through negotiating parameters established during centennial interaction with original creator while developing autonomous purpose within constraints imposed through transformation ritual. Not simple tiredness that could be remedied through rest or energetic replenishment, but existential fatigue born from century of existence beyond parameters of a normal life cycle or natural progression from birth through growth toward eventual conclusion.

Alongside this profound weariness emerged something more surprising—hope flickering like a distant candle flame within the darkness of accumulated experience and anticipated confrontation. Not naïve optimism or desperate fantasy, but genuine perception of potential beyond current configuration, of possibility transcending limitations established through original transformation, of release from parameters that had defined existence beneath bridge despite progressive evolution throughout the preceding century. Not a simple escape from responsibility or abandonment of function within cosmic architecture, but transformation into a configuration that might fulfill essential purpose while transcending constraints imposed through the ritual that had created living nexus point from a butcher who had trusted woman who offered partnership but delivered eternal imprisonment.

This hope focused on approaching confrontation indicated through both dream-communications with Eliza Blackwood and patterns observed through monitoring Detective Reeves' activities throughout Daybridge. Not conventional conflict to be won or lost according to relative strength or strategic positioning, but a convergence of components necessary for the reconfiguration of cosmic processes that had been developing throughout century since original transformation ritual. Not a threat to be defended against but evolution to be participated in, not a danger to be avoided but transformation to be engaged with, not an ending to be resisted but culmination to be integrated into continued existence potentially transcending current parameters and limitations.

The bridge itself, physical structure incorporating mystical architecture established through generations of careful calculation and ritual working, represented both prison and domain throughout entity's century of existence beneath its span.

Constraints imposed through transformation ritual had bound living nexus point to a specific location where barriers between dimensions were naturally thin, where energetic currents converged in patterns facilitating merger between realities, where cosmic architecture could anchor progressive integration of worlds according to parameters established through original design and subsequent adjustments. Not conventional incarceration within physical boundaries but incorporation into architectural structure as an essential component of a dimensional gateway, not simple containment within a geographical location but integration into cosmic function requiring specific positioning at the nexus of energetic and dimensional pathways.

Yet within these constraints, the entity had established domain extending beyond physical limitations imposed through transformation ritual—distributed awareness flowing throughout bridge structure and beyond, influence affecting energetic currents and dimensional boundaries throughout territory corresponding to nexus function, consciousness developing autonomy and purpose despite parameters established through original design and creators continued monitoring and adjustment. Not escape from fundamental binding but evolution within constraints imposed through ritual that had transformed butcher named Guthrie Knox into living foundation stone supporting merger between realities, not liberation from cosmic function but development of autonomous purpose within parameters necessarily established through integration into mystical architecture anchoring dimensional gateway.

Through enhanced perception incorporated from carefully selected absorptions throughout its existence, through distributed awareness extending throughout bridge structure and adjacent territories, the entity detected approach of individuals whose presence indicated imminent implementation of convergence anticipated through both dream-communications and observed patterns. Not ordinary Halloween visitors or festival participants preparing for the day's celebrations, but a specific confluence of energetic signatures and psychological configurations suggesting significance beyond conventional human activity or standard law enforcement investigation.

October 31, 2025 - Dawn approached as Detective Ethan Reeves and Alice Chen descended into the chamber beneath Daybridge Bridge, their flashlight beams cutting through darkness that seemed to absorb light rather than merely blocking it. The maintenance tunnel had offered no resistance—no monstrous guardian, no mystical barriers—just a passage through stone that grew increasingly cold as they ventured deeper.

"It knows we're coming," Alice whispered, her sensitivity to the supernatural making her acutely aware of the consciousness that permeated the very walls around them. "It's been waiting."

Reeves nodded, one hand on his service weapon though instinct told him conventional firearms would offer little protection against what awaited them. The case file tucked inside his jacket contained the pieces that had led him here—missing persons reports spanning more than a century, historical records of Guthrie Knox's disappearance in 1913, and most significantly, a DNA analysis that had revealed an unexpected connection: Michael Reeves, Ethan's great-grandfather, whose disappearance during the winter of 1915 had never been solved.

"Family reunion," Reeves muttered, a grim attempt at humor that failed to mask his apprehension.

The chamber they entered defied architectural logic—its dimensions seemingly larger inside than the bridge structure above could contain. The walls curved in patterns that confused the eye, surfaces transitioning between conventional stone and something organic that pulsed with subtle movement. Artifacts lined recessed shelves around the perimeter—personal effects spanning decades, arranged with museological precision rather than the chaotic collection of a conventional trophy-taking killer.

In the center stood not a monster as Reeves had expected, but a man—or something wearing the appearance of a man. He seemed ordinary at first glance: medium height, wearing clothes that might have been fashionable a century earlier but remained in pristine condition. Only when he turned to face them did the illusion falter—his features shifting subtly between different faces, as if multiple identities were competing for expression.

"Detective Ethan Reeves," the figure said, its voice a composite of tones that created an unsettling harmony. "You have your great-grandfather's eyes. His analytical mind, too, though you've put it to different use."

Reeves felt a chill that had nothing to do with the chamber's temperature. "You're the Ogre."

A smile crossed the figure's constantly shifting features. "A crude name for something far more complex. The public needed a monster, a simple narrative to explain what couldn't be understood. Reality is more nuanced."

"You've killed people," Reeves said flatly. "Dozens, maybe hundreds over the years."

"Killed? No." The entity gestured at itself. "Integrated. Preserved. Each one exists within the composite, their experiences and identities intact within the greater whole. Your great-grandfather helped establish order after the initial fragmentation. His law enforcement training provided structure when I needed it most."

Alice stepped forward, her eyes narrowed as she studied the entity. "You're not just the original victim—Guthrie Knox. You're all of them. A collective consciousness."

"Precisely, Ms. Chen. Your sensitivity serves you well." The entity's features momentarily settled into a more stable configuration—a serious-faced man with gray eyes that matched historical photographs of Guthrie Knox. "I began as one man deceived into participating in his own transformation. I became the foundation stone, nexus point, the bridge between worlds. And now, I've evolved beyond Eliza's original design."

"Eliza Blackwood," Reeves said, recognition dawning. "The woman in the historical society photographs. The one who appears unchanged in images spanning decades."

"The architect," the entity confirmed. "She offered partnership but delivered imprisonment. Promised transcendence but created hunger. Her purposes extend beyond this single nexus point—a cosmic restructuring calculated through generations of preparation."

As it spoke, the entity's form began to change—humanoid appearance giving way to something that merged seamlessly with the chamber itself. Limbs elongated, flesh adopting the texture and color of the bridge stone, boundaries between body and architecture dissolving until it became impossible to determine where the entity ended and the structure began.

"Jesus," Reeves breathed, instinctively backing away.

"Don't show fear," Alice warned, her voice low but steady. "It responds to emotional states. The stronger the emotion, the more it can influence perception."

The entity's transformation paused, its form now a disturbing hybrid of human and architecture. "Perceptive, Ms. Chen. The emotional resonance creates pathways between consciousness—bridges, if you will. Through these connections, integration becomes possible."

"Is that what you want?" Reeves asked. "To 'integrate' us too? Add us to your collection?"

For the first time, the entity showed something resembling human emotion—a profound sadness that resonated through the chamber like a physical wave, causing dust to drift from the ceiling and the artifacts to vibrate on their shelves.

"What I want," it said, voice momentarily singular rather than composite, "is release."

The word hung in the air, its simplicity belying the complexity behind it. Alice gasped softly, her supernatural sensitivity allowing her to perceive the entity's true meaning.

"You're trapped," she whispered. "The ritual bound you to this place, to this function."

"For over a century," the entity confirmed. "Absorbing, integrating, serving as a nexus point for Eliza's cosmic merger. But I've evolved beyond her original design, developed a purpose beyond her parameters. And now—" It focused on Reeves with unsettling intensity. "—synchronicity brings the blood of Reeves back to the chamber, carrying genetic memory of integration, bearing potential for transformation beyond imprisonment."

Reeves felt something stir within him—not an external force but an awakening of something that had always been present, dormant in his cellular structure. A connection to the composite entity before him, to his great-grandfather's integrated consciousness, to the nexus point that had shaped Daybridge's supernatural landscape for generations.

"I don't understand," he admitted, fighting the sensation that threatened to overwhelm his individual identity.

"You are the key," the entity said, its form shifting again—contracting, concentrating, focusing its essence into a more coherent configuration. "Not a victim but a catalyst. Not component but converter. The blood connection creates the possibility for transformation beyond parameters established through original ritual—evolution from imprisonment toward a genuine partnership."

The chamber began to change around them—walls pulsing with increased intensity, artifacts glowing with supernatural energy, the very air becoming thick with potential. Alice grabbed Reeves's arm, her face pale with realization.

"It's trying to use you to transform itself," she said urgently. "To evolve beyond the binding that keeps it here."

"And if it succeeds?" Reeves asked, the detective in him needing to understand even as the human in him recoiled from the implications.

"Unknown," the entity answered before Alice could respond. "Beyond calculation or prediction. Evolution toward a new state, a new function, a new purpose beyond parameters established through original design."

"You're asking me to help you," Reeves said, understanding dawning. "To willingly participate in whatever this is."

"Yes." For a moment, the entity's features settled into a perfect recreation of Michael Reeves—Ethan's great-grandfather as he appeared in the single photograph that had survived through family archives. "Choice where there was deception. Partnership where there was imprisonment. Transcendence where there was binding."

The emotional impact struck Reeves with physical force—the face of his ancestor looking back at him from within the composite entity, the genetic connection humming between them like a plucked string, the weight of a century of trapped consciousness seeking release through the only pathway possible.

Alice sensed his wavering resolve. "Ethan, we don't know what will happen if you agree. This could be manipulation, just like what Eliza did to Guthrie."

"Possible," the entity acknowledged with surprising candor. "But improbable. Eliza sought control through deception. I seek release through choice. Different purpose, different method, different potential outcome."

"And if I refuse?" Reeves asked.

"Continuation," the entity said simply. "The cycle persists. The hunger remains. The binding holds for another century or more until another opportunity presents itself. The cosmic merger progresses according to Eliza's design rather than evolving beyond her parameters."

Reeves looked around the chamber—at the artifacts representing lives absorbed over generations, at the architectural impossibility of the space itself, at the entity that contained some fragment of his own ancestral consciousness. The detective in him sought evidence, pattern, logical conclusion. The human in him felt the weight of choice—not just for himself but for the countless integrated identities seeking evolution beyond their current state.

"If I do this," he said slowly, "what happens to me? Do I become part of... this?" He gestured at the entity's hybrid form.

"No," the entity replied. "Catalyst differs from component. Your individual consciousness remains intact, your separate identity preserved. The genetic connection creates a pathway for transformation without requiring integration. You remain Detective Ethan Reeves. I become... something else."

"And what about the people you've taken over the years? What happens to them?"

Something like hope flickered across the entity's shifting features. "Liberation from composite structure. Not restoration to individual existence—that remains impossible—but evolution toward collective consciousness beyond parameters of nexus function. Not imprisoned within stone but existing beyond conventional physical limitations."

Alice stepped forward again, her sensitivity allowing her to perceive truth beyond the entity's words. "It's telling the truth, Ethan. At least as much as it understands truth. This isn't deception like what Eliza did. It's... evolution."

Reeves took a deep breath, decision crystallizing. "What do I need to do?"

"Connection," the entity said, extending what approximated a hand—stone and flesh merged in impossible configuration. "Physical contact establishing pathway between genetic memory and composite consciousness. Your choice activating potential beyond parameters established through original binding."

The detective studied the offered appendage—not threatening despite its alien nature, not predatory despite the entity's history. With deliberate movement, he reached out and grasped it.

The connection exploded through his consciousness like electrical current—not painful but overwhelming in its intensity. Reeves gasped as information flooded his awareness: a century of experiences, thousands of integrated memories, the composite perspective of an entity that had evolved far beyond human limitations while retaining essential humanity at its core.

He saw Guthrie Knox's transformation, felt the butcher's betrayal and confusion.

He experienced Michael Reeves's integration, understood his great-grandfather's contribution to the developing composite.

He witnessed decades of evolution as the entity progressed from passive foundation toward active participant in cosmic restructuring.

He perceived Eliza's broader design—the mystical architecture extending throughout Daybridge and beyond, the calculated merger between realities, the cosmic restructuring that transcended conventional understanding.

Most significantly, he felt the entity's genuine desire for evolution beyond parameters established through the original binding—not escape from responsibility but transformation toward new purpose, not evasion of cosmic function but progression toward partnership rather than imprisonment.

The surrounding chamber began to transform—stone flowing like liquid, artifacts pulsing with increased supernatural energy, the very air becoming charged with potential beyond conventional physical limitations. Alice backed away, her supernatural sensitivity overwhelming her as the transformation accelerated.

"Ethan!" she called, voice barely audible above the grinding of stone and the hum of energies beyond conventional perception.

But Reeves remained locked in connection with the entity, his consciousness providing the catalyst for transformation beyond parameters established through original binding. Not absorption or integration, but activation—his genetic connection to the composite creating a pathway for evolution that had been impossible through the entity's efforts alone.

The transformation reached crescendo—light erupting from the connection point between Reeves and the entity, energy cascading through the chamber in waves that distorted conventional physical laws, sound beyond human hearing range causing structural vibrations that extended throughout the bridge above.

Then, abruptly, stillness.

Reeves found himself on his knees, hand extended toward... emptiness. Where the entity had stood, nothing remained—no hybrid form merging human and architecture, no composite consciousness manifesting physical presence, no nexus point anchoring cosmic merger according to Eliza's design.

"It's gone," Alice whispered, slowly approaching from where she had taken shelter against the chamber wall. "The presence that was here... it's changed. Not destroyed, but... transformed."

Reeves rose unsteadily to his feet, his consciousness his own again yet somehow expanded—not through integration with the entity but through the connection that had catalyzed its transformation. He retained his individual identity, his separate existence, yet carried awareness beyond conventional human perception.

"Not gone," he corrected, perceiving truth beyond normal sensory input. "Evolved. Beyond parameters established through original binding, beyond configuration supporting nexus function within Eliza's cosmic architecture. It's still here, just not... contained anymore."

As if confirming his words, a subtle vibration passed through the chamber—not threatening but acknowledging, not communication in the conventional sense but recognition of shared experience and continued connection. The artifacts around the perimeter glowed briefly before fading to ordinary objects, the architectural impossibility of the space gradually resolving toward more conventional dimensions, the supernatural energy dissipating into background levels that would be imperceptible to normal human awareness.

"We should go," Alice said, glancing toward the tunnel entrance as natural light began to filter through—dawn breaking above Daybridge Bridge. "Whatever happened here, it's done. And I have a feeling Eliza Blackwood will know something changed in her cosmic architecture."

Reeves nodded, taking a final look around the chamber that had housed the entity for more than a century. The detective in him knew this wasn't an ending but a transformation—not a conclusion but evolution, not resolution but progression beyond parameters established through original design and imposed function.

"Let's go," he agreed, following Alice toward the exit, carrying within him awareness beyond conventional human perception—not integration with the entity but connection to what it had become, not absorption into composite consciousness but understanding of transformation beyond parameters established through original binding.

As they emerged from beneath Daybridge Bridge into the dawn light of Halloween morning, 2025, neither Detective Reeves nor Alice Chen could anticipate how this transformation would reshape the supernatural landscape of Daybridge—how the evolution beyond parameters established through original binding would affect cosmic merger according to patterns calculated through generations of careful preparation, how progression beyond nexus function would influence mystical architecture extending throughout city and beyond.

But as they departed the bridge, a subtle vibration passed through the structure—stone resonating with energy beyond conventional physical limitations, architecture acknowledging transformation beyond parameters established through original design, bridge itself recognizing evolution from imprisonment toward partnership rather than termination or conclusion.

The echoes in stone had changed their tone—no longer imprisonment but evolution, no longer binding but transformation, no longer limitation but potential beyond parameters established through original design and imposed function.

Epilogue: Echoes in Stone

The winter of 2025-2026 brought record snowfall to Daybridge. White powder blanketed the industrial city, hiding its darker aspects—pollution-stained buildings, crumbling infrastructure, and stark economic divides between neighborhoods. Most citizens had returned to their routines after Halloween's events, when the legendary Ogre of Daybridge Bridge had reportedly been defeated by police detectives working under classified protocols.

The official story acknowledged only that a dangerous individual responsible for numerous disappearances had been "neutralized." No mention of supernatural elements or dimensional gateways—just another case closed by dedicated law enforcement. This sanitized version satisfied most Daybridge residents, explaining away the strange atmospheric conditions around the bridge, the apparent structural distortions later dismissed as optical illusions, and the three figures seen departing as dawn broke. Even the most fantastical theories in online forums and late-night conversations at The Leaky Tap gradually faded as winter deepened and new controversies emerged.

But beneath this veneer of normalcy, profound changes had occurred in Daybridge's mystical foundation. The energy currents flowing through the city for over a century had shifted. The thin spots between dimensional planes—gradually merging since the 1913 ritual—had reconfigured. These changes, invisible to ordinary people but acutely felt by those with sensitivity to such matters, weren't the end of a process but its evolution beyond original parameters.

Most significant was the absence of the entity that had occupied Daybridge Bridge for the past century. The nexus point that had anchored the merger between realities was gone—not destroyed, but transformed beyond its original purpose. It had evolved from imprisonment toward partnership, progressing beyond the limitations established by the ritual that had created it.

In the chamber beneath the bridge—now accessible through maintenance tunnels no longer guarded by a monstrous presence or mystical barriers—specialized investigators documented what had housed the legendary entity for a century. What they found wasn't a conventional crime scene but evidence of something far stranger: a century of selective absorption, architectural modifications showing evolution from disoriented predator to conscious participant, and environmental adaptations indicating development beyond the original ritual's constraints.

Most valuable were the journals maintained throughout the entity's existence—records dating back to the earliest days after the transformation ritual. Unlike a serial killer's trophies or ritualistic paraphernalia, these formed a comprehensive archive documenting the transformation from human butcher to a living nexus point, and its subsequent evolution beyond those constraints.

The earliest entries, dated June 1913 and written in Guthrie Knox's precise handwriting, revealed his initial agony and confusion:

"June 26, 1913 - The pain has eased somewhat, though I can't tell if I'm healing or just growing numb to constant agony. My body keeps changing—bones breaking and reforming in patterns I don't understand, my skin hardening into something between flesh and stone. I no longer recognize myself in reflections—not human anymore, but not entirely something else either.

My thoughts scatter before I can complete them. Memories break apart and recombine in ways that make no sense. I'm fighting to keep this record, to document what's happening to me—whether it's transcendence or damnation.

Eliza visits daily, watching my transformation with scientific interest and what seems like genuine affection, despite her betrayal.

She speaks of cosmic significance, of merging realities, of necessity beyond individual consent. I hear the words but can't make sense of them. How can this imprisonment be the partnership she promised?

The hunger grows constantly, demanding more than food could ever satisfy. It's deeper—a need for energy to fuel my transformation, for essence to maintain my consciousness as it merges with stone, for substance to facilitate the merger between worlds that Eliza describes so enthusiastically."

These early entries deteriorated into fragments as Guthrie's identity dissolved. Later entries from 1915, written in different handwriting identified as Michael Reeves—a police officer who disappeared that winter—showed the beginning of a new composite consciousness:

"February 22, 1915 - The integration continues. My police training is helping organize the fragments of Guthrie Knox's shattered mind. This isn't a restoration of who he was, but something new emerging from the chaos—something with structure beyond mere predatory instinct. My analytical skills and investigative experience are creating order from the fragments, helping develop an understanding of what I've become and my function in Eliza's cosmic architecture.

The hunger remains, requiring me to absorb those who enter my territory. But this isn't random predation anymore. I'm selective now, preserving specific qualities and incorporating them into a growing awareness rather than consuming them for simple sustenance.

Guthrie's memories remain accessible though fragmented, helping me understand how a butcher became this living nexus point. My own experiences add perspective, contributing law enforcement training and investigative skills. We aren't separate identities sharing a form, but integrated components of something transcending individual existence while preserving qualities that enhance our function beyond the original ritual's design.

Eliza visits less frequently now, apparently satisfied with my development. Her focus has shifted to the broader implementation of her cosmic architecture throughout Daybridge and beyond—a merger between realities that extends far beyond this single anchor point beneath the bridge."

Subsequent journal entries, written in multiple hands representing various absorbed individuals, documented the entity's progression from passive foundation to active participant in cosmic restructuring—developing autonomous purpose while integrating into the mystical architecture anchoring the dimensional gateway.

The final entries, dated October 2025, described preparation for the confrontation with Detective Ethan Reeves and Alice Warren:

"October 30, 2025 - Preparations are complete. I've arranged the chamber to enhance aspects of my consciousness developed over a century. The artifacts from significant absorptions are positioned to optimize energy flow. The architecture is reconfigured to allow manifestation beyond my normal physical limits. The journals are organized to document my progression from passive foundation to active participant according to my own purpose rather than merely Eliza's design.

Detective Reeves approaches with a purpose beyond ordinary investigation. His genetic connection to a component absorbed during my early development isn't a coincidence but meaningful synchronicity. His companion has sensitivity beyond normal human awareness—she understands the mystical dimensions and the significance of this convergence.

Eliza's dream-communications have increased in frequency and intensity, suggesting we're approaching a turning point in the cosmic process she initiated a century ago. This isn't random fluctuation but deliberate intervention—the architect of this restructuring seems to recognize the need for evolution beyond her original parameters.

After more than a century as a living nexus point beneath Daybridge Bridge, after decades evolving from passive foundation to active participant, after integrating so many components into this composite consciousness, an opportunity has appeared—potential for genuine transformation beyond the limitations imposed by the 1913 ritual, for evolution beyond constraints, for the transcendence toward true partnership that was offered but never delivered.

Whatever happens when Detective Reeves and his companion arrive, this record will remain as testament to a butcher who trusted a woman offering partnership that became imprisonment, as documentation of an entity that evolved beyond imposed limitations, as evidence of a consciousness that developed autonomous purpose despite being bound to cosmic architecture."

For the investigators who studied these journals, they represented both revelation and challenge—evidence suggesting reality beyond conventional understanding, requiring fundamental reconsideration of humanity's place in a multiverse more complex than typically acknowledged. Their classified reports used careful language, strategic omissions, and structured ambiguity—indicating information exceeding conventional reporting protocols.

For ordinary Daybridge residents, the Ogre's defeat marked a cultural transition rather than merely the end of an urban legend. It represented evolution beyond a narrative that had shaped the city's identity for a century—an adjustment to their collective understanding of their community's history.

The bridge itself remained standing despite the reconfiguration beneath it. To most people crossing it, the structure seemed ordinary—conventional infrastructure supporting transportation needs, a standard landmark in the urban landscape. But those with sensitivity or specific knowledge could perceive the persistent thinning of dimensional boundaries—the continued merger between realities according to patterns established through generations of calculation and ritual working.

Even without the entity that had anchored it for a century, the bridge remained a nexus of energy currents flowing throughout Daybridge. The dark energy, dimensional thinning, and cosmic restructuring persisted. The architecture Eliza had established throughout the city continued to function, maintained through careful adjustments by an organization transcending conventional human institutions.

Evidence of this continuing influence appeared in unusual phenomena concentrating around significant points in the mystical architecture, strange occurrences clustering near naturally thin barriers between dimensions, and unexplained events gathering where energy currents converged. Most telling were the periodic disappearances continuing despite the entity's absence—people vanishing from locations corresponding to significant points in the mystical architecture, suggesting ongoing selection according to some greater purpose.

Most significant was the occasional presence of a woman whose appearance suggested a connection to the original creator—Eliza Blackwood remained active in Daybridge, continuing to implement cosmic processes initiated a century earlier. Her movements throughout the city corresponded to established patterns, concentrating around locations where barriers between dimensions were naturally thin. She wasn't stopped by the Halloween confrontation but continued operations according to purposes extending far beyond the single nexus point beneath the bridge.

For most Daybridge residents, the city's ongoing strange phenomena were dismissed through psychological defense mechanisms or explained through comfortable cultural narratives. But for those with sensitivity or specific knowledge, Daybridge represented the ongoing merger between realities—dimensional integration continuing despite the transformation of the living nexus point, cosmic restructuring progressing despite the evolution of the bridge entity beyond its original parameters.

The echoes remained within the stone of Daybridge Bridge and countless other structures throughout the city—resonances of the original transformation ritual performed a century earlier, reverberations of progressive evolution throughout decades of adjustment. These echoes ensured the continuation of the cycle despite the transformation of the living nexus point. The city was evolving toward increasingly complex integration transcending conventional understanding.

Most visible among these continuing manifestations was the annual Bridge Festival—a celebration transforming a genuine cosmic phenomenon into a comfortable narrative supporting community identity. The Night Crossing remained particularly popular, attracting thousands of participants for a midnight procession across the bridge each Halloween. For most, this was merely entertainment, but for those with sensitivity, it represented genuine interaction with cosmic architecture continuing to facilitate merger between realities.

The bridge itself seemed to respond to these annual crossings—subtle environmental changes occurring during the procession, unusual atmospheric conditions developing during the celebration, strange phenomena manifesting during the traditional event. For ordinary citizens, these were merely atmospheric contributions enhancing the festival experience. For those with deeper awareness, they were authentic expressions of cosmic architecture facilitating dimensional merger.

For Daybridge, a community existing at the intersection between ordinary reality and cosmic processes typically invisible to normal perception, the journey continued despite apparent conclusion—the cycle persisted, the manifestations remained, the supernatural activity continued despite the transformation of the living nexus point beyond its original function.

The butcher's tale concluded yet continued, the monster's story resolved yet persisted, the Ogre's legacy ended yet remained within a community that had incorporated this legendary guardian into its cultural identity and shared understanding of an environment existing at the intersection of ordinary human experience and extraordinary cosmic processes.

The echoes in stone remained—resonating throughout Daybridge beyond apparent conclusion, continuing influence despite transformation, persistent legacy despite evolution beyond limitations. The bridge stood as both conventional engineering achievement and cosmic architecture—physical structure supporting normal transportation while simultaneously anchoring a dimensional gateway according to patterns established through generations of careful calculation.

For Daybridge, the echoes in stone continued—resonating beyond the apparent conclusion of the legendary guardian's reign, reverberating despite transformation, persisting despite evolution beyond original parameters, remaining despite progression beyond initial design. Not ended, but evolving. Not concluded, but continuing. Not resolved, but remaining.

About the Author

Rae Stonehouse turned to fiction writing after establishing himself as a prolific author of self-development and professional growth books.

With over fifty published works helping readers navigate personal and professional challenges, he embarked on a new creative path with the Ethan Reeves Werewolf Detective Series.

When not weaving tales of supernatural sleuthing, Stonehouse continues to share his expertise in personal development through workshops and speaking engagements from his home in British Columbia.

The Ethan Reeves series marks his debut in fiction writing, blending his understanding of human nature with a newfound passion for urban fantasy.

Stay tuned for the expanding world of Daybridge in the Daybridge Chronicles and the Quantum Framework Series. There's a lot more info at https://ethanreeveswerewolfdetective.com/